GONE WITHOUT A TRACE

Books by Patricia Bradley

Shadows of the Past
A Promise to Protect

GONE WITHOUT A TRACE

A NOVEL

PATRICIA BRADLEY

Revell

a division of Baker Publishing Group
Grand Rapids, Michigan

Published by Revell
a division of Baker Publishing Group
P.O. Box 6287, Grand Rapids, MI 49516-6287
www.revellbooks.com

Printed in the United States of America

Library of Congress Cataloging-in-Publication Data
Bradley, Patricia (Educator)
    Gone without a trace : a novel / Patricia Bradley.
        pages ; cm (Logan Point ; Book 3)
    ISBN 978-0-8007-2282-1 (pbk.)
    I. Title.
PS3602.R34275G66 2015
813'.6—dc23   2014047674

This book is a work of fiction. Names, characters, places, and incidents are the product of the author's imagination or are used fictitiously.

15   16   17   18   19   20   21   7   6   5   4   3   2   1

In memory of my mother, Frances Bradley

Prologue

A little before midnight, a small jon boat skimmed across the lake located just outside of Logan Point. The electric trolling motor hardly broke the deathly quiet of the first hours of the New Year. The man at the tiller pulled his coat tighter with his free hand and lowered his head against the cold, dense fog that shrouded him.

The fog was both a blessing and a curse. No one could see him, but neither could he see anyone. In the bottom of the flat metal boat lay a black bag, and his gaze kept returning to it. If he was caught dumping it, he would pay more than a fine this time.

A low horn raked his senses, and he jerked his head around. Dead ahead through the thinning fog, twin lights from a barge bore down on him like avenging angels.

He swore. There weren't supposed to be any barges coming downriver tonight. He gunned the thrust on the trolling motor, barely getting out of the barge's path. The wake rocked the small boat, and he fought the dizzying motion.

That had been close, but at least now he knew he was in the deepest part of the lake. He decreased the thrust, putting the boat in a controlled drift. Once he regained his balance, he hefted the weighted bag. The boat rocked in the water and almost tipped over as he slid the body over the side.

He risked a light on the water and within seconds only ripples gave evidence of his deed. He paused briefly to stare at the widening rings and then pointed the twelve-foot boat toward shore.

This was not an auspicious beginning to the New Year.

1

The vacant warehouse in downtown Memphis reeked of decayed wood, dust, and mold spores. Livy Reynolds stood backed against a square brick column, her SIG Sauer at the ready. Her breath made little puffs of white smoke in the cold February air even as sweat trickled down the side of her face. It was a lousy way to start off the week.

She chanced a peek around the brick to survey the cavernous room. Straight ahead, a stairwell led to a second level, on her right a double doorway opened to the outside. Six feet from her lay the skeleton of a bird that had flown into the building but hadn't been able to find its way out. She scanned the columns that lined the room. Mac was behind one somewhere to her left. The bank robber could be anywhere.

From the corner of her eye, she glimpsed Mac in his Kevlar vest as he darted to a column nearer the stairway. She knew what he was doing—if the thief made it to the upper level, they'd be open targets. Where was backup?

The gunman fired. The bullet chipped the brick by her partner's head.

"Give it up," Mac yelled. "No need to die today."

Another bullet answered the demand. In the silence that followed, Livy pressed against the brick column, her heart pounding against her ribs, her mouth too dry to even wet her lips. A vision of Justin Caine appeared beside her, and she squeezed her eyes shut.

The gunman ran to the stairs, shooting toward Livy's position. Mac whipped around the column and returned fire. Caine's image disappeared, and Livy pushed herself away from her hiding place into the open. The gunman fired again, and a piece of brick broke off, grazing her cheek.

Her brain slipped into slow motion. His face came into focus. Her mind recorded the gunman's eyes as they bored into hers, his blond hair sticking out from the Redbirds baseball cap, the thin mustache. The blood rushing through her head drowned out all sound.

Livy brought her gun up, finger on the trigger. *Center mass.* Her eyes blurred, and once again Caine appeared between her and the gunman. She hesitated, unable to shoot.

The gunman turned toward Mac.

"No!" Her scream echoed in the empty warehouse as she pulled the trigger. The shot went wide, and the gunman fired. She could almost see the bullet's trajectory toward her partner before it knocked him backward.

The outside doors burst open, and a deafening explosion filled the room as a flash of light blinded Livy. She dropped to the floor and covered her head before she realized it was a flash grenade deployed to disorient the gunman. When her head quit spinning, she rose to her knees, still holding her head. Someone touched her shoulder, and she flinched.

"Sorry, Detective."

With her ears ringing, Livy read the SWAT officer's lips rather than heard him. Then the shaking started. First in her arms that she hugged to her stomach. Then to her whole body.

She turned, seeking Mac. She'd let him down. He had to be okay. Officers hovered over his unconscious figure on the floor.

A man with a medical bag raced past her, followed by more men with a stretcher.

"You all right?"

She couldn't stop her teeth from chattering. "Mac? Is . . . is he okay?"

Darkness passed across the officer's eyes. "I think he will be. Paramedics are just getting here."

Mac had on his vest. He couldn't die. She pulled her gaze from the scene and back to the officer. "The gunman?"

His lip curled. "He folded like a baby when he recovered from the flashbang and saw that beam of light on his chest. Cuffed and ready to be transported."

The ringing in her ears had lessened, and Livy caught most of what he said. She struggled to her feet and staggered when she saw Mac with his shirt ripped open and electrodes on his chest.

The officer caught her. "Take it easy," he said. "You'll be dizzy until the effects of the explosion wear off."

Again, time crawled to a standstill as the paramedic spoke, his mouth opening and closing as he instructed everyone to step away. The medic at Mac's head sat back, and the officers surrounding them moved, glancing at each other the way only fellow officers could. The paramedic pressed the shock button, and Mac's body jumped. She jumped as well, and real time returned.

"We have a rhythm! Let's transport."

A flurry of activity erupted as her partner was loaded onto a stretcher. A first responder noticed Livy and asked if she'd been checked out.

"I'm fine. Take care of Mac."

Because *she* hadn't.

■ ■ ■

The next afternoon, Livy fired ten rounds at a target thirty-five feet away. She brought the target close. All ten rounds had hit the bull's-eye, and Justin Caine was nowhere in sight. But then, he couldn't be. She holstered her gun and removed her shooting glasses and earplugs. It had taken her most of the afternoon to work up the nerve to come to the firing range. Now it was time to talk to her partner.

The drive in the waning light was much too short, and in less than fifteen minutes, she rang Mac's doorbell. Her insides quivered like Jell-O, and she wasn't certain she could do this. But she had to try. At the hospital, she'd seen the question in his eyes, a question he hadn't been ready to ask, and she hadn't been ready to answer.

Livy wasn't sure even now she could tell Mac what happened in the warehouse. She'd gone over the details with Captain Reed. The department psychologist would be next. So far, no one had asked about her mental state at the time of the shooting, but she knew it was coming.

Mac's front door opened, and Livy took a step back. She hadn't expected his ex-wife to be here.

"Livy, I'm glad you're here. Mac was wondering why you didn't come by this morning." Julie's smile crinkled the skin around her eyes. She stepped aside for Livy to enter. "He's in the den."

Questions crowded Livy's mind as she walked through the living room to the den. She knew Mac and Julie had a "friendly" divorce, but even so, she'd been surprised to see her at the hospital. Especially since he'd been injured. Danger in Mac's job was the reason Julie had left him. And now here she was at the house. Not that it bothered Livy in the least.

All thoughts of Julie left her when she rounded the corner into the den. Mac sat in his recliner, much paler than she expected. She avoided looking into his eyes. "Well, you're looking great. I see you're still hooked up."

Mac touched the monitor on his belt. "Yeah. The doctors want to make sure the old ticker doesn't kick out of gear again."

Livy sat stiffly in a chair across from him and placed her hands on her knees.

"Are you okay?" Mac asked.

Still not looking at him, she nodded.

Julie entered the room and picked up a glass beside his chair. "I, ah, think I'll run to the grocery and pick up a few things for you. Your pantry looks like Old Mother Hubbard's."

When they were alone, Mac cleared his throat. "The doctor didn't want me to be here alone, so Julie's staying a few days."

Livy didn't know why that news bothered her. It wasn't like they had a romantic relationship. She licked her lips. "You don't owe me an explanation."

"I know, but we're partners, and I don't know, I just wanted you to know."

Silence fell between them. She took a deep breath. She had to get this over with. "Look, I'm—"

"What—" Mac spoke at the same time.

"You go first," she said.

"Okay." He leaned forward. "What happened yesterday in the warehouse?"

The image of the teenage boy she'd shot flashed in her mind. She rubbed her hands on her jeans. "I don't know. One minute I'm fine, the next Justin Caine is in there, standing next to me." She lifted her gaze, blinking back the tears that scalded her eyes as the night eight weeks ago, when she shot and killed a seventeen-year-old suspect, replayed in her head. "I . . . I'm sorry, Mac. I let you down, but it won't happen again."

He started to rise, and she held up her hand. "Don't get up. I'm okay. I promise." If he tried to comfort her, she would lose it, she knew she would.

He studied her for a minute. "Maybe you just need a little more time. It's only been two months since the shooting. You shot Caine in the line of duty, and there's no shame in having trouble with killing someone. I'd be worried if you weren't."

"I keep playing it over and over in my mind, trying to make it come out different. Maybe if I'd waited for backup or—"

"Backup wouldn't have changed anything. It was dark in that alley—you had no way of knowing it was a toy gun. You told him to stop. To give it up, right?"

She had, hadn't she? Livy replayed the scene for the millionth time. Stopping at the convenience store for a soda, hearing someone demand money, seeing the robber with a gun, and then chasing him into a dark alley. *"Put the gun down! Now!"*

"Of course I told him, but what if he was trying to give me the gun?"

"Did he say he wanted to do that?"

"No. He didn't say anything."

"Then quit second-guessing yourself. The kid had just robbed that store with what looked like a real gun. And even though you were off duty, you were doing your job."

Mac always knew what to say. She clasped her hands together in her lap and picked at a hangnail. "I worry that you could've been killed yesterday because I freaked out."

He ran his hand over his mouth, and she caught the hesitation in his eyes. Her stomach sank to her knees. "If you have something to say, spit it out, Mac."

"Okay. I think you need to see the department psychologist again."

If she did, she'd be sitting behind a desk all day, viewing surveillance video. "I can handle this. I went to the firing range before I came here. All bull's-eyes."

"Shooting at a target isn't the same thing as facing someone with a gun. At least take the rest of the week off."

"I took off yesterday and today. Besides, Ellsworth didn't take time off after that drug bust went bad, and he shot and killed someone."

"That was different."

"Why? Because I'm female?"

"You know me better than that. Look, I know when you need a little time to pull it together."

"This time you're wrong." She held the gaze he leveled at her. "I'm fine. I promise."

His eyes narrowed. "If you don't want to see Dr. Robinson, go to someone in private practice, because if you don't, what happened in the warehouse will happen again. And next time the outcome might be different, Olivia."

Mac's words rang in her head all the way to her apartment. He didn't think she was mentally fit for duty. What if he was right? She let herself into her dark apartment and flipped on a light, revealing a room that needed more decoration. She'd moved into the high-rise a year ago to be closer to downtown and hadn't taken the time to add her personal touch. Maybe she'd take Mac's advice and do that this week. She had vacation time coming—three years' worth. But what would she do after buying a few pictures and table decorations? Ramble around the empty apartment? No. Weekends she didn't work or spend in Logan Point were bad enough, and because she focused most of her time on being a cop, she had no close relationships other than family, hadn't had a serious date since a college romance that went bad. Come tomorrow morning, she'd be on the job.

Like she did every evening, Livy slipped her holster from around her waist and placed it on the bookcase. She flipped through a stack of movies. Maybe she'd live vicariously through a movie romance while she ate supper. In the kitchen she rummaged through her cabinets for something to eat. Mac's cabinets weren't the only ones that were bare. Sighing, she turned to the freezer and took out a frozen dinner. Sirloin tips and wild rice with mushrooms.

Fifteen minutes later, she sat in front of the television, watching two women with guy problems swap homes in different countries.

"And all that funny stuff, those years of your life that you wasted, that will eventually begin to fade." Livy mouthed the words Iris spoke. Later when the old scriptwriter explained what a "meet-cute" was, she clicked the movie off. Maybe she could find a soccer game somewhere.

Because tonight she just couldn't watch a movie that ended with "and they lived happily ever after." Those endings only happened in the movies.

2

After getting less than three hours' sleep, Livy called in to tell her supervisor she wouldn't be in until noon. In the wee hours of the morning, she'd decided if Mac wanted her to see a psychologist, she'd go to see her friend Taylor. Taylor Martin Sinclair was a psychologist, even though her expertise was in victim profiling.

At eight o'clock she dialed Taylor's cell phone.

"Yes ma'am?"

Livy chuckled. "How did you know I wanted something?"

"Let's see. It's Wednesday morning, and you never take time to eat during the week, so you're not asking me to meet you for lunch, therefore you must need something."

"Ha-ha. How do you know I wasn't going to ask how you and Nick are doing?" Just thinking about the happy couple reminded her of the movie last night . . . and her empty life. "Are you teaching today?"

"No, that's tomorrow. What do you need?"

"A little of your time. Unless you and Nick have something planned."

"He's out of town. What time do you want to come?"

"How about right now?"

"I'll have coffee ready by the time you get here. Maybe even a little breakfast."

Livy didn't tell her friend she had no appetite. "See you soon."

It took Livy thirty minutes to drive to the Martin farm in Logan Point. When she turned in to the drive that took her past the Martin house, then Oak Grove, she noticed the old home place had a fresh coat of paint.

A quarter of a mile past Oak Grove, she pulled into a newly paved drive and climbed out of her SUV. Nestled against the tree line, the Tudor-style home they'd had built was a perfect fit for the couple. Taylor met her at the door along with the aroma of yeast and cinnamon.

"Wow, something smells wonderful," Livy said.

"Mom gave me her recipe for cinnamon rolls."

"Aren't you the old married woman now?" Livy looked her friend over. "But it seems to be agreeing with you—you look great." And Taylor did; even without makeup, she glowed.

"Well, you look tired. Hang your coat on the rack and grab a cup of coffee. The rolls will be out of the oven in five minutes."

Livy poured her coffee and picked up the French vanilla creamer beside the pot. She always drank her coffee black, but maybe it was time for a change.

"Try it," Taylor said. "You need to open yourself up to different possibilities."

"I don't think adding cream to my life will make much difference. And what if I ruin my coffee?"

"It's a start. And if you don't like it, the pot's full."

Had she gotten so regimented that changing something as small as what she put in her coffee was a huge decision? She unscrewed the cap and poured a liberal dash into her cup.

"That wasn't so hard, was it?"

Livy crossed her eyes and took a sip and almost spit it back out. "How do you drink this? It's too sweet, and now my coffee tastes like cough syrup."

Her friend laughed. "My, we're grouchy today. At least you tried it. Now, do you want to tell me what's going on?"

18

Livy dumped the coffee and rinsed the cup before refilling it. She sat at the kitchen island and cradled the cup in her hands. "I almost got Mac killed this week."

"How?" Taylor took the rolls from the oven and placed them on a trivet.

Livy had expected a little more reaction, but then, very little ruffled Taylor. "I didn't have his back in a shoot-out. He took a bullet in the chest. Of course he had on his vest, but the impact caused an arrhythmia."

Concern flashed in Taylor's eyes. "Is his heart still out of rhythm?"

"No, it was only temporary. He's okay now."

"Good. Why didn't you have his back?"

"I caved under pressure. My shot went wild."

"It's still the kid in the alley."

Tears burned Livy's eyes, and she didn't try to hold them back. Taylor was the one person she could be herself with. "I can't stop reliving it, or thinking about how his family must feel."

"Listen to me. That kid is the one who decided to rob a convenience store with a toy gun that looked so real that if you laid it side by side with a real revolver, no one could tell the difference. Even the store clerk thought it was real."

"But it was dark in the alley. Just a streetlight from the corner. What if I read him wrong? Why would he rob a store with a toy gun, anyway?"

"I don't know. The paper said he had emotional problems in the past. Almost OD'd on painkillers once."

"You're thinking suicide by cop?"

"It's possible. You told him to put his weapon and himself on the ground, right?"

She nodded. "Three times."

"And he didn't do it."

"I hear what you're saying, but I can't wrap my mind around it. It's made me question my judgment . . . and God."

"*You* are questioning God? You're the one who always reminded me that nothing was too big for him."

Livy looked away from Taylor and stared at the flames licking the logs in the fireplace. "God has the power to change any circumstance. Why did he put me in that store just when that kid robbed it? Five minutes earlier or later and Caine would still be alive, and I wouldn't be dealing with the aftermath of his stupid choices."

"Don't you see, Livy? It was Justin Caine's choices that caused his death. Not you."

"Maybe so, but all I can think about is that a seventeen-year-old boy is dead, and I could have prevented it if I'd handled it differently or if I hadn't been there at all."

"You have to readjust your thinking. Are you still seeing your department psychologist?"

Livy shook her head. "He released me. If I go back to him, I'll be given a desk job again, and that almost drove me crazy the first time. Would you consider seeing me professionally? Walk me through this?"

Taylor's blue eyes softened. "That's not my field. You need someone who specializes in post-traumatic stress."

She folded her arms across her chest. "I am not having PTSD. Would you at least consider it?"

"Let me do a little research first, and in the meantime, maybe you need to take a leave from your job, something you should have done after the shooting. If I remember right, you didn't take any time off."

She sounded like Mac now. "It's dead wintertime. If I don't work, I'll just sit in my apartment and brood."

"Then come home to Logan Point. Help Kate with her pottery." Taylor smoothed a strand of Livy's hair back. "But whatever you do, don't cut your hair again. It's just now the right length."

Livy picked at a hangnail. Some people rearranged furniture when they were unhappy with their life. She changed her hairstyle.

This might be one of those times. Being a cop was her life, and she didn't know how to do anything else. But whose fault was that? "Okay, I won't cut it, but I'm not taking a leave. That would be running from my problem. The only way I'll get my confidence back is to keep doing my job."

"At least consider it." Taylor placed a hot roll on a plate and handed it to her. "Right now, eat this."

The aroma of cinnamon and butter teased Livy's taste buds. She took a bite of the warm roll, and the melt-in-your-mouth taste sent a wealth of good memories through her. She glanced at Taylor. "These are almost as good as your mom's. Remember how she always seemed to know when the three of us needed a little something extra?"

"Problem fixers. That's what she called these," Taylor said.

"Yeah." Livy sighed. "I'm afraid a cinnamon roll won't fix my problems anymore."

■ ■ ■

Alex Jennings examined the photograph his boss handed him. It looked like a selfie with the blonde-haired beauty staring confidently at the camera, her blue eyes wide and a saucy grin on her lips. His heart rate increased. His first big case. Maybe.

"Samantha Jo Woodson has been missing for two days. She didn't show up for work Monday, but her boss waited until today before she called the emergency number the girl had given her." Delores Mathis tapped her pencil on the massive oak desk that took up much of the space in her tiny office. Her Texas drawl drew the words out. "State Senator Robert Woodson has hired us to look into his granddaughter's case."

Alex scanned the information on the second sheet that the owner of Mathis Private Investigations had handed him. "How did a spoiled Texas debutante end up in Logan Point, Mississippi, working as a waitress?"

"That's the sixty-four-thousand-dollar question."

He glanced once again at the photo. "How old is she?"

"Twenty-one."

He would've guessed eighteen.

"After her second year in college, she dropped out, said she wanted to go to Nashville and be a singer. Isn't Senator Woodson your grandfather's colleague?"

Alex nodded and unrolled the cuffs on the white dress shirt he'd worn this morning. Woodson served on the opposite side of the political fence in the Texas State legislature from Josiah Jennings. Although in their seventies, both men still wielded power in Texas politics.

"Your grandfather still bugging you to take the bar exam?"

"Oh yeah. Neither he nor my father has let up the pressure. Which reminds me, I have a lunch date with the senator." He checked his watch. "In twenty minutes."

"I wondered about the dress shirt this morning." She smiled. "Do you want this case?"

Alex cocked his head, studying the woman he worked for. He'd met her three years ago when she came to the airfield where he gave flying lessons, looking for someone to fly her to Houston. He'd offered his services. On the flight, he learned Dee was the sole investigator in the agency she'd started ten years earlier, this after spending twelve years as a Dallas homicide detective.

When they arrived at Sugarland Regional Airport, he'd been intrigued by this woman who looked like everyone's Aunt Bea. Brown hair styled in a simple cut, nothing remarkable about her face—she would blend into any setting. That was her secret, she'd told him. No one ever saw her. He wanted to know more and offered to drive her around Houston since he was familiar with the city. They talked about the case she was working on, and he made a few observations, and she offered to hire him on the spot as a consultant.

Since then, he'd worked several cases for her, never anything big or important, and he wanted to know why she was handing off a case as big as this one to him. "I figured you just wanted me to fly you to Logan Point."

"Nope. It's all yours since I have to be available to testify in court in the morning." She made a face. "Probably all week, and this case needs someone on it yesterday. There's a small airport on the outskirts of Logan Point and a bed and breakfast nearby. I'll call and see if you can stay there—just keep up with your expenses."

A tremor ran through him. Maybe if he solved this case, his grandfather would drop the campaign to get him to take the bar and join the family law firm. "As soon as I get back from lunch, I'll get right on this."

"Well, for Pete's sake, comb your unruly hair before you meet your grandfather."

He smoothed his hand over his head.

"I meant with a comb."

At exactly twelve thirty, Alex walked through the back door of the estate where he'd spent most of his childhood after his parents' divorce. Behind his back, he carried a bouquet of daisies he'd picked up at the florist. Eloise, the family cook, turned from the stove.

"Alex, you're one minute late. The senator will be fit to be tied."

"No ma'am. I'm right on the money." He pulled the flowers out. "For you, milady."

Red started at the base of her throat and rose to her cheeks. "Don't know what you mean, bringing me flowers," she said as she took them. "You ought to be finding some beautiful lady to give these to."

He sniffed the air. "But she wouldn't bake chocolate brownies for me."

"Get out of here before your grandfather's blood pressure goes up."

He laughed and kissed her cheek. "Going."

His smile faded as he went through the dining room door and spied Josiah Jennings waiting in his usual place at the table. A stack of papers lay to the left of his plate. When he saw Alex, he glanced at his watch. "Not quite late," he said.

"Good afternoon to you too, Grandfather."

"Sit so I can say the blessing, and Eloise can begin serving."

Alex slipped into his chair and bowed his head and waited for the same prayer he'd heard at every meal he'd ever eaten at this table.

"Bless us, O Lord, and this food we are about to receive from your bounty. Amen."

"Amen," Alex repeated as Eloise entered the room with their salads. He'd never been able to figure out how she knew the precise moment his grandfather would be finished praying. Unless she stood at the door, listening.

They ate in silence, Alex wondering why he'd been summoned to the house. He figured the stack of papers on the corner of the table had something to do with it, but before he could ask, his grandfather cleared his throat.

"Are you still seeing the Townsend girl?"

His grandfather had asked him to lunch to talk about his dating life? "No, Beth went on to greener pastures."

Josiah cocked his head to the side. "Just what do you do to these girls that scares them away?"

Did it always have to be his fault? Granted, it probably was, given his aversion to marriage, but why did his grandfather automatically assume Alex was to blame? "Beth was looking for a ring and a house with a white picket fence."

"And you're not?"

Hardly. Not after the turmoil of his parents' divorce, one that he had been caught in the middle of. The idea of marriage sent cold tremors down his back.

"Nope," Alex said, responding to his grandfather's question.

Tired of the direction of the conversation, he pointed toward the papers. "What do you have there?"

"Don't point with your fork," his grandfather said. "It's your application to take the bar exam."

His stomach took a nosedive. He should have stayed with the topic of his love life. "Who said I was taking it?"

"I do. You've got to do something with your life other than goofing off."

"I'm doing okay teaching people how to fly."

A muscle twitched in his grandfather's cheek. "I rue the day I ever bought you that plane."

His grandfather might rue the day he paid a hundred thousand dollars and change for the 1970 Bonanza F33A, but his bribe had saved Alex's sanity. Flying was all he'd ever wanted to do since he was fourteen and his mother took him up in her Cessna. He'd soloed at sixteen and had become a certified flight instructor by the time he was eighteen.

"The plane served its purpose. I went to law school, even graduated in the upper half of my class. Besides," Alex said, "I do have another paying job."

His grandfather snorted. "What, following wayward husbands around for that private investigation agency?"

Alex clamped his jaw against the words that threatened to spill from his lips as Eloise appeared and whisked the salad bowls away. He waited as she served their plates of quiche lorraine and lemon asparagus and then beat a hasty retreat. "Mathis Private Investigations is a top-notch company, and I'm working on a pretty big case right now. A missing girl."

"I didn't say it wasn't a good company." Josiah took a bite of quiche. "Dee Mathis gave you the Woodson case?"

"How do you know about the case?"

"I recommended her, but I had no idea she would turn it over to a novice."

"Thanks for the vote of confidence." Alex cut a small bite of quiche. If his grandfather thought enough of the agency to recommend it, why was he so opposed to Alex working there? The answer came immediately. Anything Josiah Jennings couldn't control, he opposed.

The older man cocked his head. After a minute, he said, "I'll make a deal with you. You solve this case, and I'll never mention the bar exam again."

"Deal." Alex would do almost anything to get his father and grandfather off his back about taking the bar.

His grandfather held his finger up. "However, if you fail, I expect you to apply to take the test by the end of the month, and if you don't, I'm done with you. I will not be a party to you wasting your life."

The quiche stuck in Alex's throat. The implication that he was presently wasting his life stung, but did he want his future riding on this one case?

"Think you can't solve it?"

Heat seared Alex's face. "It's still a deal," he said. "But I expect you to live up to your end of the bargain."

Josiah leveled a gaze at him. "When have I ever not? By the same token, I will expect you to do the same. And although the filing date for the July exam ended at the end of January, I have it on good authority that in your case, the date can be extended to March thirtieth. I would prefer if your application was in by the end of February."

"Three weeks? You expect me to solve this case in three weeks?"

"That's the deal. Take it or leave it."

Alex had no choice now. His grandfather had backed him into a corner, and the only way out was to find the missing girl. And he would do it. He had to.

If he had to practice law, he would die a slow and sure death.

■ ■ ■

As Livy drove to Memphis, she couldn't keep her mind off the meeting with Captain Reed. She was pretty sure he was going to request that she be recertified at the shooting range. But if he asked her to see the department psychologist, she was going to say no. She didn't need anyone in the department to know how messed up her thinking was. An hour later, Reed confirmed her suspicion in a meeting with her partner.

"You want me to run the shoot/no-shoot course at the range?" Livy swallowed the lump lodged in her throat.

Captain Arlin Reed nodded. "Mac here thinks it'll be a good idea. He's shooting it with you, as well. And then you both have sessions scheduled with the department psychologist."

She glanced at Mac. Had he told the captain she hadn't covered him Monday?

He met her gaze. "In case you're wondering, I told Arlin you're still dealing with the aftermath of the December shooting."

"Fine. Let's get this over with." She rose from her chair. "Are you riding with me or meeting me there?"

He glanced away. "Meeting you. I'm, ah, meeting Julie for a late lunch afterward."

"Fine."

A pain shot through her right eye. Not a migraine. Not now. On the drive to the range, she practiced relaxation techniques. But when she stood at the firing line, waiting for a target to pop out, the muscles in her shoulders knotted. *Relax. Go slow.* The target slid out, a figure with a gun in his hand. She fired. Another target, no gun. She let it pass. Three more targets with guns.

Another target, farther back this time. Livy hesitated, then she fired, hitting it dead center. Except . . . the target was a no-shoot. She didn't have time to think before a target popped out, closer this time. Was there a gun? She blinked. Yes. The target disappeared before she could fire, and a target twenty-five feet away popped up. Again a split-second hesitation before she fired, missing it.

Her hand shook, and she lowered her gun. If this had been for real, she would be dead. Or her partner. She stepped back, trying not to throw up.

"You okay, Olivia?" Concern weighed in Mac's voice.

She turned, her legs almost buckling. One look told her he'd seen what had happened. She holstered her gun. "Looks like you're right. I'm not fit for service."

3

Five minutes out from the Logan Point airport, Alex radioed his position to the air traffic controller and was cleared to land. He set his Bonanza down on the runway and taxied to the front of the small terminal, stopping where a lanky man with wooden chocks directed him. With an airport this small, it was probably the guy he radioed. Even so, the quality of the airport surprised him. A brick terminal, long runway. Someone had invested money here. A cold north wind whipped his clothes as he climbed out of the plane and shook hands with the man. "Sam" was written over the pocket of his khaki shirt, and long johns extended beyond his cuffs.

"Will you need fuel?"

"Yes, but it can wait until morning." He'd see how long he'd be in Logan Point before renting a hangar. Alex grabbed his bag, then ducked his head against the cold and hurried inside with Sam.

"Sure thing. How long are you planning to be here?"

That would depend on what he found out this afternoon. "I'm not sure, but can you tell me where I can find a car rental place?" As he'd flown in, he'd noticed there weren't any businesses around the airport.

Sam nodded his head in the direction of the front doors. "There's a courtesy van you can use. It's free for four hours if you think you can conduct your business and get it back by . . ." Sam checked his watch. "Seven—that's when they close the terminal and everybody leaves."

"Thanks, but I believe I'll go ahead and rent a car."

"The town is a ways down the road. Nearest car rental is probably eight, ten miles." He handed him a card. "Call and they'll pick you up and take you back to the agency."

Alex started to dial the number, but his curiosity got the best of him. "What happens if someone flies in and no one is here?"

"Happened once before we staffed this place. A corporate big shot flew in and forgot to tell anyone he was coming, and he had to walk to town. Eight miles. In July. That was before cell phones."

Nice to know. Alex dialed the number and arranged for a car. After he disconnected, he freshened up in the restroom and then wandered around the nicely furnished waiting room in the terminal while he waited. He noted the sophisticated computer system and was once again impressed with the Logan Point airport.

Sam pointed toward a wooden podium. "Appreciate if you'd sign our book. We like to keep up with where people come from, where they're going."

Alex obliged, with Sam looking over his shoulder. When he finished, Sam nodded. "Texas. Thought I recognized that accent."

"Are you good on accents?"

"Yep. There's a young lady down at Molly's Diner that talks like you."

His pulse quickened. That had to be the Woodson girl. "Do you know her?"

"Samantha Jo? Just from the diner. She's a real good waitress—never gets the orders messed up. Haven't seen her this week, though. You family?"

"Friend of the family. The last time you saw her, was she upset or anything?"

"Naw, maybe a little jumpy. She's a pretty little thing. Nothing's happened to her, has it?"

"Do you know if Samantha Jo had a boyfriend?"

He shook his head. "Never saw her anywhere but at the diner and never heard anybody say she had a boyfriend. Of course, I wouldn't know what she did when she worked at Johnny B's."

"Johnny B's?"

"It's a big truck stop on the other side of town near the bypass. You never did say if you thought something happened to her."

No, he hadn't. The front door opened, and they both turned toward the sound. "That's your car rental people."

"Thanks. Appreciate your help."

A late model blue Impala sat at the curb when Alex and the car rental agent exited. After he took care of the paperwork at the car rental agency, he used his GPS to find the sheriff's department. That was something Dee had drilled into his head. Stop in and let the local law enforcement know what you're doing in town. He'd done her one better by calling and talking with Sheriff Ben Logan before he left and making an appointment.

Sheriff Logan's handshake was firm but not bone crushing. That was always a good thing. Showed that the other person, often a law officer, didn't have anything against PIs. The sheriff appeared to be in his early thirties, like Alex. "Thank you for giving me a little of your time, Sheriff Logan." He took the chair offered. The office was larger than Dee's back in Dallas, but the oak desk reminded him of hers. Several photos of an older man adorned the gray walls.

"Call me Ben, unless you plan on breaking the law," he said with a grin.

"I don't. Just trying to find out what happened to Samantha Jo Woodson for her folks."

"That was quick—them hiring a private detective."

"I don't think it was any reflection on you . . . they're just worried. Hiring our company makes them feel like they're doing something."

"I can understand that," Ben said, nodding. "Molly called me yesterday when she didn't show up for the second day. Samantha Jo had worked for her a month and was always punctual, never called in sick. We went to her apartment and got the manager to let us in. It was neat, nothing out of place, and while I don't know what all she had there, clothes were hanging in the closets, other stuff was in the drawers."

On the paperwork Alex had read, a mention was made of a church she attended. "Did anyone see her at church Sunday?"

"She attended Center Hill, same place I go. I don't remember seeing her, but that doesn't mean she wasn't there."

"Do you know if she worked Sunday?"

"Molly isn't open on Sundays." Ben stood. "Why don't you follow me over to the diner? If I'm there, Molly might open up a little more than if you go by yourself. And while you talk with her, I'll call around and ask if anyone saw Samantha Jo on Sunday."

Molly's Diner was like the little diner down the road from the hangar back in Texas. Except there were no checkered tablecloths. Instead, Formica tables filled the diner and a row of stools with black vinyl seats fronted a counter—same family atmosphere, though. Molly sized him up as Ben introduced them. He thought even Ben's introduction might not be enough until she stuck out her beefy hand. "I hope you can find that little girl."

"So do I," he said as Ben excused himself to make the calls.

"I feel bad about not calling someone 'til yesterday, but I didn't want to hover too much."

After he questioned her about basic things and received the same answers he already knew, he tapped his pen on the tablet. "Do you know why she left the last place she worked?"

"Johnny B's?" Molly rolled her lips in. "Said she didn't like the hours, but now that I think about it, she mentioned once about some guy that creeped her out. She never said that's why she left, though."

Ben reentered the diner. "I can't find anyone who saw her Sunday at church."

"So she may have been gone three days," Alex said.

"It's beginning to look that way." He turned to Molly. "Do you remember what she wore to work Saturday?"

Molly frowned. "Jeans. I know because that's all she ever wore, but I don't remember about the top. Let me ask one of the other girls." She turned to a tall blonde filling the salt and pepper shakers. "Lindsay, do you know what Samantha Jo wore to work Saturday?"

The girl cocked her head and thought a minute. "She wore that pretty blue top. I wanted to get one like it, but she said it came from some shop in Texas. She acted like it might be expensive."

"Could you go with us to identify it if we find it?" Ben asked.

"Samantha Jo wears some of the coolest clothes. I'd love to see in her closet." The waitress shot a questioning glance at Molly, who nodded. "Let me take off my apron."

Outside the diner, Ben asked, "It's not too cold, why don't we walk? It's only two blocks."

A few minutes later, as they neared an older apartment complex, Alex turned to Lindsay. "Did she have a car?"

"An older model white Malibu," the girl replied.

The white Malibu sat in the apartment parking lot, but no blue top was found in her closet or anywhere else in the apartment.

"I can't believe she has three pairs of J Brand jeans." Lindsay turned from the closet door, her eyes wide. "And look at this. A tie-dyed sweater from MSGM."

"MSGM?" Ben repeated.

"It's an expensive line of clothing," Alex said. When Ben gave him a sidelong glance, Alex chuckled. "It's a brand that Nordstrom's carries. My last girlfriend shopped there, and I accompanied her shopping sometimes. You wouldn't believe the prices."

Ben rested his hand on his Glock. "That means she disappeared probably Saturday, either voluntarily—"

Lindsay waved her arm toward the closet. "No woman in her right mind would go off and leave these clothes."

"So the possibility she was abducted is very real." Alex swept his gaze around the room. Even with fresh paint, the apartment didn't compare to what Samantha Jo was accustomed to. What was she doing in Logan Point in the first place? He shifted to face the waitress. "Did Samantha Jo mention why she came to Logan Point?"

"I think she ran out of money and couldn't afford to stay in Memphis."

That explained a lot. "Does Samantha Jo have any friends?"

Lindsay shook her head. "When she first came to town—I think it was around Thanksgiving—she came into the diner with this cocky dude. He strutted around like a banty rooster. I thought he was her husband, but after she came to work here she told me he was just her boyfriend and that he left her high and dry right after Christmas."

"Does this guy have a name?" Ben asked.

"Seems like she called him Cody."

"How about a last name?"

Lindsay looked toward the ceiling. "Uh, Jones, no, maybe Smith . . . no . . . oh, wait, I remember—it was Wilson. One time he put their dinner on a credit card and it bounced and Molly said it bounced like a Wilson basketball. Then he paid with cash. Cody Wilson."

"Do you know if she knows any of her neighbors in the apartment complex?"

"Only me. I live three apartments from here, and the units on either side of her are empty."

So no one would have heard a scuffle in the apartment, probably not even a scream. Maybe Molly still had the receipts, and

34

he could track the Wilson boy down. But at least he had a few leads, and someone back in Texas should know if she dated this Wilson kid there.

Ben locked the apartment, and they walked back to the diner, where Molly told them she'd get her accountant to find the credit card receipt. As they walked to their cars, Alex sifted through the information he'd learned. "This Johnny B's—what kind of truck stop is it?"

"It's a big trucker plaza. Nice hotel with a pool, two restaurants, one with twenty-five-dollar steaks, the other more like Molly's only updated with a coffee shop. There's a nightclub and a separate sports bar on the other end of the plaza. He leases everything out except the original diner and coffee shop. A lot of truckers and tourists as well stop at Johnny B's because of the easy access, good beds, and even better food. Where are you staying?"

"A bed and breakfast. The Potter's House, I think. I have the address in my GPS."

Ben gave him a strange look.

"What, is it a bad place?"

"Oh, not at all. Kate Adams is a great cook and her place is really nice. It's just something I remembered. Her daughter Robyn left town a little over two years ago, and no one's heard from her, except for one note and a phone call. She worked at Johnny B's."

■ ■ ■

Mac wasn't the only one to see Livy's failure. Captain Reed pulled off his headphones. "My office. Thirty minutes."

Livy nodded and removed her safety glasses and headphones, avoiding Mac's eyes.

"Olivia, I'm sorry."

She didn't want Mac's pity. "Don't be. It's not your fault."

"I wasn't saying it was, only that I know how much being a detective means to you."

No, he didn't. She'd thought he did, thought that he was like her—being a Memphis homicide detective was the only life she had. But he had Julie now, and she had . . . nothing. Did she even know who she was if she couldn't be a detective? She stuffed the headphones in her bag. Failure. The word chased itself through her head. She swallowed down the lump in her throat that threatened to choke her.

Mac put his hand on her arm. "There's no shame in being human. Give yourself time to work through the December shooting. You'll get your confidence back. I know you will."

At least he was still her cheerleader. She raised her gaze and caught him checking his watch. "Thanks. Go on and meet Julie. I'm fine."

"You sure?"

She nodded, not trusting herself to speak.

"Come on and we'll walk out together."

"No. I need a few minutes by myself before I meet with Reed."

"I'll check on you later today, okay?"

"I'll be fine. My aunt in Logan Point invited me to dinner, and it may be late before I get home." Questions swirled through Livy's mind, questions she wasn't sure she wanted answers to. She stared at her shoes. "Who do you think they'll partner you with?"

"It'll only be temporary, Olivia. You're my partner."

But what if it wasn't temporary?

■ ■ ■

With the sun setting behind her, Livy left her apartment and joined the rest of downtown Memphis headed east. She ran her hand through her hair and then glanced in her rearview mirror. Switching from dress clothes to jeans and a pullover wasn't the only change she'd made after leaving Reed's office. At least going from blonde to strawberry blonde wasn't as drastic as whacking her long hair off.

The earlier meeting with Reed had gone the way she expected. He'd given her two options. Take a leave or man a desk. Either way, she had to pass a psychological eval and a firing test before she resumed her duties as Mac's partner. She was to let him know in the morning which it would be.

Could she even sit behind a desk all day again? For six weeks after the Caine shooting, she monitored security cameras, a job straight from purgatory. But monitoring cameras was better than entering other detectives' notes into the computer. She didn't think she could bear to see what the others were doing and not be a part of it.

Livy took the Bill Morris Parkway and joined even more cars. She should have waited forty minutes to let traffic move out, but Kate served dinner at six sharp, and she didn't want to be late.

■ ■ ■

The Potter's House Bed and Breakfast. And below that sign another proclaimed Kate's Pottery Shop. That explained the name of the bed and breakfast. Alex turned into the drive and studied the two-story house through the bare limbs of a gnarled oak tree. An old house, probably predating the Civil War. He liked the gables and the wooden structure, but he wasn't sure he wouldn't prefer a hotel over staying in someone's home. But for whatever reason, this was where Dee put him, and he was eager to talk with the owner about her daughter. She just might not be eager to talk with him.

A cold north wind accompanied him up the steps to the front door. It opened before he rang the bell. "Mrs. Adams?"

"Kate," she corrected. "Come on in out of the cold."

The aroma of bread baking tickled Alex's nose as he stepped through the doorway and set his suitcase down in the warm foyer. Kate Adams wasn't quite what he expected. Jeans and a man's white shirt erased the image of a matronly innkeeper in a flowered dress and sensible shoes. Although she did have the sensible shoes. And while she appeared to be in her early sixties, matronly was never a word that would be associated with the woman wearing her hair in a long braid down her back.

"Would you like to look around the house before I show you to your room?"

"Sure." He followed her into a paneled room filled with books.

"This is obviously the library," she said. "Feel free to read anything in here—some of these books date back to when I was a child in the early fifties. Three or four of them belonged to my mother."

"I doubt I'll have time to read while I'm here, but it's a beautiful room." He followed her to the formal dining room, then into the kitchen.

"Supper is every night at six, and there's no extra charge." A bell dinged, and she opened the oven and took out two golden loaves of bread. "Most of the time it's just me and my husband, Charlie. But tonight my niece is joining us, along with my son-in-law and granddaughter."

"I don't want to intrude."

"You won't be. They're used to my guests joining the dinner table."

His stomach reminded him he'd skipped lunch. "Then I accept."

He glanced at his watch as he retrieved his suitcase from the foyer, then followed her upstairs. Only an hour until supper and he'd wanted to ask about her daughter. But one of the first things he'd discovered as an investigator was that asking questions before establishing a little bit of rapport usually netted less information. And who knew where the conversation might go around the dinner table.

"I'm putting you in the Porcelain room. It's connected to a bathroom, and usually I remind my guests to knock before entering, but seeing how no one else is here, it won't be necessary."

"Porcelain room?" Alex said.

"I thought it would be appropriate to name my rooms after different types of pottery. There are several porcelain pieces in here." She opened the door and waited for him to enter. "It was originally my oldest daughter's room."

The daughter who went missing? Alex caught the words while they were still a thought, and instead, scanned the bedroom that held a dark cherry double bed and matching chest. He pointed to an openwork jar with a lid. "Did you make this?"

"I did. Anything ceramic in the house, I probably made." She tilted her head slightly. "When your boss called, she said you were a private investigator."

"I am." Alex waited, sensing more than idle curiosity.

"I want to hire you to find my daughter."

"Mrs. Adams, I'm already working—"

"It's Kate, and it wouldn't take much of your time."

This was more than he bargained for. True, he'd hoped to discuss the missing daughter, but he hadn't expected her mother to want to hire him. "Why don't I put my things away, and then we'll discuss this further downstairs?"

Kate smiled. "Great."

Something told him Kate wouldn't take no for an answer, and while he had initially thought the two cases were related, until he heard the whole story, he wouldn't know. If he decided they weren't, he'd have to turn her down, at least until he found Samantha Jo.

After Alex transferred his clothes to the chest, he called Robert Woodson and inquired about any boyfriends Samantha Jo had. Woodson was emphatic that she had no boyfriend by the name of Cody. After hanging up, Alex stored his shaving kit in the bathroom and went to the kitchen. Kate had made herself a cup of tea. "There's a pot of coffee by the oven."

Evidently he didn't look like a tea man. "I actually enjoy an occasional cup of lapsang souchong." He smiled at her surprise.

"Earl Grey is pretty good too. But I think I'll pass on drinking anything right now." He sat at the table opposite Kate. "Tell me about your daughter."

"First, whatever we discuss, I'd prefer you not mention it at supper."

"No problem."

She took a deep breath. "Robyn left two and a half years ago, and other than a message on my son-in-law's answering machine and a letter to me three months later, we've heard nothing. Chase— that's my son-in-law—thinks she'll come back when she gets ready, but I don't think it's that simple."

"What did the message and letter say?"

"I listened to the message, and she just said she was sorry." Kate took a folded paper from her pocket and held it out to him. "And this is the letter she sent."

"Do you still have the envelope?"

"It's in my jewelry box. Do you want me to get it?"

"Not if you remember where it was postmarked."

"That I know. Knoxville, Tennessee. And my niece—the one who's coming to dinner—mailed her description and a photo to the Knoxville Police Department, but that's been a dead end."

He nodded and unfolded the paper and read the simple handwritten words. *I'm sorry, Mama, I wish I could come home, but I can't. Tell Abby I love her.* The date was just before Christmas two years ago. "She left in September?"

"Yes. She worked the evening shift at the Grill and Coffee Shoppe out at Johnny B's truck plaza, and no one's seen her since."

While Alex was sure coincidences happened, the disappearance of two waitresses who'd worked at the same restaurant, even years apart, was suspicious. "She didn't take any clothes?"

Kate shook her head. "That's why I've always believed she didn't go voluntarily."

He glanced at the letter, really no more than a note. "But if that's true, why not just come home instead of sending this? Knoxville isn't that far."

"Eight hours, and that's what Chase says. He thinks she ran off with someone."

"Were they having problems?"

"No more than most young couples. They argued over money, and Robyn wanted to work and Chase wanted her to stay home. I know she was depressed because she'd gained back all the weight she'd lost plus some, but she loved Abby. I just can't imagine her running off and leaving her."

Alex rubbed his jaw. "Do you know Samantha Jo Woodson?"

"Name's familiar. Why?"

"She's a waitress at Molly's Diner. Before that, she worked at Johnny B's at the Grill and Coffee Shoppe until some guy made her uncomfortable enough to quit. And she's missing."

"Just like my Robyn."

"Possibly."

The back door opened and a young girl ran in, bringing the scent of cold with her. "It's freezing, Nana."

Kate shot him a warning look. "We'll discuss this later." She hugged the child. "I'd like you to meet someone. Alex Jennings, this is my granddaughter, Abby Martin."

"I'm pleased to meet you," he said. The door opened again, and the girl's blonde ponytail bounced as she turned toward it.

"Daddy, come meet Mr. Jennings."

Alex stood as Chase Martin entered the kitchen. He could see where Abby got her beanpole frame, even though she was a much smaller version. Kate's son-in-law stood at least six one and could easily carry another fifty pounds. But Abby didn't get her blonde hair from him, unless it would turn dark as she got older.

The man shrugged out of his canvas Carhartt coat and then extended his hand. "I'm Chase Martin. Nice to meet you, Mr. Jennings."

He accepted his hand. "Just call me Alex."

"What brings you to Logan Point?"

Alex hesitated. "Business."

"You'll have to come back this summer and visit our lake." Chase turned to Kate. "Charlie said not to wait supper on him. He wanted to change the oil in the tractor before he quit for the day."

"I declare, that man doesn't know when to stop. Maybe he'll be here by the time Livy gets here."

"Aunt Livy is coming? Yay!" Abby glanced at Alex. "She's not really my aunt, but I call her that anyway."

Livy must be the niece Kate had mentioned. "What kind of tractor do you have?" he asked Chase.

"John Deere."

The door opened again, and two more people joined them.

Charlie and Livy, obviously. Or at least he hoped. He didn't think the kitchen could hold many more people.

"I thought you were going to work on the tractor," Kate said.

"I couldn't find any oil," Charlie said as he hung a red baseball cap on the coatrack. "I'll pick up some in town tomorrow."

When Charlie saw Alex, he nodded and Alex returned the nod, but it was the petite strawberry blonde who had caught his attention. And not just his.

"Aunt Livy, you changed the color of your hair!"

"Do you like it?" Livy asked and whirled around, fluffing her hair.

Kate grimaced. "I don't understand why you keep changing it, but it's better than some things you do to it."

Livy's blue eyes sparkled as she hugged Abby, and dimples popped in her cheeks when she laughed at something the girl said. She looked up and caught him staring.

"Oh!" Her cheeks turned pink. "I didn't know you had a guest, Kate."

Kate made the introductions and then told everyone to grab a plate and help themselves. As they gathered around the kitchen table, Alex paused. He couldn't imagine his family sitting down for a meal anywhere except the formal dining room. Everyone grew quiet as they grabbed the hand of the person next to them.

Abby nudged him and held out her hand. "We always hold hands when we ask the blessing."

He took her hand, and she pointed her head toward Livy. "Oh," he said. Livy stretched her arm across the table, and he slipped his hand into hers. As he bowed his head with the others, the warmth in Livy's fingers sent a shiver up his arm.

"Our dear heavenly Father," Kate said, "what a blessing to be able to gather our family at this table. Thank you for each of them, and thank you for bringing this nice young man to share our meal. May you use each of us in your kingdom. Bless this food to the nourishment of our bodies. Amen."

Abby and Livy squeezed his fingers when Kate said amen, then withdrew their hands. Alex's thoughts lingered on Kate's prayer. So different from his grandfather's. It was almost like Kate was having a conversation with God. He didn't know people did that. He looked up as Abby nudged him again. Livy held a plate of thick-sliced bread, waiting for him to take it. "I'm sorry," he said and took the plate. "I guess my mind was woolgathering."

Abby giggled. "What's woolgathering?"

"Daydreaming. You know, like you do when you're supposed to be doing your homework," Livy said, then shifted her gaze toward him. "What brings you to Logan Point?"

"Business," Chase replied.

"I figured that," she retorted, making a face at him. She turned to Alex again. "What type of business brought you here?"

He always felt self-conscious explaining what he did. Most people either glamorized it or looked at him like he just crawled out from under a rock. He should have worked on a cover story.

"He's a private investigator," Kate said, saving him the trouble.

"Really?" Abby's voice rose an octave. "He's like you, Aunt Livy."

He turned to Livy, and a pained expression crossed her face. She definitely fell into the latter category. "I gather you're not a private investigator?"

"Hardly. I'm a homicide detective for the Memphis Police Department."

4

A private investigator. Who would have thought the handsome stranger would do something so sleazy. Not that Livy thought all PIs were sleazy. But the ones she'd encountered who were any good were retired police officers, and Mr. Jennings was too young to fit that bill.

"Maybe you can find my mommy."

Abby's words stilled the room.

"That's a thought," Charlie said.

Kate squeezed her husband's hand. "I agree."

Her aunt had mentioned a private investigator in the past. Had she brought this Alex Jennings to Logan Point? No, Kate would have told her if she had.

"I'm sure Mr. Jennings is much too busy," said Chase.

The PI frowned. "Please, Mr. Jennings makes me sound all serious and organized, and anyone who knows me will assure you, I'm anything but that."

Livy frowned. "If you don't take your job seriously—"

"Didn't say that," he said. "But I'll probably be here for a few days, so just call me Alex."

"Well," Kate said, "I think discussing this with *Alex* in view of hiring him is a perfectly logical thing for us to do. Especially since he's already working on a similar case. Samantha Jo Woodson has gone missing the same way our Robyn did."

Samantha Jo, the girl who had recently started coming to church, the one who had taken Livy's self-defense course? She, as well as everyone else, turned to stare at Alex. A splotch of red spread across his face. Livy leaned forward. "Is Samantha Jo really missing? Or did she go off with that Cody Wilson boy that she came here with?"

"We don't know."

"We?" Livy asked.

"Ben Logan and I talked with her boss earlier today. So far, no one has seen her since Saturday—she just seems to have left."

Abby's eyes grew round. "That's just like what happened to Mommy."

This was a conversation her niece did not need to be a part of. "Alex, where are you from?" Livy asked.

His eyebrows pinched together, but when she shifted her eyes toward Abby, understanding crossed his brown eyes, and he gave a slight nod. "Dallas area. How long have you been a detective?"

So the mysterious Mr. Jennings didn't want to talk about himself. "Six years. What do you do when you're not being a private investigator?"

"I'm a flight instructor at a small airport outside Dallas."

Her stomach clenched. The man flew airplanes? Like her dad?

"What do you do when you're not detecting?"

Livy narrowed her eyes. "I—"

"She doesn't do anything," Kate said. "She's always detecting, as you say."

Livy opened her mouth to protest and closed it. She hated admitting her aunt was right. When had she let her job take over her life? Or maybe the better question was why.

Chase tapped his daughter on the head. "Finish your meal, pumpkin, we need to get home so you can do your homework."

"Aw, Dad, I want to stay and talk to Mr. Alex about finding Mommy."

"He's much too busy to take on anything like that. Right?" Chase said, turning to Alex.

Livy hurt for her niece. And Chase. They both missed Robyn so much. But like Chase, she didn't want Abby to get her hopes up that this PI could find Robyn.

"I'm pretty busy . . ." Abby's shoulders drooped, and Alex took a deep breath. "I tell you what. If I run across any information about your mom, I'll let your dad know."

"Really?"

"Really."

Livy would have to give Alex points for trying to let Abby down easy, but she would reserve judgment on his professional abilities. She hadn't been able to find her cousin, and she doubted he would either.

Silence fell around the table as everyone focused on eating. After Abby finished her chocolate cake, Chase pushed back from the table. "Thanks for dinner, Kate. With Mom out of town, we've been struggling." He glanced at his daughter. "Are you ready?"

Livy stood and took out her phone. "How about a photo before you two leave?"

Chase moved away from his daughter. "Not me."

She laughed and snapped a shot of Abby posing with one hand behind the back of her head, the other on her hip, then one of her blowing kisses. "Thank you very much. I'll post these on Facebook. Tell all your friends."

After the door closed behind Abby and Chase, Livy picked up her dish. "Let me help you with these before I leave."

"No, that's what I'm for," Charlie said, taking the plate from her hands.

"And dishwashers," Kate added. "I'd rather you talk with Alex and tell him what you've found in your investigation of Robyn."

Livy sat back down as something inside her resisted, maybe because Alex had a case to work on while she faced weeks behind a desk. But he must be pretty reputable or Ben wouldn't have given him the time of day. She made a mental note to check with Logan Point's sheriff in the morning. Get his impressions of Alex.

"Let me grab my notebook," Alex said.

In spite of Kate's protest, Livy helped with the dishes while Alex went upstairs, and they quickly had the kitchen cleaned.

Charlie hung his drying cloth on the rack. "And ladies, I'm going to bed."

"Good night," Livy called after him.

"Why don't you stay the night?" Kate asked. "You have clothes here."

The offer tempted her. The thought of going home to her empty apartment and staring at the four walls until bedtime turned her stomach. "Which room did you give Alex?"

"Bailey's."

The other end of the hall. If she stayed, at least they wouldn't be running over each other. "I think I will."

"Good. I'll put fresh linens in your room." Kate turned to go upstairs and stopped. "Did you get the email from your dad saying he'd be home in a couple of weeks?"

"Yeah, I received it." She'd heard his broken promises before, but this was one time she could really use his support. "Do you think he'll come this time?"

"I had a good talk with him a few days ago and told him he needed to come home. He promised he'd fly in soon."

Why did she even care about the man who dumped her and her sister on Kate when Livy was seven? A memory of riding on his shoulders surfaced. *Because he'd been so different before my mother died.* Unexpected tears stung Livy's eyes, and she blinked them back.

Kate's expression softened, and she put her arm around Livy.

"He's a good man, but sometimes I could just shake that brother of mine when he doesn't stay in contact with us."

Livy flicked a tear from her cheek. "I'm fine, and don't worry about the linens. I'll get them when I go upstairs."

"You'll do nothing of the sort. I'll put them on your bed."

After Kate went upstairs, Livy settled in her usual spot at the table while she waited for Alex to return. She glanced around the kitchen. Funny how Kate and Charlie's house was more home to her than her own apartment, even though she hadn't lived here in ten years. She jerked her head around as Alex blew into the kitchen.

"I'm sorry," he said. "I had a phone call from Samantha Jo's father."

"No problem. Anything new?"

"Not really. He had a couple of names for me to check out in Nashville."

She'd heard Samantha Jo sing in church and could see how she might make it in Music City. Alex sat at the table and placed a yellow legal pad beside him. The private investigator reminded her of someone. The dark hair and eyes. Broad shoulders . . . the way he carried himself, not cocky but with confidence. Her heart fluttered. The Brazilian soccer player. No wonder her heart beat faster when she was around him. She loved to watch Kaka play, and not just for the sport.

"Samantha Jo hasn't been seen since Saturday night." He glanced up at Livy. "Did she ever mention why she came to Logan Point?"

"She told me she wanted to be a singer but ran out of money. She worked in Memphis for a couple of weeks before coming here. She thought Logan Point would be safer."

"Okay. That tracks with what I got out of her parents earlier today. They wanted her to go to college, and she wanted to go to Nashville. They weren't paying for that, didn't think her voice was strong enough to sing professionally. So she struck out on her own. They received a call from her before Thanksgiving, and she was stuck in Memphis with no money and her Malibu had broken down. They offered her a bus ticket home and to send her to college. She hung up on them."

Livy shook her head. "And arrived here right after that with Cody Wilson. What was that girl thinking?"

"She wasn't." He looked up from the pad. "How about your cousin? Did she leave in a vehicle?"

Livy nodded. "She had a little Frontier pickup."

"And you haven't been able to trace it?"

"The motor number has never shown up for titling or even car tags."

"So she's either running it with expired tags or it's been scrapped."

"Or dumped somewhere." Alex was thorough. She'd have to give him that. "How long have you been a PI?"

"Three years."

"Any background in criminal justice?"

"A little. I have a law degree, and I specialized in criminal law."

"You're a criminal defense lawyer?"

"I didn't say that. I think you have to pass the bar before you can practice law. And seeing as how I've never taken it, no, I'm not a lawyer." A smile teased at the corner of his mouth. "And from your tone, you'll probably be glad to know my dad is the district attorney in Dallas."

For once, Livy was at a loss for words.

"Back to your cousin," Alex said. "Did she ever mention anyone at work who bothered her?"

"I didn't talk to Robyn much during that time. She had withdrawn. I think she and Chase were having a few problems. Nothing that couldn't be worked out, at least that's what I thought . . ." Livy tried to shrug off the guilt that dogged her for not paying more attention to her cousin. "Looking back, I think she was depressed. It bothers me that I didn't tune in to that when we were together."

"People often hide depression."

"Why haven't you taken the bar exam?" She knew it was none of her business, but she couldn't help it. The question kept bugging her, because in spite of what he said about not being organized, Alex Jennings was very put together. Maybe he just didn't have follow-through, like her dad.

He gave her a double look. "What?" He waved his hand. "Never mind. I know what you asked. I just can't believe you asked it."

"I think that's a perfectly natural question to ask after someone says they have a law degree."

His eyes narrowed. "If I answer it, do you think we can get back to this case?"

"Forget I asked. I didn't know it would become a federal case."

"Thank you." He checked his watch. "Oh, wait. It's almost nine, and I have to call my boss. Do you think you could take time to talk again in the morning? Or even better, do you think you could help me with this case? I really need someone local to go around with me to places like the truck plaza, and I hate to ask Sheriff Logan to take up more time with me."

Livy mulled his question. She had little patience for people who didn't follow through. People like her dad. But Alex seemed sincere in trying to find Samantha Jo. Maybe she should at least give him a chance.

"I have a job that comes first," she said. One she didn't really want to go to. And if Alex knew she had lost her confidence, he might take back the offer. But at least working on this case would give her something to look forward to after shuffling papers all day, or even worse, watching security monitors. "However, since I'm mostly doing paperwork right now, I'll see if I can take off tomorrow afternoon. You're right that you'll get a lot more out of folks around here if I go with you." Maybe she should tell him about the Caine shooting. No. Mr. Got-It-All-Together wouldn't understand, and they were only going out to Johnny

B's. She wouldn't even need her gun there. "Can you wait until after lunch?"

"I'll wait. I want to go back and talk to Molly at the diner and then check out Samantha Jo's apartment again. I can do that in the morning." He studied her for a minute. "Why are you sitting behind a desk?"

She lifted her shoulder in a half shrug. "It's too complicated for a two-minute conversation, and you have to call your boss. Maybe tomorrow, when we'll have more time." She stood. "I think I'll get ready for bed."

Livy had reached the door when he called her name. "Yes?"

"I haven't taken the bar because I don't want to be a lawyer."

She stared at him. That opened a whole new set of questions. Like why he'd gone to law school in the first place if he didn't want to practice law. But he was already dialing his cell phone. The answer would have to wait until tomorrow.

■ ■ ■

"Daddy, do you think Mr. Alex can find Mom?"

Chase paused in his reading of *The Black Stallion*. Abby's blue eyes held hope, the very thing he had been afraid of, and he didn't want to crush it. Especially not right before bedtime. She'd already lost enough sleep the past two and a half years worrying about her mother. "I don't know, pumpkin. Why don't we talk about this in the morning? Right now you need to get your beauty rest so you can knock the socks off those fifth grade boys in your class."

"Aw, Daddy. Boys are . . ." She made a face. "Icky. Except for TJ. He's not so bad."

How he wished Abby would keep that attitude. He smoothed back a tendril of blonde hair. She would be quite the knockout in a few years. A few short years. He dreaded the day when she told him she was too old for him to read to her. She yawned. "Why don't we finish this tomorrow night?" he said. The issue with

Robyn must really be bothering her if she couldn't keep her mind on her favorite book.

"Okay." She snuggled into her pillow. Her eyes popped open. "Wait! We didn't say our prayers."

She climbed out of bed and knelt beside where he sat on the bed. "God, thank you for the hundred on my test today. And for dinner tonight at Nana's, and for . . . just everything. Bless Daddy and Nana and Gramps and Granna Martin, and Aunt Livy and that nice Mr. Alex. Would you help him to find my mom? And bless Mom wherever she is. Amen."

Her prayer tore at his heart. Abby saw the good in everyone and everything. Sometimes he'd give anything to go back to believing good could be brought out of any situation. He clenched his jaw. Robyn had destroyed that. "Okay. Time to get that beauty rest." He tucked her in. "See you in the morning."

In the kitchen, Chase glanced at the envelope on the table before rummaging through the cabinets for something sweet. It was a bad habit he'd picked up, but as he looked at the almost empty shelves, he realized it was one that wouldn't be satisfied tonight. Tomorrow, the grocery store. With a sigh, he picked up the envelope. Divorce papers. All he had to do was sign them. He didn't understand what was so hard about it. Robyn wasn't coming back, and he needed to get on with his life. Not that he ever expected to marry again. He'd never trust another woman with his heart.

Once he signed them, he'd have to tell Abby. And Kate. And Charlie. His mother already knew and didn't approve. He worried his bottom lip with his teeth, until finally he folded the papers and put them back in the envelope. He didn't have to sign them tonight. He picked up the legal document and took it to his office. Until he was ready, he didn't want to risk Abby finding it.

After Chase showered and climbed into bed, he stared up at the ceiling. *Are you up there, God?* Abby's simple prayer earlier had reminded him that it'd been a while since he'd prayed. His mind flipped back to the days before Robyn left. They had argued day and night about money, her working . . . the last straw had been when she had to work the evening shift.

"What about Abby?" he'd said. "You won't be here when she gets off the school bus."

"Don't you dare criticize the way I take care of Abby," she'd argued back. "You know I'm a good mother. Your problem is I won't be here when *you* get home, but why would you care? You never say anything unless it's to criticize me. 'Do you need to eat that dessert? I thought you were worried about gaining weight. Why did you buy Abby another pair of jeans? Can't you at least stay on budget?'"

She'd mimicked his voice, and even now, his angry words shamed him. He rolled over, but his thoughts came with him. When had their life and marriage been reduced to nothing more than hurtful words and silence?

One thing Robyn had been right about. She was a good mother. That's what made it so hard to understand why she left. What if she didn't leave voluntarily? No. He squeezed his eyes shut, trying to get rid of that thought. He'd rather believe she left them for the reason she left on the answering machine. *I'm no good to anyone like I am. I need to discover who I am, so please, don't try to find me.*

He clung to that message, believing she left it of her own accord. Because if he didn't, he'd have to accept that she might be dead.

5

Robyn Martin shut the hall door and willed her rubbery legs to turn around. How had Will Jensen gotten into the living room of the safe house? How did he even find it? The Tennessee/Virginia state line split Bristol in half, and the shelter was on the Virginia side. Either way, it was a good thirty miles from his home in Kingsport. Outside, the fluorescent streetlight flickered and went out. Her heart rate jumped another notch. She'd asked the city to replace that light a month ago. Somewhere in the back of the house, a door opened and closed. Her director getting the woman and child out of the house.

"I want my wife and daughter. They're mine."

She wanted to tell him they weren't property, but Jensen stood with his hands fisted at his side, his feet planted wide, and his eyes bulging. If he were a volcano, he'd be ready to blow. She twisted a ring on her finger, listening for the wail of a siren or some indication that the Bristol, Virginia, police were on the way. Hearing nothing, she took a deep breath. "Mr. Jensen, you seem to be a reasonable man."

Robyn kept her voice low and even. She ran her gaze over him, trying to detect whether he had a gun, and didn't see anything that indicated he might be carrying. "And I'm sure you want what's best for your family. Right?"

Confusion edged into the man's face. "What do you mean?"

"You frighten them when you get angry like this. But I know you have a lot to be angry about. Losing your job, your mother dying . . . would your mother want you to frighten your daughter?"

"How did you know—she told you, didn't she?"

"She's worried about you. And I am too. The Bristol police are on their way. If you're still here when they arrive, you will be taken to jail. You don't want that, do you?"

He opened and closed his fists. "They'll take my side."

"Will they? Did they the last time?"

Indecision crossed his face. A faint siren wailed. "You don't want to be here when they arrive," she said.

His tongue darted out, swiping his lips. "You tell her . . . you tell my wife I'm coming back. You tell her that." He whirled around and stalked out the door.

Robyn made it to the sofa before her legs turned to jelly. She braced her elbow on the sofa arm and supported her head with her hand and took deep breaths. Within a minute, the drive filled with police cars. Still trembling, she pushed herself off the sofa and forced herself to walk to the door he'd left open. She had to let them know Jensen had left the premises.

"He's gone," she called. Another car pulled in front of the safe house, and her director climbed out, followed by Jensen's wife and daughter. Maybe Jensen wouldn't return tonight. By tomorrow, his family would be at another safe house. Hopefully one he wouldn't find.

Two hours later, Jensen's wife and daughter had been moved to another safe house, but Robyn couldn't get the nine-year-old girl off her mind. Small for her age, but a spunky little thing. Like Abby. The thought ambushed her just as the kettle she'd set on the stove whistled. She shoved the thought from her mind as well as the one that came after it. She couldn't go home.

Robyn turned the eye off and picked up the kettle, halting with it halfway to her cup as the lock in the door clicked. She relaxed as the director of the safe house entered the kitchen. Besides being the director, Susan was her best friend in Bristol.

"You startled me. I didn't think you'd get back so soon." Robyn poured boiling water over a bag of herbal tea, releasing the peach-flavored scent.

Susan Carpenter kicked off her shoes and placed her purse on the table. A satisfied smile stretched across her brown face. "The transfer went quicker than I expected. Is there any more tea?"

Robyn pushed the tin toward her, then took her cup to the table. A few minutes later, Susan joined her, easing her bulk into the chair.

"You did really well tonight. Handled the situation like a pro."

"Thanks." In the past two and a half years, she had spent enough time in therapy and classes to handle any situation. Any except going home to Logan Point.

Susan's phone dinged, and she checked it. "Oh, how sweet," she said, and looked up. "My daughter put the new baby's picture on Facebook. See?"

She handed Robyn the phone. "She's beautiful." Robyn scrolled through the other photos of the baby, then looked up. "Do you mind if . . ."

"No, feel free."

In spite of the resolve she'd made the last time she went to her cousin's Facebook page, she typed Livy's name in the search bar and waited for her page to come up. For some reason, the photos Livy posted were visible even though Susan wasn't friends with her cousin. Her heart almost stopped when a picture of Abby materialized. She must have been in a playful mood, posing like a 1950s calendar girl. She shut her eyes. Why did she do this to herself? It only made not seeing her daughter worse.

"Don't you think it's time to set things right?" Susan's voice broke the quiet in the kitchen.

Her fingers sought the wedding band she'd had repaired after the doctors cut it off in the ER. "I can't."

"What happened to you was not your fault."

"I'm not completely blameless. Chase tried to get me to quit Johnny B's." She looked up from the phone and brought her hand to her face. "The man said he would kill me if I ever told. Almost did, anyway."

"Still no memory of him or what happened?"

She shook her head. "Nothing's changed since the last time we talked about this. The only thing I remember is hanging around Johnny B's for a little while after I'd gotten off from work. I was drinking a soda, somebody asked for more ice, and everyone else was busy, so I took care of it. The last thing I remember is not feeling well and thinking I might be taking the flu."

"He probably put GHB or rohypnol in your drink and then followed you outside." Susan squeezed her hand. "I know I sound like a broken record, but it wasn't your fault. Go home to your family. Let them help you heal."

The image of a hawk with its talons extended flashed in Robyn's brain. Her stomach cramped, and sweat broke out on her face. She hugged her arms to her chest.

"Take a deep breath," Susan said. She grabbed a paper towel and wet it. "Here, put this on your face."

Her stomach heaved. "Pan!" She motioned with her hand, and Susan grabbed a pan, shoving it under her chin. Seconds later, her supper came up.

"I'm sorry. I shouldn't have pushed you." Susan handed her another wet towel.

Robyn pressed the towel against her lips. She shook her head. "Not your fault. I saw . . ." She licked her lips and tried to make sense of what she'd seen. "It was a bird. Like a hawk, and it had its talons like this." She formed her hands into claws. "Like it was grabbing something."

"Do you still think the man had a tattoo?"

"I don't know. Whatever he gave me wiped out so much of that night. I don't even remember him beating me, or you helping me, only how bad I hurt when I woke up in the hospital here in Bristol."

She picked up Susan's phone again and opened the Facebook app. Abby's laughing face appeared, and she choked back tears. "I wish I could go home. But what if he's there, waiting for me? Even here, I don't feel safe."

"I don't think he'd recognize you if he saw you. You look nothing like you did thirty months ago."

Robyn eyed her friend. She may have lost weight and colored her hair, but she was pretty sure anyone from Logan Point would recognize her.

"Hand me my phone." Susan took the phone and said, "Smile."

In spite of herself, Robyn smiled, and the camera flashed. "This is dumb."

"Just wait." Her friend scrolled through her photos. "This is you a month after you came here."

Robyn looked at the photo. Yeah, curly red hair, overweight, big nose that she'd always hated, only bigger because it had been broken. In her mind, that was the way she still looked.

"Now look at what I just took."

She scrolled to the photo Susan indicated. Blonde hair now and straight as a board, courtesy of a flat iron. When her jaw had been wired shut, the pounds melted off, and she now wore a size six instead of a sixteen, and the big nose—it was gone too. She'd had so much trouble breathing after the man smashed it a plastic surgeon had offered to repair the damage. The nose she'd always wanted was the only good thing that had come out of that night.

She'd trade it for the old one in a heartbeat just to go back to the day before it all happened and make different choices. Quit her job like Chase had been bugging her to. Go back to school. Any number of choices.

"I'll loan you my car. You could go back and check things out. No one would have to know who you are."

She stared at Susan, an idea formulating in her mind. If she could just see Abby, know that she was all right. She looked at her photo again, really seeing the difference. It was time to stop seeing the old Robyn when she looked in the mirror, and start embracing the new one. If she went back, no one would recognize her. She could slip into town and slip back out.

"What will you do for a car?"

"I can drive the van. Go, Robyn. Set yourself free."

Free. Would she ever be free? Not as long as that man was out there. But if she could just see Abby one more time . . . She breathed a deep breath through her nose and exhaled. "Okay. First thing in the morning."

■ ■ ■

He searched the internet like he had every night for two and a half years, typing in every variation of Robyn Adams Martin he could find. He'd thought Robyn would be grateful that he'd saved her from those men at the grill. But she'd fought him and had escaped. But he would find her, and when he did, she would be punished.

He even checked Olivia Reynolds's Facebook page. Reynolds had made her photos public. Only one reason the detective would do that. Reynolds knew her cousin was out there somewhere, and she thought if Robyn saw pictures of her daughter, maybe she would come home.

Outside, north winds howled, moaning through the trees like banshees. Or was that . . . He better go and see. He shut the computer down and shrugged into a down coat, feeling the pockets for the syringe. Satisfied, he hurried to the barn, stopping once to pick up a rock.

The voices had made him build the cage—a place to keep the one they chose to replace Sharon. He'd argued. He didn't need a replacement. It was better to turn the mothers loose with a warning to quit their waitress jobs. But they wouldn't listen and chose Tina.

He shifted the rock to his left hand. Thinking about the waitress from Gulfport made him sad. At least he'd learned a few things because of her. Blackout windows, and he'd reinforced the cage. And he no longer unlocked the door unless the girl was knocked out.

Near the door, screams blended with the wind. He wished she wouldn't make him do this. He hated using the drugs. But he couldn't have her screaming like that. It would disturb his mother. He pulled a pair of night goggles from his coat pocket and slipped them on before entering the pitch-black barn. She stood at the cage, gripping the bars, and he smelled her fear. Sour, acidic pheromones. Years of smelling his own had honed his senses. He stood a little taller. He was the giver of life . . . or death.

"Let me out of here!"

How did she do that? Know he'd come into the barn. She yelled again. Really, it'd been four days. Hadn't she figured out she wasn't leaving here? "All this yelling," he said. "Stop it."

"Please," she sobbed. "Let me go. I promise I won't tell anyone. My father. He'll pay you whatever you ask."

"Sharon, I don't want money." He kept his eyes on her as he hesitated at the door to the cage. So beautiful. Like an orchid. But that blonde hair. "Why did you bleach your hair, Sharon?"

She turned toward his voice. "I've told you over and over again. I'm not Sharon. My name is Samantha Jo Woodson. My grandfather is a state senator in Texas. He'll pay whatever you ask."

He'd have to dye her hair back to its natural color. Tomorrow he would pick out the right shade of red, and tomorrow night she would change her hair to its natural color, or he'd sedate her and do it himself.

He slipped the prefilled hypodermic syringe from his pocket. From the other pocket he took out the rock he'd picked up and threw it against the wall of the cell as he unlocked the door. She whirled around, and he slipped inside the cage.

She felt the air in front of her.

Silently he slipped behind her and grabbed her in a choke hold, quickly injecting the rohypnol in her neck. Just as quickly, he let her go and slipped back out of the cell, locking it. "I wouldn't have to do this if you would just be quiet."

She collapsed in a heap. "Please, please let me go."

"Listen to me, Sharon." He whispered the words. "You're not leaving me again. If you would just accept that you're so much better off here with me instead of working where those men watch you. Did you know they watched you?"

"No." Her voice faded.

"You're mine, Sharon. Only mine."

6

By eleven Thursday, Livy thought she would lose her mind. She could not sit in this cubicle behind a desk for however long it took to get her confidence back. Did she even want to be a cop any longer? She'd tossed and turned half the night wrestling with that question.

Maybe it'd be easier to look for something else to do with her life. Like what? Being a homicide detective is all she'd ever wanted to do. Was she going to let the tragedy with Justin Caine take her dream away? Resolve surged up from inside her. No. But sitting behind a desk, shuffling papers, would not get her confidence back.

Do you think you could help me with this case? Alex Jennings's question last night surfaced in her thoughts. Nothing about the case required a gun—just following up on leads. Maybe if she really threw herself into helping Alex solve Samantha Jo's case, it would be the boost she needed to get past what happened with Caine. She closed the folder and walked to Captain Reed's office. "Can I talk to you?"

He motioned her in. "Close the door. Have you made an appointment with Dr. Robinson?"

"No. I want to see someone else. Taylor Martin, I mean Sinclair." She had trouble remembering to use Taylor's married name.

"The profiler who helped us last summer with the Wilson case?"

Livy nodded. "I want to take a leave of absence until I can figure out what's going on in my head."

"I think that's a good idea. When do you want to start your leave?"

"How about right now? I can't shuffle papers indefinitely—I'll go crazy."

"Fill out the paperwork before you leave." He studied her for a minute. "You'll get your confidence back, Livy. Killing someone, even in the line of duty, is a hard thing to deal with."

"Have you ever . . ."

"Yes."

He glanced down at his desk, and when he looked up again, she read the same pain in his eyes that haunted her.

"I believe it's something a good cop never gets over. You have to compartmentalize and not open that box, or it will eat you up."

Livy didn't want to say it, but compartmentalizing was easier for men—their minds automatically separated things into boxes. For women, on the other hand, everything was connected. It was harder for women to put distance between themselves and anything that affected them emotionally. But she nodded. No reason to give the captain another reason to keep her benched. "Thank you, sir. I'll stay in touch and let you know how I'm progressing."

Outside Reed's office, she searched for Mac and found him in the break room. "How are you today?"

"Okay. Still sore, but no more arrhythmia. You?"

Mac's voice was guarded, almost like he was walking on egg-shells. She'd give anything to have their easy camaraderie back. "I just asked for a leave."

The pinched brows relaxed. "That's great. I know you'll be back and better than ever. You just need a little time."

"I know."

He hugged Livy, surprising her.

"I wasn't trying to hurt you when I told Reed that you were

having trouble. Olivia, I care about you. You're like a kid sister, and I was just trying to look out for you."

She pressed her lips together. Three years they'd been partners, and somehow she'd missed that Mac thought of her like a sister. She never had a brother to look out for her, only a cousin—Ben Logan—and come to think of it, Mac and Ben treated her the same way. Somewhere in the back of her mind she had this fantasy that one day Mac would look at her and see more than a partner.

She didn't know whether to laugh or cry from embarrassment. At least she'd never told him her feelings, and hearing him say the words *kid sister* was kind of a release from something she never had. This might be the time to let him know she was glad Julie was back in his life. "Look, I hope you and Julie can work things out."

He startled. "I . . . I don't know what you mean."

She stared at him. She'd observed the way his ex looked at him. Was it possible he didn't know that Julie was still in love with him? "You'll get it, just give it time."

As she walked out of the Criminal Justice Center, Livy could have sworn she heard a door close. She turned to look back. Concrete and glass. She remembered the first day she walked through the glass doors. Excited. Anxious. Fearful. All of it rolled into a dream come true. She pressed her lips together and nodded toward the building. She would be back.

So why did walking away feel so final?

Livy drove to her apartment and picked up a few clothes. No sense in trying to stay in Memphis if she planned to work in Logan Point with Alex on the two cases. And as for the counseling sessions, she would bring that up the next time she talked to Taylor. Maybe she didn't even need them. She locked the dead bolt on the door of her apartment, once again sensing finality. It was as though she was starting a new chapter in her life, but on the drive to Logan Point, she couldn't get the old chapter off her mind, Mac and Julie in particular.

How long had it been since she'd had a serious relationship? Too many years to count. Men just didn't live up to her expectations. *Mac did.* Yeah, but they didn't have a dating relationship, and if she went beneath the surface of those feelings, she knew what she'd find. Mac was desirable because he was unattainable—just like the soccer player she drooled over on TV. She'd always known he still carried feelings for his ex-wife and therefore that made him safe to care about. So why was it so difficult for her to fall in love?

Like she had to ask. The men she'd dated in the past were a lot like her dad. Here today and gone tomorrow. And what was it with picking the same man over and over, except for their name? Was she subconsciously attracted to men like her dad?

Jeremy Reynolds had showed her early on that men could not be depended on. Her father would rather be off flying his airplane in Alaska than keeping his promise to come home for her birthday. Year after year until she quit reminding him of the date. And he never remembered on his own. Not once in the last fifteen years. Oh, a week later, maybe, but never on her birthday.

Which reminded her not to get caught up in Alex Jennings and his laid-back personality either. Any man who flew small airplanes probably had the same wanderlust her dad did. Alex already had one thing in common with her dad—he didn't follow through, or he would have already taken the bar exam. And his explanation that he didn't want to practice law didn't wash. Who in their right mind worked for a law degree if they didn't want to practice law?

■ ■ ■

Alex sat at the traffic light, drumming his fingers on the steering wheel. February was a short month, reminding him he had little time to waste in finding Samantha Jo. So far he had nothing. She could easily be off with her boyfriend. Or she could've gotten the urge to move on to Nashville. But she would not have left her J Brand jeans behind. It took a certain personality to wear the two-hundred-dollar jeans. His last girlfriend wore them, and she wouldn't be caught dead in anything else. *Dead*. Not a word he wanted to associate with this case.

When the light changed, he turned and drove slowly around the town square. It was a charming little town with storefronts reminiscent of the fifties and sixties, only newer looking. Evidently a huge restoration had taken place not long ago. He parked the Impala in front of the jail and climbed out. He'd heard the weatherman report that the temperature would be close to sixty. That was what he loved about the South. It usually didn't stay cold long. When he went inside the sheriff's department, the receptionist looked up. "It's Alex, isn't it?"

"I'm surprised you remember me." What was her name? Millie? No. Maggie. "Is Ben around, Maggie?"

"Let me buzz him." She spoke into the phone, then nodded. "He said to come on back. Third door on the right."

Alex walked down the hall and located Ben's office.

"I'm glad you came by," Ben said when Alex entered his office. He nodded toward another man sitting on the sofa. "Alex, Wade Hatcher, my chief deputy."

Alex shook the outstretched hand.

"We were just going over to Samantha Jo's apartment to comb through it. Want to come along?"

"You bet. I'll follow you."

At the apartment, each man pulled on latex gloves and took a room. In the kitchen, Alex sorted through the mail on the counter. Nothing but utility bills and advertisements. He went through the drawers, then the pantry. Nothing unusual other than Samantha Jo was very tidy. He turned and ran his gaze around the small room, looking for anything out of place. On one wall, a whiteboard listed her schedule at the diner for the week. He stepped closer. An envelope had been stuck behind the board, and he removed it.

Childish letters spelled out her name and address. "Ben, I might have something here."

The envelope had been opened. He slid the paper out. The same lettering. *I warned you, but you didn't listen. Quit the job at Johnny B's or else.*

"What do you have?" Ben asked.

Alex handed him the letter as Wade joined them. "It looks like a threat."

"Why didn't she report this?" Wade asked.

"Maybe it's from her boyfriend. That Cody Wilson kid," Alex said.

"Turns out that wasn't his name. The credit card was stolen, and the boyfriend had maxed the card out just prior to using it at Molly's."

"The owner didn't report it?"

"The real Cody Wilson didn't know until his bill came in, and that was in December—it was a card he didn't use much. How about Samantha Jo's parents? What'd you learn from them?"

"They'd never heard of him." Alex flexed his fingers. The urgency to find Samantha Jo gnawed at him.

Ben scratched his jaw. "Let's go see if ViCAP has anything similar to this case reported."

Two hours later, the three of them pored over the results of the queries. "One hundred and three cases of waitresses in the eighteen-to twenty-nine age range who disappeared and haven't been found."

"Look at this," Wade said. "Five cases where waitresses reported being abducted and left in strange places. Each of them had received anonymous notes at some point before their abductions."

"Does it mention what the notes said?" Ben asked.

Wade looked closer at the sheet of paper. "They were warnings for the waitresses to quit their jobs and take care of their children."

Alex leaned forward. "But why would he take Samantha Jo? She didn't have a child. And this note doesn't mention one."

"Good question. Perhaps he thinks she does," Ben said.

Wade pointed to the note. "This sounds like it's not the first note she received."

It didn't make sense. But then crime never did to Alex. He looked over the ViCAP sheet again. "Could any of the women identify their captor?"

"No. In each case, the waitress had no recollection of how they got to where they were dumped." Wade read a little further. "Lab reports show traces of GHB, but no sign of sexual assault."

"Where did these attacks occur?" Alex asked.

"Kentucky, Ohio, South Carolina, North Carolina, and Tennessee."

Ben stood and walked to the whiteboard in his office. "Give me the location with dates."

Wade read the names and dates. "Columbia, South Carolina, January two years ago; Cedar Point, North Carolina, May, four months later; Henderson, Kentucky, August of last year; Nashville, Tennessee, October of last year; Cincinnati, Ohio, a month later in November."

The sheriff paused. "He's escalating . . . unless some of the abductions weren't reported."

"Let's check these out—get the full report," he said. "Wade, you take the first two, and I'll do the others."

A text chimed on Alex's phone. Livy. She was on her way to Logan Point. He texted his location and received a reply. "Livy Reynolds is picking me up, and we're going to Johnny B's."

"Livy? Coming here in the middle of the day?" Ben exchanged looks with Wade. "She's not working?"

"Said something about taking off this afternoon. From the way she talked, I don't think she's working on a case."

Ben lifted his eyebrows.

Wait a minute. Livy was a homicide detective in Memphis. She should be busy. Alex folded his arms. "What's going on?"

Ben doodled on a piece of scrap paper, and then he tossed the pencil on his desk. "Something happened back in December. She'll probably tell you about it after she gets to know you."

"What happened?"

Ben seemed to struggle with telling him.

"I can always google it," Alex said. "But if it's something I need to know, I'd appreciate—"

"It's not a secret," Ben said, and Wade nodded in agreement. "Livy interrupted an armed robbery one night before Christmas, chased the guy into a dark, dead-end alley. Told him to put his gun down, but he wouldn't comply. Started toward her, and she shot him. Turned out to be a seventeen-year-old boy with a toy gun."

"He also had a switchblade in his pocket," Wade said. "Everyone seems to forget that."

Alex held up his hand. "I don't understand."

"She's had trouble dealing with the boy's death. Feels she should have known it was a toy. The department review of the case found nothing wrong with her actions."

Alex could only imagine how difficult it would be to deal with killing anyone, even in self-defense, but a kid with a toy gun would be so much harder. "So, she's second-guessing herself?"

"Yeah."

The information was useful to know, but he didn't see that it would affect Samantha Jo's case. He simply had to find her, and he didn't expect it would involve guns or shooting. Although he had brought his 9mm Glock along with him and was proficient in using it. His father had seen to that.

Ben stood. "Do me a favor and don't mention that we discussed this. She'll tell you in good time."

"I won't." Alex knew better than to expect Livy to tell him what had happened. Information like that was shared only with someone you trusted. And trust took time. He hoped to be out of Logan Point and back to Dallas by the end of the week.

Ben's phone buzzed, and he picked up the receiver. "Thanks, Maggie." He hung up. "Livy's on her way back."

Alex stood and slipped his hand into his pocket, jingling his change. The sooner they got started, the sooner he could close this case.

"Well, what have you guys discovered?" Livy asked as she entered the room.

After Ben gave a summary, she frowned. "So we may be dealing with a serial killer? Or at the least, a serial abductor?"

"No one's died that we know of yet. Wade and I will be contacting the sheriffs in the counties where those five abductions occurred. Should know if those cases fit this profile."

"Speaking of profile," Livy said, "have you run this case by Taylor?"

"No. I'll text her and ask her to stop by today after she finishes teaching. Oh, and I don't think you'll learn anything at Johnny B's. I was out there yesterday asking questions."

"It's worth a shot," Livy said. "Maybe your questions triggered a few new memories."

"Who's Taylor?" Alex asked.

"A good friend. A victim profiler," Livy said. "And she's Chase's sister. Maybe Samantha Jo's case will shed new light on Robyn's." She turned to Alex. "Are you ready to see what we can discover at Johnny B's?"

He'd been ready. "Your car or mine?"

7

Outside the jail, Livy glanced at Alex. He seemed nervous . . . or anxious. "Kate's house is on the way to Johnny B's. You want to drop your car off there? And Kate probably has something in the fridge we can eat."

He checked his watch. "Noon already? I am hungry. Let's do that."

A few minutes later, Livy turned into her aunt's drive behind Alex's blue Impala. Maybe over lunch she'd get a little more information on what they'd found at Samantha Jo's apartment this morning.

"Chicken salad is in the refrigerator," Kate said when they entered the kitchen.

"Sounds good," Alex said.

"It always is." Livy took the bowl out and sliced a piece of her aunt's sourdough bread as Kate set plates on the bar. She had no idea how Kate ran a successful pottery shop and found time to cook. She glanced at Alex. "Bread?" When he nodded, she cut two more slices. "Why did Ben check with ViCAP on this case?"

"I found a note at Samantha Jo's apartment, warning her to quit the job at Johnny B's. It sounded like maybe she'd received an earlier one. Did Robyn ever receive anything like a note?"

"No," Kate answered. "Chase and I searched the house from top to bottom after she left, trying to find a clue of why. We didn't find anything like that. Everything at the house looked like Robyn thought she was coming back. No clothes or shoes were missing, and she'd put sausage from the freezer in the refrigerator to thaw for breakfast the next morning. I'll never believe she left home that day with intentions of never returning."

Which would mean Robyn didn't leave voluntarily. Livy's muscles tightened. Which opened the very real possibility she was dead. Except, she had mailed Kate a letter after she left. And she'd called Chase and left a message. Livy focused on that as she finished her sandwich. Fifteen minutes later, she placed her paper napkin on the plate. "You ready?"

Alex nodded. "Good sandwich, Kate. Thanks."

"Glad you enjoyed it." Kate turned to Livy. "I'm so glad you took off this afternoon. Now I can deliver an order of mugs if you'll pick Abby up at school."

"At three?" When Kate nodded, she checked her watch. That would give them a little over two hours at Johnny B's. Should be plenty of time. "I'll pick her up."

When Livy pulled into Johnny B's complex, Alex whistled. "This is like a mini strip mall."

She laughed. "Yeah. There are all sorts of shops here, from food to clothing to even a game room. He's making a fortune leasing it all out—except for his original diner and coffee shop. That's where he hangs out. A lot of truckers really like this place, and not only truckers but tourists and local folks as well."

Livy drove around to the side, past a long row of eighteen-wheelers.

"Some of these look like they have sleepers. Why would they stop here?"

"To eat, take a shower, and sometimes just to have a long bed to stretch out in." She pulled into a parking space in front of the neon sign that proclaimed Johnny B's Grill and Coffee Shoppe. "If we're lucky, Johnny B will be here."

"Just who is Johnny B? Is that his name?"

"Johnny Baxter is his legal name, but no one calls him anything but Johnny B. He saw a place like this out in the Pacific Northwest. Somewhere around Seattle, I think. Anyway, about ten years ago, he opened up the first section of the plaza. It was a really nice convenience store where truckers could get diesel, a shower, and food. Word spread through the trucker world, and he soon was adding on. As far as I know, he runs a clean place. No drugs and his waitstaff at the lounge a few doors down have been instructed if they are aware that a trucker is going out on the road, no alcoholic beverages. Says he's not going to be responsible for some family getting hit head-on by a drunken truck driver. There are no alcoholic beverages sold at the grill. This is a place where a trucker—or anyone—can get a decent meal and good coffee."

"I'm sure you questioned him when Robyn left?"

"I did, Ben did, even Chase. Johnny B was shocked. Said he never saw it coming. Said she never flirted with any of her customers, was just always pleasant and friendly, but not too friendly."

"Here's hoping he has information on Samantha Jo."

Livy hesitated. Logan Point was a small town, suspicious of strangers. "I need you to pose as a tourist. I'll ask the questions and—" She broke off as a frown creased his brow. "Something wrong?"

"I don't know. Did I just lose control of this case?"

"I don't know what you're talking about. We need a plan, and I'm providing one. Even if I'm with you, people inside the diner might not open up to a private investigator. What's your problem?"

"I know we need a plan, but I thought we might come up with one together."

Livy stared at him. Together? And where did he get off telling her how to do her job?

"There! That's the problem."

"What?"

74

"It's written all over your face." He folded his arms across his chest. "You don't respect my abilities because I'm a private detective. Just because you're a cop and I'm not doesn't mean I'm stupid. Before we go any further, we need to get this out of the way."

"That's ridiculous." Or was it? Maybe unconsciously she had leaned that way. "Just how do you suggest we handle this?"

"I'll go in as a tourist, like you said."

She huffed. "If you agree with me," she said through her teeth, "what's the problem?"

"Your high-handed tone, that's the problem. Don't talk down to me. You've done it ever since we met."

Is that what she'd done? Probably. She tilted her head, taking in his firm jaw and chiseled lips. Alex Jennings was not a pushover. She liked knowing he'd stand his ground. "I apologize."

"Thank you. And I agree that you should ask the questions. That *is* what you were about to say?"

"Yes. Once I'm asking questions, you can chime in, like you had heard about the case."

"I like that, but I think I should go in first and order. That way it'll give time for everyone to look me over and hopefully decide I'm not a cop or private eye."

She hated to admit he was right. "Okay, go ahead. I'll check my email."

After he'd entered the diner, she clicked on the email app on her phone. The sheriff in Knoxville whom she'd emailed earlier today had replied. Nothing new on Robyn's file.

After ten minutes, she climbed out of her SUV and walked toward Johnny B's, noticing a note in the front window advertising that Johnny B's was hiring a waitress. Probably not Samantha Jo's job since she'd quit a month ago.

Inside the diner, Livy paused to let her eyes adjust to the darker atmosphere. Alex sat at the counter. She recognized three locals at tables near the front. One of them was finishing up his lunch while the other two had coffee cups in front of them as they were surfing the internet.

She counted eight customers she didn't recognize seated at other tables. Over-the-road truckers, she figured. She spied Johnny B at the end of the counter behind a cash register, wearing his customary white shirt and black pants. The buttons on his shirt strained to contain his ample belly. Finding him here meant this must be their lucky day. A smile stretched across his face when he spied her.

"Detective Olivia Reynolds. You're a sight for sore eyes. What brings you to my place today?"

"Need to ask a few questions about one of your former waitresses. And that's Livy to you, mister." She grinned but was dead serious. Other than her father, no one but Mac had ever gotten away with calling her Olivia.

"I told Ben Logan yesterday everything I know about Samantha Jo Woodson. Can I buy you a cup of French Market?"

"I think I'll pass today." Johnny B knew she didn't like chicory, but he always asked anyway. She slid onto a stool in front of the owner. "Did you know someone threatened Samantha Jo because she worked here?"

Johnny B's eyes widened. "No way. This is a decent place. I mean, you got truckers here, and they get a little too friendly sometimes, but Samantha Jo never led any of them on. Who was it?"

"If I knew, I wouldn't be here. Did you ever see anyone take a special interest in her?"

"Half the men who came in here, that's all. She's a pretty girl." He slid a handful of bills into the register. "Ask any of these men. Jason there"—Johnny B pointed toward one of the three men she'd recognized—"now, he never would ask her out, but he wanted to. And Timothy over there, he got red-faced every time she came around him, just like Bobby over there."

Livy shifted to where she could see the men. "Do you think they'd mind talking to me?"

"All you can do is ask."

"Might help if you encouraged them."

"Yes, Olivia." Johnny B rapped a glass on the counter. "Okay, gents, you all know Olivia Reynolds. She wants to ask you some questions about Samantha Jo. You help her out. Okay?"

Livy shook her head at Johnny's use of her full name as she walked to the tables. She paused at the counter beside Alex as he sipped his coffee. She stared at the menu on the wall that listed the different coffees. Taylor's words rang in her mind. *You need to open yourself up to different possibilities*. Why not? She dug three dollars out of her pocket. "Johnny B, I think I'd like a hazelnut latte, if you don't mind."

He made a face, and she laughed. That was worth the inflated price of the drink. "If you don't approve of lattes, you shouldn't sell them."

She acknowledged Alex as she waited for the waitress to make her latte. He was close enough to the tables to follow their conversation. "Afternoon," she said. "Passing through town?"

"Something like that." He pulled out a twenty and pointed to the coffee mugs behind the counter for sale. "I'd like to buy two of these," he said to the waitress as she handed Livy her cup.

Livy stared at the cup. Whipped cream in coffee? What had she ordered? She took a sip and forced herself not to gag. No way would she let Johnny B know it was her first latte or that she didn't like it.

She shifted her attention to Jason Fremont, a local hunter, trapper, and taxidermist. He always seemed to belong in another era with the leather vests he'd made from skins he'd tanned. His table was between Timothy Nolan's and Bobby Cook's. "Hey, guys. Do you mind if I sit here, Jason? That way I can talk to all three of you at the same time."

"My pleasure, Detective Reynolds." The lanky trapper closed his computer and sat up straighter in his chair. "But I have to wonder why you're here asking questions. You're a Memphis cop."

The usually quiet Jason surprised her. She didn't have a ready answer and took another sip of the drink as she scrambled for one. The latte was growing on her. "Well—"

"Yeah," Timothy Nolan said. "Did Ben Logan call you in on the case?"

She studied the part-time trucker. He lived with his elderly mother on a farm near the river. Where Jason was quiet, Timothy was outgoing. "No, Ben didn't call me in, but he's aware I'm asking questions. As to why I'm here, Samantha Jo is my friend."

"She's a sweetheart." The statement came from the rotund Bobby Cook. He pushed his plate back, then picked up his soda and took a long draw. "Somebody said Samantha Jo went missing Saturday," he said as he put the bottle on the table and used the back of his hand to wipe his mouth.

"No," Timothy Nolan said. "I saw her Sunday."

Livy jerked her head around. "Really? Where?"

"Pulling out of the driveway at her apartment. I was on my way to McDonald's to get breakfast since Molly wasn't open. I asked her if she wanted to join me."

"What'd she say?"

"Said she didn't have time. Had somebody she needed to meet."

Livy set her mug on the table and pulled out her notebook. "Did you tell Sheriff Logan this?"

"He didn't ask." Timothy's eyes widened. "And I just remembered."

"See." Livy jotted his statement in her notes. "Maybe you'll remember something else."

"I talked to her Saturday at Molly's," Bobby said. "And she didn't say anything about leaving."

She turned to Bobby. He had been a few years ahead of her in class, but she knew him from visiting his mother with Kate when she was a kid. She'd been "poorly" in Kate's terms, and her aunt regularly took bread or vegetables out to her. "How's your mother?" she asked.

"Like she's always been. Around the house the main topic we discuss is her ailments and meds. She rarely gets out. Never cooks. That's why I eat here or down at the diner all the time."

She hid a smile with a sip of her latte. Mrs. Cook had always enjoyed discussing her health with anyone who would stop and listen. "What did you and Samantha Jo talk about?"

"I always let her do the talking. She wanted to be a big country singer. Johnny B let her sing here one night, and she ain't half bad."

"Not half bad? You're crazy," Timothy said. "She has a great voice. And one day, she might make it in Nashville if she gets a good break."

It was evident the two men thought she'd left Logan Point for Nashville. "Did she ever mention anyone she might stay with in Nashville?"

Bobby snorted. "She thought that kid she came here with was going to stake her, but he didn't have enough money to stake anybody. And then he run off and left her. It's a wonder she didn't get pregnant."

"That's no way to talk about Samantha Jo." Low and fierce, Jason Fremont's voice stilled the other two men. "She never slept with that boy. Not that he didn't try. I think that's why he up and left her. And she paid her share of the bills."

Livy turned to the trapper. "How do you know this, Jason?"

A blush spread up his neck and across his face. "I just know."

"Do you know where she went?"

"No, but I know she didn't run off with nobody. And that kid she came here with—wasn't anything going on between them."

"When did you see her last?"

"Friday night. We went to the movies after she got off work."

"Didja kiss her?" Bobby elbowed him.

"None of your business what I did or didn't do."

Livy shifted in her chair so she could see Alex in her periphery. He'd swiveled his stool around and was openly listening in. "Are y'all talking about that girl who went missing?"

The three men turned to stare at him. "I couldn't help but over-hear," Alex said.

Bobby folded his arms across his chest. "Who are you?"

He stood and extended his hand to Bobby. "Alex Jennings. I'm looking for a job here in Logan Point."

Livy gripped her pen. Where in the world was Alex going with this? As Bobby hesitantly shook Alex's hand, Johnny B stood and walked to the tables.

"Do you know how to cook? Not sure if you'd be interested, but I need a cook for the evening shift."

Livy shifted her focus to Johnny B. He'd been paying more at-tention to their conversation than she'd realized.

"I put myself through college cooking at a local hamburger joint." Alex tilted his head as though he were considering the job offer. "Let me think about it, and I'll let you know tomorrow."

"Good deal," the restaurant owner replied.

Timothy leaned forward, staring at Alex. "How'd you know about Samantha Jo?"

"I was at Molly's Diner earlier today, and everyone was talking about it."

Alex's gaze slid past Livy, and she turned. The other men in the room stared their way. Since she had their attention, she might as well use the opportunity. Livy slid off the chair and walked where all of them could see her. She counted ten other men in the room and a couple of local women. "I guess you've figured out we're looking for Samantha Jo Woodson, who used to be a waitress here. If you have any information on her whereabouts, I'd appreciate it if you'd come and talk to me."

She turned back to Jason, but he'd slipped out the door.

"He didn't want to talk to you anymore about Samantha Jo," Bobby said. "He's been sweet on her ever since she worked here."

Livy studied the other two regulars. "How long have you been eating here?"

They looked at each other. "I've been coming ever since it opened," Bobby said. "Johnny B doesn't allow drunks, so I don't have to worry about getting into no fights to have to explain to Mama."

"Yeah." Timothy jerked his head toward the men sitting at tables. "We've all been coming here since it opened." He turned and squinted as he surveyed the room. "Except maybe George there. How long you been coming, George?"

George lifted his shoulder in a shrug. "Couple of years. Why?"

"Do any of you remember my cousin Robyn?" Livy asked.

"That girl that ran off and left her kid?"

Livy turned to look at Timothy just as her watch chimed an alarm, and she checked it. Time to pick up Abby, but first she wanted to hear what Timothy had to say about Robyn. "You knew her?"

"We all did. I always liked her. Never could understand why she worked here, though. I mean, it's a nice place, but she never seemed the type to work in a diner. But then, neither did Samantha Jo."

■ ■ ■

Robyn's alarm went off at five, and she rolled over, feeling for the snooze button. It had taken her until one to relax enough to sleep, and four hours' sleep wasn't enough to make a long trip on. Five minutes later, her alarm went off again, and she groaned. *Get up.* Unless she wanted to stay in Logan Point overnight, she needed to get on the road, and she pushed herself out of bed. She had to leave by six if she wanted to get a glimpse of Abby as she left school.

After a quick shower, she slathered Amazing Grace lotion on her dry skin. Abby had always loved the scent. What if . . . She brushed the thought away. No way would Abby get close enough to smell the lotion. By six, Robyn was on the road, thankful the morning sun would be behind her. The cities passed by almost in a blur. Kingsport, Knoxville, Chattanooga.

The closer she got to Logan Point, the more Robyn wondered if she'd lost her mind. What if someone recognized her? What if the man who abducted her recognized her? But the desire to see her daughter overrode all her doubts and planted another question. What would it take to go home? More strength than she had right now. But one day . . .

She refocused her thoughts and laid out a plan. It was a beautiful day and warm for February, so a lot of people would be stirring, maybe enough that she wouldn't stand out in a strange car. She checked her watch. She should arrive in Logan Point before school let out. Maybe she could drive by and see Abby standing in the parking lot. Or, if she arrived early enough and Abby still had recess her last class period, she might even be on the playground. Robyn could drive by on the street that ran parallel to the school and possibly see her daughter.

She arrived in Logan Point a little after two and stopped at the McDonald's near the bypass and fortified herself with a cup of coffee. At two thirty, she drove past the playground filled with fifth graders practicing soccer.

So many. Impossible to tell which one was Abby. Or if it was even her class. Wait. A soccer ball rolled toward the fence that kept the children from running out into the street. A blonde-haired girl ran to get it, and for a tiny second their eyes met before the girl kicked the ball back to the group. Abby. Robyn's heart beat so fast she thought it would jump out of her chest.

Seeing her was like an addictive drug. Now she wanted to see her again. But she didn't dare drive past the playground again. She turned at the next street and drove to the service station across from the school and waited, hoping no one would notice her.

Robyn glanced toward the playground. The students had gone

in. It must be almost time for school to dismiss. Yes. Cars had begun to line up, and an SUV she recognized joined the line. Livy. She had expected her mother to pick Abby up, not her cousin. She slid down in the seat. The cop in Livy would notice anything unusual. Now she was afraid to follow them. She'd thought that perhaps if her mother made a stop, like Walmart or the grocery, she could observe her daughter again. But Livy was a different story.

The line began to move quickly, and Livy's SUV passed by again with Livy driving and a man in the passenger seat. Robyn hadn't seen a second person in the car earlier. But Abby was in the backseat. In spite of her fear, the lure of being close to her daughter pulled her out of the parking lot. She expected Livy to turn right at the stop sign—toward home—but she turned left. Where was she going? The park. It was nearby. Abby must have talked Livy into taking her.

She couldn't believe her luck and followed them into the park and around to the lake, parking some distance from where they pulled in. Robyn sat in the car for a few minutes, watching as Abby ran down to a bench near the water's edge. Livy and a man who towered over her cousin trailed after her. Livy carried a paper sack. Bread for the ducks, she'd bet.

Robyn grabbed the camera she'd brought, thinking she might use the long lens to capture a shot of Abby, but this was so much closer than she ever thought she'd get. She snapped several from inside the car, but then she hung the camera around her neck and grabbed her purse. If she could just get a little nearer. She climbed out of the car and walked toward a bench near where Abby threw bread for ducks to gobble up.

Several people passed her on the walk, and she glanced around as a light wind touched her cheek. Quite a few people had taken advantage of the warm temperature and had come to the park to walk. A few people had their dogs on leashes. She glanced up at the blue sky interwoven with streaks of white plumes from planes taking off and landing at the airport in Memphis. She dropped her gaze to four teens throwing Frisbees. And Abby stood less than a hundred feet from her with Livy and the man Robyn didn't recognize.

Robyn had thought she could do this. Sneak into Logan Point, get a glimpse of her daughter, and then leave. Now she wasn't so sure. Seeing Abby and Livy made her want more. She wanted to gather her daughter in her arms and never let her go. She wanted to see her mom and dad and Chase. The vault where she kept those desires cracked open. Maybe she *could* return. Maybe Chase *would* believe her.

Movement overhead caught her eye as a bird swooped in front of her car. A red-tailed hawk. Her muscles tensed as it dove like a missile to the ground where a small squirrel hunted for acorns.

"No!" Robyn waved her arms. Too late. The hawk grabbed the squirrel in its talons. A scream came from somewhere to her left. She hurled the only thing she had in her hands. Her purse. The startled bird released the squirrel and flapped back.

"Get away, bird!" Abby's scream froze Robyn as the girl ran toward her.

The hawk abandoned all thought of its prey, and the squirrel took off to a nearby oak. "I think the squirrel is safe," Robyn said, keeping her voice low. What if someone recognized her voice? She'd perfected her boss's Virginia accent, but still . . .

Abby bent over and picked up Robyn's purse. "You saved him," she said, handing her the purse.

By now, Livy had reached them. "Good throw."

Robyn could not still her heart that had taken off like a jet. "I've never seen that happen before," she said.

"Sometimes those red-tailed hawks can be quite bold."

Yeah. Like the man who abducted her. The hawk had looked exactly like the tattoo she'd seen on his body. Why couldn't she remember where on his body? She risked a glance at Livy and almost didn't breathe. Her cousin was staring at her.

Livy held out her hand. "I'm Livy Reynolds, and the young lady here is Abby Martin." She waved to the man who had remained behind. "And that is Alex Jennings."

Robyn shook Livy's hand. "Susan Carpenter," she said, borrowing from her boss again. She faltered when Abby held out her hand, and then took it, imprinting the warmth of Abby's small fingers in her brain. "Thank you for getting my purse. Well, I better be going."

"You're not from around here," Livy said.

"No." Robyn slid her wedding band back and forth on her finger. If it were anyone other than Livy, she would dismiss the statement as curiosity. Somehow she'd aroused Livy's suspicion. "I'm on my way to Memphis for a job interview."

"I live in Memphis. Who are you applying with?"

She searched for a name. "FedEx."

Livy nodded. "Good company. You remind me of someone, just can't put my finger on who." Suddenly enlightenment reflected in her face. "My cousin. You remind me of my cousin."

Robyn froze, not daring to breathe. "R-really?"

"Yes. She's a missionary in Mexico." She turned to Abby. "Doesn't she remind you of your aunt Bailey?"

Abby cocked her head to the side, studying Robyn. "A little bit."

Robyn wasn't sure she could speak. She had to say something that would be opposite of what Robyn would say. "Lucky her. They say we all have a double."

Livy chuckled. "Yeah. What made you stop here at the park? I mean, it's a little out of the way if you're going to Memphis."

"Excuse me?" At least Livy blushed while Robyn searched for a plausible reason to be here.

"I'm sorry. I tend to ask too many questions sometimes."

"I do have to leave." She smiled at Abby. "Maybe the hawk won't come back."

"Did you stop to take pictures?" Abby pointed to the camera around her neck.

Now Abby was curious. The question needed to be settled or it could look as though she had something to hide. Which she did. "Not really. I've been driving a long time and thought maybe walking a little would stretch my legs. I asked at McDonald's if there was a park nearby. And voila, here I am. It was nice meeting you both."

She turned and forced herself to walk slowly back to her car. She'd bet her blood pressure was at stroking level. When she slid behind the steering wheel, she noticed Livy and Abby had followed her. She waved, and they waved back. She pressed her hand against her lips. *Just get out of the car. Tell Livy, explain what happened thirty months ago.* A mental picture flashed in her mind—the hawk swooping to grab the squirrel, bold as daylight. Just like her kidnapper.

She held back the tears until she was out of the park. She didn't want to be afraid. She wanted her life back. But how did she stop living in fear when she didn't know who her abductor was?

8

Alex shifted on the concrete bench. He had only one reason for being in Logan Point, and that was to find Samantha Jo, and sitting at a park was not getting it done. He'd been a little surprised when Livy wanted to stop at a convenience store and pick up bread before going to the school. To feed the ducks, she'd said. At the park. That was when he figured out she planned to take her niece somewhere other than home. He had to stay sharp to follow her conversation sometimes.

He reviewed what they'd learned at Johnny B's. Jason was in love with or at least had a crush on Samantha Jo, but he didn't seem her type. A hunter and trapper. Visions of frontier days flashed in his mind. Alex didn't know people still trapped wild game. But Livy had explained after they left that mostly all Jason trapped was beaver, and only because they were such a nuisance. Alex wasn't sure how he felt about a taxidermy business. He'd never liked the moose head that hung in his grandfather's den.

The other two men seemed nice enough. Timothy, along with Jason, appeared to be in his early thirties, and Bobby clearly was older, in his late thirties. All three of the men believed she'd taken off for Nashville. Tomorrow, he'd fly up there and make the rounds of record producers to see if she'd made contact with any of them.

Leave her photo too. Perhaps if she showed up, they would contact him.

His gut told him she hadn't gone to Nashville. If she had, those expensive clothes would have gone with her. A girl like Samantha Jo didn't go off and leave a tie-dyed sweater that cost over three hundred dollars. And then there were those cases of the waitresses who'd been abducted and released. He took out his phone and called Ben Logan. When he answered, Alex asked if he'd learned anything about the cases.

"Not yet," Ben said. "There were too many customers at each of the diners who could have administered the drug. The detectives in each state are faxing their reports. After I read those, I'll send one of my deputies to interview the waitresses."

"Do you know if any of the regulars at those diners have quit coming?"

"If that information isn't in the reports, I'll definitely send Wade to find out."

"If you'll clear the way, I'll fly to Nashville tomorrow and see if I can interview the waitress there." He preferred a firsthand report any day over a written one.

"I'll call the detective working the case and let him know you're coming," Ben said.

Alex told Ben he'd be in touch and disconnected, then checked on Livy. He couldn't help but notice the difference in her when she was around her niece. Lighter. That's what she was. Although at this particular moment, she seemed puzzled as she and Abby walked toward the parking lot. They waved to a woman who was backing out, then after the car pulled away, Livy took out her phone and seemed to be texting.

As Livy and Abby walked toward him, he took the opportunity to watch her without being obvious about it. She wasn't like most women he knew. The wind had tousled her hair, but that didn't seem to bother her. Earlier today, he'd seen a photo that looked like it'd been taken when her hair was much shorter, spiky even, and blonde. The look she'd given the camera was sassy. Sassy. That was what he liked about her. With a start, he realized he'd better be careful about liking her at all.

■ ■ ■

As the tan Camry backed out of the parking spot, Livy used her phone to key in the license plate number on the front of the car. She turned to Abby. "Do you want to run get the bag we left at the bench?"

Abby ran to retrieve the bag, and Livy dialed a friend at the Department of Motor Vehicles. After she answered, Livy gave her the license number. "It's a Virginia tag."

"Can I call you back? I'm swamped right this minute."

"Sure." She hung up and tapped her phone against her palm. Something was off about this whole scenario. And she couldn't shake the feeling she knew this Susan Carpenter. Was it that she looked a little like her cousin Bailey? Except her cousin had darker blonde hair, whereas this Susan's was almost platinum, but some of her mannerisms were like Bailey's. But it was more than that. A gut instinct. But about what? Abby returned, and she took her by the hand and walked toward Alex. She'd bet he was chomping at the bit to leave.

"Are you ready?" he asked when they reached him.

"Um, yes." She'd been right. Livy glanced back to where the car had been parked.

"Who was the lady?"

"She *said* her name was Susan Carpenter."

"She was nice," Abby said.

"Yes, she was. Do you want to run get in the backseat and buckle up?"

"Yes ma'am."

Alex didn't say anything until Abby was out of earshot. "Something bothering you about the woman?"

"Am I that obvious? The whole thing seemed weird. She was nervous. And I can't figure out what she was doing here." Livy slowed her pace, wanting to get a handle on her thoughts before she drove Abby home. The kid could pick up on worry better than she could.

"What do you mean?"

"She had Virginia tags—I've called the tag number in to DMV—and said she'd been driving a while and wanted to stretch her legs. But why did she drive all the way to the park when she could have simply walked around any of the fast-food parking lots just off the bypass? And why did she come through Mississippi from Virginia when it would've made more sense to go through Nashville?"

"You'd make a good cop," he said.

"You think?" Livy eyed him. She never knew when he was serious. His chiseled lips curved into a smile, and her heart quickened when he winked at her. She'd noticed before how thick the lashes that fringed his eyes were. So not fair for a man to have thicker lashes than she did. She drew her gaze from his face. This was not good. She couldn't let his looks distract her. Where was she? Susan. "I got the strangest vibes . . . like I know her from somewhere. At first I thought it was because she looked like my cousin Bailey, but it's more than that."

"I didn't get a good look at her. I noticed she was a little taller than you, but what'd she look like?"

"I think it was those wedge shoes that made her taller. Straight blonde hair—I liked her hairstyle." She might try that all-one-length style the next time she had the urge to cut her hair. "She had brownish, hazel eyes."

Livy's cell phone rang, and she glanced at the caller ID. "My friend in DMV." She answered. "What'd you find?"

"A tan Camry registered to one Susan Carpenter in Bristol, Virginia. No outstanding warrants."

"Thanks. Do you mind emailing me a copy?" Her friend agreed to send the information, and Livy hung up.

"Find out anything?"

"The tag confirms she's who she said she was. Susan Carpenter." Livy relayed the rest of the conversation. "I think I'll google this Susan Carpenter and see what I can find out about her."

Abby climbed out of the SUV and waved. "Aunt Livy, are we going home or can I play some more?"

"We're going home."

As they drove out of the park, Abby spoke up. "I like that lady. She smelled like Mom."

She glanced at Abby in her rearview mirror. "What do you mean?"

"When I handed her the purse, I could smell the perfume Mom used to wear."

"Really, honey?" Livy said.

Abby nodded. "Are we going to Nana's or is Daddy home yet?"

Livy exchanged glances with Alex. "Nana's. Did the woman look familiar to you, Abby?"

"A little."

An hour later, Livy leaned over her laptop with Alex sitting beside her. She typed Susan Carpenter, then Bristol, Virginia, into Google. Several hits returned.

"This Susan person gets in the newspaper a lot."

"Yeah." Livy clicked on a link, and when the link came up, she skimmed the article. She clicked another link, and a photograph of a dark-skinned woman in her sixties popped up. The caption read "Susan Carpenter at ribbon-cutting ceremony." "That's not the woman we saw today."

"You sure?" He glanced at the photo. "Oh no, I don't suppose it is. Did your query bring up any other women by that name in the Bristol area?"

She clicked back to the original query. "No, all the links are connected to the Susan Carpenter associated with the Wings of Hope Ministry."

Alex typed on his tablet. "The Tennessee-Virginia line splits Bristol and is a little over an hour and a half from here by air. You want to take a little trip?"

She swallowed. "Fly?"

"It's the only way I know to get there in an hour and a half. It'll take the lady you met today over seven hours to drive it. We could be there and have the situation checked out before she arrives in Bristol."

"But it'll be dark soon."

"I'm both IFR and VFR rated. I have—"

"What's IFR rated? And VFR?"

"Visual Flight Rules. Instrument Flight Rules. I'm rated for either one. I also have a private pilot license, and I'm a certified flight instructor." He typed on the tablet again, and after a pause looked up. "And the weather is perfect for flying. Full moon, no fronts, no storms, no clouds expected here or Bristol. What do you say?"

She still didn't know what the two acronyms meant. Perhaps if she'd paid more attention when her dad tried to talk to her about flying, she would know. But her mom had passed her fear of flying on to Livy, and she'd never wanted anything to do with planes or flying.

And now Alex wanted her to fly at night. In a small plane. No was on the tip of her tongue, but what if the woman she met today was Robyn? For the first time, Livy allowed the question to surface. She hadn't looked like her cousin. The last time she saw Robyn, she weighed at least fifty pounds more than the woman today. And had curly red hair. *Dye and a flat iron.* She'd had hazel eyes, and Robyn's eyes were bright blue. *Contacts.*

She smelled like Mom. It was a wild hunch, but she'd acted on crazier hunches before. She swallowed. "Let's do it."

"As late as it is, we may want to stay over and return tomorrow.

I'll pack a bag and then go to the airport, refuel, and do the pre-flight inspection while it's still daylight. We'll leave as soon as you get there."

By the time Livy arrived at the airport, she'd decided she'd lost her mind. She didn't know Alex. At the very least she could have googled him, seen if he had any outstanding warrants or plane crashes. *Get a grip.* Alex was a certified flight instructor. *So he said.* Why would he lie? The argument raged in her head. She took out her phone and clicked on Google and typed his name in. Several hits came up. Alex had a web presence.

The first link took her to a newspaper article in Dallas. *Alex Jennings, grandson of State Senator Josiah Jennings, obtains instrument rating.* She skimmed the article on her screen. So Alex was from a wealthy family. She never would have guessed from the way he acted. And he *was* a certified flight instructor, among other things. Her face burned. It was better to know than to wonder. Now if she just didn't throw up on the flight to Bristol. She grabbed her overnight bag and entered the terminal building.

"Hey, Miss Livy. About time you showed up around here again."

She turned. Sam Golding. Before her father had taken off for Alaska, Sam had been a fixture at their house.

"Hi, Sam." He hadn't changed. Still skinny, maybe not as tall as she'd thought he was, but then she'd grown. Even so, he still towered over her. "How's your wife?"

"She passed away a couple of years ago. Heart attack."

"I'm sorry." She really needed to stay in the loop better. She depended on Kate to keep her informed on what was going on in Logan Point, but sometimes Kate forgot to mention things.

Alex slipped in through the side door and nodded at the airport manager. "I'd like to rent that hangar I mentioned yesterday for a few days."

"Sure thing. There's a nice roomy one on the end. And we have a plane tug you can use to roll it in."

"That's great. I'll write you a check when we get back." Then he turned to Livy, and she warmed at his teasing smile.

"Are you ready?"

"As I ever will be."

"That Bonanza is a sweet plane," Sam said.

A sweet plane. Very reassuring. She followed Alex through the glass door to the taxi area, where the plane waited.

"Did you tell Kate where we were going?"

"No, just that we had a lead on Samantha Jo's case. I didn't want to get her hopes up only to have her disappointed." She had to walk faster to keep up with the long-legged pilot. "Do you think Robyn holds the key to Samantha Jo's disappearance?"

"I hope she does, because if not, I don't have a clue where to start looking other than Nashville." He climbed up on the wing and opened the door to the plane, and then he gave her a hand up before climbing into the cockpit.

Livy climbed in after him, and once she was settled, she glanced at all the gauges. "I hope you know what all of these thingies are supposed to do."

"Me too." He kept a straight face as he handed her the earphones. "This *thingy* will make talking on the flight easier and protect our ears."

She slipped the earphones on, aware of how close Alex was, and when he leaned over to adjust the headset, she caught a light woodsy fragrance. With precise movements, he flipped switches and pushed and pulled plungers before turning the key on the engine. She swallowed hard when the prop turned once and quit.

"It never starts on the first try." He turned the key again, and the engine fired up. "See?"

As Alex spoke into his microphone to Sam, requesting permission to taxi and take off, she swiveled around, looking for any incoming planes.

The plane rolled toward the runway, and once there, Alex revved the engine. The plane raced down the tarmac, and they were soon airborne. As the plane rose higher, he circled the airport and flew east. Below her, the lights of Logan Point glowed in the dusky evening.

"You okay?" Alex's voice sounded far away.

"I'm fine. It's beautiful."

"Oh yeah. This is my favorite time of day. Poets call it the gloaming—when it's not quite day or night."

For a while neither spoke. Tension eased from Livy's body as the light dimmed into night, and stars that seemed close enough to touch emerged. A sigh escaped her lips. She didn't know what she'd been so frightened of. And it wasn't like this was her maiden flight. Her dad had taken her up in a friend's plane when she was a child and again later as a teen after he bought his own plane. Now she regretted not going up with him more often.

Time passed as the plane droned across the sky. They occasionally made small talk as Alex constantly checked the dials and the window. He glanced at her. "Glad you came?"

Livy nodded. "I'm glad you talked me into it."

He gave her a thumbs-up, and she laughed. "So, how did you get to be a pilot?"

"It's a long story."

"We still have at least an hour. Go for it." When he didn't say anything, she glanced toward him. Stiff shoulders. Fingers tapping the throttle. Alex definitely was uncomfortable with the question. "Look, I didn't mean to pry."

He shook his head. "You're not. On my fourteenth birthday, my mom flew from California to Dallas in her own plane. She took me up for a ride—that was my birthday present along with ten lessons at a little airstrip outside of Dallas."

"What did you mean about her flying from California? She didn't live with you?"

"No. My parents divorced when I was nine. Dad got custody of me because . . . he was a Jennings. Mom quit fighting him about it when I was eleven—that's how long the court case dragged on."

That explained the reluctance. "I'm sorry." She knew what it was like to lose a mother. In some ways, losing one to divorce could be harder than death. "At least your dad wanted you."

He didn't answer for a minute. "It wasn't so much about wanting me as making sure Mom didn't get me."

■ ■ ■

Alex had hated being a pawn between the two of them, actually three, counting his grandfather. Theirs was not a "civil" divorce, either in division of property or the custody of their nine-year-old son. Joe Jennings brought all of his connections and his skill as a prosecuting attorney into the battle, and Alex really couldn't blame his mother for giving up and taking what his dad offered in the end—a substantial cash settlement in exchange for giving him custody of Alex. He spent two weeks in the summer with her in California and one week either before or after Christmas. How he'd hated the grilling his father always gave him when he returned from California.

He scanned the airspace, looking for blinking lights. No other planes showed up on his radar, but still, he checked. Livy shifted in her seat, peering out the window. Back at the airport, Sam had told him a little about Livy's dad, Jeremy Reynolds. That he'd gone off to Alaska to fly tourists into the bush after his wife died, leaving his two daughters with his sister, Kate. Alex had a better understanding of Livy's aversion to flying , but he hated that she'd let her dad sour something so wonderful. If he hadn't had flying, Alex didn't believe he would have survived.

"So . . ." Livy's voice came through the earphones. "How long before you soloed?"

"Soloed? You know the lingo."

"Yeah. Picking up some of it couldn't be helped since my dad is a pilot. He used to fly for one of the big commercial companies before he took off for Alaska. But I'm sure you already know that—you spent a good thirty minutes with Sam before I got there."

He laughed. "He does like to talk. But to answer your question, I soloed on my sixteenth birthday." He glanced toward her. "Why didn't you ever learn to fly?"

"Lots of reasons. My mom was terrified of flying, and she passed that on to me. After she died, I guess it was to get even with my dad. One of those cut your nose off to spite your face kind of deals. I was just so mad at him."

"I know that feeling."

"Yeah, I guess you do. My dad's never been responsible. Oh, I guess he was before Mom got sick. But it's like her illness triggered something in him. After she died, he just ran away from everything."

"What was wrong with her?"

"Bone cancer. We all knew it was only a matter of time, but Dad . . . he wouldn't accept it. Kept saying she would beat it. He encouraged her to do things she shouldn't. He thought if she would eat certain things and exercise, she would get better. The day she fell and broke her hip, he was staying with her. My sister and I were at school.

"We had already come to live with Kate and Charlie in their big house—actually my grandparents' house. Dad encouraged my mom to get out of bed. He was trying to get her to exercise, and I know he meant well, but she fell, broke her hip, and didn't survive surgery. After that, he just went off the deep end. Bought a plane with some of her insurance money and flew off to Alaska."

No wonder she didn't want to fly.

She touched his arm. "I'm sorry. I didn't mean to spill my life history."

"Sometimes it helps to talk to someone."

She sighed. "I guess. When did you get your first plane?"

Livy had a habit of abruptly changing the subject. "That's another story."

"Good. Maybe it will take my mind off of landing."

"I was twenty-three and in my last year of college. My grandfather wanted me to go on to law school. You know, carry on the family business. I didn't want to, but my grandfather knew exactly the right carrot to dangle in front of me. He made me an offer I couldn't refuse. An airplane. Not just any airplane, but this one. A Beech Bonanza F33A. All I had to do was go to law school. I took the offer."

"That was an expensive bribe. And you've never taken the bar."

"That wasn't part of the deal. I think he figured if I put in the time and effort to get the degree, I would take the exam."

"Your family is all about control, aren't they?"

Livy had never met his family, yet she had them pegged. "You could say that, at least on my dad's side. My mom . . . she just encourages me to break the ties."

"Why don't you?"

Yeah, Alex, why don't you? "It isn't that easy." He shot a glance at her. She leaned toward him, obviously interested in his answer. He couldn't remember the last time a woman had been that interested in him after they discovered he was the black sheep of the Jennings family.

"Why isn't it?"

"For one thing, I really do love my dad and grandfather, and I want to make them proud of me. I want to prove I can be successful without being a lawyer. Finding Samantha Jo would do that. I don't mean that's why I took the case, but it is a side benefit. If I find her, they'll get off my back about the bar. But, if I don't find her by the end of the month, I have to register for the exam and take it in July. I figure after that there will be a lot of arm-twisting to join the family law firm."

"Wow, Alex. That's a lot of pressure."

"It's the deal I made." One he was beginning to regret.

"They surely wouldn't disown you if you didn't take it."

He glanced at her and raised his eyebrows. "They definitely would."

"What if you fail?"

"That's not an option."

"Air traffic control, this is Cessna N Victor 1245—" The voice on the radio broke up.

Alex glanced toward his left and observed the blinking lights of another plane in the distance. "We're not too far out." He switched on his microphone. "Tri Cities Tower, Bonanza N3541C, 20 miles West, at 5000 feet, landing Tri-Cities airport with weather information Bravo."

The tower responded almost immediately. "Bonanza N3541Charlie, enter left base for runway 23, report left base."

Alex spoke into the mic once more. "Bonanza 41Charlie, left base for runway 23."

"41Charlie cleared to land runway 23."

The runway lights came into sight, and Alex guided the Bonanza between them. "Here we go," he said and heard Livy suck in a breath. "It's going to be fine."

The landing went without a hitch. After they climbed out of the cockpit, he guided her toward the terminal, resting his hand on the small of her back. He leaned his head toward her. "That wasn't too bad, was it?" he said softly.

She glanced up at him. "No. I never realized how beautiful night flying could be. I might even get someone I know to give me flying lessons . . . if he's around Logan Point long enough."

"Yes!" Alex pumped his fist. "I knew if I could get you up in the air, you'd want to fly. Everyone always does."

She put her hand on her hip and cocked her head. "That wasn't my first pony ride."

Livy's face had the same glow he'd seen time and again when

the flying bug bit. And in that moment under the lights of the terminal building, she was the most beautiful woman he'd ever seen. The intensity of her blue eyes, the dimples in her cheek as a grin teased her face, the way her blonde hair curled toward her face. It all came together like a thunderbolt and wrapped around his heart. "What made the difference?" He hadn't meant for the words to come out so husky.

A slow blush crept into her face. She lifted her hands, her fingers pointing upward. "When we first took off and night was closing in and the vastness of the sky . . . I don't know how to explain it. There was just a peace I haven't felt in a long time."

"You don't have to explain it. I know what you mean." For a second, he held her gaze. He could get lost in those eyes. Then the door to the terminal opened and people streamed out. The moment was gone. "We have the return flight to look forward to," he said.

She nodded mutely, and he knew she'd felt what he had.

Just what he needed. One more complication.

9

Livy waited while Alex rented a car. She had the address her friend at the DMV had emailed her already programmed into her phone. Her thoughts trailed back to the flight from Logan Point. It had been so different from what she'd expected. She could see how flying could get addictive, how it could be an escape . . . one her dad took. But did it have to be at his family's expense?

She brushed the thought off and scanned the area for Alex. The memory of his teasing smile sent warmth through her chest. What had happened out under the lights? She pressed her lips together. That was a question she didn't have to ask. She knew exactly what happened. And it wasn't happening again. She had enough trouble in her life without adding an attraction to a Texas flight instructor. Just because she understood why he might love flying, she couldn't dismiss how much he was like her dad. Running from responsibility.

He never should have accepted the airplane if he wasn't going to fulfill the requirement. Oh, he'd said taking the bar wasn't part of the deal, but it had been understood, she'd bet money on that. No, he had a duty to his family. Just like her dad had a duty to her and her sister, Jennifer. She collected her thoughts as Alex strolled toward her.

"Ready?" He jingled the keys to the car he'd rented. "Look

for a blue Jetta. They didn't have anything bigger, but it actually has a GPS."

"Good." A tingle shot through her arm when he laid his hand on it and guided her toward the door. Once in the car, she fastened her seat belt and typed in the address. A British voice instructed them to turn right out of the parking lot. "Cool. I like that." She turned to Alex. "On, Jeeves."

"I think Jeeves was a valet, you know, a man's man, not a chauffeur."

"He drove him once, I know. It was after a cricket game."

He turned to stare at her. "You watch *Jeeves and Wooster*?"

"It's not against the law, is it?"

He laughed, and she loved the sound of it.

"No, but it's hard to believe we both like the same thing."

He had a point there. Jeeves spoke again, directing them to turn left at the next light. He caught her eye, and they both burst out laughing. "Okay," he said. "We can't double over laughing every time the man speaks."

"I'll do better," she said. "Promise." And pressed her lips together, but it was no use. Laughter erupted. "I think that high altitude messed with my brain."

"And the excuse before was?"

She laughed. She didn't know when she'd bantered so easily with someone of the opposite sex. But now it was time to get down to business. "I'll be serious. No more laughing."

Alex kept a straight face and drove where the GPS directed. Twenty minutes later, they pulled up to a ranch-style brick house. She checked her watch. Eight forty-five. None of the windows were lit up. "Do you think she's gone to bed already?"

"I saw a light at the back of the house as we approached. Let's go see."

They climbed the steps to the front door and rang the doorbell. Livy jumped and pressed her hand to her chest when an intercom asked their business. "We, ah, we're looking for Susan Carpenter."

"Your name, please, and your reason."

She felt silly talking to a tan box. "I'm Detective Livy Reynolds and the gentleman is Alex Jennings. We're here to ask you a few questions."

"Could you hold your badge up where the camera can see it? It's above the door."

Livy held her shield up and silence followed, then the lock clicked and the front door scraped open. Susan Carpenter stood almost as tall as Alex's six-two frame, and in spite of her sturdy size, her poise reminded Livy of a runway model. A smile graced her face.

"Detective Reynolds, come in. Your friend too." The well-modulated voice added to the impression of calmness and self-assurance.

Livy glanced at Alex. He seemed as puzzled as she was. She stepped through the doorway into a dimly lit living room.

"Let's go back to the kitchen, if you don't mind. I have guests in the bedroom next to this room."

They followed her to a brightly lit kitchen. A yellow Formica table centered the room. Yellow gingham curtains covered windows that had been frosted over. A whiteboard listed meal times and duties. What kind of house had they come to? She studied this Susan Carpenter who had been the subject of the newspaper articles and the director of Wings of Hope Ministry. Things fell into place, sort of. Livy tilted her head. "Do I know you?"

"I used to be a model; maybe you saw me in a magazine ad. Won't you please sit at the table? I'll make us a pot of coffee."

A spicy scent wafted from a pot on the stove as Livy sat on one side of the table while Alex took the other. She realized they'd been so focused on getting to this house, they hadn't eaten.

Susan Carpenter poured water in a coffeemaker and turned to them. "I have spaghetti if you'd like a plate."

Alex's stomach growled. Susan smiled and opened a bread box, taking out a loaf of French bread. "I guess that's my answer. Fix you a plate, and then we'll talk."

The spaghetti was delicious. Susan sat at the end of the table, nodding when they expressed their thanks. She turned to Alex. "I think I know why Livy is here, but not you."

Alex paused with a fork of spaghetti halfway to his mouth. "I'm a private investigator, working on a case of a missing girl."

"I see."

Livy smeared butter on a piece of the bread. "You seem to know me. Why is that?"

"We'll get to that later. What brings you here?"

Alex leaned forward. "We met a person driving your car and using your name in Logan Point today. When we checked your name out, we had some questions."

Susan's slow easy smile appeared again. "Yes, I'm sure you did. Did you recognize the woman?"

"Not exactly," Livy said. Pinning this Susan Carpenter down was like grabbing an eel. "I don't ever remember seeing her before, and she reminded me a little of my cousin, but my cousin is in Mexico. Yet I felt as though I knew her. It was strange. Almost as strange as this conversation we're having right now."

The coffeemaker dinged, and Susan stood and poured each of them a cup of coffee, then looked over her shoulder. "Cream or sugar?"

"Black for me," Alex said.

"Me too."

Susan set the cups down and reclaimed her position at the head of the table. Livy placed her elbows on the table and tented her fingers. Susan still carried herself gracefully, and Livy could imagine her twenty years and thirty pounds ago. Her complexion, straight hair, and slightly almond eyes hinted at an Asian heritage mixed with the African. Livy couldn't figure out why she answered every question with another question. "Who was the woman posing as you today?"

Susan stared into the mug she held, gently rubbing her finger on the handle. "Let's talk about this house first."

There she went with the diversion again, but Livy had a hunch if she wanted information from her, she'd have to play her game.

Alex cocked his head. "What about this house?"

"Do you know what it is?"

They both shook their heads.

"You googled me, but not what I do."

"The article I scanned mentioned something about training and jobs for women," Livy said.

"Once we saw the woman in the park wasn't you, we didn't have time," Alex said. "I wanted to get into the air before dark."

"So that's how you got here so quickly." Then she straightened her shoulders. "Look around this kitchen and tell me what you see."

Livy bit back the *what* that almost sprang from her lips. She ran her gaze over the large room that held a recliner and sofa on one end. On the other end, white cabinets lined the wall. She noted the sunny curtains, the clean white floor, and the plaque over the sink. *You are my hiding place; you will protect me from trouble and surround me with songs of deliverance.*

"I see a homey place," Alex said.

"I see a safe place." Livy tilted her head. "This is a shelter, right?"

Susan's broad smile lit up her face. "You're both right. The woman you met in Logan Point today is my assistant here. Last night she stood up against an abusive, drunk husband while I took his family out the back."

Livy's shoulders slumped. They had come all this way for nothing. Her earliest school memories were of protecting Robyn from bullies. Her shy cousin had been an easy target because she wouldn't stand up to them. No way it had been Robyn who stood up to the abusive husband.

"And while my assistant was able to stand against this man, she can't face her own fears. She's in a prison not of her own making. Over two years ago, I found her battered and beaten in a rest area on the highway outside of town." Susan stared at a point on the wall behind Livy.

Livy leaned forward, drawn into the story by Susan's compelling voice. "What had happened to her?"

Her gaze shifted until it caught Livy's eyes. "She didn't know."

"How could she not?" Alex said.

Susan turned to him. "Lots of reasons. I called the police, and they came and took her to the hospital. She had a concussion, a broken nose, three broken ribs, and she'd been drugged. GHB."

"The date-rape drug." The thought of what the woman she'd met in the park earlier had gone through sickened Livy. "Was she . . ."

"No. That was the strange part, and to this day, she hasn't been able to remember much of what happened that night."

"Why didn't she go back to her hometown?"

Susan's cell phone beeped, and she glanced at it, then slid it back in her pocket. "I need another cup of coffee. How about you two?"

Alex handed her his cup. "Probably won't sleep, but fill it up."

Why was Susan telling them this story? What did it have to do with them? She studied her as she handed Alex his coffee, then sat down again. Again Livy was struck by her gracefulness. That coupled with her calm, gentle manner made it easy to see why women trusted her.

"She's terrified of returning home."

Alex frowned. "Why?"

"Because she's afraid people won't believe her," Livy said. She'd worked rape cases for a year before joining the homicide division and didn't know how many times she'd heard women say no one would believe they weren't at fault.

Susan nodded. "The man who did those terrible things to her is still out there, and she doesn't know who he is. He could be someone she might see every day . . . or only on Sunday," Susan said.

"But you've encouraged her to go back." Livy knew that from her tone.

"I don't think she'll ever be free until she does."

"What's her name?" Alex asked, and Livy held her breath, waiting to see if Susan would answer.

"Robyn Martin. And according to the text, she'll be here in a couple of hours."

■ ■ ■

Robyn shook her head, trying to stay awake as the highway stretched on and on under the full moon. Another hundred miles. Had to stay awake. She checked the clock. Twelve thirty. She'd driven the last two hundred miles on automatic, barely aware of the small towns she passed through. Over and over, her mind replayed the afternoon.

To be so close to Abby . . . Livy . . . and not tell them who she was. What would it hurt if she had? The image of the hawk answered that question. He was out there, waiting to swoop down and capture her again. And if Abby was with her, he would take her daughter as well. No. She couldn't risk it.

But what if she went back to Logan Point for the sole purpose of catching this . . . this creature. He wasn't human. No human could have beaten her the way that man did. She flinched, remembering the way his fists had pounded her face, her body. Three broken ribs, broken nose, battered face. But the physical injuries had healed.

What if Livy figured out who she was? *God, please don't let that happen.* Robyn had come to rely on God since the attack. He'd brought her this far, he wouldn't let her world come crashing down again. But she hadn't been able to give him her fear. She'd tried. But every time she thought she had, it raised its ugly head, gripping her body in paralyzing weakness. When it hit, she couldn't move, she couldn't speak, and she could barely breathe. She heaved a sigh, so tired of living her life under this cloud.

If she could just remember something about the man other than the tattoo. Or even how she'd gotten to the rest area where she escaped from him. Bits and pieces of riding in something that night seemed like a dream when she tried to remember. Whatever type of vehicle he'd carried her away from Logan Point in had been spacious, like a big car or truck, maybe. An eighteen-wheeler blew past her, rocking the little Camry. Why couldn't she remember?

A loud pop jerked her attention to the road. Seconds later the unmistakable whop-whop of a flat tire was confirmed as the steering wheel pulled to the right. Robyn slammed on the brakes and muscled the car to the side of the road. She flipped the emergency flasher on and rummaged in the glove compartment for a flashlight before she climbed out of the car. Moonlight cast the surrounding area in shadowy figures. Her shoulders slumped as she walked to the front passenger side and stared at the decidedly flat tire.

Headlights from an eighteen-wheeler topped the hill she'd just climbed and slowed. A shiver ran down her back. What if . . . All sorts of images bombarded her mind. Why hadn't she found a motel and waited until daylight to travel? Her blood pulsed in her head as the truck pulled onto the shoulder and the driver hopped out. Seconds later the gravel crunched as someone walked toward her and then rounded the end of the trailer.

"Having trouble, ma'am?" The man lumbered toward her.

His voice sounded kind. "Flat tire."

"Do you know if you have a spare?"

Please let there be a spare. "It's not my car." She hated the way her voice broke. Now he'd know she was afraid of him.

"My name is Walter Cronkite." He stuck his hand out, but she could only stare at him.

Walter Cronkite was a newscaster and dead. Tears scalded her eyelids. Of course it wasn't *that* Walter Cronkite. How could she be so silly?

"No need to tell me yours. I only told you mine because you look scared to death. I usually get a laugh out of it since I don't look anything like that newsman and he's passed on."

She offered him a quivery smile. "Thanks. It is kind of scary being on the road alone at night."

"Yes ma'am, it is. Now, let's see if we can find that tire."

Walter knew his way around Camrys and soon had the tire out. When he bounced it on the ground, he groaned.

"What's the matter?"

"It's flat, ma'am. Let me jack up the front of your car, and we'll take the flat tire and donut here to a plaza about three miles up the road and get them fixed."

She stared at him. Get into the truck with him? Yeah. Unless she wanted to stay here on the road until he returned. Not hardly. "Let me get my purse." She needed to text Susan and let her know what happened and that she'd be later than she'd told her earlier.

Once in the big rig, Robyn tried to relax. The man had been nothing but kind. He pulled the truck out onto the highway and shifted gears until it was rolling down the road. "Thank you," she said.

"Just doing what I hope someone would do for my wife in the same situation."

"Your wife is a lucky woman."

He shot a look her way. "Wish you'd tell her that."

"I'm sure she knows it." She settled into the seat. Unease crept into her chest. The cab of the truck seemed familiar. And it shouldn't—she'd never ridden in a semi before. She gripped the handrail. She'd done that before. But when? Robyn tried to get enough saliva to lick her lips, but her mouth was dry. A memory flashed in her mind. Country music. Trying to move. Hurting. A bed. She squeezed her eyes shut.

"We're almost there."

His voice cut into the memories. She was here. Safe. But once . . .

"Is this a sleeper cab?"

"What?" Walter turned to stare at her.

She realized how that must sound and threw up her hand. "I mean, I . . . I've never seen the inside of a semi. I just wondered how hard it was to sleep in your truck." She wasn't making sense, but now that the thought had grabbed her, she had to know.

"Oh. Nah, it's not bad. While I'm getting your tires fixed, look around."

He pulled the rig into the plaza and parked on the side. After he closed the door, Robyn touched the curtain that separated the cab from the sleeper. She jerked her hand back. Did she really want to go there in her mind? She breathed evenly, willing her body to relax. She had to know. She climbed out of the seat and through the curtain and then sat on the bed with her eyes closed and waited.

Her hand flew up, shielding her face. She shrank back from the edge of the bed into the corner. She flinched as another blow hit her shoulder. Her eyes flew open and she blinked, banishing the memories. She ran her hand over the edge of the bed. Memories surfaced again. They had stopped at a rest stop on the interstate, and she had pretended sleep. But when he got out of the truck, she'd watched him go to the restroom. That was when she escaped. She'd half stumbled, half run to the women's restroom and smack into the arms of Susan Carpenter.

With shaky legs, Robyn climbed out of the cab of the truck. She breathed the cold February air, not even wincing at the pain it caused her windpipe. She was alive. And she had another piece to the puzzle of that night. If she could only remember his face. But had she even seen it?

10

Robyn paid the service attendant and thanked him for bringing her back to her car and mounting her tire. She'd been so grateful he'd offered. Walter had been so nice, but she hadn't believed she could get back into the eighteen-wheeler again. She checked her watch, then texted Susan she'd be home in ninety minutes. She looked forward to returning to her everyday routine.

Four cups of coffee should keep her awake until she rolled into Bristol at three. While she'd waited for the attendant to repair the tire, she'd journaled everything that had happened in the last twenty-four hours. Seeing Abby, Livy, having the courage to make the trip—most of her life she had been afraid to do anything alone, something she'd never understood. No one in her family was like her. Her mother was the strongest person she knew, and her sister Bailey served as a missionary in Mexico. That took courage. And her dad had served on merchant ships until his two daughters were teenagers. So what happened with her? She'd always been afraid to try anything new, scared even to ride horses, always a follower and never a leader. But that was slowly changing. *I can do all things through Christ who strengthens me.*

When she held on to that verse, she stretched beyond herself. Trouble was, she didn't always hold on to it. But tonight she had, and now she knew a little more about that horrible night that changed her life. She couldn't wait to get back to the shelter and tell Susan.

A little over an hour and a half later, Robyn pulled into the drive at Hope House. A blue car she didn't recognize sat in front of the house. Probably not a woman hiding from an abusive husband, but Susan hadn't mentioned having company. She pulled all the way behind the house where a light shone through the kitchen window. Surely Susan hadn't waited up. No. Just left a light on, that was all. Robyn unlocked the door and eased into the kitchen. Someone was wrapped up on the sofa, and another person slept in the recliner. Had there been such an influx of clients that there was nowhere for them to sleep? Footsteps padded down the hall from Susan's bedroom, and she came through the door.

"I thought I heard a car," she said. Whoever was on the couch stirred.

"What's going on?" Robyn whispered.

"Your friends are here."

Robyn backed against the door as Livy pulled the blanket away from her face.

"Robyn! You're back."

She swayed as the room moved. A band squeezed her chest, making her unable to breathe. Livy? Here? "How . . ." Her knees buckled.

"Catch her! She's fainting."

Hands grabbed her, and she felt herself being lifted in strong arms and placed on the couch. Susan placed a wet cloth on her head. "It's going to be all right, baby. It's going to be fine."

Robyn struggled to sit up. "I'm okay." She turned, searching for Livy. "How did you get here before I did?"

Livy squeezed her hand. "Alex over there flew us in his airplane."

She glanced toward the recliner. Alex? Oh yeah, the good-looking guy with Livy and Abby. She took a shuddering breath. They hadn't come all this way just to say hello. "How did you find me?"

"I ran your license plate and then looked Susan Carpenter up on the internet. When we found her"—Livy glanced toward Susan and smiled—"it was obvious you'd given us a fake name."

Robyn should have known Livy would do something like that. She glanced up to find her cousin scrutinizing her.

"You've changed so much," Livy said.

"And you've dyed your hair again. I think I like it strawberry blonde."

Her cousin shrugged, then she picked up Robyn's hand. "It's still there."

"What's there?"

"The blue mark where you stabbed the pencil into your hand and the lead broke off. See." She pointed to a small blue dot at the base of Robyn's thumb. "Why didn't you contact me?"

"I . . . I couldn't. First, I was too ill, but later, if I thought about it, I had a panic attack." She glanced up at Susan. "Did you tell them what happened?"

Susan nodded. "I thought it'd be easier if they knew before you returned."

"Thank you. I think tonight I discovered how I got to the rest area. Earlier, I had a flat tire and a long-haul trucker stopped to help me." She smiled at Susan. "Your spare was flat as well, and he drove me in his truck to the nearest service station. During the ride I almost freaked out because inside the truck seemed so familiar. While the trucker saw to my tires, I explored the sleeper part of the cab. I'm almost certain my abductor kept me prisoner in a sleeper cab."

"Do you have any idea why the man chose you?" Alex asked.

She shook her head. "I remember so little about that night and even the days before it happened."

He took out a pen and notepad. "Let's write down what we

know. Okay?" She nodded and he continued. "Your abductor was a man."

Again she nodded.

"Do you remember anything at all about him?"

She searched her memory. "Only the hawk."

"What hawk?" Livy said.

"He had a tattoo somewhere on his body of a hawk."

Alex nodded. "I'm working on a case in Logan Point. A twenty-one-year-old woman has disappeared, much like you did. She worked at Johnny B's until she received a warning to—"

"What did you say?" Robyn's stomach sank to her knees. How had she forgotten the note?

Alex leaned toward her. "Did you get a note?"

"Yes." She whispered the word. She pressed her hands to her temples. "I thought it was a prank and just threw it away. I never connected it to the kidnapper."

"Exactly what was in your note?" Livy asked.

Robyn shuddered. She didn't want to remember. "Quit your job and stay home with your child," she whispered.

Livy and Alex exchanged glances. "Do you remember when you received it?" Alex said.

She slid her fingers down the side of her face and rested her chin in her hands. "At least a month before he . . ."

Tears threatened to spill from her eyes, and Livy patted her arm. "Let it rest. Don't think about it right now. In fact, why don't we all let it rest until morning?"

"Good idea," Susan said. "I have two extra bedrooms, Livy, if you and Alex want to stay here."

"That would be great."

"I'll get our bags from the car," Alex said.

Susan stood. "And I'll get fresh linens."

When they were alone, Livy took Robyn's hands. "I can't believe we found you. I've missed you so much."

Robyn blinked back tears again. "Me too."

Livy touched her face again. "You look so different, and I bet you wear smaller sizes than I do. Even Chase won't know you."

Chase. He didn't know her before she left. "How is he?"

"He's missed you."

She'd like to believe that.

"He'll be so glad to see you. Everyone back home will be." Livy hugged her again.

Home. Livy thought she was going home. Exhaustion seeped into every muscle in Robyn's body. She wouldn't tell Livy tonight that home wasn't happening. She didn't have the energy to argue with her cousin who put duty above everything else.

■ ■ ■

Livy took the overnight bag Alex handed her, glad he'd suggested bringing one. "Thanks."

"Where's Robyn?" he asked.

"Her room."

"Do you think she'll go back with us?"

"I don't know." Livy had seen the fear in Robyn's eyes when she mentioned home.

"Maybe the question I should ask is, is she ready to take her life back?"

Livy wasn't sure she liked the direction the conversation was going. "What do you mean?"

"The key to solving her case and Samantha Jo's is locked in Robyn's memory. All that's needed is a trigger. Like what happened when she rode in the eighteen-wheeler."

"You're not suggesting that we ask Robyn to be bait, are you?"

"Not at all. She wouldn't be bait—not if we kept her identity secret. You didn't know her, and no one else will."

"You mean, we take her back with us, but we don't tell anyone who she really is?"

"It wouldn't be for long. She could get a job at Johnny B's or even Molly's Diner. Evidently the man frequents both places. Once she's in familiar surroundings, her memory may come back. It does in amnesia cases sometimes."

"But she doesn't have amnesia. He drugged her. That's an entirely different thing."

He palmed his hands up. "It's just something to think about tonight and talk about in the morning."

She rolled her shoulders, trying to unkink the tight muscles in her neck. She could only guess at how tired Robyn was. *Robyn.* It was almost unreal to touch her and know she was safe. "Let's sleep on it."

"That's what I meant."

■ ■ ■

Sunlight peeped through the curtains, rousing Livy from a restless sleep. The aroma of bacon came from the kitchen. She cracked her eye open to look at the clock on the wall. Seven thirty. She thought about turning over and catching more sleep when a light tap on the door killed that idea. "Come in."

Susan stuck her head in the doorway. "Alex sent me to see if you were up. There's a frontal system coming in from the west, and he feels you need to return to Logan Point before it gets there."

"Is Robyn up?"

"Yes. She and Alex are talking. Breakfast is on the table, and the two families staying here have already eaten."

Livy scrambled out of bed, her lifelong habit of protecting Robyn kicking in. She didn't want Alex talking Robyn into something she wasn't ready for. She threw on a pair of jeans and a sweater and hurried down the hallway, mentally preparing an objection to whatever Alex had proposed.

"Seeing Abby, being that close to her—"

Livy burst into the kitchen and glared at Alex. "I thought you and I were discussing this, not you and Robyn."

"You were asleep, and Robyn and I started talking, and the conversation led to Robyn returning to Logan Point. It's her decision, anyway."

Robyn leaned forward in her chair. "What I was saying when you came in—seeing Abby made me realize I can't stay away any longer. I'll do anything to get my daughter and my life back. I'm tired of running."

The objection died on Livy's lips as the deep yearning in Robyn's voice shot an arrow to her heart. If she had just been around when her cousin received the note, or if she'd *really* looked into the case after Robyn went missing, whoever abducted her might be in custody now. Two and a half years would not have been lost.

It wasn't only the yearning that stopped her but the steel in Robyn's voice that made her finally realize she was not dealing with the Robyn of old. The one who couldn't make a decision and the one who had attracted the bullies. This was a new and courageous Robyn, who was ready to be used as bait for the animal that had kidnapped her. The memory of Justin Caine flashed in Livy's mind. What if it went terribly wrong? "It could be dangerous."

"Livy is right," Alex said. "I'll do everything I can to protect you, and I know Ben will as well. And Livy, of course."

Susan took her by the hands. "Don't rush your decision."

Robyn nodded. "But you think I should do it."

"I think you should at least think about what they're saying. Ask yourself if you'll be content here now that you've seen Abby."

Robyn hugged her arms to her stomach. "It's scary, but I want my life back."

"Then we need to make a plan. Does anyone want coffee? Livy?" Alex asked.

Maybe caffeine would clear her head. "Thank you."

Alex poured a cup of coffee and handed it to her, then poured his. "First," he said, "if you go back with us, we'll have to keep everyone in the dark, at least for a while."

Robyn caught her breath. "Do you think that's absolutely necessary?"

"Unfortunately," he said. "It's the only way we can keep you safe."

She nodded, but the pinched look on her face made Livy wonder if Robyn could do it. Livy wasn't even sure she could pull it off, knowing how much Kate wanted to find her daughter and Abby wanted her mother back. What a can of worms they had opened.

Robyn straightened her shoulders. "If that's the only way, I guess I have no choice. What's the rest of the plan, and how will we pull it off?"

"I've been thinking about that," Alex said. "This guy seems hung up on waitresses, and he's a regular at Johnny B's. The restaurant is looking for a waitress—"

"You want me to go back to Johnny B's? I don't know if I can do that." She chewed on her thumbnail.

"You won't be alone," Alex said. "Johnny B offered me a job the other day, and I'm going to take it—I can hang around before or after work if that's what it takes to be there when you're there."

As Robyn played with the wedding band on her ring finger, Livy hurt for her cousin. She understood where Alex and Susan were coming from—the only way Robyn could ever be safe was if her abductor was caught. But what if they talked her into returning and something terrible happened—like he kidnapped her again. Her pulse accelerated, and a chill shivered down her back. If she encouraged Robyn to go back and it went south, the outcome could be the same. Her hands would be stained with Robyn's blood. "I think we need to scrap this plan." Livy folded her arms across her chest.

The other three stared at her.

"Robyn doesn't need to go back until we catch the kidnapper. Using her as bait is too dangerous."

Alex stretched out his hands. "But Robyn is our only link to him, and we aren't using her as bait. Our guy won't recognize her, just like you didn't."

"But she doesn't remember anything about him."

"She might if she was in familiar surroundings. If she smelled his cologne or saw an action like . . . lighting a cigarette. Anything might trigger a memory the way riding in the truck did."

"It's too risky."

Robyn held up her hand. "Stop talking like I'm not here." She turned to Livy. "Stop trying to protect me. I'm not a six-year-old afraid of my shadow anymore."

Robyn's words struck a nerve. She'd always been her cousin's protector, and now Robyn wanted her to back off? She clamped her jaw tight before she said something she'd regret.

"I want to do it," Robyn said. "I can't live like this. I've been scared long enough. I want my life back, my family. I can't go on without Abby. And if returning to Logan Point will get my family back, then let's do it."

Did Robyn have any idea what she was getting herself into? Livy put her hands on her hips. "You can't tell anyone who you are. Can you do that?"

"I can for a little while. Just to be near Abby and seeing her will be enough until we catch him."

"Good," Alex said. "We need to decide on a name for you to use and whether we tell Ben who you are."

"I'll be who I've been for the past thirty months—Sharon Arnold," Robyn said.

"Sharon? Why Sharon?"

"I don't know, but the name popped into my mind at the hospital when the police asked who I was. It's hard to explain, but it fit somehow."

"Sharon it is," Alex said. "And I think Ben should be in on the secret." A pained expression crossed his face, and Livy noticed it. "What?"

"I told him I'd fly to Nashville today and interview the detective handling the case of the waitress who was kidnapped. I need to call Ben and get him to set up another appointment."

She nodded. "I'd like to go with you when you go." Then she turned to Robyn. "How do you feel about telling Ben who you are?"

"I think I'd feel better if he knows what's going on."

"Then we're all in agreement." Livy tapped her fingers on the table. "Have you thought about where she's going to live? I don't think she can stay with Kate unless we tell her the truth, and if Kate's around Robyn long, I can promise you, she will figure it out."

"I've been thinking about that. The apartment building where Samantha Jo lives had empty units. If we could find two together, Robyn could take one and I could rent the other and set up an intercom so I could hear if anyone entered the apartment."

He seemed to have it all planned, but Livy couldn't help but worry. This wasn't a game where she or Alex could blow the whistle and stop the action. Even though her cousin didn't look like the old Robyn, Livy could tell that her mannerisms had not changed. "You'll have to be careful interacting with people," Livy said.

"What do you mean?"

"You still have the same mannerisms you had before. And you're supposed to be a stranger, so you'll have to forget what you know about people in Logan Point. You can't seem to be too familiar with them."

Alex turned to Robyn. "Livy's right. You need to play a role, and you'll need a cover story. We'll work on that on the flight home, and we need to leave in the next hour."

Livy's stomach growled. "Do I have time to eat?"

A grin tugged his lips. "From the sound of your stomach, I'd say we better make time. You eat and I'll go on to the airport and get the plane fueled and run through my preflight inspection." He turned to Susan. "Can you drop them off at the airstrip?"

"Sure. I better get dressed, though. My robe might stretch the boundaries of acceptable clothing." She winked at them.

As Robyn started to leave, Livy stopped her. "Can you stay a minute?"

"Sure. How about I pour us another cup of coffee."

"I want a hug first. I didn't get one last night." Tears stung Livy's eyes as she wrapped her arms around her cousin. "I never thought we'd see each other again."

"I know. Neither did I."

"And I can't believe the way you've changed. Every time I look at you, it takes me a minute or two to get used to the new you."

"The first time I looked in the mirror after the doctor operated on my nose, I couldn't believe the change either. I loved it, even with the swelling and black eyes." Robyn ran her finger down her nose. "You know how much I always hated that big hump."

Livy sipped her coffee. "It was never as bad as you thought, but it's not just your nose. I can't get over how trim and fit you are. Are you working out?" Robyn always hated to exercise.

"I lost all the weight because my jaw was wired together, and I'm keeping it off with exercise. Don't let this freak you out, but I'm lifting weights, and jogging, and rock climbing."

"Rock climbing?" It was a sport Livy had loved when she was younger, but she'd never been able to get Robyn or Taylor interested in it. "Inside or out?"

"This winter I'm stuck with the training wall, but as soon as the weather breaks, I'll be outside. Maybe we can try it together."

"That would be great." Livy hugged her again, hardly able to believe she was talking to her cousin face-to-face. "Everything . . . it's just mind-boggling."

"I know." Robyn smoothed a wrinkle in her pants. "Look, I'm sorry if I hurt your feelings earlier."

"I don't know what you're talking about." But Livy knew exactly what Robyn meant. She needed to learn how to keep her emotions from showing on her face.

"When I told you to quit trying to protect me."

Livy shifted in her chair under Robyn's intense gaze. "But I've always looked out for you."

"And I appreciated you coming to my rescue when we were kids." Robyn looked away for a minute and then turned back to Livy. "But if you hadn't," she said, her voice softer, almost apologetic, "I might have learned how to take up for myself."

Heat filled Livy's cheeks. "I never meant to do that."

"I know you didn't, and I didn't say that to hurt you . . . this is hard." Robyn's eyes filled with tears, and she blotted them with a napkin and took a breath. "It's just that I need to fight my own battles."

Livy sighed. She did have a tendency to fight others' battles. It made her a good cop, but maybe she did take it to extremes sometimes. "I'll try to remember that." She found a grin. "If I do it again, just tell me to back off."

"I will."

Livy squeezed her cousin's hand. "You've grown up a lot in the past two and a half years."

Robyn returned the squeeze. "How are Mom and Dad?"

Livy smiled. "Kate is . . . Kate. Strong, always depending on God. She never believed you just walked away."

Tears gathered in her eyes again. "That sounds like her. And Dad?"

"You won't believe this, but he hasn't had anything to drink since you disappeared."

Robyn's eyes widened. "You're kidding. That's wonderful, but you make it sound like my leaving had something to do with it."

"It did. Charlie believed he failed you somehow, that his drinking was one of the reasons you left." Her cousin hadn't asked about

Chase, confirming Livy's suspicions that all had not been well between the two.

"It was so hard not letting everyone know where I was, but I'm glad some good has come from this ordeal."

"It's still hard for me to understand why you didn't call me. Like it or not, I've always run the bullies off, and now that I'm a cop, I have a gun." She tried to make a joke of it, but it stung that Robyn hadn't trusted her enough to get in touch.

"You can't imagine how fear paralyzed me. For the first year, it was all I could do to get through each day. I couldn't handle one more thing. Just as paralyzing was the belief that no one would think I was telling the truth."

"You know I would have believed you."

"Chase wouldn't." Robyn whispered the words. "I'm sure he'll find a way to blame me."

"He was a suspect for a few days, until you called and left a message. Were you two having problems?"

"When did we not? He kept pushing me to go back to college. To lose weight. To come out of my shell." She picked at a hangnail on her finger. "If I hadn't been pregnant with Abby, Chase never would have married me."

"I believe you are way off base on that one. You're the only woman Chase has ever loved."

She snorted. "I don't know why."

"Robyn! Where's that confident person I saw minutes ago?"

"Just being honest." She looked away. "Two and a half years ago I was overweight and depressed and didn't care whether I lived or died. It took almost dying and two years of therapy to get to the point where I wanted my life back." She picked at the hangnail again. "I wonder how Chase will like the 'new' me?"

"He's going to be surprised, for sure. But you're the same person, stronger, for sure, but still that sweet, loving Robyn I grew up with."

"Always the encourager." Robyn gave her a quick smile. "Enough about me. I'm not the only one who's different, and I want to know what happened. But first, tell me about Alex."

Livy ignored the comment about her being different—she didn't want to go there. "What about him? We just met two days ago."

"Two days or a hundred, I can tell you one thing, he's mighty fine." Robyn wiggled her eyebrows. "And I noticed he seems very considerate of you. Flying you up here . . . fixing your coffee this morning."

Livy searched for words and came up empty. "I don't know what you're talking about."

Robyn grinned. "Okay, have it your own way. So, what's happened in your life to make this change I sense in you? And it doesn't feel like a good change."

Livy stiffened. She wasn't sure if she liked the bold way her cousin asked questions. "What do you mean?"

A slight frown creased Robyn's brow. "I've never seen you hesitate like you did about me going back to Logan Point. As long as I can remember, you were always our leader, even more than Taylor, and always ready to right a wrong." Robyn gulped a breath. "Oh, I saw where Taylor got married. Is he a good guy?"

Livy nodded. "One of the best. But how did you know?"

"Susan subscribes to the online *Logan Point Gazette*. Is Taylor home for good?"

"Already teaching at the University of Memphis." Livy stretched. "We better get dressed if we're going to leave here on time." She felt Robyn's gaze boring into her and looked up. "What?"

"Are you sure there's nothing going on between you and Alex?"

"Yes, I'm sure." She sat up straighter. "Our relationship is purely business—he wants to find Samantha Jo Woodson, and I wanted to find you, which I've done. And since I want to catch the man who did this to you, I'll continue to work with him, but there is absolutely nothing romantic between us. Never will be."

Robyn raised her eyebrows, but she dropped it. "How about your job in Memphis?"

Livy glanced away. They were back to that. She stood and picked up her coffee cup. "I've taken a leave."

"Sit back down here and tell me what's happened. Thirty months ago, you wouldn't even take a vacation. What gives?"

Livy shook her head. "We don't have time to get into it."

"We can take five minutes so I can at least know how to pray for you."

She didn't want to talk about Justin Caine. "Mac suggested I take a leave, and let's leave it at that for now. We'll have plenty of time to discuss it later."

"It took me two years of therapy to understand that hiding a problem only makes it worse. Are you getting help for whatever it is you don't want to talk about?"

"I'm talking to Taylor."

Robyn shook her head. "Taylor is too close to you. She won't tell you the hard stuff. Besides, counseling isn't even her field."

Livy checked her watch. "We need to get packed if we're leaving for Logan Point."

"You can't run away from your problems," Robyn said. "Believe me, I know."

11

Alex gripped his cell phone, his voice hollow inside the hangar. "The first of March is still almost three weeks away. I'm not coming home right now just to fill out paperwork for the bar exam."

"Three weeks isn't very long," his grandfather said. "Your father and I are very much interested in seeing if you follow through this time."

He kicked the front tire on the Bonanza as a south wind whistled around the metal building. It'd be the first time his dad showed an interest in three years. His relationship with him had always been rocky, and it had always seemed like his dad never had time for him unless it had to do with one-upping Alex's mother. It had taken Alex until he was grown to figure out it was a generational thing. Josiah manipulated his son and criticized everything he did while doting on his grandson.

Now he could understand why his dad had checked out of his life early on, but it still hurt, especially since Alex's refusal to take the bar had driven a wedge between him and his grandfather. "Once I find Samantha Jo, the bar exam becomes a nonissue."

"*If* you find her."

"I'll find her." And not because it was part of some deal with his grandfather, but because she was a living, breathing person. He ended the call and massaged his jaws where he'd clenched them.

He loved his grandfather, but it was getting harder and harder for Alex to respect him. State Senator Josiah Jennings had wielded power in Texas for so long, he'd lost sight of what was really important.

Josiah. Alex tried to remember when he'd started thinking of his grandfather by his first name. Probably when he walked the halls of the state capitol building with him and saw how political deals were made, or sitting at the dinner table with his father and grandfather and other Texas legislators. Talk about what went on behind closed doors.

It was only in retrospect that he realized his grandfather had been grooming him even then to eventually take what the senator thought was Alex's rightful place in state politics. First become a practicing lawyer and then run for office after he had a few years of practice behind him. They probably had his dad's job of district attorney in mind.

Just last month, Josiah had announced his retirement, and Alex had heard his father was gearing up to run for the senate position. He'd probably win, and the pressure to bring Alex into the fold would intensify.

It'd been their plan all along, and Alex had been naive to think otherwise. He'd actually believed his grandfather understood his love of flying when Josiah gave him the Bonanza on his twenty-third birthday. Nothing was said about it being a bribe to attend law school, at least not until after he'd flown it. At that point, he would have done anything to keep the plane. His mother had warned him, but Alex hadn't listened. She'd been right—the plane had just been another way to control him.

He was surprised his grandfather had agreed to the deal involving Samantha Jo. Well, not really, considering Josiah didn't believe Alex would find her. He would prove him wrong, because it was either find her or take the bar . . . or be disowned.

In spite of his frustrations at his dad and granddad, he didn't want to be disowned, and not because of his grandfather's money. It was about being a Jennings and a Texan. The name was rooted deep in Texas history—all the way back to the Alamo. It was a heritage he wanted to contribute to, just not as a lawyer like his dad or a politician like his grandfather.

Alex pushed the problems with his family out of his mind. Time to do his preflight inspection, and he didn't need anything to distract him. In the air was no time to discover he'd overlooked something during his checks. As soon as he finished checking the fuel for water or trash, his other problem intruded. He couldn't understand why Livy was against Robyn returning. He hoped she wouldn't keep second-guessing him.

He took out his phone and dialed Ben Logan. When the sheriff answered, he said, "Can you reschedule the appointment with the Nashville detective and meet with me and Livy this afternoon? In private."

"Where are you? I tried to call earlier and it went to voice mail."

"I'm at an airport near Bristol, Tennessee." Alex glanced at the side of his phone. "My phone's on silent. Sorry. Is anything going on? Has Samantha Jo surfaced?"

"No, nothing like that. Evan McCord has been trying to reach Livy, and she's not answering either."

"Maybe her phone is on silent as well. I'll tell her when she arrives here at the airport."

"She's with you then?"

"Yes, we were following a lead. That's what we want to talk to you about."

"Can you meet me at my house by two thirty? Livy will give you directions."

Alex checked his watch. It was almost ten. If the girls would just come on so they could get in the air. He glanced toward the terminal building and relaxed. Livy and Robyn were coming through the glass doors. "We should make that easily."

After stowing their luggage, Alex helped both onto the wing before he climbed into the pilot's seat. Once they were settled with Robyn in one of the backseats and Livy in the front beside him, he handed them both earphones.

"So we can talk," Livy said with a grin at Alex.

He couldn't keep from smiling back. She seemed to have shaken the mulligrubs, and her live-wire personality had resurfaced.

"You'll love this, Robyn. I promise." Livy bounced in her seat. "And I'll get to see what the trip looks like in the daytime."

Alex couldn't believe this was the same person he'd had to practically bribe to make the trip yesterday. "I talked to Ben Logan and set up a meeting at his house for two thirty. We'll go from there."

He turned the key, and the prop caught the first time. Livy raised her eyebrows, and they laughed together. "Did Ben reach you?"

She shook her head.

"He indicated someone by the name of Evan McCord was trying to get in touch with you."

"Mac?" Livy's brows pinched together, and she took out her cell phone. "It's dead, and I forgot to bring my charger. I'll call him later."

He wanted to ask who Mac was, but she might tell him it was none of his business. And she'd be right. He hadn't thought to ask Ben if Livy was seeing anyone. Maybe he should. With her looks, it'd be hard to believe someone wasn't pursuing her, and he may have just imagined that there'd been a spark between them last night.

After getting clearance, he taxied out to the runway and took off into a clear blue sky. Almost immediately they encountered strong headwinds that would slow the flight. Two hours later, dark thunderheads banked to the west. Twenty miles back, they had encountered small pockets of turbulence, so Alex was glad to see the small airport.

While he piloted the plane, Livy and Robyn spent the first part of the flight coming up with Robyn's cover story. They decided that Livy had met "Sharon" in college, and they had renewed their friendship on Facebook. When Sharon lost her job, Livy offered her a place to stay while Sharon looked for a new job.

After that the flight had been quiet, except for a few comments from Livy as she tried to figure out where they were. He suspected they were all thinking about what would happen next.

Once on the ground, he taxied to the hangar he'd rented from Sam the day before while he'd waited for Livy to arrive. That it had an airplane tug was a bonus. No pushing the plane into the hangar. A gust of wind whipped through the opening between the buildings as he closed the door and ran to the terminal building where Livy and Robyn waited. Livy opened the door and he ran in, just ahead of the rain. At least his plane was out of the weather.

"Why don't we take my SUV?" Livy said. "After we talk to Ben, we'll have to drive back by the airport to go to Kate's. We can get your car then."

He nodded, and Livy borrowed a rain slicker from Sam and dashed out to pull her car under the drive-through. Alex glanced at Robyn. She had grown paler the closer they got to Logan Point. He wanted to point out that Sam, who hovered nearby, hadn't known her and no one else would either. "Sharon." Alex took her by the arm. "I don't believe I introduced you to Sam."

Robyn startled, and then her face flushed, putting a little color in it. She held out her hand. "Sharon Arnold," she said. "Alex was kind enough to give me a ride here. Tomorrow I'll have to find a way to Memphis to look for a job." She tilted her head. "Unless you know of one around here? I was a waitress at my last job."

Sam rubbed his chin. "Plenty of those jobs here. I heard Johnny B's was still lookin' for a waitress. And Molly's Diner too."

"Thank you so much." She flashed him a brilliant smile, and his face turned red.

Alex raised his eyebrows. *See, you can do it.* Livy's horn sounded, and he nodded to Sam. "I'll be back in an hour or so to get my car."

"No hurry. It's not going anywhere."

As he held the passenger door for Robyn, he said, "Piece of cake."

"I didn't know what you were doing at first."

"But you caught on. You'll do just fine."

"She'll do fine at what?" Livy said.

"Just practicing a little," Alex said. "Let's not tell Ben right away who Robyn is. See if he has a clue."

"Not a bad idea, for a PI."

He made a face at her. Looked like it was going to take him becoming a cop to get any respect.

A little before two thirty, Livy pulled into a long drive and stopped by an electric gate to key in the code. Alex shifted in his seat and looked around. A two-story white brick was to the right, and a ranch style was to the left. "Why the tall fence and electric gate?"

"A few years back, a drug dealer tried to get to Ben's dad. The big house is Sheriff Tom's." She turned down the drive to the ranch style. "This is Ben's."

Evidently Ben had been watching for them, because he opened the door before they knocked. They stepped into a large room that served as a living room, den, and kitchen. It was a man's room. Paneled, blinds, no curtains, leather furniture. Alex liked it.

A boy who looked to be the age of Robyn's daughter shrugged into a raincoat.

"My son, TJ," Ben said to Alex. "School dismissed early today, and my mom is taking him to the movies."

The pride in his voice struck a nerve. The sheriff wasn't much older than Alex, but he seemed so settled and knew what he wanted out of life. He glanced at Livy as she kidded with the boy. As much as she liked kids, why hadn't she already married? Maybe she was like him and hadn't met the right person.

A horn tooted and Ben tousled his son's hair as the boy raced for the door. "Either me or your mom will pick you up later."

After TJ left, Livy nudged Ben. "The big day is Valentine's Day. Right?"

A broad grin flashed across the sheriff's face. "Yep. And TJ is already officially a Logan."

Evidently Alex missed something, and he shot a questioning glance at Livy.

"It's involved, but the short version is Ben's getting married to Dr. Leigh Somerall. And I say it's about time."

"You're right about that too. Nothing fancy, just us and a few of our friends at church that evening. Are you coming?"

"Of course I'll be there."

Ben grinned again and then shifted his gaze to Robyn. "Who's your friend?"

Alex waited for Livy to speak, but she nodded for him to take the lead. "We've come up with a plan to catch whoever took Samantha Jo, and she's part of it."

■ ■ ■

He eased into the barn and closed the door. Yesterday he'd raised the blackout shades after he'd realized Sharon needed sunlight. She'd finally quit screaming, probably because she'd lost her voice. He tugged at the ski mask. It'd felt good outside where it was cold, but inside the barn, it itched.

He stood for a moment, his gaze drawn to the girl in the cage. Yes, the red hair looked much more natural. His mother had agreed with him as well. She should; it was the same color she'd used for years. He swung a plastic bag back from his shoulders, and Sharon looked up. Once again he smelled her fear, and smiled.

"Thank you for leaving the shades up." She spoke barely above a whisper.

He'd known she'd come around. He lowered his voice, altering it just in case she might remember talking to him. "You're welcome. I've brought you something to read while I'm gone."

"You're leaving?"

She was upset. His heart lifted. She was coming around ever so much faster than the last girl. He shook his head. That one had been a mistake. How had he ever thought she might be his Sharon?

"I'm only leaving for a day. There's food in this bag and bottled water." He set it on the floor outside the bars. This was a short trip to Nashville. Just long enough to turn the girl's purse in and get Ben Logan and Olivia Reynolds looking in a different direction. "You can open it and pull what you need through the bars." He'd learned that lesson with the last one as well. She'd talked him into opening the door and then tried to escape.

"What if this place catches on fire?"

"It's not going to. You should be comfortable enough with heat and food and water and something to read." He narrowed his eyes as tears formed in her eyes. If she started screaming again, he'd have to sedate her.

"Why are you doing this to me?"

"It's for your own good. Being a waitress isn't a job for a woman like you. Those men only have one thing on their mind. I'm just trying to protect you."

"Then turn me loose. Please," she sobbed.

"Oh, Sharon." His voice hardened. "I know what you want to do. You want to be with those men. Just like . . ." He shook his head. "Don't you understand? You're mine now. You'll never be free again."

■ ■ ■

Rain drummed on the roof as Robyn consciously relaxed her muscles under Ben's curious glance. She in turn watched his face for any sign of recognition. If he didn't know who she was, this crazy plan they'd concocted might work. She held out her hand. "Sharon Arnold."

The sheriff shook her hand. "Ben Logan. Why don't we sit at the kitchen bar and one of you tell me what this plan is."

"Mind if I make some coffee?" Livy asked. "We didn't get a lot of sleep last night."

"Sure. Coffee is in the cabinet over the coffeemaker. Creamer is in the refrigerator."

As they gathered around the island, Alex pulled out her stool. He seemed to be a nice man. And certainly smitten with Livy. Not that she figured her cousin knew. For such a good detective, Livy had never been too observant when it came to men who were interested in her. She glanced at Ben. His engagement announcement had been in the online edition of the *Logan Point Gazette*, and she almost blurted her congratulations out. That was what Livy and Alex had cautioned her about—being too familiar. She sat back and let the other two lay out the plan.

"Rob—ah, Sharon here received one of those letters like Samantha Jo." Alex's face flushed. "She didn't quit her job, and a few weeks later, the sender abducted her."

She flinched under Ben's scrutiny. "And he let you go?"

"Whatever he gave me wore off, and I escaped."

"So you know what he looks like?" Excitement crept into the sheriff's voice.

Thunder rumbled overhead, and she took a deep breath. "No. I have very little memory of that night."

Livy set a cup of coffee in front of Robyn. "But she does remember some things. Like, she was in a semi."

"And he had a tattoo," Robyn added. If she could just remember where it was on his body. "It was a hawk, or now that I think about it, it could be a falcon. Whatever it was, it had its talons extended, like this." She formed her fingers into claws.

Ben took the cup of coffee Livy offered. "I still don't know what your plan is," he said.

Livy poured another cup of coffee and handed it to Alex. "We believe whoever kidnapped her also abducted Samantha Jo."

"And those other waitresses," Alex said. "We think he either lives around here or comes through here on a regular basis. I plotted the other locations where a waitress had been kidnapped, and Logan Point is on a direct route to each one of them."

"We decided I would get a job at Johnny B's. Two people who worked there have been kidnapped—he's probably a regular." Robyn took a sip of the hot coffee. "And maybe something will trigger a memory, his cologne or his voice. I'm hoping I'll remember his face."

"But he'll recognize you. And either run or abduct you again."

"No, I doubt he'll know me."

He searched her face, and again no recognition showed in his expression. "Your name isn't Sharon, is it?"

"No."

"I'm assuming your appearance has been altered since he kidnapped you. How long ago did it happen?"

"Thirty months." She didn't waver under his gaze.

"Thirty months . . . that's when . . ." He stared at her. "Are you telling me you're Robyn Martin? But . . . you look so different. Your hair . . . you're so thin. And Robyn had blue eyes. I know. I looked at the description enough."

"Contacts. Flat iron. Plastic surgery after he beat me senseless. That tends to make a person lose weight." Tears burned her eyes. Coming home stirred up emotions she'd long buried.

Ben grabbed her up in a bear hug. "Abby and Chase and your mom and dad will be so happy."

She stepped back and threw Livy a plea for help.

"We can't tell them just yet."

Ben turned to Livy. "What? Why not?" Then he slapped his head. "Of course we can't for the very reasons I mentioned."

Alex said, "The more people who know, the more likely the kidnapper will find out."

"Can you do it?" Ben's brows lowered as he stared at her. "Be around your family and not give yourself away?"

"I hope it won't be for long. Alex and Livy seem to think it'll only be a couple of weeks at the most."

Ben scratched his temple. "I hope they're right. What do you remember about the night he kidnapped you?"

"Not a lot."

"Did you finish your shift at Johnny B's?"

She nodded. "But before I left, I remember setting my canned drink down to help one of the waitresses with her order. That's when he must have put the drug in."

Ben made notes on a tablet. He looked up. "Do you remember any of the customers who were there?"

Robyn closed her eyes. She'd turned that night over and over in her mind for over two years. "Bobby Cook, Timothy Nolan . . . Johnny B was there. Tommy, the short-order cook. The tall skinny guy that wears all the leather—"

"Jason Fremont," Livy said.

Ben leaned forward. "Anyone else?"

She searched her memory bank. "One of the game wardens was there . . . Sully Anderson. He was mad about losing his job because of budget cuts. There were others, I know, but right now I can't think of anyone else."

"If you do, jot their name down."

"I just hope being at Johnny B's will trigger more memories the way riding in that eighteen-wheeler made me remember being in the cab of a semi." Robyn twisted the wedding band on her finger. "Of course, the first thing I have to do is get a job at Johnny B's."

Ben laughed. "That won't be a problem. Saw him in town today. He's looking for a waitress. But . . ." He held up his finger. "You need someone with you for protection. I can't put a deputy there all the time. It would look suspicious." He turned to Alex. "Ever work as a short-order cook? Johnny B mentioned he needed one."

Alex grinned. "I'm way ahead of you. He offered me the job yesterday."

Livy bumped him with her shoulder. "Think you can handle it?"

"I'll have you know that when I was in college, I worked at a local Burger King, flipping burgers. Sure, I can handle it."

Knowing Alex would be there bolstered Robyn's courage.

"Since I'm not working, I can hang around Johnny B's some too," Livy said.

"How come you're not working?" Ben asked.

She hesitated. "Captain Reed and Mac thought I needed a little vacation. Which reminds me, I have to call Mac. Can I use your land line?"

Ben nodded. "It's on the wall."

Robyn had the impression Livy's vacation wasn't a surprise to him, and as soon as things got settled, Livy was coming clean with her.

"Okay, we need to figure out where Robyn is going to stay."

"How about the apartment building where Samantha Jo lived? Didn't look to me like it was fully rented," Alex said. "I thought we might get side-by-side apartments."

"How about furniture? Do you have any?"

Alex winced, and Robyn's hopes sank. She hadn't thought about furniture, and evidently, neither had Alex.

"I'd offer to let you stay with my mom and dad, but that would arouse suspicion." Ben drummed his fingers on the granite counter. "How about the hotel at Johnny B's?"

"*No!* I . . . I can't stay there. It's going to be hard enough working at the diner, but to be that close to where he took me twenty-four hours a day. I can't do it."

"How about if she stays with us—at the bed and breakfast?" Livy shifted her gaze to Robyn.

Her muscles tensed. Deep within her, Robyn realized it was what she wanted, but could she be that close to Abby, or the others for that matter? What if she did something to give herself away? What if the man discovered who she was and came after her . . . and Abby was hurt? Her fingers shook, and she pressed her hands together. *You can do this.* She had to. She couldn't live the way she'd been living, fearing her own shadow, living apart from her family. She fingered her wedding band again.

"Are you okay, Robyn?" Concern laced Livy's voice. "We can call this off if you want to."

This was her chance. To what? Live in fear for the rest of her life? She lifted her chin. "No, I'm fine. It's the only choice we have. Let's do it."

12

The rain had dwindled to a mist by the time they left Ben. Livy pulled up to the security gate, and the gate opened. "You don't mind riding with Alex to the house, do you? Mac wants me to meet him at Molly's Diner for a cup of coffee. He said it was important."

Robyn hugged her body with her arms. "Don't worry about me. I can do this on my own."

She didn't sound as though she could.

"Would it bother you if we tagged along, sat at different booths?" Alex said from the backseat. "I'm starving and imagine Robyn is too. We'll grab a late lunch."

Robyn relaxed visibly in the seat beside her. Livy should have thought of that option, but after her conversation with Mac, her mind had created all sorts of scenarios. They all ended with him saying he'd made a mistake and wanted her back as his partner.

She shot Alex a thank-you look in the rearview mirror. "That's a great idea. Then afterward I can drop you off at the airport to pick up your car and we can all go to Kate's together."

"We're a team." Alex reached over the seat. "Give me a high five."

She slapped his hand all the while shaking her head. "You're crazy."

"I think he's nice," Robyn said and high-fived him as well. "A full stomach will help me do what I have to do tonight. Do you . . ."

Livy glanced at her cousin. "Do I what?"

Robyn's throat tightened, and she swallowed. "Do you think Abby will be there? Or Chase?"

Her stomach took a dive. She hadn't thought about that, but of course Robyn had. "I don't know. I haven't spent enough time at Kate's to know the routine." She touched Robyn's hand. "Let's just take this one minute at a time." A memory of something Abby had said hit her. "Oh, and you need to find a different perfume."

Alex winced. "I'd forgotten that."

"Perfume? I don't wear perfume. What are you two talking about?"

Alex leaned toward the front seat again. "That's one of the things that got us started investigating who you were. In the car after Livy and Abby met you in the park, Abby remarked that you smelled like her mom."

Robyn covered her mouth with her hand. "I can't believe she remembered. But it's not perfume, it's Amazing Grace lotion. I'll get a new kind."

Livy tapped her fingers on the steering wheel. How many other small things like that were there to trip them up? Anxiety struck like lightning. Maybe this wasn't such a good idea. She brushed the thought away. Somehow, she had to stick to Robyn like a shadow—if she'd let her.

Alex tapped her on the shoulder. "Let me out before you get to Molly's. That way no one will see us all get out of the same car."

"Good idea." As Livy turned onto the town square, she saw that Mac's '64 Mustang was sitting in front of Molly's Diner, and she pulled in beside it. He'd been restoring that car ever since she'd known him.

She paused inside the door as Robyn took a table in the back. Mac sat by the window and lifted his glass of tea. She walked toward him and he stood, making her do a double take. "What was that for?" she asked when they were both seated. She glanced up as Alex came in.

He lifted one shoulder. "My mama always taught me to stand in the presence of a lady."

"And what was I when we were working?"

"My partner and that doesn't count. I didn't look at you as a lady then." He shook his head. "Wait, that didn't sound right. But you know what I mean."

"Gee, thanks." Things seemed almost normal with Mac, and a weight lifted from her heart. For the first time since she came through the door, she took a good look at him. He had color in his face again, and it was good to see a twinkle in his gray eyes. But he seemed a little nervous. "What was so important that you had to see me today?"

"Do you want a drink? Coffee? Tea? Soda?"

"I think I'll get a sandwich and tea, but I'm paying." No way was she letting him get the ticket. She motioned to the waitress who had just left Robyn's table and gave her an order for a chicken salad sandwich and tea. Then she turned back to Mac.

He stirred his drink with the straw. "Where were you today?"

Her hopes crumbled. Mac was evading the subject, so Livy knew she wasn't going to like whatever he wanted to discuss. "Flew in from Bristol, Tennessee, with a friend and—" She caught herself before she said Robyn's name. "Sharon."

He stared at her. "*You* flew in an airplane? Big or little?"

She sat a little straighter. "A Bonanza. I think I'm going to take lessons as soon as we wrap up the case." Maybe then she'd have something to talk with her dad about.

"You're working on a case? Does Reed know about this?"

"I'm just helping Ben out—it's not my case. I'm on a leave of absence, remember?"

"Livy, the whole purpose of the leave is for you to rest and get your perspective back. That's not going to happen if you throw yourself into another case. Have you made an appointment with Keith Robinson?"

"I'm not seeing the department shrink." She fell silent as their waitress brought her plate. He definitely wasn't here to ask her to return to work. "Thank you," she said. "Now, did you come here to tell me something or to get on my case?"

"I'm just worried about you."

Livy took her time cutting the sandwich into four triangles. He wasn't being forthright, and she was tired of playing his game. When she finished, she picked up a triangle and bit into it. Although Molly's chicken salad was always tasty, today it filled her mouth like sawdust. She guzzled the tea.

"I'm resigning from the force."

Livy stilled her body. Surely she hadn't heard him right. She looked up into his gray eyes. Yeah, she'd heard him right. Her stomach churned. He couldn't resign. Mac was the only partner she'd had since becoming a detective. "Why? You love being a detective."

He dropped his gaze to the table, and she wanted to make him look at her and say it wasn't true. "Tell me you don't love it."

Mac lifted his eyes. "I love Julie more."

"But how do you just stop being a detective?"

He leaned back in his chair and folded his arms across his chest. "You're not making this easy."

"I'm just trying to understand."

She waited, and a minute passed as Mac stared out the window. "After that bullet hit me Monday, things changed. Lying in that hospital bed with my heart beating like a ping-pong ball on crack, it came to me. Is this all there is? Get up every morning, go to the CJC, catch the bad guys, send them to jail, and they come out the back door—or maybe even the front door—before I can get in my car." His voice was low and intense as he raked his hand through his hair. "Yeah, I love being a detective, but I want a life. A wife, kids, house, ball games—all of it. And I want it with Julie. You know as well as I do I can't have both."

Livy's heart thumped against her chest. What would it be like to love someone like that? Would Mac wake up one day and regret the choice he made? She studied his face. Even as uncomfortable as he was telling her he was resigning, peace radiated from him. "What will you do?"

"I've accepted a job as a security consultant for a company in Atlanta."

"Atlanta? You're moving too?"

"Julie thought . . . no, we both thought it would be for the best. Cut the ties. No looking back."

Livy stared down at the napkin she'd twisted into a long spiral. "It won't be the same."

He patted her hand. "Life isn't static. It's always changing, and we have to learn to change with it. You're a good cop, and you'll do fine with a new partner."

No, she wouldn't. Mac was the only partner she wanted. What was she going to do without him?

"Livy, I'd like your blessing."

She jerked her head up. That wasn't fair. But he was her partner, and she couldn't hold him back from what he wanted to do. She squared her shoulders and looked into his eyes. "I'd be lying if I said I was happy about you leaving, but if that's what you want, I wish you well." She almost choked on the words.

He held her gaze. "Thanks. Now, tell me about this case you're working on."

■ ■ ■

Robyn rode with Livy to the house they both grew up in. "This will be the first big test—getting by Mom."

Livy laughed. "Yeah, she can smell a lie a hundred miles away."

"Don't I know it." Robyn wasn't too worried about her dad. But then there was Chase. Her heart beat faster, just thinking about him. How would he react when the truth came out? Before she'd been kidnapped, their marriage had disintegrated into silence and sleeping in separate beds. She'd actually considered divorce, even thought Chase might have already gotten one while she was missing. That he hadn't gave Robyn hope.

She stared out the window, the landscape a blur. The last two and a half years had given her time to step back and take a hard look at their marriage. Their problems hadn't been all Chase's fault. She hadn't tried to make it work, believing he only married her because she was pregnant with Abby. That, in turn, had left her filled with guilt—she'd known it was wrong to sleep with him, and while he hadn't accused her of trapping him into marriage, she was certain he thought it.

Sometimes she wondered if subconsciously she *had* trapped him, because she definitely wasn't his type. Chase was handsome and out-going, and he would not have picked a plain Jane introvert like her.

"Are you okay?"

Livy's words drew her back to the present problem. "As good as I can be until we get the man who kidnapped me." Robyn smoothed a wrinkle from her pants. "How about you? You've been quiet since your meeting. Is everything okay with Mac?"

Livy's fingers tightened around the steering wheel. "He's leaving Memphis."

"What? He's quitting the police department?"

"And getting back with his ex-wife."

"Did you and Mac—"

"No."

Livy's answer came a little too quickly.

"We didn't have that kind of relationship. In some ways, it was even closer. He was my partner." She grunted. "It does feel a little like a divorce, though."

Robyn had waited for Livy to tell her why she'd taken a leave of absence, but so far she hadn't opened up. It wasn't good to bottle up emotions, and that was what her cousin seemed to be doing. "I read online about the shooting before Christmas. How are you handling that?"

Livy's face paled. She didn't respond, and the hum of the tires filled the silence between them. Finally, she gave a shrug. "I'm getting there."

"That's the reason for your leave, right?"

"Yeah." She turned her right blinker on. "We're almost home."

Like Robyn didn't know that, but it was obvious Livy didn't want to discuss the shooting. Maybe in a day or two, she would open up. "Does Mom know you're bringing someone?"

"I called Kate earlier and told her I was bringing a paying guest, but don't worry about the money. I'll take care of it."

"I have money. Susan paid me quite well, and I haven't had anything to spend it on other than college."

"College? That's great. I always hated that you didn't go back after Abby started school."

Nothing more was said as Livy pulled into the drive and parked behind the house. "Well, this is it. Shall we go in?"

As they climbed out of the car, Alex's blue Impala pulled in behind them. Robyn waited and let them go into the house ahead of her. With her insides ready to jump out of her body, she stepped over the threshold into the lighted kitchen. Everything was exactly the way she'd pictured it all these months. She swayed as memories bombarded her. How many times had she come through that back door and smelled cookies or bread baking in the oven and yelled, "Mom, I'm home!"

"Kate, I want you to meet my friend, Sharon Arnold."

Robyn snapped her attention back to the present. She bobbed her head, schooling her voice to sound like the Virginia dialect she'd perfected. "Pleased to meet you, Kate."

145

That felt strange, calling her mother by her given name. Very strange. Her mother looked good. Hair a little grayer, but she still stood straight, and peace reigned in her face, as it always had.

"Livy says you'll be here for a few days."

"Yes ma'am." She tried to catch the words, but it was too late. In Virginia, most of the women her age didn't say "yes ma'am" or "no ma'am." Hopefully, her mother wouldn't know that.

"Manners too." Kate smiled.

Robyn breathed a little easier. But then she realized she needed to ask about the cost. "Uh, Livy didn't say how much your nightly rate was—"

"Livy also said you didn't have a job, so why don't we wait and see what you can pay. Right now I don't have any paying guests other than Alex, and if you're willing to help out around here, there'll be no charge."

"Th-thank you." Robyn's heart swelled. Her mom had not changed one bit, always ready to extend a helping hand.

"Nothing to thank me for. Let me show you where you'll be staying. It was my daughter's room before she married."

Robyn almost couldn't get her feet to move. She would be staying in her old room? She glanced sidelong at Kate. Did she know? She didn't appear to. She followed her mother up the stairs to the room she'd grown up in.

"There's nothing fancy here, but I think you'll be comfortable." Kate stepped back, and Robyn entered her old room.

"Thank you." She set her suitcase down, remembering when her mom had changed the room from purple walls and posters of the Backstreet Boys into something out of *Country Living*. She ran her hand over the white eyelet bedspread that covered the four-poster cherry bed. The bedspread had been added since she'd been gone. She tried to think like someone who had never seen the house. "It's beautiful. From what I've seen, you have a lovely home."

146

"I hope you'll enjoy your stay with us. My husband should be in soon. He's helping our son-in-law get his tractor ready for spring."

Something Chase's uncle always did. She almost blurted out something about Jonathan. She shouldn't have come here. There was too much to trip her up. And just being with her mother and not saying who she was made her heart ache.

"How did you and Livy meet?"

"Through a mutual friend. Susan Carpenter." Too late, Robyn realized that wasn't their cover story. "Actually, we went to college together, and lost touch. But Susan brought us back together."

"Yes, my granddaughter, Abby, was telling us about meeting her in the park. Something about a hawk."

Abby. None of them had considered that she might remember the name Robyn used. Now she understood the meaning of weaving a tangled web. She would have to avoid her daughter, and that brought more heaviness to her chest. She'd so looked forward to at least being around Abby.

"We'll talk more at supper. Oh, and Abby will be joining us. Her dad as well, if he and Charlie get finished with the tractor."

Again, Robyn tried to think of what a stranger would ask or say. "Does she live nearby?"

"The farm next to us. She uses an old lane that connects the two places and will ride over on her four-wheeler if it isn't raining."

When did Abby get a four-wheeler? Was Chase out of his mind? She wasn't big enough to handle one of those machines. "Aren't those things dangerous?" The words were out of her mouth before she could stop them.

"That's my sentiment exactly. She's not afraid of anything, and her daddy lets her do far more than I think he should. But at least the four-wheeler has a good headlight, and it is a short distance." Kate turned to leave. "Supper is at six."

"I may not come down. My head is killing me, and I'm awfully tired."

Her mom stared at her, a slight frown on her face. "My daughter Robyn had headaches. They could lay her quite low sometimes."

"I feel for her." The door creaked as Robyn closed it behind her mother. She sank into the wingback chair in the corner of the room and pressed her hand to her mouth. This was so much harder than she'd envisioned. She didn't even want to think about going down for supper tonight.

■ ■ ■

Alex checked his watch as he came down the stairs. Almost six. And something smelled inviting. Livy and Robyn had disappeared into their bedrooms after they'd come in, and he didn't know if either of them would be coming down for supper. He hoped Livy did. He wanted to know more about this Mac. Her body language in the diner had piqued his curiosity. She definitely hadn't been happy with whatever Mac had told her.

When he entered the kitchen, soup was bubbling on the stove as Kate took a black skillet of golden brown corn bread from the oven. Her granddaughter was busy setting the table. He hadn't expected Abby back tonight; the child could pose a problem if she mentioned she'd seen Robyn in the park. Did Robyn know she was here? "Good evening, Miss Abby." He bowed.

She curtsied. "Evening, Mr. Alex." She went back to setting the table. "Do you know if Aunt Livy and the new person will be at dinner?"

"I will," Livy said from the door. "But I don't think the other guest is eating. She has a headache." Livy glanced around. "Kate, what do you want me to do?"

"How about putting ice in the glasses for the tea."

"My mom used to have headaches."

Alex winced. Robyn should have picked a different excuse. He needed to see about getting her a furnished apartment. Tomorrow.

His cell phone rang, and he unhooked his phone from his belt. Johnny Baxter. Alex had called and left a message that he'd like to take him up on his job offer. He stepped into the hallway to answer. "Hello."

Johnny B got to the point right away. "Got your message. Can you start tomorrow at three?"

"Sure."

"Come in half an hour early and we'll discuss salary."

"Sounds like a winner." Smiling, Alex hung up and went back to the kitchen. "I start my new job tomorrow afternoon."

Livy set a glass down. "Really? That was fast." She turned to Abby. "How was school today?"

Her thin shoulders lifted in a shrug. "Okay. TJ Logan asked me if I'd sit with him at our class party on Valentine's Day."

Livy put her hand on her hip. "You're too young to be thinking about parties with boys."

"Oh, Aunt Livy, it's not like that—it's school. He just wants me to sit with him. Besides, I'm almost eleven."

"Not until next summer," Kate said.

Alex hid his smile. He totally agreed with Livy and Kate. Kids grew up too fast these days.

"Mr. Alex, are you going to give Aunt Livy a valentine?"

"Abby!" Livy's face lit up like a red balloon.

"I bet she'll get a lot of valentines," Alex said.

Abby rolled her eyes. "I don't think so. She doesn't have any boyfriends." She looked up at Alex. "You do like her, don't you?"

Heat crawled up his neck. He was pretty sure he and Livy matched now. "Ah, yeah, sure."

She nodded, satisfied. "That's what I thought. So have you thought about what you're going to give her? She doesn't like flowers, you know."

"Abby Martin!" Livy's mouth opened and closed. "You stop this nonsense right now."

"I thought I might give her a goldfish." He enjoyed seeing Livy flustered. "How about if I take her up in my airplane?"

"That's better." Abby cut her eyes toward Livy. "But a nice dinner would be more romantic."

"Abby." Kate's voice held a warning. "That's enough."

She ducked her head. "Yes ma'am."

Alex heard the girl mutter something under her breath when she passed him. He could have sworn she said she was just trying to help.

Kate cleared her throat. "It doesn't look as though Chase and my Charlie are going to make it, so let's say the blessing, and then you can fill up your bowl with soup, and there's salad on the table."

Once again, Kate's prayer was like a one-sided conversation with God, then the dinner table was quiet as everyone enjoyed the hearty beef soup and corn bread. When they'd all finished, Kate set a bowl of banana pudding on the table, and Alex suppressed a groan. If he stayed here much longer, he'd gain ten pounds.

Kate turned to Livy. "Have you checked your email?"

"I haven't had time."

"Well, you probably have another message from your dad, like I did. He said he would see us real soon."

"Did he say why?"

Something in Livy's tone made him look up. Her facial expression mirrored how he'd feel if he discovered his father was coming.

"No. Just that he definitely was coming."

"I wouldn't plan the reunion meal just yet. He'll probably cancel."

"Livy." Kate's voice held a mild reproach before she turned to Abby. "Get your jacket, and I'll run you home. It's too cold and dark for you to go home on the four-wheeler."

"I'll clear the table while you're gone and dry the dishes in the sink," Livy said. She picked up the drying towel.

"And I'll help." Alex winked when Abby shot him a look of approval.

After they left, he stacked the bowls. "Abby is quite the little matchmaker."

She pointed her finger at him. "You shouldn't encourage her."

"I think she had a pretty good idea. Do you really not like flowers?"

Livy shrugged. "I like roses."

He nodded his approval. "When is Valentine's Day, anyway?" When she stared at him, he said, "I know it's February 14, but what day is that?"

"Well, this is the seventh, so Valentine's is next Friday." She picked up a pan on the stove.

"Okay. How about it? Dinner, maybe dancing, Friday night?" She hesitated and he said, "Or are you going out with Mac that night?"

"No. I'm going to a wedding. Ben's—remember?" She set the pan down with a thud. "But why would you think I was going out with him? Mac and I were partners. That's all."

Relief surprised him as he held his hands up in a defensive action. "Sorry. There just seemed to be a lot of intensity between you two this afternoon at the diner."

Livy pinched the bridge of her nose. "No need to be sorry. It's not your fault. It wasn't the best meeting I've had with him." She threw the dish towel on the counter. "I need some fresh air."

She hurried out the back door, leaving him with his mouth gaped. She'd freeze to death out there. He'd seen her coat on a hook in the hallway beside his when he'd come downstairs. Alex grabbed both of them and hurried outside after her. She stood shivering under the giant oak that lifted its bare branches to the sky. Tears glistened on her face, and her arms hugged her body.

"I thought you might need this." He slipped the coat on her shoulders.

She wiped her cheeks with the back of her hand. "Thanks."

Alex shrugged into his coat. "It's not too bad out here, just misting a little. Want to take a walk?"

"You don't have to do this." She stared at the ground.

He glanced down at her, and his heart caught. She had no idea how vulnerable or beautiful she looked. He ducked his head where he could see her eyes. "What if I want to?"

A small smile tugged at her lips. "Thank you."

They walked for a few minutes in silence under the overhead lights that lined the drive. He glanced down at her. "Did Mac bring bad news?"

She nodded. "He's leaving Memphis."

"Wow, that is hard. Any particular reason?"

Her chin quivered, and she pressed her lips together. "Me, partly."

"You? How could you—"

"I had his back, and I froze, and he was shot."

"When?"

"Monday."

"Wait a minute. How could he have been shot Monday and look fine today?"

"He had his vest on, but it caused an arrhythmia and his ex-wife came to the hospital and now they're getting back together and moving to Atlanta because she doesn't want him to be a cop."

"Whoa—slow down a second. Let me process that." Mac might not have had a romantic interest in his partner, but Alex wasn't sure Livy could say the same. "So you think it's your fault that he's quitting the force?"

She nodded.

"That doesn't make sense. If he was still in love with his ex-wife, it was only a matter of time before he figured out what he wanted."

"He didn't want to be partners with me anymore."

Her whispered words fell into the silence of the night. That was the real problem. He could think of nothing to refute her words, so he remained quiet.

"That's why I took a leave of absence. I have to figure out if I can be a cop."

"Ben says you're a good cop."

"You've been talking to Ben about me?"

"No, it just came up."

"I used to be a good cop, but . . ."

"But?"

She sucked in a breath and slowly let it out. "I killed a seventeen-year-old boy in December. He'd just robbed a convenience store with a toy pellet gun. But I didn't know it was a toy. I told him to put it on the ground, but he didn't. Then he raised his arm with the gun in his hand. I don't know why he did that." She closed her eyes. "I was cleared of any wrongdoing, but I can't put it behind me. That's what made me freeze the other day with Mac. And again at the shooting range. I failed my shoot/no-shoot test."

"Aw, Livy, that's tough." He'd never even shot at anyone, much less killed a person, so he couldn't say he knew how she felt. But he did know what it was like to fail. Maybe that was the real reason he resisted taking the bar exam—he didn't want to fail and see the disappointment in his father's eyes. His heart ached for her as he took in her slumped shoulders and the hurt radiating off her body. "Give yourself a little time."

"Yeah, that's what everyone keeps saying. But while I'm trying to get my head together, no one wants to be my partner. And I can understand since I'm not sure I'd want to be my partner."

Alex stopped in front of her and put his hands on her shoulders. "Cut yourself some slack. You were only doing your job when the boy was killed. It wasn't a mistake. This bad time in your life will pass—everything does, good or bad. And until then, I would be honored to be your partner."

Her eyes searched his face. "You would?"

"Yes ma'am," he said and was rewarded with a tremulous smile. He didn't understand how Livy had gotten through the barrier he'd built around his heart, but somehow she had. Maybe it was because she wasn't from Texas, so she didn't know anything about his family's background or their wealth and social position. Unlike most of the women he dated, she had no ulterior motives.

A quarter-sized snowflake landed on her cheek, then another. Her blue eyes widened. "It's snowing." Wonder filled her voice. They looked up, and thousands of flakes swirled through the air. "We haven't had snowflakes this big in years."

"See if you can catch one." He stuck his tongue out, and a snowflake landed on it, wet and cold.

She held her arms out and turned her face up to the sky. "It's like we're in a snow globe."

Laughter danced in her eyes and then bubbled from her lips, and Alex laughed with her. Livy's childlike joy spread to him, and for a few minutes, he forgot the case, he even forgot his grandfather's ultimatum. The spirit within him soared, and he grabbed her hands and swung her around as the flakes swirled. Briefly, they danced to the music of the silent night, the flakes adorning her hair like diamonds.

Livy whirled around. "Race you to the house!" She took off running, and he ran after her, catching her near the light pole beside the old oak. She hooked her arm in his, and they walked toward the back door.

"You're pretty fast," he said.

She butted him with her shoulder. "You're not so bad yourself."

Alex swung around in front of her again. "Wow. A compliment from the lady who never gives them."

She stopped and looked up at him, her blue eyes luminous in the shadowy light. She made him feel like he could do anything, even hang the moon. Snow continued to surround them, muting all sound except for the beating of his heart. Livy leaned in to him as he trailed his finger down her cheek, the touch sending shivers to his heart.

What was he doing? He dropped his hand and took a step back. His last relationship had moved too quickly and ended in disaster when his girlfriend had wanted the whole package—a ring and a house and children, and all he could see was the disaster his parents' marriage had been. Their breakup had been bitter, even though he'd warned her up front he wasn't marriage material.

He hadn't even given Livy that speech, and it was a little late now. "Livy. Short for Olivia."

Her eyes darkened, and she narrowed them. "Don't *ever* call me that."

"That's a beautiful name. Why don't you like it?"

"It's what my father calls me."

13

Robyn parted the curtains of her window. Snow covered the grass. She didn't remember hearing anyone mention it was going to snow. Surely her mother hadn't let Abby ride that four-wheeler home. It'd been all she could do to keep from going downstairs while her daughter was there. She was so fearful of doing something that Abby would recognize. No, it was better to stay away from everyone until they caught the man who had kidnapped her . . . and probably that other poor girl.

Her stomach rumbled, and she wished she hadn't told her mom not to bring a tray up. She checked her watch. It was after nine. She'd heard Alex and Livy come up an hour ago, and her mom not long afterward. Perhaps she could ease down the stairs and get a bowl of soup, maybe even a piece of corn bread. No. She might run into her dad. But her stomach growled again. "Okay, okay," she muttered.

The second step from the top creaked when she put her weight on it. How many times had that board gotten her caught as a teenager coming in late from a date with Chase? She should have remembered it.

The kitchen light was on, surprising her. Dad must not be in yet. Robyn pulled the soup from the refrigerator and ladled a cup into a bowl. She debated whether to warm it or not. She didn't

156

want to run into her dad tonight. She was too tired to be on guard. Surely one minute wouldn't matter.

The microwave dinged just as the back door scraped open. And she froze as her dad entered the kitchen.

"You must be one of Kate's guests." Dad's raspy voice hadn't changed.

His face, leathery from years on the ocean, was the same, and tears sprang to her eyes. Thank goodness she hadn't taken her contacts out—her blue eyes were the only thing about her that hadn't changed. She ducked her head so he couldn't get a full view of her face. "Yes, and you must be her husband," she said, careful to stay in her Virginia accent.

"Do you think there's any more of that soup, Charlie?"

Her heart stilled. Chase was on Charlie's heels. Who was staying with Abby? She almost blurted the words out. But then, Abby was almost eleven, and only a quarter of a mile away. Besides, she could be with his mother, Allison. She nodded toward the refrigerator. "Plenty in there."

"Oh, I thought you were Livy."

"No, not Livy." Robyn softened her voice, hoping he would not catch any nuance of her former accent. She glanced at him and caught him staring at her. Red crept up his neck. She had to do something that was totally un-Robyn-like. She touched her finger to the side of her chin and cocked her head to the side and smiled. "And you are . . . ?"

A sheepish grin crossed his face. "Chase Martin. Did you say there was soup in the fridge?"

"Yes, and it's quite good." Robyn glanced at the bowl in her hand. The soup hadn't heated through and through, and now that she'd been caught, she might as well get it hot. She put it back in the microwave for another minute. While she waited, she studied Chase. Her husband had lost weight, and he had a few streaks of gray in his dark hair, but other than that, he looked good. Too good.

She took the bowl out and turned around, almost bumping into him. Their eyes locked, and a tingle went through Robyn. His intense blue eyes had been a stumbling block for her since the day she realized she was in love with him way back in the seventh grade. "I guess you're waiting for the microwave." She stepped out of his way.

"What did you say your name was?"

She hooked a strand of her hair behind her ear. "I didn't, but it's Sharon Arnold."

A frown flickered in his eyes. "Are you staying here long?"

"Not too long. I hope to be moving into my own place soon." She looked down at the soup. "I think I'll take this upstairs. It was nice meeting you."

She escaped from the kitchen and hurried up the stairs. He hadn't recognized her. The thought chased through her head. This plan actually might work. Now, if only whoever abducted her took the bait. *What if it was someone who wasn't in town?* He had to be. She just couldn't consider that he wasn't.

■ ■ ■

Livy plugged her phone in to charge it and then climbed into bed with a yellow legal pad and a pencil. Tonight had been magical in the snow. They'd been like kids until . . . Alex had meant to kiss her, she knew he had. She wondered what happened to make him drop his hand like her skin had burned it.

It was just as well. Not that she went around kissing men anyway—since she'd become a cop, she hadn't had time for relationships. They took too much energy. Besides, there was no need to break her eight-year losing streak.

Eight years? Had it really been that long? It wasn't that she didn't have opportunities. When she first became a cop, several of the men she worked with had asked her out, but dating someone she worked with hadn't seemed like a good idea. She'd known the relationship wouldn't go anywhere—they never did, and then working alongside someone she'd maybe kissed would have been awkward. Being a female detective was difficult enough without complicating matters.

And the same held true with Alex. Besides the fact that he was a private investigator, which until recently equaled not quite good enough to be a cop, he was from Texas. She didn't do relationships well, let alone long-distance relationships. She tapped the pencil against the notepad. Knowing a relationship between them could never work was kind of freeing. She could enjoy being around him without getting her heart broken. She just had to make sure she didn't lose sight of the could-never-work factor.

Livy couldn't believe she was wasting time thinking about a non-relationship with Alex; she focused on the legal pad. She liked to freewrite sometimes about a case, but with no more information than she had, it was a little early for this case. What she could do was list a few things they needed to watch for after Robyn went to work at Johnny B's. Livy assumed she'd apply for a job tomorrow.

Mannerisms. Livy had noticed a few that her cousin used in the past two days, like hooking a strand of hair behind her ear and chewing on the inside of her mouth. These two things in particular reminded her of the old Robyn. Livy needed to caution her again to be aware of every movement she made. Livy tapped the pencil on the yellow pad, and her thoughts went to the banana pudding in the refrigerator. Maybe there was some left. She slipped on a housecoat and went to the kitchen.

Voices reached her at the foot of the stairs. Charlie must be home. She pushed the swinging door open. Chase looked up from the table and squinted at her.

She frowned at him. "What are you doing?"

"Just making sure this time it really is you. Last time you were someone named Sharon."

She almost stopped breathing. Chase had seen Robyn? "You

think Sharon and I look alike?" She hadn't considered the possibility of them being confused with one another.

"I just saw a woman that wasn't Kate in her kitchen and assumed it was you. Once I really looked at her, I knew it wasn't. She reminded me of someone, though."

She swallowed. "Anyone I know?"

Chase drained the glass of milk he was drinking and wiped his mouth with a napkin. "I don't know. If I figure it out, I'll let you know."

Livy removed the banana pudding. "Oh, she probably has one of those familiar faces. Want some?" She held the bowl out, and he took it. "I thought I heard two people in here."

"You did. Charlie just went up the back stairs." He spooned a healthy portion on his plate. "Nobody makes banana pudding like Kate."

Livy glanced around the room. "Where's Abby?"

"Mom came home, and she's spending the night with her."

Livy filled her bowl, then returned the pudding to the refrigerator and sat at the table across from Chase. "How's it going with you?"

"So-so." He waved his hand back and forth then placed his spoon on the table and sat back in his chair. "I'm thinking of filing for divorce."

Livy stopped with her spoon halfway to her mouth and returned it to the bowl. She searched for something to say. "How soon?"

"Probably next week. The papers are already drawn up. I know you don't approve, but I have to get on with my life."

"I don't approve, but I do understand how you feel. Would you consider waiting a month?"

"Why?"

"I've taken a leave of absence, and I plan to focus on finding out exactly what happened to Robyn." They had to find the guy who kidnapped her soon. Livy didn't know how much longer she could keep the truth from everyone.

"Even if you find my wife, I don't think there's anything you can tell me that would keep me from going through with the divorce."

"That will be up to you." She knew Chase. Once he knew the whole story, he would never follow through with it. "Deal?"

"I don't know. I'll have to think about it."

■ ■ ■

A little past noon on Saturday, Robyn straightened her shoulders and followed Livy inside Johnny B's Grill and Coffee Shoppe. Inside the building, familiar smells vied for her attention. The oiled wooden floors, roasted peanuts, a steak sizzling on the grill, garlic biscuits from the oven. And the sounds. Plinking noises from the video games in a side room could barely be heard over the twang of a guitar from overhead speakers. Ice clinked in glasses, and beneath it all, vibrancy hummed throughout the room. It was a whole other world, and overlooking it all was a portrait of Johnny B's mother, dressed in a pink waitress uniform. She spotted Johnny B at his usual place at the end of the counter.

Livy made her way through the tables, and Robyn followed. She stood back a little as her cousin spoke to him. He glanced her way and nodded, then motioned her over.

"It's all yours," Livy said as she passed her. "I'll be outside. Ben called while I was talking to Johnny B. I need to call him back."

"Thanks." She smoothed her hands on her pants, just in case they were sweaty.

Johnny B shook her hand, then looked her over. "So, you're looking for a job? Ever do this kind of work before?" His expression said he doubted it.

"Yep," she said. "Waitressing helped put me through college."

He peered over his glasses at her. "If you have a college degree, what are you doing here?"

"Can't find a job."

"What's your degree in?"

She had expected the third degree and decided the truth would serve her best. "Psychology."

He snorted. "That and a buck and a half will get you a cup of coffee here. You gotta have a master's to do anything with it."

"I know. I'm planning on getting a master's in social work."

He tilted his head toward her. "I like you. Can you start this afternoon?"

From what Livy had said about him being shorthanded, she'd expected that. "What time?"

"Three, so you'll have a couple of hours to train before it starts getting busy. I have enough help tomorrow, but on Monday, be here at four. By the way, where are you staying?"

"At Kate Adams's bed and breakfast."

His eyes widened. "Pricey."

Robyn gave a shrug. "She's not charging me anything. Livy put in a word for me, told her what a hard time I've been having."

He nodded. "Kate's like that. How do you know Olivia Reynolds?"

Livy would toast his buns if she heard him use her given name. "We connected on Facebook. She's the one who talked me into coming to this area."

He nodded. "I hope you're up to the job. This is a busy place."

"I see that." She turned and scanned the restaurant. Most of the tables were filled, and with truckers coming in all hours of the day and night, the restaurant would stay busy. She was glad he'd given her the same shift she'd worked before. "Thank you for the opportunity."

"Save your thanks until eleven. See if you still feel the same way. Oh, and uniforms are simple. Black slacks, white blouse—you furnish your own." He glanced down at her high-heeled boots. "And you better wear some good walking shoes."

She walked to the door, releasing a pent-up breath. First step accomplished. She didn't see Livy and continued to the car, where her cousin sat with her cell phone pressed against her ear.

Robyn slid in on the passenger side and waited for her to get off the phone. From the look on Livy's face, something had happened.

"How'd it go?" Livy asked as she ended the call.

"Hired me. You look as though you just got bad news."

Livy drummed her fingers on the steering wheel. "Samantha Jo's wallet showed up in Nashville at a bus stop."

"So she's not missing any longer?"

"No, she's still missing, just not from here. The police think it dropped out of her purse, but I don't buy that she lost it."

What if the girl's disappearance wasn't linked to her own abduction? Robyn flexed her fingers. Would Alex pull out and go to Nashville? She liked the idea that he would be at the diner while she was working.

Three hours later, Robyn adjusted her apron and glanced through the opening to the kitchen, where Alex flipped a burger. His presence reassured her, and she turned her attention back to the young waitress training her. It was so hard to not tell Callie that she knew how to enter her order into the computer. Johnny B hadn't changed anything since she'd been gone. But Callie was nice, and even though Robyn had been waiting tables when the girl was in grade school, she held her tongue.

Callie patted her arm. "If you run into anything you don't understand, just let me know. It'll just be me and you until four. If you'd like, you can work the cash register and counter. That way you won't have to keep up with so many orders at one time. But if someone comes in and I'm busy, I'd appreciate it if you could catch them."

"Sure thing." A customer slid onto one of the stools at the counter.

"Do you want me to stick around for your first order?"

"I think I can do it." Robyn took out her pad, not that she needed one. Jason Fremont would order a ham on rye bread and a cup of their strongest coffee and then find his regular table. She wiped the counter in front of him. "Hi, I'm Sharon. What can I get you today?"

He looked her over. "You're new."

Give the guy a Kewpie doll. She smiled. "But only today."

"What do you mean?"

"I'll only be new today. Tomorrow I'll be a seasoned pro."

He laughed. "Oh yeah. I see what you mean. You'll fit in just fine around here."

She set a glass of water in front of him. "Do you need a menu?"

"No, I'll have a ham on rye bread with a cup of your strongest coffee."

"Coming right up." She entered the order into the computer and picked up the pot of coffee. After she'd filled his cup, she walked to the end of the counter, where another regular waited for his cup to be refilled. Bobby Cook drank dark roast as well. "Fill your cup, sir?"

"Well, howdy, little lady. What kind of coffee you got there?"

"Colombian dark roast."

He shoved his cup toward the edge of the counter. "Appreciate that. Saw Callie training you. Been in town long?"

She filled his cup. "No."

"You married?"

She was glad she'd taken off her wedding band. "Not anymore."

"You have any children?"

Bobby hadn't changed either. "A little girl, but she's with her grandmother. I'm hoping we can be together real soon."

The door opened, and two men came in and sat at a table. Cowboy boots, vests, phones on their belts. Truckers, she'd bet. She looked around for Callie but didn't see her. Robyn picked up menus and two sets of silverware and walked around the counter to their tables. More remarks about her being new that she responded to with a smile. "What can I get you?"

The older of the two men handed her the menu back. "Same thing I get every time. The daily special and a cup of joe."

Robyn jotted the order down. She rarely heard coffee called a cup of joe except from the older drivers.

The other driver handed her his menu. "I'll take the same thing."

Callie came from the back, and Robyn gave her the truckers' orders.

"Thanks. I see we're getting busy."

Robyn turned around as the door opened and several more people entered, one or two she remembered. "Yeah."

An hour later as she filled water glasses and set them on a tray, the sense of someone watching her made her skin prickle. She glanced up and surveyed the room. Could he be here? She scanned each customer, seeking . . . she didn't know what she expected to find, maybe something that would shout this is the one, but no. Everyone looked normal.

She picked up the tray of glasses and took it to her station. She'd moved out onto the floor after another waitress came on duty, and had three tables she needed to take orders from. She set a water glass on the first table, recognizing Timothy Nolan. In fact, she had recognized several people from when she'd worked here before, and some of them were truck drivers who had been regulars. After she delivered the other waters, she came back to Timothy. When she worked here before, he usually ordered a hamburger in the evenings. "Are you ready to order?"

He gave her a curious look. "Is your name Sharon?"

She paused with her pen in the air. "How did you know?"

"I think Johnny B is calling you." He pointed toward the end of the counter, where Johnny sat.

"I didn't hear him. I'll be right back." She hurried to where Johnny waited at the cash register he'd taken over after the diner had become so busy. "I'm sorry, but I didn't realize you called me."

He laid a bundle of credit card receipts in his money box and slid it under the counter before he answered. "Nothing important. Callie found this note on a table you helped her with. Table twelve, I think she said." He handed her a small white envelope with "Sharon" neatly printed on the outside.

Her fingers shook as she took the envelope by the edges. Even though the handwriting didn't look like the writing that had been on the note she'd received before, Ben might want to try to get fingerprints from it.

"Here, I'll open it for you." Johnny B took the note and slid his knife under the edge and sliced it open.

"Thanks." She didn't remember him being so impatient. She removed the folded piece of paper, and a fifty-dollar bill fell out. Her mouth dropped open. "Fifty dollars?"

"You made an impression on somebody."

Robyn didn't think she'd ever gotten a fifty-dollar tip before. She read the note. *You did a great job. Looking forward to seeing you again.* It wasn't signed. She turned and scanned the room. "I don't remember where table twelve is."

"It's in the corner."

A shiver ran down her back. "But . . ." She shook her head. "I didn't wait on that table."

"Well, you certainly knocked somebody's socks off."

Was it possible she had already made contact with her abductor? Or was it just a lonely truck driver trying to be nice? She slid the envelope into her apron pocket where she kept straws. "I better get back to work."

Robyn returned to Timothy's table and took his order, which indeed turned out to be a burger and fries, and as soon as she entered it into the computer, she walked to the kitchen in search of Alex. He had hamburgers going on the grill, a basket of French fries in his hand, and an overwhelmed look on his face. "Where's the main cook?"

"Taking a break." He dumped the fries into a warming tray, and wiped his forehead with the back of his hand. "I hope he comes back real soon."

"I need to talk to you when you get a chance."

"Sharon, you have customers," Callie called from the dining room.

"See you later." She hurried from the kitchen, passing the cook on the way. The restaurant was filling up with the supper crowd. She had forgotten how popular this place was with families on Saturday evening. Poor Alex. But at least he had help now.

"Customers at table nine asked for you to wait on them," Callie said as she poured water in glasses.

Robyn glanced at table nine, and her heart sank. Her mom and dad with Chase and Abby. And Livy, not looking too happy. She grabbed silverware and took it to their table. "Evening, folks. Are you getting the night off, Kate?"

Kate smiled at her. "Absolutely. But I didn't realize you had a job here."

"It just happened today."

Abby looked up from the paper she was coloring, and her eyes widened. "Aunt Livy, it's that Susan we met at the park."

Robyn's stomach churned. There would not have been a good time to run into Abby, but this was absolutely the worst.

Chase stared at her. "I thought you said your name was Sharon."

"No, Daddy. Her name is Susan."

"Oh no, honey," Livy said quickly. "You must have misunderstood. This is Sharon and she's staying with your nana."

Four pairs of eyes stared at her while Livy avoided her gaze.

"Well," Chase said. "Which is it?"

"Order, Sharon!" Alex's voice boomed from the kitchen.

"Ah, let me catch that while you decide what you want to drink." Robyn collected herself while she picked up Timothy's hamburger and fries. Maybe Abby would drop the issue. But it had drawn attention to her, something she did not want, especially from Chase. She set Timothy's plate in front of him and then hooked a strand of hair behind her ear before she thought. Livy's warning rang in her head, and she almost reached to undo her action.

"Thank you, Sharon." Timothy unfolded his napkin. "How has your first day been?"

"Busy. Would you like more tea? Or dessert?"

"No, take care of your other customers. But maybe later."

She chewed the inside of her cheek as she walked to table nine. "Have you decided on your drinks?" As they gave her their drink order, Robyn sneaked a glance at Abby and caught her daughter staring at her. Before Abby could say anything, she hurried to her workstation for their drinks.

"I thought you said you were getting a job in Memphis," Abby said as Robyn set a glass of Sprite in front of her.

She should have known her daughter would remember. "It didn't work out. Have you all decided what you'd like?" After she wrote down their orders, she collected the menus. "Thank you."

As she walked to the computer, once again she had the sense someone was watching her. Once she finished entering the orders, she scanned the room. Everyone seemed preoccupied with their food rather than paying attention to her. But she couldn't shake the feeling. Most of her customers were people she'd waited on two and a half years ago. All of them normal people. Not one looked like some crazy maniac who went around kidnapping women and beating them half to death.

Had she been the crazy one to come back?

14

Alex poured frozen potatoes into the deep fry basket and lowered it into the hot oil. He'd lost his mind, agreeing to be a short-order cook at Johnny B's. He hadn't worked this hard in years. But it probably would only be for one day. With Ben's news that Samantha Jo's wallet had been found in Nashville, he'd be flying up there in the morning. Alex was pretty sure Ben would be closing the case in Logan Point. Maybe Samantha Jo had left on her own. Still, it wouldn't be a bad idea to talk to the detective who handled the case of the waitress who was abducted.

"Hey, Alex."

He lifted the other basket of fries out of the oil and set them to drain before he looked up to see what the kitchen manager wanted. "Yeah?"

"Have you had a break?" Eddie said.

He shook his head. "There hasn't been time."

"Well, things have slowed, so take twenty."

He didn't have to be told twice. He untied his apron and hung it on a peg. Robyn looked as though she wanted to talk earlier. Maybe she could take a break as well. He poured a cup of coffee and pushed through the swinging door to the main dining room. There weren't many empty tables, maybe five out of twenty-five in the main dining area, and he chose the one closest to him. As

169

busy as this place was, he didn't understand why Johnny B didn't expand. He had the room. He waved at Robyn, and when she finished refilling a customer's cup, she walked toward him.

"Callie, would you watch my tables a minute? I'm going to take a short break," she said. She grabbed a cup and filled it before she joined him at his table. "You look tired."

"In Texas we say, I'm plumb tuckered out." He ran his gaze over her. She seemed frazzled. "You okay?"

Robyn used a napkin to take an envelope from her apron. "Someone left me an unsigned note with a fifty-dollar tip in it. I came back to talk to you about it, but you were swamped. I thought Ben might want to check it for fingerprints. I didn't even wait on whoever left this."

He took it, making sure he touched only the napkin. The lettering was nothing like the writing on Samantha Jo's note. "It may be nothing more than someone wanting to make an impression on you."

"Wouldn't they have signed it?"

"You'd think. Anything else out of the ordinary?"

She picked at a hangnail on her thumb. "I have the strangest sense someone is watching me."

"Have you seen . . . ?"

"No. It's only an eerie, creepy feeling."

"Maybe it's your imagination."

"I thought about that, being here again, and that could be it. And it could be the note and tip. Then Abby remembered that I said I was Susan." She braced her elbow on the table and rubbed a spot just over her left eyebrow.

"Maybe this wasn't such a good idea. Do you want to call it off?" He hoped not. She was the only lead he had to finding Samantha Jo.

She slid her hand around to massage her neck. Finally, she looked up. "It's too late to quit now. I want my family, my life back. Besides, this is just the first night. Maybe tomorrow night will be better."

"I hope so." He caught a glimpse of Livy out of the corner of his eye, and his heart skipped a beat. He shifted so he could see her full on. High heels? And not just high heels, but outrageous high heels. How did she walk in them? His gaze traveled up, noting her shapely calves and the way her red dress showed off her curves. He wouldn't normally describe Livy as smokin' hot, but tonight the description fit.

She stopped at their table but didn't sit down. "Anything happening tonight?"

Alex filled her in on the tip and Robyn's sense that she was being watched.

"I've tried to watch and see if anyone paid more attention to Robyn than normal, but Abby has kept me busy with questions."

"I had hoped she wouldn't remember that I called myself Susan that day in the park."

"I think I can fix that. She's coming home with Kate and me to spend the night, and I'm going to tell her you're working undercover with Alex."

"Do you think that's a good idea?" Alex said. He'd hate to see this case unravel because of a ten-year-old girl's questions. "What if she talks about it at school and it gets back to whoever is abducting these women?"

"I won't tell her what case you're working on."

"That might work," Robyn said. "Is Chase riding with you?"

"He came in his car, said he had some shopping to do." Livy squeezed Alex's arm. "You look tired. Do you think you can handle this job?"

"Ha-ha. It's hard work—you ought to try it sometime."

"Nah, I think I'll leave that to you, Mr. Private Investigator. Whenever I went undercover, it was always with vice." She winked at him and clicked away on her high heels.

"Livy," he called after her, and she turned around. "You clean up good."

Her face flushed, and she waved him off.

Robyn punched his arm when Livy was out of hearing range. "What's going on with you two?"

"What do you mean? We're just working this case together."

"I don't buy that." She leaned toward him. "There is an obvious attraction between you, and I don't want Livy to get hurt."

"Wait, we're just kidding around."

She shook her head. "What I've seen isn't kidding around. Livy is falling for you, and if you're not interested, then you need to back off. She's been hurt before, and this thing with the boy who was shot before Christmas and now Mac has made her vulnerable."

He didn't shy away from her gaze. "I'll never hurt her."

"Good. Because if you do, you'll have me to answer to."

■ ■ ■

"I'll get the check." Chase picked up the bill for their meal. While coming to Johnny B's hadn't been his idea, he wanted to do something special for his mother-in-law.

"This was going to be my treat," Kate said.

"You treat us three or four times a week. I'm going to have a cup of coffee and a piece of that strawberry cake that keeps calling my name. Anyone else want a piece?"

"Oh, Daddy, cake doesn't call your name."

"Yeah, it does, pumpkin. Listen." He cupped his hand to his ear, and under his breath whispered, "Chaaaase . . ."

Abby laughed, and that made him happy. She had come so far from the broken little girl who kept looking for her mommy. He simply didn't understand why Robyn had left them. And now he'd pretty much promised Livy to wait a month before filing for divorce. He glanced at the table where she stood talking to Alex and the woman he'd met last night at Kate's. Something was going on with those three, and he was curious as to what it was. Curious enough to stick around after Abby and Kate left with Livy so he could talk with Sharon. Maybe Alex too, if he wasn't busy. He would ask Livy, except it would do no good to try to get anything out of her.

Livy waved good-bye and walked toward their table. She had been on edge lately. Kate had said something yesterday about Livy taking a leave of absence from her job with the Memphis Police Department, and he figured it had to do with the shooting she'd been involved in. But tonight she looked different. Right now her face was flushed and her eyes bright. If he didn't know better, he'd think she was attracted to the private investigator.

"Everyone ready?" Livy asked.

"I'm having dessert. You want any?" he asked.

Livy rubbed her stomach. "I couldn't eat another bite."

"Me either, Daddy."

"Or me," Kate added. "And I need to get home and get a few things done so I can attend church in the morning."

"See you all at church tomorrow, then," he said. After they left, he looked around for Sharon to order the coffee and cake. She was at the cash register, and something about the way she stood seemed so familiar. She wrote on a ticket, then stuck the tip of the pencil in her mouth, wetting the lead, and then wrote something else. With a start, he realized Robyn used to do that. Sharon looked around and caught him staring, and he held her gaze briefly before lifting his cup. She grabbed the coffeepot and walked his way.

"Coffee?"

"Please. And a piece of that strawberry cake."

When she returned with the cake, he cocked his head to the side. "What brought you to Logan Point?"

She hesitated. "I was going to Memphis for a job interview, but when I stopped here, I liked the town."

"And my daughter somehow thought your name was Susan."

Her lips tightened. "Yes. Not sure why."

"How do you know Livy?"

"Facebook."

The answer had come quick. Quick enough to make him wonder if it was true.

"I better get back to work."

"The restaurant isn't busy. Can you sit down for a bit? I'd like to get to know you a little better. After all, you're staying with my mother-in-law, and you'll probably be around my daughter quite a bit."

Her shoulders stiffened, but she sat in a chair across from him. "Is that the reason for the third degree?"

"I guess I'm just surprised that you've made friends with Livy and Alex so quickly. Or did you know him before you came here?"

"Look, I admire that you want to protect your daughter, but you don't have anything to be afraid of as far as I'm concerned. I'd never hurt your child. I'm just trying to get on my feet and start over."

"Starting over is an admirable goal, and I didn't mean to grill you." He smiled. "Kate said you were from Bristol. Is your family there still?"

"No. I lived at a shelter for abused women while I finished my degree."

A shelter? Somehow he couldn't put this confident woman together with an abusive husband, but it would explain her unease around him. And why she didn't want to talk about her past. "I'm sorry. I can be rude sometimes."

The barest of color tinged her face, but she gave him a slight nod.

"Can we start over?"

"And do what?"

He scratched the side of his head. "Well, we'll probably be running into each other. I know tomorrow I'll be eating Sunday dinner with Kate and Charlie, and I'm assuming you'll be there. I'm in and out of their house all the time, and I'd rather it not be awkward, especially if Abby is around."

She sighed. "Sure."

Abruptly, she held out her hand. "Hello, I'm Sharon Arnold. You must be Chase Martin. Pleased to meet you."

He didn't quite have that in mind, but he'd have to admit, it was a little funny. He took her hand and was surprised at how soft it was. "And I'm pleased to meet you, Ms.—" He glanced at her left hand. No ring. "Should it be Miss Arnold?"

"Ms. is fine. Or just Sharon."

She smiled, and his heart caught. He hadn't noticed just how beautiful Sharon Arnold was until now. She had the most unusual hazel eyes, and her silky blonde hair curved delicately under her chin. So different from Robyn's wild red curls. *Robyn.* Maybe it really was time to move on.

■ ■ ■

She couldn't believe she was flirting with her own husband or how easy it was to talk to him. And that he was flirting back. It had been so long since he'd shown interest in her. Not that she could blame him—she'd pushed him away for years, believing he only married her because of Abby. When this was all over, could they possibly put their marriage back together? It was too much to hope for. She stood. "It's been nice chatting, but I do need to get back to work."

"What time do you get off?"

"Eleven." She checked her watch. "Three hours." It had been a long day.

"I didn't see a car at Kate's. Do you have a way home?"

"Alex gets off the same time I do."

"What's with that? He's not a short-order cook. What kind of case is he working on?"

She had no idea how to answer him. "You'll have to ask him. But I wouldn't do it here."

"You're probably right."

He stood, towering over her. "Any time you need a ride, let me know."

"Why, thank you, Mr. Martin." She busied herself clearing the table and then took the dirty dishes to the kitchen. When she came out, he waved and walked out the door. She tried to swallow but couldn't get past the lump in her throat. It wasn't fair. She grabbed a broom and started sweeping. How did her life get in such a mess?

■ ■ ■

He closed the door to his mother's room. She'd eaten such a small amount, but maybe it was because he'd waited so late to feed her. He should never have hung around Johnny B's so long—until after eight—but he'd been fascinated with the new waitress. He sighed and returned to the kitchen and quickly made a sandwich for Samantha Jo. Despite what the voices said, he'd finally concluded she would never be his Sharon. She was too young for one thing, too skinny, as well. And she kept lying to him, saying she didn't have any children. He hated lying. He wasn't sure what he was going to do with her. He put the sandwich and a bag of chips on a tray with a soda. Had to feed her, though.

He paused outside the barn door, thinking again of the new waitress at Johnny B's. She was afraid of something. He could smell it, just like he could smell Samantha Jo's fear. He'd heard her say she had a child, a daughter. She should be home taking care of her. He'd already seen the truckers eyeing her, and he knew what they were thinking. Just like with his Sharon. But something wasn't quite right with this new Sharon. He couldn't put his finger on it. Maybe it was because she reminded him of someone. But who? That didn't come to him. But it would. Just like he could smell her fear, he never forgot a face.

It was an omen—that her name was Sharon. Maybe she was the one. He sighed. But then, what would he do with Samantha Jo? He pulled the ski mask down over his face and entered the barn. Moonlight filtered through the windows, and a single lightbulb dangled from the rafters over the cage.

He used a different voice every time he talked to her. Today he would use his soft, Irish accent. "Aire you hungry, lass?"

"Who are you today? Some Scottish dude?"

Her sarcasm irritated him. "Lass, I can take the sandwich back."

"No. I'm sorry."

"Ya know the drill." He smiled as she sat on the bed and waited for him to slide the tray through the slot.

"When are you going to let me out of here?"

He backed away from the door. "When I know you'll stay. And when ya quit your lying."

She took the napkin off the plate and picked up the sandwich. "I haven't lied to you. I don't have a child. Why did you take me, anyway?"

"I keep telling you, I'm saving the children."

"Yeah, right."

"You think I'm stupid." He could hear it in her voice. Did she forget he was smart enough to kidnap her? Sweat formed under the ski mask. Maybe he'd put her in the dark. Then he could take the mask off. He walked to the switches that controlled the light-bulb and the blinds, but before he flipped them, he took the night goggles off the hook. In a matter of seconds, it was pitch dark inside the barn. He yanked the ski mask off and slipped the night goggles on.

She covered her face with her hands. "No! Don't do that. I'm sorry. You're not stupid."

"Too late, lass, but if you're good, I may flip the switches when I take my leave."

"Please," she whimpered.

"Eat your sandwich."

She raised the sandwich in the air as if to throw it away.

"I went to a lot of trouble to make that. If you throw it on the floor, you'll know the next time you get food . . . or any light in here. Now do what I said."

She lowered her hand and bit into the sandwich. Gradually her face changed. "Okay, I get it—you're saving the children, but how did you do it?"

"What?"

"Kidnap me."

His chest swelled as he thought of his ingenious plan. Should he tell her? He'd told his mother, but as usual, she didn't even comment. She was like everyone else who thought he was stupid. How he longed to show them all how wrong they were. What would it hurt to tell Samantha Jo? She would never leave here. Not alive, at least.

"Was I the first person you kidnapped?"

"No. I usually turned them loose."

"What do you mean?"

"It's like a game. I always sent the note first to warn them. It was plain enough—quit your job and stay home with your child. You know, like I sent you. Only most of the time I don't mail it. Just leave it on a table with their name on it."

"And you never got caught?"

"I wasn't crazy enough to leave it on the table where I sat. It was such fun to watch their reaction when they opened it. I would have loved to have seen your reaction. But they were just like you. None of them ever quit their job until I kidnapped them." He couldn't understand why they didn't follow the instructions. "Why didn't you do what the notes said?"

"I thought it was a joke. Or meant for someone else."

Hmm. Evidently, he would have to reword the note. "After I was certain the waitress intended to keep working, I executed the next phase of my plan. I waited until their shift was almost over and slipped GHB into their drinks."

"How? Why didn't someone see you?"

"Diners are busy and no one thinks someone will spike their drinks—after all, it's a diner, not a bar. I always sat next to the waitress's water station. If she wasn't drinking anything, then I knew I wasn't supposed to take her. But if she'd poured herself tea or coke, it was a sign."

He laughed, keeping his voice low.

"Don't do that. It . . . it sounds so evil."

"I'm not evil! Do you know what happens to children of wait-resses when their mother comes home? They're beaten. And they never have a birthday party." His voice rose until he was shouting.

She shrank back on the bed.

His anger disappeared as quickly as it had come. "I'm sorry. I didn't mean to frighten you. If all of you had just done what the note said." His voice cracked. "But I never hurt anyone. I always dropped them off where they would be safe until the drug wore off." Except for Tina. The voices had chosen her to become Sharon, not him. She would have had a good life with him, and he would have never hurt her if she hadn't tried to escape.

"How did you get them into your car?"

"Some I didn't. They're still on the list. But sometimes after they started getting sick, they would come outside to get fresh air, and I would be waiting."

"I don't understand. If you were going to drop them off some-where, why did you build this cage?"

"Because the—" He couldn't tell her about the voices, that they'd told him to build it. She would think he was crazy. And he wasn't. "It's for Sharon."

"Who is this Sharon? And why do you have a cage for her? If she loves you, she'll stay without being a prisoner."

He pressed his hand to his head. She was confusing him.

"Why did you put me in here?"

"You were different. You were like Robyn, except you didn't have a husband."

"Robyn? Tell me about her."

"Not today." He walked to the door. All these questions had his head spinning. And he didn't want to think about Robyn.

At the door, he slipped the goggles off and hung them on the peg. Once outside, he reached back and flipped the switches. She'd been good. He would reward her. Even if she had opened the door to memories of Robyn.

With a jolt, he realized Robyn was the first waitress the voices told him to keep, but he'd said no—she was married, and he wasn't a home wrecker even though she wasn't happy. He'd seen her crying after that husband stopped by the truck plaza. He'd just wanted to help her, make her understand she needed to stay home with her daughter. She'd been the third waitress he'd kidnapped, and he truly intended to drop her at another location.

But the GHB hadn't worked on her like it was supposed to. He'd almost been to the town where he planned to drop her off with another note warning her to quit her job when she came to. She'd fought him. Heaviness weighed in his chest. She'd made him hit her. After she saw his face, he'd injected her with Versed and planned to bring her back to the farm until he could decide what to do. But she'd managed to escape. He'd decided long ago that she didn't remember what happened or she would've come back and had him arrested.

He'd almost stopped after Robyn. The newspaper accounts had scared him that badly. With the first two, there'd been no newspaper account—he'd kept a careful watch. But the voices wouldn't shut up. Just like they wouldn't shut up about building the cage. Five months later, he encountered the waitress in South Carolina . . .

Outside the barn, he welcomed the cold air that cleared his head and checked his watch. Not quite ten. He walked to the house and climbed into his pickup.

He had a sudden urge to see the new waitress.

15

Sunlight filtered through the curtains Sunday morning, waking Robyn from a restless sleep. She glanced at her watch. Seven thirty. Unless something had changed, her mom had been up for at least an hour and a half and coffee was made. Maybe she could slip downstairs and grab a cup of coffee and get back to her room before anyone saw her. She didn't want to play twenty questions this morning.

Abby sat at the table eating cereal when she entered the kitchen, and she almost turned around until Abby saw her. "Good morning." She poured her coffee, glancing at her daughter. Abby was watching her, a guarded look on her face.

"Aunt Livy said you're helping Mr. Alex and that's why you said your name isn't Susan. But you're not supposed to tell stories."

"I know." She had to bring Abby around. They couldn't let her go around asking questions at the wrong time. Robyn sat at the table. "Do you watch TV?"

Abby nodded.

"What I'm doing is like what those actors on TV do. I'm playing a role."

"Are you trying to catch a bad guy?"

Robyn nodded. "I am."

"Then I guess it's okay. It's just that my mom always said you had to tell the truth, even when it hurts."

To sit this close to Abby and not gather her in her arms and tell her how much she loved her made Robyn ache. "Your mom's right."

"So, what is your name?"

Robyn hesitated. One lie brought another. "Why don't you just call me Sharon for now?"

Unblinking, Abby stared at her. Finally she nodded. "Okay. For now."

She relaxed a little but kept her guard up as Abby played with her cereal.

Her daughter looked up. "Why haven't you asked where my mom is? I know somebody has told you she's gone away."

"They have." She pressed her lips together, searching for the right answer. "It's none of my business. I think if my mom was gone, I wouldn't like people asking me about her."

A frown line pinched Abby's brow, then all at once the frown faded, and a grin started at the corners of her mouth and quickly stretched across her heart-shaped face. "I like you. That's exactly what my mom would say, and sometimes you kind of even sound like her. She left a couple of years ago, but she's coming back. I know she is."

Robyn's heart stilled in her chest for a second. She had to be more careful with her speech patterns. "I'm sure there's a very good reason why she hasn't come back."

"Abby, where are you?" Livy's voice came from the living room. "You need to get dressed or we're going to be late to church."

Abby spooned the last of her cereal into her mouth and put the bowl in the sink. "I'm coming." She started to the door but hesitated. "Are you coming to church with us?"

"Not this Sunday. I'm still tired from yesterday. I think I'm going to catch a nap."

"Good, then you'll be here for lunch." Abby tossed her a smile before she hurried out of the room.

Not if she could get out of it. Watching her words and the way she said them, guarding her every gesture—it was too much. She glanced up when Alex came into the kitchen dressed in a sport coat and tie. "You're going to church?"

"Thought I would since I'm not flying to Nashville until later this afternoon." He poured a cup of coffee. "You're not?"

She shook her head. "I'm beat, and I need to be on top of my game tomorrow. I have a gut feeling the man who abducted me is hanging around watching, and I can't afford to make any mistakes." She tilted her head. "Do you think Samantha Jo is in Nashville?"

"I don't know. Her wallet was found there, but with everyone asking questions and looking for her, whoever took her could have planted it at the bus stop to draw attention away from Logan Point. According to the Nashville Police Department, she hasn't claimed it yet."

Her cell phone rang. Johnny B's Grill and Coffee Shoppe showed on her ID. "Hello?"

"Sharon, Johnny B here. One of the morning waitresses didn't show up, and you did a good job yesterday. Could you cover for her, at least through the lunch crowd?"

No matter how good a job she'd done, the only reason he'd called was because no one else wanted to give up their Sunday. She didn't hesitate, though—at least she wouldn't have to be here for lunch. "Let me ask if I can get someone to run me over there."

She turned to Alex. "Do you have time to take me to work? Johnny B's is shorthanded this morning."

Alex nodded. "Maybe I should stick around there for a while too."

Robyn spoke into the phone. "I have a way. What time do you want me to come in?"

"Ten would be great. Thanks."

The line went dead, and she laid her phone on the table. "Thanks for taking me, but you don't have to change your plans. Whoever this guy is, he's not going to make a move during the day. There would be too many people around."

Alex nodded. "Keep me posted on how you're doing . . . say, every thirty minutes? And see if you can work the day shift tomorrow since I'll be in Nashville."

"Sure, but really, don't worry. I'll be fine. I think Livy will hang around."

At five minutes before ten o'clock, Robyn put her purse in her locker and tied an apron around her waist. Johnny B introduced her to Tonya, one of the other waitresses on the shift, then when she walked through the restaurant, she recognized several more regulars from two years ago. Most of them she'd enjoyed serving, but one or two had been complainers. The food had never been right or the coffee was too weak, and they'd been stingy tippers as well. But, she couldn't imagine any of them being her abductor. Still, someone from this diner, either employee or customer, had kidnapped her, and she believed his identity was locked somewhere within her memory. She was counting on him saying or doing something that would release it.

Callie beamed at her as Robyn picked up a ticket book. "Thank goodness you could come. I didn't look forward to working the whole restaurant with just Tonya."

Robyn shrugged. "I need the money."

"You want to take the middle section of tables? I'll work the back, and Tonya can get the front."

"That sounds good to me." Robyn nodded toward the four customers in her section. "Have they all ordered?"

"Jason and Bobby haven't ordered. The others are waiting for their food. I'll take care of that."

"Which one came in first?" Robyn asked.

"Jason." She started to leave, then turned back. "Did you hear about the car that went through the railing at the lake?"

"No. Was anyone hurt?"

184

"The driver escaped from the car, but so far the woman hasn't been found. It happened sometime before daylight. I think they're going to drag the lake."

"How terrible for the families involved." The sense of loss lingered in Robyn's mind as she filled a water glass and walked to Jason's table.

"Good morning." She set the glass in front of Jason. She'd seen him around town all her life. Trapper, fisherman, single, and always polite. She'd been about ten when her dad took her to the taxidermy shop Jason's father owned. Seeing all the stuffed animals had scared her at the time. Would still frighten her. "What can I get for you today?"

"Coffee to start with," he said. "I see you came back—wasn't sure you would."

"Yeah. This seems to be a good place to work. I'll get your coffee." If Jason was her abductor, there were no warning bells going off. She stopped at Bobby Cook's table. "I'll be back to get your order, but can I get your coffee?"

"You can take my order too. I want the usual."

Ham and eggs, sunny side up, with biscuits and sawmill gravy. "Since I don't know what the usual is, I'll be right back. Black?" He grunted an affirmative. Bobby was on the borderline. Most of the time he was amiable, but he could get real cranky. She couldn't see him kidnapping women, though. Seemed like he'd been an over-the-road driver once but worked as a sales rep for a food distributor two years ago. She didn't know if he still drove a big rig. Maybe she could work that question into the conversation.

She nodded to Johnny B behind the cash register as she picked up a tray and two cups. He spent most of his time here at the grill, and he was here the night someone put GHB in her drink. But he didn't drive a big rig. Or did he? Somewhere she'd seen a photo of him beside a big Kenworth. She poured a cup of chicory.

"You look like you need a refill." She set the steaming cup beside him.

"Thanks, Sharon, and especially for coming in."

"Glad to do it. Like I told Callie, I need the money." She hesitated. "You ever drive one of those big rigs out there?"

He grinned. "Years ago, when I was young and handsome." He pointed to a row of photos on the far wall. "That's me, third photo from the end."

"Why'd you quit?" She glanced where he pointed.

"I had this dream of a restaurant. Mama there"—he pointed again at the portrait of the waitress in pink—"she financed it."

His tone indicated she was asking too many questions. But she had learned he'd driven a big rig once. Even so, Robyn had trouble believing Johnny B was the one who kidnapped her. "Well, I hope you enjoy your coffee."

She walked to Jason's table and set his coffee down. "Are you ready to order?" She poised her pen as more people drifted in.

"I think I'll go with sausage and eggs."

"Biscuits or toast?"

"Biscuits." He glanced up and met her gaze. A blush spread across his face, and he looked away. "Uh, does anyone ever say anything about Samantha Jo?"

The skin on her neck prickled. "Who's Samantha Jo?"

"She, uh, used to be a waitress here. Then she went to work at Molly's Diner. And now she's gone. I just wondered if anyone around here has heard from her."

"I haven't heard her name, but I'll ask."

She moved two tables over to deliver Bobby's coffee and get his order. He didn't surprise her, ordering his usual.

"I heard Jason ask about Samantha Jo."

"Like I told him, I don't know her, but I'll ask."

"He was in love with her, you know, and I think she was kind of sweet on him. For a while there, he quit coming to the grill and ate at Molly's Diner." He chuckled. "Only when Samantha Jo was on duty, though."

Did Alex and Livy know Jason was in love with the missing waitress? She'd have to check and see. "I'll get this out as soon as it comes up." She started to walk away and turned back to Bobby. "Are you a truck driver?"

"Used to be, but it got too hard on the old back."

A few minutes later, as she entered the orders, she felt the sensation that she was being watched again. She scanned the room. Everyone looked normal, and she felt a little foolish. Maybe her brain was playing tricks on her. Or maybe her awareness was just heightened.

No, she believed with every fiber in her body that someone who frequented this restaurant was her kidnapper, and he was here today, watching her. Maybe not this minute, but he had been. She studied each man who had been a regular thirty months ago. Johnny B was working on his receipts. Jason and Bobby were doing something with their phones. Timothy had come in, and he was staring at her, but in a "wait on me please" sort of way. And there was Mayor Holloway. He was a semi-regular.

She tried to remember how many of them drove tractor-trailers. But what if it was simply a truck driver who made Johnny B's a regular stop and not someone who lived here? Tears of frustration burned her eyes. Unless one of them made a move on her, the game was at a dead end.

Six women had received warnings and then were kidnapped. What did they all have in common? She tried to remember what she'd read in Alex's reports. Children. They'd all had children. Did Samantha Jo have children? She'd have to ask Alex or Livy. But maybe that was something she should play up. That she had a child she could be with if she didn't have to work.

Should she wait until Alex was there? No. Might as well plant the thought now. She smoothed her apron. Time to try her theory out.

16

Livy glanced up as Alex slid into the pew beside her at Center Hill Church.

"Did you hear about the car that went into the lake?" he asked.

She shook her head. "Was anyone hurt?"

"I heard the driver was okay, but his passenger is missing. They're dragging the lake."

"Do you know if it was anyone local?"

"Someone said the car had a Tennessee tag."

Probably from Memphis. Even though she most likely didn't know the people, the news weighed heavily on her. The organ began to play softly, and as she settled back in the pew, the blue envelope next to the hymnal reminded her she hadn't written her check for the offering. She took out her checkbook and dashed one off and tucked it into the envelope like she did every week.

Her pen hovered over the small boxes on the envelope that she always checked off. Present. Check. Bible brought. Check. Daily prayer time. Maybe a half check. Same for Bible reading. She needed to do better this coming week. As she stood for the first song, her mind wandered from the hymnal. When did she become so OCD about checking things off a list, especially when it came to God? The answer came in the next breath.

Always.

If she did her part—follow the rules—God would do his. Livy refocused on the music, but by the time the song ended and she was seated again, more questions intruded. So what happened in the alley? Why didn't God let her know the Caine boy didn't have a real gun? Why didn't he do his part? Whoa. Livy squirmed in her pew. This was wrong. Blaming God was like inviting lightning to strike her. She tried to take the thoughts back, but thoughts were like words. Once out there, they couldn't be called back but instead unleashed even more questions. Like where was God in the warehouse when she froze? And when she lost her job; although technically she hadn't lost her job. Yet. She tugged at her scarf. Had someone turned the heat up?

Alex leaned over. "You okay?"

The congregation stood for another song, and she grabbed her coat. She didn't know what was wrong, but the room was so stuffy she had to get out. "I'll see you after church."

She squeezed past him and hurried out the door. Once outside, she stood with her hands on the small porch railing and inhaled the cold, fresh air as the February sun bathed her face. She had no explanation for the panic that had just happened. None. The door opened again and she sensed Alex beside her. "I'll ask you again. Are you okay?"

Livy shook her head.

"What's wrong?"

She cut her gaze to him and again shook her head. How could she explain something she didn't understand?

He glanced down at her booted feet and took her hand. "Feel up to a walk?"

She didn't want to go back inside the church, so with her hand in his, she followed him down the steps to the sidewalk beside the street. They walked for five minutes in the fifty-degree weather with neither speaking. Livy measured her steps so she wouldn't step on the cracks and then gave up. She caught a glimpse of a few buttercups that had pushed their green stems through the brown grass, and in a few yards, yellow crocuses brightened the landscape.

"Eloise always said I was a good listener . . . if you want to talk," Alex said.

"Who's Eloise?"

"The cook at my grandfather's house."

"You had a cook?"

"And a maid and a yardman."

"Wow, your mom was a lucky lady."

They walked a few steps before he answered. "My mom didn't like being waited on or someone working in her flowers. And then she left."

Stick your foot in your mouth, Livy. "I didn't mean to bring up a painful time in your life."

He shook his head. "I'm past it now. Besides, life was a lot calmer after she left."

"It was that bad, huh?"

"My first memories are of them yelling at each other. Arguments that rivaled the Fourth of July fireworks before she called it quits. And when they weren't fighting, the tension was thick enough to slice."

They walked in silence for a minute, and then he sighed. "Propriety is everything to my father's side of the family, especially Grandfather. He's retiring as state senator, and my father is set to follow in his footsteps with the expectation that he'll probably run for national office one day. Truthfully, in six years, Grandfather believes my dad will be elected the next United States senator from Texas."

"How about your mom? Is that what she wanted your dad to do?"

"She hated the political life that was expected of her." He

laughed, but it wasn't a happy laugh. "Mom didn't do the teas and luncheons or any of the social scenes in Dallas. She definitely didn't fit Grandfather's image of who Dad was supposed to marry. As for my mother, the Jenningses' rules and regulations smothered her free spirit, and then there was her penchant for antiestablishment friends."

"Why did your dad marry her? Didn't he know what she was like?"

"I think they met during his rebellious period."

She laughed. "So the father is like the son?"

"Hardly. And why would you say that?"

"You don't see refusing to take the bar as rebellion?"

He sighed. "I never thought of my dad and me as being alike. That's scary."

"On the way to Bristol, you said you were nine when your mom left."

He nodded. "She wanted to take me with her, but my grandfather put his foot down. At the time I was angry. Thought she chose her freedom over me, but I realize now that the only way she could have kept me was to stay and accept their way of doing things, and she couldn't do that. They would have killed her spirit, who she was. Sometimes I wish I were more like her."

She understood his dad and granddad's penchant for rules. Rules grounded her. "But you've turned out okay, so what's so wrong with rules? Or lists, for that matter."

"Nothing, as long as there's room for exceptions. And I didn't mention lists." He cocked his head toward her. "Don't tell me you're a list maker."

"What's wrong with marking things off a list?"

"Did I say there was?"

She focused on the cracks in the sidewalk. "No. I think it's God who doesn't approve of my lists."

"What?" He stopped walking and swung around in front of her.

"Back in church I was marking those little squares, you know, things you did during the week like read your Bible and—"

"Do you think God's really interested in those things you ticked off?"

"You . . . you don't?"

"I've always thought it was about a relationship, not about *doing* things or following rules."

"I believe that as well, but how do you know if you're pleasing God if you don't have some way of measuring it?" She lifted her gaze to his warm brown eyes and tried to ignore the tremor that raced through her body.

He lifted his eyebrows. "Do you read your Bible because you want to or so you can mark it off a list?"

When was the last time she'd read Scripture for the comfort it brought? Or for just learning more about who God was? Her heartbeat thundered in her ears. Not since the shooting. "Have you ever gotten mad at God?"

"A time or two, like when my mom left. But then, I was mad at everyone. What are you mad at God about?"

Her fingers stung from the cold, and she shoved them into her coat pocket. "I've always been taught he's all seeing, all powerful, so why did he put me in that alley with the Caine kid? Why didn't he stop me from shooting him?"

"So that's what this is about."

She shifted her gaze past him and caught a glimpse of red against the side of a white house. Camellias. Her favorite winter flower. *Where were you, God?* "Why do you think he didn't?"

When Alex didn't answer, she slipped her hands out of her pockets and rubbed them together while she blew on them. "Tough question, huh?"

"Well, I'm not exactly a theologian, but it seems to me everyone is responsible for their own actions. You were doing your job, your duty if you will, and this kid was breaking the law. He robbed someone, and then he didn't follow orders when you told him to put the gun down. He made the choice, not you, and because he did, that one decision impacted not only him but you and a lot of other people."

"But I should have known it was a pellet gun and not real."

"How were you supposed to know?"

Livy opened her mouth to protest, but the words died on her lips. She couldn't have known. "Why didn't God stop it? I've always done my part. I've gone to church, I've helped the poor, I've given money—"

"Has God been there for you before?"

She looked away from his warm brown eyes, remembering when her mom died and how hurt she'd been. She searched for God then and found peace. And when she made detective, the joy she'd felt that her prayer had been answered. She turned her gaze back to Alex and nodded.

"Then I think you have a choice to make. Either you trust God or you don't."

"That's easier said than done sometimes." But Alex was right. Maybe she was asking the wrong question. Maybe she should ask herself why she felt so guilty about the shooting. She hadn't chosen to be in that alley. She didn't know it was a toy gun and not a real, lethal automatic. And it was Justin Caine who chose to disobey her command to put down the gun, real or not. He made those choices. Caine was the criminal, not her.

If she continued to let what happened hold her hostage, she wouldn't be any good to anyone. For the first time in months, a portion of the heaviness lifted from her heart. She knew it would return, but for right now, this moment, she felt free.

"Thanks," she said and blew on her hands again.

"You're cold." He cupped her hands in his.

A shiver that had nothing to do with being cold ran up her arms. She raised her gaze and almost got lost in his brown eyes. If he kept looking at her that way, she'd be toast.

■ ■ ■

He put the bowl of soup where his mother could reach it. Sometimes it was so hard to be civil to her. Especially when he remembered the way she treated him. Locking him in a closet when she brought her *friends* home from whatever greasy spoon she worked at. He flinched, remembering her anger after they would leave. And the stripes on his back and legs from the belt.

"Eat your lunch," he said. "Or do you want me to feed you?"

The last time he'd forced her to eat, she'd almost choked. Said he was cramming it down her throat. Nothing he did ever satisfied her. So why did he even try? The walls of the room closed in on him, making it hard to breathe. Let her starve if that's what she wanted to do.

He left the bowl on the table and closed the door behind him with a bang. In the kitchen he poured another bowl of soup and placed it on a tray with crackers he'd brought home from Johnny B's. Maybe Samantha Jo would appreciate his efforts.

His gaze rested on the square envelope on the kitchen table. He'd scribbled Sharon's name on the front along with the address for Kate Adams's bed and breakfast. He'd heard Johnny B say that was where she was staying, and that Kate wasn't charging her anything.

He'd come home from Johnny B's and written the warning after he'd overheard Sharon talking about her daughter back in Virginia. That was where she should be—home with her child, not in Logan Point working as a waitress.

He picked up the card with a napkin. No need to take a chance on leaving fingerprints. Mail or leave it at the restaurant? If he mailed it, it'd take two days to reach her. He shook his head and tucked the card inside his coat. That was too long. He'd leave it on a back table so one of the other waitresses could find it . . . or maybe even leave it in the employees' break room. It was right across from the restrooms. A smile curved his lips upward. She would soon know that *he* knew where she was staying. That would freak her out.

As he walked to the barn, he wondered if the passenger from the wreck had been found yet. He'd heard they were dragging the lake. *What if* . . . No, she would never be found. He'd dropped her body in the channel, right in the middle of the lake. If the river current had moved her body at all, it would be downriver and not in the lake.

Heaviness stooped his shoulders. Why did she have to make him so angry that night? He never would have hurt her. At the barn door, he stopped and pulled the ski mask over his face. Maybe someday he could let Samantha Jo see his face. If she ever stopped resisting him.

"Lunch," he called in a soprano voice. That hurt his throat. Instead, maybe he'd just whisper, or maybe he'd get one of those voice synthesizers. He couldn't take a chance on her recognizing his voice. Not yet, anyway. Not until he was certain she wanted to stay. Then he'd reveal who he was. He could almost imagine the admiration in her eyes when she learned his identity and how smart he was. A genius, actually. She'd never guess, not in a million years.

He was encouraged that ever since he'd returned from Nashville, there'd been change for the better in Samantha Jo. She'd stopped screaming, for one thing. And he was pleased she'd put on the new clothes he'd bought her.

"Did you hear me?" he whispered.

"I'm not hungry." Her voice sounded listless. She was on the bed, sitting with her legs crossed.

What was it with these women and not eating? First his mother, now Samantha Jo. He set the tray on the floor and slid it through the bars. "You need to eat."

"I don't want to be drugged again."

"I promise there's nothing in your food." He'd only given her enough drugs to knock her out when she wouldn't quit screaming. "I don't want to hurt you. I want us to be friends."

She bit her lip. "Why should I believe you? You kidnapped me and keep me locked up."

"But it's for your own good. And the good of your child. You've never told me if it's a boy or a girl. I walked by the school twice last week when children were on the playground, thinking I might see if any of them looked like you."

"I told you, I don't have a child." Samantha Jo leaned her head back against the wall. "Why do you keep insisting that I do?"

He couldn't be wrong about that, the voices couldn't be wrong. "Why are you lying to me?"

She raised her head and stared straight at him. "Why is it so important that I have a child?"

He blinked. "Be . . . because I'm saving the children."

"Saving them from what? Tell me about it."

She was just toying with him. Pretending to want to know. He stared through the bars. No, that was interest in her eyes. "If you'll eat, I'll tell you."

She leaned forward on the bed. "You promise there are no drugs in it?"

He put his hand behind his back and crossed his fingers. There was only a little antianxiety medicine in the soup, nothing that would knock her out. "I promise."

She took the bowl and began eating. "So tell me. Why are you saving children?"

"I don't want them to go through what I did."

"You've said that before." She paused with the spoon halfway to her mouth. "What happened to you?"

He sat on the barn floor near the cage. If she could see the scars on her back, she wouldn't have to ask. "My mom was a waitress, and sometimes she would bring her 'customers' home with her.

That's when she locked me in a closet, and sometimes it was two days before she remembered me."

"That's terrible. Was she sorry about it?"

"No. She would be angry that I hadn't called to her. And she would take a belt to my back, my legs, anywhere it would reach. But if I did yell and let her know I was still in the closet, she'd get just as angry and the same thing would happen."

"Why didn't you tell someone?"

"She would have killed me."

She was quiet for a minute. "That's a bummer. But I don't—" She stopped halfway, and seemed to be thinking. "So how do you decide which children to save?"

"I just know."

"If I did have a child, don't you think he or she might be worried about me?"

"So, you do have a child."

"I said if."

She was playing games again. He stood. They'd talked enough for today. "I'll be back with your supper later."

"Do . . . do you think you could give me something besides those hunting magazines to read. Please?"

He studied her. She looked so vulnerable. "Do you have a boy or a girl?"

She hesitated and seemed to struggle with answering him. "A . . . boy."

He smiled at her. "Good girl. I'll see if Mother has any books she'll let you read."

"Your mother knows I'm here?"

He smiled again. "Oh yes."

■ ■ ■

After lunch, Livy went upstairs for her gun. Standing on the sidewalk, talking to Alex, it had seemed so easy to know she'd done nothing wrong, but how would she react in a tight situation when she or her partner looked down the barrel of a real gun? Of course, she wouldn't know the answer to that until she was in that tight situation, but she had a plan.

There was a new target range in Logan Point that had the practice course she'd failed last week, and she would start the plan off with it. Then Livy planned to talk to Taylor about setting up regular appointments for counseling—if she would see her. If not, she'd get her to recommend someone.

She met Alex at the bottom of the stairs and couldn't help noticing the way butterflies filled her chest when his chiseled lips parted in a smile. No. Wrong time in her life to fall for someone like Alex. Someone who didn't follow through after three years of law school. Someone who would be leaving when this case was finished.

Someone like her dad.

He eyed the gun in her hand. "Where are you headed?"

"Practice shooting at an indoor range. Want to come along?" She couldn't believe she had just done that. She definitely didn't need an audience if she couldn't handle the course. Maybe he would decline. "Wait, don't you have to fly to Nashville?"

"I decided to wait until in the morning. As of thirty minutes ago, no one has claimed Samantha Jo's wallet, and since I can't talk to any of the record producers or agents today, there's no need to fly up there this afternoon. Do they furnish guns or do I need to grab mine?"

"Yours is fine. Mississippi is an open-carry state. Just be sure to not conceal it."

As he turned to walk away, his cell rang, and he glanced at it. "It's my granddad. You go ahead, and I'll meet you there. What's the address?"

"I don't know. I can tell you how to get there." She shot him her wicked grin. "But, you're a detective. You can find it."

198

"Does this place have a name, or am I supposed to figure that out too?"

"Logan Point Shooting Range. Simple enough?"

He nodded and answered his phone. "Good morning, Grandfather."

Livy slipped out the back door and hurried to her car. Maybe his grandfather would keep him on the phone long enough for her to get in a practice round or two.

The new Logan Point Shooting Range surprised her. Spread out over five acres, it included both indoor and outdoor ranges with several options. If it had been warmer and less windy, she would have used the outdoor range. There was even a paintball field well away from the firing ranges. She opened her case and took out her headphones. Now to get in some practice shots before Alex arrived.

"Livy." Ben Logan's voice sounded behind her. "I'm surprised to see you here."

She turned around. "What are you doing here? Why aren't you at the lake investigating the car that went off the bridge last night?"

"I come here every Sunday afternoon. Dragging the lake is a slow process, but Wade has it covered. Besides, I'm just ten minutes away, and he'll call me if I'm needed."

"What was the cause of the accident?"

"The driver registered .25 on the Breathalyzer." He shook his head. "People do stupid things."

"And everyone pays," she said. "Have you talked with Nashville PD today about Samantha Jo's wallet?"

"Touched base a few minutes ago. No one has come forward to claim it."

"So are you closing this case out?"

"Not just yet. Alex said he was flying up there tomorrow, and I'm thinking about going with him to talk with the waitress who was abducted last year. Something about that wallet deal doesn't sit right with me."

"I think Alex has a problem with it too."

"I like Alex," Ben said. "Seems to be competent."

"Yeah, for a PI." She added a grin to the comment since Alex had proven himself competent on many levels.

"I heard that," Alex said.

Livy hadn't seen him arrive, and a cringe shivered through her. He wouldn't know she was joking. She turned around, and the question in his eyes made her want to kick herself. She held her hand up. "And I was smiling when I said it."

His brown eyes held hers, and then he gave a slight nod. He turned to Ben. "Any new information on the waitresses?"

"Wade tapped into the National Incident-Based Reporting System last night and discovered three more kidnappings that fit our profile. Two taken and released before Robyn and a waitress in Gulfport who went missing just after Christmas."

"Where's Gulfport?" Alex asked.

"South Mississippi," Livy said.

"I contacted the sheriff in Harrison County, and he's faxing the report. I planned to call you two when it came in, then the car went off in the lake. All my men are working it. My dispatcher will call when it comes in."

Alex turned to Livy and winked. "Until then, why don't you and I do some shooting?"

Her heart lifted, and suddenly it didn't matter that she wouldn't have any practice shots. "Sure."

"Which course are you shooting?" Alex asked.

She could take the easy way out and shoot the regular targets. But she'd never been one to take the easy way. "The shoot/no-shoot."

Alex's eyebrows went up. He remembered it was the one she'd failed. The three of them walked to the course.

"Oh, look." He pointed to a sign. "You can do the course with a partner—even compete against each other. What do you say?"

"Wouldn't you rather shoot the course with Ben?" She tried to keep the desperation out of her voice.

"Nope. Didn't tell Ben the other night I would be his partner."

"I'll be your scorekeeper-slash-referee," Ben said.

She tamped down the nervousness that crawled into her throat. She could do this. "You're on."

They signed up and were assigned their spot. Alex carried a 9 mm Glock, a gun she'd wanted to try out. Maybe he'd let her before they finished. After all three had put on headphones, Ben had them stand with their backs to the target range. "This will be a little more realistic. When I say go, turn around, assess the situation, and fire or not fire according to the target. Don't pay any attention to each other's target—just focus on yours. Got it?"

They both nodded. She held her gun with both hands, waiting. Heat flushed her face, and sweat trickled down her back. *Come on, Ben.*

"Go!"

They both turned. Ten yards away, a target popped up, a robber holding a gun. She fired. At the same time, Alex fired his gun. Target after target popped up, some lethal threats, others not. When the last target went down, Livy knew she'd aced the course, and after she'd exchanged the empty magazine for a full one, she holstered her gun and then turned to Ben for verification.

His wide grin confirmed her assessment. "You both did good. A hundred percent for both."

She high-fived Ben and Alex.

"We're not done. Can't have a tie. How about the firing range?" Alex turned to Ben. "Would you be scorekeeper again?"

Ben's cell rang, and he held his hand up as he answered. "Hello." As he listened, the smile on his face faded. "I'll be right there."

"Did they find the body?" Livy asked.

"Not exactly. They found *a* body. It was wrapped in a heavy-duty black plastic bag and weighted with concrete blocks." He slipped the phone back on his belt. "And Wade says she's wearing some sort of waitress uniform."

Alex's Adam's apple bobbed up and down. "Is . . . is it Samantha Jo?"

"Wade didn't think so, but he couldn't be sure."

Livy gripped her gun. If she'd only tried harder to find Robyn, this woman might not be dead.

17

It couldn't be Samantha Jo. Alex fought the anxiety that slammed his gut. "Can I tag along to the lake with you?"

"No need. The coroner has been on call all day, and the body is already on the way to the hospital. After a preliminary exam, it'll go to Jackson for the autopsy. But we'll get her prints and at least verify whether it's Samantha Jo or not."

"Jackson, Mississippi?" Livy frowned as she packed her gun and headphones in her bag.

Ben nodded. "All of our autopsies are done there."

"Each county doesn't do its own?" Alex asked. As far as he knew, in Texas each county conducted their own autopsies.

"Afraid not."

"Any chance we can get Memphis to conduct it? Half the lake is in Tennessee. I know the coroner there," said Livy.

"I'd have to give Tennessee the case, and I don't want to do that."

"No," she agreed.

"How long will it take to get the results back?" Alex wasn't certain he agreed with Ben about holding on to the case if Memphis could do the autopsy sooner.

"Good question, but we'll get enough information before we send the body to ascertain whether or not it's the missing waitress from Gulfport."

"Then do you mind if I go with you to the hospital?" Alex said. Ben nodded. "Won't be pleasant."

"I'm coming as well," Livy said. "Oh, wait. This makes everything different. Robyn is at Johnny B's by herself. I'm going to pass on the hospital and shadow her. If our guy dumped the body, finding it may send him around the bend. Robyn's already said she thought someone was watching her, and I want to be there if this guy decides to target her. If he does, he'll have to come through me."

"And me," Alex added. "I'll join you there as soon as I know whether or not it's Samantha Jo."

The wind had kicked up as they exited the building. Livy's car was parked near the entrance, and he felt the urge to tell her to be careful as she walked to her car, but he knew she wouldn't appreciate it. "I'll come to the truck plaza as soon as I can."

She nodded and they waited until she'd unlocked the door and sat behind the wheel before continuing on to their cars. Alex jammed his hands into his pockets as they walked to the end of the parking lot. "Did Wade say why he didn't think it was Samantha Jo?"

"According to him, the body is fairly well preserved, and he thinks the victim is too small and too old to be your girl."

Relief washed over him as he climbed into the Impala and followed Ben to the hospital. According to the report his boss had given him, Samantha Jo was five eight and only twenty-one. Didn't sound like Samantha Jo.

His earlier phone conversation with his grandfather came to mind.

"So you haven't found her yet," his grandfather had said. "Do you really expect to?"

"Yes." Alex had held his temper. "I still have three and a half weeks."

"Three," his grandfather corrected.

"You almost sound like you hope I don't find her."

"That doesn't even dignify a response." And the line had gone dead. Alex had called him back and apologized, but he was so tired of walking on eggshells around his father and grandfather. Not that his dad ever called. Alex had accepted a long time ago that he and his dad would never have the kind of relationship most fathers and sons had.

When he was a kid, he'd carried the burden of believing it was his fault. He was grown before he learned what the problem was. In his grandfather's eyes, no task his dad completed pleased him. Even if his dad did a good job, instead of praise, Josiah rained down criticism—his dad should have gone about the task differently . . . or he didn't do it the way Josiah would have, therefore, it wasn't as good.

And then Alex came along, and his grandfather doted on him. The sad part was, Josiah loved his son—he just never showed it. Maybe Alex should reach out to his dad when he returned to Texas. Except that would only give him an opening to pressure Alex about taking the bar, which if he did and passed, would pretty well solve the current problem between them. Until Alex didn't join the law firm.

Right now, though, the most important thing for Alex was to find Samantha Jo Woodson. Not for himself or to prove his grandfather wrong, but because she was a young woman with her whole life in front of her. She had a family who loved her. He had to find her.

At the hospital, he caught up with Ben at the front entrance, then accompanied him to the morgue. Outside the door, the sheriff handed him a mask. "It will help some."

This wasn't the first morgue Alex had visited. The first time he hadn't been prepared and tossed his cookies. This time even though he was prepared, the mask didn't begin to cover the smell of the body on the stainless steel table centered in the small, cold room. But his food stayed down. The coroner used scissors to finish the opening Wade had started on the black bag. Even to Alex's untrained eye, the body bore no resemblance to Samantha Jo Woodson.

The coroner stretched a measuring tape from her head to her feet. "Our Jane Doe is five four," he said into a recorder.

"And Samantha Jo is five eight," Alex said. His relief was tempered by the knowledge that the woman on the table had a family somewhere, and even though it wasn't the girl he was looking for, the person responsible for this victim's death probably had Samantha Jo. He had to be found and stopped.

"How long before an autopsy will be performed?"

"Depends on how backed up Jackson is. We're going to get fingerprints and take a few photos today," Ben said, "just in case something happens to the body between here and Jackson. And we'll go ahead and get her weight and take X-rays of the teeth—we can do that without disturbing the body."

Alex was on Ben's heels when he left the morgue. As they got off the elevator on the first floor, he asked if Ben still planned to fly to Nashville with him in the morning.

"How long are you going to be up there?"

"Half a day at most. I've put together an email to send out first thing tomorrow to all the record producers and agents. Her family indicated she'd been in contact with a few of them, and those are the ones I want to talk face-to-face with. I plan to take her photo around to their offices, see if any of the receptionists remember seeing her lately."

The front doors opened automatically as they approached. Ben rested his hand on his gun. "I'd like to talk to the cop who received the purse. See if he can describe the person who turned it in."

Alex nodded. "I believe the purse is a red herring, but it's a lead I can't afford to ignore. It'd be great if we found her, or found someone she'd contacted in the last week. Think you can be ready to leave by six? According to the weatherman, the temp is going to be in the forties, and I should be back by noon—unless we get a lead."

"I'll meet you at the airport a little before six." Ben stopped at his car. "Where are you headed now?"

"To get the plane ready, and then to Johnny B's. You?"

"Johnny B's. I don't want Livy or Robyn there without cover. I believe our Jane Doe is connected to all the other cases of kidnapped waitresses, and whoever killed her is still out there."

"Assuming she is connected, why do you think he killed her?"

"Probably for the same reason he beat Robyn to where she wasn't recognizable. Have you seen the photos the police took in the ER at Bristol?"

Alex shook his head. "How did you see them?"

"I called the chief of police, and he emailed them. I don't know how she lived through the beating he gave her."

"And this animal probably has Samantha Jo. I just hope she doesn't do anything to set him off." Alex rubbed his hand over his eyes. "One more thing. Do you believe this is the work of someone who comes through here only every now and then?"

"No," the sheriff replied. "It's either someone who lives in Logan Point or a trucker who comes through often enough to know the best place to dump a body in the lake. While I'm at Johnny B's, I'll get Livy to help me question some of the truckers who are regulars. We'll get the drivers' names and the companies they work for this afternoon, and tomorrow while you and I companies in Nashville, I'll have one of my deputies contact the different companies for their logs. I figure if we do that for a few days, we'll catch all the regular drivers."

"Good deal." Alex climbed into his car and drove toward the airport. He'd love to help ask questions, but if he did, he'd blow his cover. His phone rang and he glanced at the ID. Johnny B's. "Jennings."

"Alex, Johnny Baxter. Wondered if you could come in for a shift. Our cook got sick."

He hesitated. If he went in to work, he'd have to forgo getting the plane ready, meaning he'd have to get up a little earlier in the morning to fuel up and do his preflight. But it would give him an opportunity to see Livy again. He wheeled the Impala in a U-turn. "Sure. Be there in ten minutes."

■ ■ ■

Livy walked into the noisy atmosphere of Johnny B's and glanced around the half-full restaurant. She didn't see Robyn. Her heart sank to her knees. What if the kidnapper had gotten her somehow? *Stop it.* Her cousin had to be in the back.

Johnny B sat at his regular place by the cash register. She nodded at him. "Have you seen Sharon?" She'd almost said Robyn. Again. She'd be so glad when they closed this case.

"She took a break." He jerked his head toward the back.

Livy pushed the swinging door open and then walked down a short hall to the small room where the employees' lockers were. It was where they also went to put up their feet and rest. The room was empty except for Robyn. She sat at a table, her face pale, her eyes closed. She must know about the body. "Hey, how's it going?"

Robyn tossed an envelope on the table. "This was on the table when I came in for my break. I decided to talk about having a daughter, and I think this is the result."

So she didn't know about the dead waitress. Livy used a napkin to pick up the envelope that looked the same as the one she'd seen at the sheriff's office. "It's from him?"

"I think so. It's similar to the one I received before."

Livy carefully extracted the note card and read the words. *This is a warning. Make sure you heed it. Go home to your daughter. Quit the job at Johnny B's or else.*

"We'll run prints."

208

"He's too smart to leave anything on the envelope or note. This is what we wanted, right?"

Livy squeezed Robyn's hands. "Yeah."

Robyn gave her a shaky smile. "One of the truckers came in, said they found a body in a black bag. Is it Samantha Jo?"

"I don't think so." Livy looked away, back toward the swinging door.

"You're not telling me something."

Livy licked her dry lips. "How soon do you get off? Can you leave now?"

Robyn shook her head. "One of the waitresses had to go home—stomach virus . . . along with the cook. I can't leave Callie shorthanded."

"Okay. I'll stick around until you get off. Have you learned anything today?"

She took a shaky breath. "Johnny B doesn't drive a semi anymore. I marked him off my list. And you don't have to stick around. I heard him call Alex in to work. I'll ride home with him."

Robyn had suspected Johnny B? "Talk to anyone else?"

"Jason, at breakfast. He makes short runs, but mostly he likes to trap and stuff animals—as in a taxidermist." She wrinkled her nose. "Did you ever see the place where he does it?"

Livy nodded. "Yep. I think I went with you and Charlie once when we were kids. All those animals . . . still gives me the willies to think about it. Do you think Jason. . ."

"Kidnapped me? I don't know. I didn't see a tattoo on his hands or his arms when he took his coat off and rolled up his sleeves." She checked her watch. "He hasn't been in for lunch yet, but he ate a late breakfast. You can question him and see what you think."

"Has he triggered any memories like riding in the semi did?"

"No. Callie and Bobby Cook say he was in love with Samantha Jo, but I suppose he could have kidnapped her if she didn't reciprocate his love—he is a little old for her." She leaned forward. "You never did answer my question."

"I know." Livy rubbed the tight muscles in her neck. "Wade thinks the body in the lake is a waitress."

Robyn sank back in the chair with her hand over her mouth and closed her eyes again.

"Are you going to be sick?" Livy looked around for a washcloth or waste can.

Robyn shook her head, still not speaking. After a minute, she opened her eyes. "Are you sure it isn't the girl Alex is looking for?"

"It's not Samantha Jo," Alex said from the doorway. "And you two really need to watch where you talk. I could hear you from down the hall. And the public restroom is just across the hallway."

Livy's stomach dipped. She hadn't thought that someone might overhear them. What if the kidnapper—now murderer—worked at Johnny B's? She stood and shut the door. "What are you doing here? I thought you were going to the airport."

"Got called in to work." He turned to Robyn. "What time do you get off?"

"Five. You?"

"Seven."

Robyn looked too stressed and tired to wait two hours for a ride home. They had to do something about getting her a car. "I'll come and pick you up," Livy said.

"Thanks."

Livy handed the envelope and note to Alex. "It was on the table when she came for her break."

He looked it over. "Anyone could've put it here. A worker, a customer who goes to the restroom . . ."

"It's been so busy this afternoon, I'm sure no one even noticed it," Robyn said. "It could've been here for a couple of hours."

"I'll check with the other workers, see if they noticed it." Livy wrapped it in a napkin and put it in her bag. "Do you know who came into the restaurant before you took your break?"

"Lots of truck drivers have stopped in this afternoon, some I know, some I don't. As for the regulars, Johnny B, Bobby, Timothy. Jason hasn't been in since breakfast. But I'm sure most of them are gone by now, although a few may be back for supper."

Livy ran her hand through her hair. Bobby Cook was a salesman, but she'd seen him driving a big, expensive pickup. "Are you certain the man who took you was a truck driver? And that you were in the cab of a semi? You know, some of those double cab pickups are fancy. Could've given you the sense of a semi cab."

Robyn slumped even farther into the chair. "I'm not sure of anything anymore. What if this goes on for weeks? I don't think I can go much longer without telling Mom and Dad and Abby who I am."

"I know. It's killing me too." Livy hugged her. "We're going to catch this guy."

Alex tapped Livy's arm. "Ben's out front, and he wants you to help him question the customers who are here." He turned to Robyn. "Are you going to be okay?"

Robyn lifted her shoulders in a shrug. "I have to be. I can't sit in here and have a pity party. There are customers to be waited on, but at least I don't have to work in the morning."

"I'm scheduled for four tomorrow afternoon." Alex tilted his head. "Same time as you?"

"Yep."

Livy stood. "I'll let you know if I find out anything," she said and walked down the hallway.

Johnny B shot a curious glance toward Livy when she reentered the dining room, and she took out a pad and pen as she walked over to him. Might as well start with him. Before she said anything, he held up his hand.

"Done talked to the sheriff. Don't know anything."

"You don't even know what I'm going to ask you."

"Tell you what, fill me in on why *you're* here asking questions, and it might trigger something I didn't even know I remembered."

She tapped the pen against her notepad, trying to decipher his convoluted sentence. "There've been a few waitresses kidnapped. We think it's an over-the-road truck driver doing it. Two women have disappeared from—"

"I knew it! I never thought Robyn left of her own accord. Tell you the truth, I thought that husband of hers might've done away with her."

Livy stiffened. "You never said that before."

He shrugged. "Would you have given any credence to my theory?"

"I don't know. I do know that Chase had nothing to do with her disappearance. Any other theories?"

Johnny eyed her over his cup as he lifted it for a sip. "Nope, just that one," he said and drained his cup, then plunked it on the table. "Are you thinking one of the truckers killed that waitress and dumped her in the lake? I understand she wasn't from here."

As far as Livy knew, nothing had been said about the victim in the lake being a waitress. "How did you know she was a waitress?"

"My cousin Gilley was in the boat that brought her up. He was there when Wade cut into the plastic. It was awful, he said. But he saw enough to know it wasn't Samantha Jo and that she wore a waitress uniform."

The joys of small towns. But she should have expected it. The search and rescue team was made up of fishermen and hunters—the good ole boy network—what one knew, they all knew.

"Got any more questions, Olivia?"

"Yeah. How long since you drove a big rig?"

His eyes widened. "Five, six years. You don't think I'm your guy, do you? Why, if I did something like that, my mama would skin me alive."

212

Livy glanced at the portrait on the wall. "How is Mrs. Baxter?"

"This part of your investigation?"

She laughed. "No. I just remember how she stopped by the house when I was a little girl to visit Kate." And scared her to death. The woman was stern. Not a funny bone in her body. "She made good cookies."

"That'd be my mama. She's doing poorly. Hardly ever gets out of bed. But she's eighty and had a good life."

Livy tapped her jaw with the pen. "You know these truckers better than anyone. Any of them capable of kidnapping or murder?"

He looked out toward the dining room, and she turned to follow his gaze. "Those are good men out there. They carry a lot of responsibility, and sure, some of them are strange, but it's hard to believe any trucker I know could do something like that. Let me think on it a couple of days."

Livy turned back to him, and he evaded her eyes. She waited. He might not know anything, but something was bothering him. Perhaps he had a hunch he didn't want to share. She reached into her pocket and took out a card. "If you think of anything, call me on my cell phone."

He took the card and stared at it, then looked up. "I'll do that, Detective Olivia Reynolds. You never said why you're involved in this case."

"I didn't, did I."

■ ■ ■

Robyn leaned against the counter, resting her back. Four o'clock. One more hour. The front door to the restaurant opened, and Jason Fremont sidled in with his head ducked low. The poor boy was so shy. Her gaze followed him to his regular spot. He and Bobby Cook and Timothy Nolan, all regulars and all hometown boys, formed a triangle. They'd frequented the restaurant when she worked here before, usually coming for at least one meal a day on the days they were in town, and then for coffee at least once between meals. She used to kid them that they just wanted to get caught up on the latest gossip.

She looked over the room, trying to remember how many of the other truckers sitting at the tables had been regulars back then. Only one or two, and Livy and Ben had interviewed them before they left an hour ago. A deputy remained behind to get information from the next wave of drivers, but Livy would be back to pick her up when she got off.

Callie breezed by her. "Did you get Jason's order?"

She shook herself from the past. "Getting his water first." After she filled a glass, she grabbed the coffeepot and a cup and added them to the tray. Jason would want coffee, and Timothy probably needed a refill. "You want the usual?" She set Jason's cup down and filled it three-quarters full, then pulled a couple of creamers from her apron.

He removed his camouflage cap and hooked it on the back of a chair at the table. "You sure catch on quick."

She froze. "I, ah, Callie mentioned you always ordered the same thing." Moving to Timothy's table, she refilled his cup. "Dessert?"

"Whatcha got?" He smiled at her.

"Your favorite, caramel cake." The words slipped out again. She must be tired to make two mistakes that close together. "And your other favorite—chocolate pie."

"No, the cake is my favorite." He stirred cream into his coffee. "What brought you to our little town? You look like a big city girl."

"Don't be tying up all her time, Timothy." Bobby raised his cup, letting her know he wanted a refill too. "She doesn't want to fool around with no Marine."

"Well." Timothy drawled the word out. "She sure doesn't want to hang out with an old army guy."

Robyn put her hand on her hip and eyed them both. "*She* doesn't want to hang out or fool around with anybody. Y'all got that?"

"Yes ma'am." Bobby grinned. "But you said you weren't married, and I haven't seen a boyfriend, so a man can dream, can't he?"

Bobby was very observant. Too much so, and he didn't forget anything. "This is regular Colombian. That okay?"

"Honey, anything you bring me will be just fine," Bobby said. "Did you talk to your daughter today?"

"Not yet." She glanced at her watch. Thirty more minutes and she could go home. Maybe Abby would be there.

"Hey, Bobby, let her get my cake, if you don't mind." Timothy leaned back and looked pointedly at the man.

"Be right back with it," she said. These three had not changed at all. She'd learned one thing, though. Timothy and Bobby were retired military, something she'd forgotten. She hurried to the computer and entered Jason's ham on rye, and then she cut Timothy a piece of caramel cake and took it out to him. "Here you go, sir."

"Thank you, Sharon. Don't let that bozo over there get too friendly."

"I don't think he means any harm." She tilted her head. "So you were a Marine. Been out long?"

"Ten years."

"And you've been driving a big rig ever since?"

His eyes warmed. "Yeah. I have my own truck and used to drive full-time, but since Mother's stroke, I've cut back a lot."

She tried to remember his mother, and a recollection of a thin woman with rouged cheeks and red hair surfaced. She'd ask Livy about her.

"Sharon, think I could get another refill?" Bobby winked at her.

"She's waiting on me," Timothy growled.

A customer brushed past her, and a familiar scent brought memories of June mornings and fresh-cut grass. Someone was wearing the same aftershave Chase wore. She turned, and a small gasp escaped her lips. Not someone, but Chase. He still used the

215

aftershave she'd picked out just before . . . Robyn straightened her shoulders. "Be right with you."

In a daze, she walked back to the kitchen to check with Alex on Jason's order. Not ready.

"You okay?" he asked.

"Chase just came in." She filled another glass with water for Chase and set a fresh pot of coffee on her tray for Bobby. Chase would order tea, not coffee. She'd bet the rent on it. First she re-filled Bobby's cup, then after smoothing her apron, she pasted a smile on her face and walked to Chase's table. "Surprised to see you here tonight."

"I told Livy I'd pick you up, and since I haven't had lunch, I thought I might as well eat while I wait." He sat back in the chair, and his grin sent her heart into orbit.

"You're going to take me home?" Her insides wouldn't be still. And that green sweater looked so good on him, making his hazel eyes almost the color of the sea. Sitting next to him in a vehicle was not a good idea.

"Thought I would. You don't have a problem with that, do you?"

"No, just wondered what happened to Livy." She twisted a strand of her hair on her finger, then tucked it behind her ear.

"She's tied up with Ben. She said you'd be off in . . ." He glanced at his watch. "Less than thirty minutes. Figure that'll give me time to eat one of Johnny B's famous BBQs. Unless you'd like to grab a bite somewhere after you get off. I could wait." The grin on his face faded. "I mean, it wouldn't be a date or anything. No. I'm sorry, you probably didn't even think . . . I really shouldn't have said anything." He closed his eyes. "I'm making it worse."

"Yeah. I think you are. But don't worry. I had lunch an hour ago, so I'm not hungry."

Relief showed in the lean lines of his face. He'd lost weight since she'd been gone. Was it possible she'd read him wrong, and

216

he'd actually grieved for her? Callie elbowed her as she passed. "Jason's order is ready."

Robyn jumped. "Oh, thanks." She turned back to Chase. "You want the BBQ and tea?" she asked.

"Yes."

Robyn felt his gaze on her back as she walked to the computer and entered his order. Thank goodness this day was almost over. So many mistakes, someone was going to catch her. After she delivered Jason's order, she retreated behind the counter with a cleaning cloth.

"You're going to rub the top off that counter," Callie said several minutes later as she filled a water glass. "And your BBQ is ready."

"Thanks. After I take it to the table, I'm clocking out."

"I don't blame you. It's been a long day."

That it had. She picked up the plate and took it to Chase. "I'll be ready when you finish."

"Why don't you put it in a to-go box, and I'll eat it at Kate's?"

"You don't have to do that. I need to make sure my customers are taken care of before I leave, anyway."

She stopped by Jason's table first, and when he didn't want dessert, she left his ticket on the table. Next she checked on two truckers in the back and took their orders. "I'm not sure who's taking my place, but Callie will make sure your meal gets to you."

One of the truckers tucked a five-dollar bill in her hand. When she protested, he held his finger up. "That's just for being so nice. See you next trip."

Her mood elevated, she laid Timothy's ticket on the corner of his table and turned to Bobby. "Anything else for you?"

"How about I take you home?"

She patted him on the shoulder. "Sorry, but Chase is doing the honors. Maybe next time." Yeah, right. Like she'd get in a truck with any of the men in the restaurant.

18

Chase chewed thoughtfully on the messy BBQ. Three tables over, Sharon talked with Bobby Cook. He'd known Bobby all his life. Usually easygoing, but he could show a temper. The look in Bobby's eyes indicated more than a casual interest in Sharon, but she seemed to be brushing him off as she turned to another customer.

Something about the way she stood reminded him of Robyn. Maybe that was why he was so drawn to her. He should have told Livy to get someone else to pick her up. Because for all practical purposes, he had asked Sharon for a date, and he had no idea why. It had seemed so natural that the words slipped out. But he was still married. And until that changed, he had no business even flirting with another woman. Even one who reminded him of his wife.

He kept her in his line of vision and noticed Timothy staring at him. He waved, and the ex-Marine nodded. Timothy was one he didn't know much about, only that he'd grown up in Logan Point. He'd gone to a smaller school on the far side of the county while Chase had attended the main county school. Then, instead of going to college, Timothy had joined the Marines. Chase finished his sandwich and leaned back in the chair, the glass of tea in his hand.

Sharon appeared at his table, her purse in her hand. "I'm ready."

"Good. Let me take care of my ticket."

Once he'd paid Johnny B, he walked ahead of her to open the door, then ushered her through it with his hand on her back. Chase caught a light, sweet fragrance as she came close to him. Odd how similar it was to what Robyn used to wear. "My truck is over here."

"Why do all the men in Logan Point drive pickups?"

He laughed. "You've noticed."

She rolled her eyes. "It'd be hard not to."

He made a muscle with both arms. "Logan Point is a man's town," he said, using his deep voice. He opened the passenger door and helped her step up into the cab. Regret stabbed him. He hadn't done that for Robyn in years. When did the romance leave their marriage? And how much was he to blame?

As he climbed behind the steering wheel, Sharon fumbled with her purse, then felt her pockets. "Oh, wait, I can't find my phone."

"Do you think you left it inside?"

She opened the truck door. "I must have. Let me go see if I can find it."

"Give me your number and I'll call it."

"Good idea, but wait until I get inside."

She told him her number, and he waited until she went through the doors before dialing it. When the call went to voice mail, Chase hung up.

Suddenly it dawned on him that he should have gone with her. What if someone abducted her? He dialed as he climbed out of the truck and hurried toward the diner, his heart racing. She answered this time, and relief swept over him.

"Finally found it in the break room. I'll be right out."

"I'm inside the door." His heart slowed as she walked out from the back of the diner.

"You could have waited in the truck," she said when she reached him.

"If anything had happened to you, Livy would skin me alive." He opened the door for her and walked her back to his pickup.

She fastened her seat belt. "Sorry for being so much trouble, but thanks for taking me home."

Something about her voice was different. He glanced at her. "Did you say you were from East Tennessee?"

She crossed her arms over her stomach. "I've lived in Bristol for a few years. Why?"

He shrugged. "No reason. It's just that sometimes I catch a different accent."

Her face colored and she twisted a strand of hair around her finger. "I've lived other places. Have you lived here always?"

"Yeah. Even when I attended Memphis University. Drove back and forth. For a while, my wife attended with me, but she dropped out." He backed out of his parking space and pulled out of the lot. He hadn't meant to make her nervous, but he wanted to know more about her. "Were you a waitress back in Bristol?"

Her sigh was soft, resigned. "For a while. Mostly I went to school for my degree and helped out where I lived."

"At the abuse shelter." Chase turned his left signal on and turned off the highway.

"You remembered."

"Why were you living at an abuse shelter? Did your husband—"

"No. I . . . was stalked and I managed to get to Bristol without him finding me. I didn't have a job or a place to live, and Susan took me in at the shelter. I just earned my degree in December."

"Abby said you were helping Alex with a case. Is it because you were stalked?"

Sharon shifted in the seat, and he took his eyes off the road for a second. She stared straight ahead.

"You don't have to answer."

"No, it's all right. I'm trying to help Alex find whoever took the Woodson girl."

"He thinks it might be your stalker?"

"Yeah."

"But . . . won't he recognize you?"

She hesitated again. "No. I've changed."

Even though she was answering him, he could tell she wasn't comfortable talking about the subject, and he didn't like making her uncomfortable. He turned right onto Coley Road. "Tell me what kind of degree you have."

Her shoulders relaxed. "It's in psychology, but I'm getting my master's in social work. I want to help other women who've been abused."

"Good for you. I wish my wife had gotten her degree." He liked Sharon. She was spunky and brave. That was where she was totally different from Robyn. He couldn't imagine his wife surviving on her own. "It must have been hard, starting over with nothing."

"You do what you have to do. I was alive, and for a while, that was enough. Now I want to get my life back."

"I'd like to help."

The look she shot him indicated she hadn't forgotten what he'd said in the restaurant. Heat crawled up his neck. "Look, about what I said earlier . . . I shouldn't have made that comment. I'm a married man, and until I change that, I have no right to ask a woman out to eat. But helping you wouldn't be the same thing."

"Are you g-getting a divorce?"

He didn't know why it was so easy to talk to Sharon. He found himself wanting to tell her about Robyn. "Considering it."

"What happened to your wife?"

"She got tired of being married to me a couple of years ago. Took off to who knows where." He tried to keep the bitterness from his voice, but when Sharon flinched, he figured he hadn't succeeded.

"How do you know that's what happened? Did you ever consider something might have happened to her?"

"I might if I hadn't gotten this call, saying not to try to find her, that she had some things to work out." He rubbed the back of his neck. "You see, we were having a little trouble. Sometimes when

221

I think back, I realize I might have been hard on her. At any rate, I figure she just got tired of me griping all the time."

"Why didn't you try to work it out?"

"I didn't know she was that mad at me."

"Did you love her?"

The question filled the cab. "Yeah," he finally said. After a few seconds, he added, "Guess I still do, especially when I think about what a good mom she was. That's when I wonder if something could have happened to her—'cause it's hard for me to believe she'd stay away from Abby this long."

"Chase—"

His side window exploded, and he threw up his hand. "What—"

The unmistakable crack of a gun sounded, and the truck lurched to the left. Someone was shooting at them. "Get down!" He steered the truck to the side of the road as another bullet whizzed by his head, exiting out the back windshield.

"The shots are coming from across the road. Get out and stay low." The truck wouldn't offer much protection, but at least they wouldn't be out in the open. Sharon scrambled from the truck as another shot rang out. A searing pain ripped through the front of his shoulder. *Got to get out.* He looked down. Blood everywhere. Chase tried to climb over the console. So dizzy.

"Chase! No!"

"Get down . . ." The words barely made it past his lips when darkness edged into his consciousness.

■ ■ ■

Robyn knelt beside the truck, her hand shaking as she punched in Livy's number. The lights from the cab of the truck cast a harsh light in the darkness. "Hello?" Livy's voice cut through the eerie silence.

"Chase has been shot! We're about a mile from the house on Coley Road. Hurry!"

"Did you call 911?"

"No, but I will." Should've called them first. The phone shook in her hand as she pressed the emergency numbers.

"911. What's your—"

"I'm on Coley Road about a mile east of Kate Adams's bed and breakfast. The person I'm with has been shot. Please hurry! He's bleeding." Robyn tossed the phone on the dashboard and climbed back into the truck. Chase lay slumped over the console, blood pooling around the gearshift. He was losing too much blood. She searched the truck for something to use as a pressure bandage, but as usual, her neat-freak husband had a pristine truck. She peeled off her coat. She had to get him on his back. *But what if moving him causes paralysis?* Which was better—bleed to death or not walk? She tried to lift him, but he was dead weight. She pushed again, and he groaned.

"Chase, I need you to help me. Try to lean back!"

His eyelids fluttered open.

"Can you hear me? You've been shot. I need you on your back. I'll try to help you." She tried to keep the panic from her voice. "Do you understand me?"

He barely nodded, and as he pushed, she tried to help him. "One more time."

She pushed on his uninjured right side as he rolled back, exposing his blood-soaked shirt.

"Hurts so bad," he whispered.

If she didn't stop the bleeding, he would bleed to death. She pressed her coat to the wound. "Stay with me. Help is on the way." He closed his eyes.

"Chase, talk to me." No response. "Please don't die. It's me. Robyn. I love you, Chase."

He couldn't die. Not when they were so close to being together again. Why hadn't she already told him who she was? Maybe this wouldn't have happened.

She clamped her teeth together. Whoever had kidnapped her shot Chase. She was as sure of that as she was of breathing. It was her fault. She'd flushed the kidnapper out, but Chase might die because of it. She kept pressure against the wound.

Car lights flashed in front of her. *Please let it be Livy.* Seconds later, her cousin jerked the driver's door open. "What happened?"

"Someone shot at us. Chase is bad, I know it." At last, sirens sounded in the distance, but she didn't let up on the pressure.

"Are you hit?"

She shook her head as red and blue lights topped the hill. "Just Chase. He's really bleeding."

"Let me take over for you."

"I've got it." She kept her coat over the wound until a paramedic climbed into the cab.

"I'll take over from here," he said. "On the count of three."

Once the medic's hands were pressing the wound, she backed out of the truck and another paramedic took her place. Chase hadn't moved. She wasn't sure he was even breathing. "Is he going to live?"

"Let us get him out of the truck so we can assess his injury."

Shivering, Robyn backed away from the scene. Her head swam as coldness spread across her face. She fought the blackness stealing her vision. Then her knees buckled, and she sank to the ground.

When she came to, a paramedic was wrapping a blood-pressure cuff around her arm, and Livy knelt on the other side of her. "What happened?"

"Be still while I get your blood pressure," the medic said.

She winced as the cuff inflated.

"Blood pressure is low," he said. "But you don't seem to be injured, so I think you just fainted."

She struggled to sit up. "How's Chase?"

Livy helped her. "They're working on him."

"Don't try to stand yet," the medic advised as Ben stooped beside her.

"What happened?" he asked.

"I don't know. We were talking and suddenly someone started shooting at us. He was trying to get me out of the truck when he was hit."

"Could you tell where the shots came from?"

"Chase's side window exploded first. Then there were more shots, and I think one of them hit a tire. The one that hit Chase came through the windshield after we pulled over." She shivered in the cold night air, and Livy slipped out of her coat and wrapped it around her shoulders. "What are they waiting for? Why aren't they taking him to the hospital?"

"They're getting him stabilized," Livy said. "You didn't see the person?"

"No. We were just talking and—"

"Do you remember who was there?" Ben asked.

She pressed her hand against her mouth, reliving the moments before they left the restaurant. "It's Sunday night, so it was mostly just the regulars—Jason and Bobby and Timothy. Johnny B. A couple of truck drivers, but everything was normal." She turned as they lifted Chase and placed him on a gurney. Her eyes burned from unshed tears.

"I think our guy saw you leave with Chase, and he didn't like it," Ben said. "We can't do much here at the scene tonight, but in the morning I'll have my deputies scour the area across the road. For now, give Livy a list of the men who were at the restaurant when you left. I'll call Taylor to see if she can meet us at my office."

"Ben, she'll want to be with Chase," Livy said.

He winced. "You're right, but she'll want to catch this guy too. Maybe we can talk at the hospital."

Chase had been shot and it was all her fault. The thought went around and around in Robyn's head like a bad song. Her eyes were glued to the scene where paramedics worked on him. He had an IV now, and they'd hooked him up to a heart monitor. She didn't like the way the amber and red lights gave his skin a ghostly cast. One of the medics approached Ben as the others lifted the gurney into the ambulance bay. "He's stabilized, but he's lost a lot of blood."

"You think he's going to make it?" Ben asked.

"Barring complications, he should. Have you notified the family?"

Robyn hugged her arms to her stomach as Ben glanced toward her. "I'll call his mother now." He took out his phone and dialed.

Livy fisted her hands. "This wouldn't have happened if I had been there to take you home."

"It's not your fault." Robyn followed her gaze, her teeth chattering. Once Chase was loaded, the driver slammed the bay doors and hurried to the front of the ambulance. Her heart ached to go with him. "If anyone is to blame, it's me. When I was pressing against the wound, I kept asking myself why I hadn't told him who I was."

She looked at Livy. "Is it time to tell the family who I am? If I don't, won't they think it's strange that I'm hanging around the hospital? Because I'm not leaving until he's out of the woods."

"Let's play it by ear," Livy suggested. "Our guy is coming unraveled, and I don't know if we can keep you safe if he knows you're Robyn."

"I don't think I was safe tonight, and Chase certainly wasn't."

■ ■ ■

In the surgery waiting room, Robyn ran her finger over a wrinkle in the green scrubs a nurse had loaned her. Her bloody clothes were in a bag at her feet. No one had questioned her being there after Livy explained she'd been in the truck with Chase and why. She glanced toward the door. Where were Livy and Alex with that coffee they'd gone after?

Across from her, Taylor paced the room, crossing paths with Charlie. Evidently, her dad had grown close to Chase since she'd been gone. Chase's mother, Allison, leaned forward, resting her head in her hand, and Ben stood in one corner, conferring with his fiancée. Leigh Somerall had treated Chase in the ER before sending him to surgery an hour ago.

Robyn approached the doctor. "Do you think he'll make it?"

The doctor hesitated, her green eyes darkening. "Nothing's ever guaranteed, but I think he has a good chance. His vitals were good, and he's young and in excellent physical shape. We should be getting another report soon."

The concern in Leigh's voice almost did Robyn in. She hadn't known her well in high school, but she hoped that would change when this was all over with.

"Thanks," she said and walked to the window. After a minute, she felt a presence at her side and turned, giving Allison a hesitant smile.

"Livy tells me you've worked all day. I want you to know, we don't expect you to stay. Not that we don't appreciate your concern."

"I want to be here." Allison had always treated Robyn like she was her own daughter, had even taken her side over Chase's on more than one occasion. Robyn would give anything if she could just reveal who she was to Allison and explain what happened two and a half years ago.

The phone rang, and everyone turned to stare at it until Allison crossed the room and answered it. Robyn held her breath as her mother-in-law nodded, then hung up.

"The bullet is out. It missed all major organs but nicked a major vein. That's why there was so much blood." She took a deep breath and released it. "But he's going to be all right."

Cheers erupted in the room. Robyn wanted to dance as tears streamed down her face. *He's going to be all right.* Sweetest words she'd ever heard. She hugged Livy and then hugged her again. Then, she caught her breath, suddenly remembering that when she thought he might die, she'd told him who she was. And that she loved him.

What if he remembered?

■ ■ ■

He cleaned the Browning 22 rifle, wishing it had been his 30-06 in the gun rack on his pickup. If the deer rifle had been there instead of the light caliber rifle, Chase Martin would be history. He ground his molars, thinking about the way Chase's hand rested on Sharon's back when they went out the door. And before that, flirting with her like he was single. Martin had Robyn, and he had mistreated her. He wasn't getting Sharon.

He'd watched Sharon this evening. She'd gotten the card, but she hadn't gone home like he'd expected. Maybe she thought it was a joke. He stroked the barrel of his rifle. That would be a serious mistake on her part.

■ ■ ■

Chase was going to be okay. Livy repeated that to herself as she hesitated outside the room the hospital director had arranged for them to meet in. She didn't care how many times she repeated those words, it didn't take away from the fact that if she had stayed until Robyn's shift ended and brought her home, it wouldn't have happened. Alex and Ben rounded the corner and walked toward her.

Alex touched her arm. "You okay?"

She gave him a shrug and didn't answer. She'd teared up a time or two in the last two hours and didn't trust herself to talk.

Ben eyed her, his eyebrows raised, then he addressed Alex. "Are you still flying to Nashville in the morning?"

"I thought I would. Are you still going with me?"

"No, not after this. Y'all go on in the room; I'll join everyone in a minute. I asked Taylor to wait for me down the hall in a consultation room. I want to let her in on Robyn's identity before we meet. Might save us a little time."

That made sense. Alex opened the door, and they entered the room. It looked like some sort of boardroom with a long conference table and chairs. A whiteboard occupied one end of the room. Livy took a seat, and Alex sat across from her. She hated waiting and checked her email on her phone.

"You never answered me," he said.

She looked up. He'd asked if she was okay. At the moment, the tears seemed in check. "Of course I am. I didn't do my job and Chase gets shot. What's not to be okay about?" She clamped her mouth shut to stop her lip from quivering.

"Being sarcastic won't help, and neither will feeling sorry for yourself. I do know how you feel—I feel as though I let her and Chase down too, but we couldn't have stopped it."

"I don't think it would've happened if it'd been me taking her home instead of Chase."

"You don't have a crystal ball to look into and see what this guy is going to do. At least no one died. And maybe it flushed our kidnapper out into the open."

"But we don't even know if it was him."

"It was him, all right. And he's already fixated on—"

The door opened, and Robyn stuck her head inside. "Oh, good. I wasn't sure if this was the place."

"It is. Come on in. Ben and Taylor will be here as soon as they talk." Livy was glad for the interruption. Alex did not know how she felt. He'd only known Chase a couple of days. She'd known him all her life.

"He said he was going to tell her who I am. I wish we were telling everyone. Has anyone called Abby and let her know how her daddy is?"

"Allison called Kate," Livy said.

The door opened again, and Ben and Taylor entered. Livy's

breath caught as a wide smile spread across Taylor's face. She knew exactly how Taylor felt as she wrapped her arms around Robyn.

"Girl, you should have let us know! Maybe we could have helped." Then Taylor held her at arm's length. "I can't believe how different you look. Who would've thought losing weight and having a smaller nose would make such a change." She touched Robyn's hair. "All that red and those beautiful curls. Gone. No wonder no one has recognized you."

Livy totally agreed with Taylor and said, "Don't worry, the curls are still there. I saw her straightening them this morning."

Robyn twisted a strand of hair around her finger. "I might keep the blonde coloring. I kind of like it."

"You don't even sound like yourself." Taylor stared at her. "And you had such blue—" Her mouth dropped open. "Contacts?"

"Yep." Robyn grinned, obviously pleased with herself. She turned to Livy. "Do you know how good it feels to get this out into the open? I can't wait for everyone to know."

Livy couldn't imagine how her cousin felt. "Did you notice how marriage agrees with Taylor?"

Taylor blushed. "I can't wait for Robyn to meet Nick."

"This is what I'd hoped to avoid," Ben said with a chuckle. "Let's get caught up later. We have a criminal to catch."

"Sorry." Red colored Taylor's face again. "Okay. Let me tell you what I think, and then we'll talk about what happened tonight and how it fits in." She moved to the front of the room by the white-board. "I've gone over the information Ben emailed me, and some of it I'm sure you've already figured out. This guy has a fixation on waitresses. I figure he was betrayed or perceived himself to be betrayed by someone close to him who was a waitress. Could've been a girlfriend or even his mother. He's a white male between the ages of thirty and fifty. He mingles well with people, and he's probably OCD. In a restaurant setting, that means he'll probably order the same thing every meal. Breakfast will be the same thing every morning, probably something like bacon and eggs. Lunch, probably a sandwich, dinner will be meat and potatoes."

"Unfortunately, that sounds like every truck driver that comes into Johnny B's," Robyn said.

Taylor laughed. "I was afraid we might have that problem." She picked up a folder and turned to the whiteboard. When she finished there were ten names on it.

"The first victim was Georgia Simmons. She lived in the Mobile, Alabama, area and was taken two years before Robyn on January 31; the second—Debbie Porter—a year later, also on January 31." She used a pointer to go down the list. "Then, seventeen months later, he takes Robyn on August 31, followed by seven more if we count the Jane Doe."

Taylor paused. "I hate to call her Jane Doe, but we don't have confirmation that she's the waitress who was last seen getting into a semi on December 29 after a fight with her husband. But to get back to the timeline, there's Tammy Morton, taken five months after Robyn and again on another January 31; four months later Carrie Thomas on May 31; three months later Linda Rogers on August 31; two months later Cora Jones, October 31; one month later Jamie Williams on November 30. And, Jane Doe, which brings us to February 1 of this year when Samantha Jo is kidnapped."

She put the pointer down. "Okay, tell me what you see here."

Livy leaned forward. "He seems fixated with the thirty-first."

Taylor beamed. "Absolutely. And three of the women were kidnapped on January 31." She pointed to Samantha Jo's name. "I believe it would have been four if she had not gone to the movies with Jason. There is something significant about January 31."

"The timeline escalated," Alex said.

"Yes. Unless there are victims we don't know about."

"Wade is combing the different databases," Ben said.

Livy stared at the board. "Are there any similarities in his victims?"

Ben pulled a stack of paper from his notes and passed them out. "Here's what we have so far on the victims. All but Samantha Jo are overweight. If the Jane Doe is his, she fits the profile as well."

Livy stopped taking notes and leaned forward. "If she's one of his victims why did he kill her? Why didn't he let her go like he did the others? And why keep Samantha Jo?"

"Good question," Taylor said. "One that I don't have the answer to. According to the notes he leaves, he's driven by a desire that mothers stay home with their children, which leads me to believe he was abandoned as a child by a waitress mother.

"He also has control and anger issues, but on the other hand, his mode of operating also suggests he is patient and extremely smart. Look at the way he stalks the women and waits to catch them alone."

"I can tell you, he definitely has anger issues," Robyn muttered.

Taylor nodded. "He depends on the drugs to keep the victim under control. When that didn't work with you, he became frustrated. And he can't handle that, so he lashed out. I believe the Jane Doe is his and something similar probably happened with her. And by the way, I'm pretty certain he's a resident of Logan Point. Wade indicated in the report that she was found in the channel of the river—the deepest part of the lake. Only someone who knew the area would know where that was."

Alex tapped his pencil on the table. "Why did he shoot Chase?"

Taylor turned and wrote *Sharon* on the board. "I believe Robyn, as Sharon, is his next victim, and I think he was jealous." She turned to Robyn. "You really need to be careful."

"I will. Becoming his victim again is the last thing I want."

Taylor nodded. "You've had a little time to think. Take us through everything you can remember about being at Johnny B's before you got off—what you did, who was there."

"I'm having trouble remembering anything," Robyn said.

"Okay. Let's try something. Close your eyes and try to relax."

She closed her eyes, and Livy breathed with her as she took a deep breath, then another one.

"Okay, take a minute to picture the restaurant. Then, tell me what you see."

Robyn sat still. "I see Chase. He's sitting right in front of me. Behind him is Jason Fremont. He ordered his usual. To their right is Timothy Nolan, and just on the other side of him is Bobby Cook. A couple of over-the-road truck drivers are behind them." She caught her breath. "And Johnny B is talking to one of the drivers."

Livy dismissed the two over-the-road drivers. They'd have to be checked out, of course, but she doubted they would be familiar with the lake. She tried to picture Johnny B on the lake. Not impossible, and the other three? She'd known them for years and hated to think it was any of them. She pulled her attention back to her cousin as she asked another question.

"What did Chase say to you?"

Robyn smiled. "He asked me if I wanted to go with him to get something to eat. And it embarrassed him when he realized what he'd said."

"Did any of the other customers hear him?"

"Probably all of them. They were all sitting close together."

"Were they all there when you left?"

Robyn opened her eyes. "I'm not sure."

Ben shifted in his chair. "You've said you thought someone was watching you. Have any of those men seemed overly protective or interested in you?"

She twisted a strand of hair around her finger. "You know how it is at a restaurant. The men think I'm single, and they come on to me."

Livy reached across the table and squeezed her cousin's hand. "You're handling this well."

"Not much else I can do until we catch this guy." She glanced around the room. "I think it's time to up the stakes—come clean with who I am."

"No!" Livy leaned forward. "If he's fixated on you thinking you're Sharon, he'll go ballistic if he knows you're Robyn."

"I don't see what difference it'll make now. He's already gone ballistic."

Ben shook his head. "But he wasn't shooting at you. If he had been, he would've been on the other side of the road. You can't tell anyone who you are unless you want to go into protective custody and disappear until we find him."

"Not doing that." Robyn folded her arms over her chest. "I thought the whole purpose of me coming back was to get him to come after me. If I disappear, he'll just go underground."

A crazy idea popped into Livy's head. One that just might work.

"What if . . ." She stopped until she had everyone's attention. "What if I pose as Robyn?"

19

W hat?" Alex stared at Livy. She couldn't possibly mean what he thought she did.

"Explain," Ben said.

"So far no one has recognized Robyn as Sharon, because she doesn't look the way she's supposed to. A lot of the features people expect have changed—hair, eyes, nose, weight, and she's not wearing glasses. We're cousins and there's some resemblance even though I don't have the old Robyn's Roman nose. But you'll have to agree my nose is bigger than hers is now. Put a curly red wig and a pair of glasses on me, and I can pass for a slimmed-down Robyn."

"No!" Alex and Ben and Robyn all spoke at the same time.

She glanced toward Taylor.

Taylor held up her hands. "Don't look at me."

"Have you even worked as a waitress?" Alex said.

"All through my senior year in high school, then four years of college is all."

The room fell silent, and Alex shifted his gaze from Livy to Robyn. He hadn't seen a photo of Robyn before her appearance had changed, but Livy might be right about one thing. "Do any of you have a photo of Robyn from two and a half years ago?"

"I might. Why?" Livy asked as she took out her phone.

As bad as he wanted to catch this guy, he wasn't sure if this was the right way to go. "If we bought into your idea, there might be a problem. Our kidnapper might not buy that you're Robyn—"

"The way she's changed," Taylor said, "I'm not even sure he'd buy that Robyn is Robyn."

"Here." Livy handed Alex her phone.

The photo of Robyn and Abby was too small, so he used his fingers to make it larger. He studied it, focusing in on her face. Wow. Robyn had totally changed. Photos tended to make people heavier than they were, but the woman in the photo weighed at least fifty pounds more than the Robyn he knew. And the difference in the two noses . . . amazing. He looked from the photo to Robyn, then to Livy. Both were about the same height, and Livy bore a faint resemblance to the Robyn in the photo. More even than the real one. He looked at Ben. "You're going to think I'm crazy, but with the right wig and glasses, it might work."

"Yes!" Livy said. "I can pick up a wig in Memphis tomorrow."

Ben held up his hand. "Wait, I didn't say I would go along with this crazy idea."

"It might be the bait we need to catch this guy," Taylor said.

"How would we handle the family?" Robyn asked.

Alex chewed the inside of his mouth. He hadn't considered what to tell them.

"If we go through with this, and I'm just saying if," Ben said, "we only tell them Livy's part. We need to wait until he's in custody to reveal the whole truth."

"Come on, Ben," Robyn said.

"I'm sorry, Robyn, but it's too easy for mistakes to be made. You want to trust your mom and dad to keep it quiet? And Abby—it'd be asking a lot of her not to tell her best friends."

Her shoulders drooped. "Yeah. I see what you mean."

Alex smiled. "If this goes like we plan, it shouldn't be long before you can tell everyone."

"Do I still go in to work tomorrow afternoon?" Robyn asked.

"No. You need to quit so Johnny B will hire me," Livy said. "But before you do that, I want you to go shopping with me to pick out an outfit you would have worn two and a half years ago."

■ ■ ■

"I can't believe you backed me up tonight."

Alex and Livy were alone in the kitchen, making a cup of hot cocoa at the stove, and her eyes glittered with excitement. The desire to take her in his arms and kiss her came out of nowhere, and he tamped it down. That would probably shake her up. "Well, I did say I'd be your partner, but you surprised me by suggesting it."

She frowned at him.

"It's a little out of the box." He stirred the chocolate milk to keep the milk from scorching.

"And you don't believe I can think outside the box?"

He raised his hand. He seemed to keep sticking his foot in his mouth. "Didn't say that. Can we start over?"

"Too late."

He loved the way her blue eyes snapped when he flustered her. "I know why you're doing it. And for the record, can I just say there's nothing wrong with going with the tried and true. It's your personality."

She tilted her head. "You are digging your hole deeper. Why do you think I want to pose as Robyn?"

"You feel guilty. In Bristol you didn't want Robyn to come back—you thought it was too risky, but you went along with us. Now you think you should have stood your ground, especially since Chase was shot. And you don't want Robyn to do it."

Two red dots appeared on her cheeks. He was right, but she'd probably never admit it.

"What did your grandfather want when he called this morning? You never told me." She smiled sweetly at him.

He dropped marshmallows into two mugs, then poured the hot cocoa and handed her one. Had it just been this morning that he'd talked to his grandfather? That conversation seemed at least two days ago. "I don't know. He hung up on me," he said as he sat down. She joined him, sitting next to him at the end of the table.

"What did you say?"

Alex took a sip and looked at her over the cup. "Why do you assume I was to blame?"

"You weren't?" When he didn't answer, she said, "Just joking."

Although he knew she was kidding, her words stung. In school, if something went wrong, it was Alex's fault. For a time, he'd even gone out of his way to get into trouble, reasoning that if he was going to be blamed anyway, he might at least get some fun out of it. "He called to see how the case was coming along, and to remind me that I only have three weeks to find Samantha Jo."

Livy touched his arm, sending a shock wave to his elbow. "I'm so sorry."

"I accused him of hoping I didn't find her."

She sucked in a breath through her teeth. "Not good."

"I could have used a better choice of words. When the body was found in the lake today, I was sure it was her body. When I saw that poor woman's swollen face, I felt so bad about being relieved. She belonged to someone. A daughter, maybe sister, and according to his track record, definitely a mother. I worry that Samantha Jo is going to end up the same way."

Livy stirred the marshmallows. "Why do you think he's changed from releasing the women to keeping them?"

"I think he's delusional, and he's getting worse. Or maybe he wants a wife, and thinks this is the only way to get one."

"If Taylor is right, he probably wants a substitute for his mother."

"Then why is he keeping Samantha Jo? She's much too young."

"Maybe he sees her the way his mother was when he was young."

Livy shook her head. "Trying to figure it out is enough to drive a sane person crazy."

"Yeah." He'd lost his taste for cocoa and took the cup to the sink. A cross-stitch hanging caught his eye. *For I know the plans I have for you. Plans for good . . .* He gripped the sink. He'd sure like to know God's plan right now. Because he didn't have one.

"Alex." Livy's soft voice was right behind him. Her hand rested lightly on his shoulder.

He turned around, and her blue eyes were wet.

"I think you could use a hug," she said and wrapped her arms around him.

"Thanks." Alex whispered the word against her hair and gently pulled her closer. She fit so perfectly in his arms. His heart thumped against his chest, and he knew she felt it, probably heard it. He'd never felt this way before. With his luck, she didn't feel the same way. He lifted her chin so he could see her eyes, and they were round and huge.

"You're amazing." He cupped her face in his hands and lowered his head until his lips met hers. A soft sigh escaped her mouth as she reached up and slipped her hands behind his head. Her lips, soft and yielding, responded to his. They broke apart, and he trailed his finger down her jaw. "I think I might just be falling for you."

"You think?" she teased.

"Would it be a good thing or a bad thing?" he asked, but before she could answer, he claimed her lips again.

When he released her, Livy rested her head on his chest. "Hmm. A good thing, I think."

"You think?"

"You are incorrigible."

"I believe I've heard that before," he said against her hair.

"From a female?"

"Oh yeah."

She leaned back, and lifted an eyebrow.

He brushed a strand of her blonde hair back. "She was at least forty years older, and I was in the third grade."

"That's better, because I think I might be falling for you too."

Right now, Alex could dance without touching the floor. Then reality set in. Tomorrow the woman he was falling in love with was going to use herself as bait. And he had to get to Nashville and check out the lead on Samantha Jo's wallet and get back to Logan Point before she did.

■ ■ ■

It was still dark when Alex eased the door to the Impala open. With any luck, he would be finished in Nashville and be back in Logan Point by one, but when he turned the ignition, all he heard was a grinding sound. *No!* He tried again and was rewarded with a series of clicks. Either the battery was gone or the solenoid switch. He rubbed his forehead. Maybe Livy could run him to the airport, and he could call the car rental and have another car delivered to the airport.

Alex pulled his phone out and hesitated. He really hated getting Livy out of bed before six, but the sooner he made it to Nashville, the sooner he would get back. He punched in her number, and she answered on the third ring. "Hello?"

"I hate to wake you, but could you run me to the airport? The Impala won't start."

"Alex? What time is it?"

"A little after five."

She groaned.

"If it weren't important—"

"No, no, that's okay. Be right down."

He made Livy a cup of coffee while he waited in the warmth of the kitchen for her to come down.

"You owe me," she said when she came through the door.

"Wow. Ten minutes. And you're beautiful at five thirty in the morning." And she was. No makeup, hair barely combed, but her blue eyes sparkled, and even more, when she looked at him, he felt like she truly "got" him.

"I'm up. You can stop with the flattery. You still owe me." She spied the coffee. "But not quite as much as it could be." She snagged the cup and took a sip. "Oh, that's good."

"I aim to please."

She rolled her eyes and then jingled her keys. "Ready?"

"Yes ma'am."

At the airport, she insisted on walking to the hangar with him, even though he told her it wasn't necessary. "Go home and get more shut-eye."

"I'm awake now. Might as well see you off."

That she wanted to be with him warmed him more than his down coat. He never expected to feel this way about anyone, not after seeing his parents' marriage disintegrate into a shouting match. He stopped and pulled her close and looked into eyes the color of an October sky. "You're pretty amazing."

Livy slipped her arms around his neck. "I know," she said with a twinkle in those blue eyes. "And so are you. And one day maybe I'll let you teach me how to fly."

"I'd like nothing better. But right now, I better get this plane checked out and get to Nashville."

■ ■ ■

As Alex went through his preflight inspection, images of her dad doing the same thing ran through Livy's mind. She hadn't heard another word from him since the email saying he planned to come, but that wasn't surprising. She wasn't that important to her father. She shook the memories off as Sam arrived and Alex fueled up.

"Thanks for hanging around," he said.

"Nothing to thank me for—it'll go on the tab you're running up, right next to getting me up at five thirty."

He laughed and kissed her lightly on the lips before jogging to his airplane.

"Nice guy," Sam said. "Oh, your dad called me. He—"

"Logan Point Tower, Cessna F6548 Juliet 10 miles Northwest, at 2000 feet, landing Logan Point airport."

Livy glanced at Sam. "A plane coming this early?"

"That's what I was trying to tell you—it's your dad."

Surely she hadn't heard him correctly. Sam hurried to the terminal building, and Livy trailed him. By the time she entered the building, Sam was responding to the pilot, then he radioed Alex, asking him to delay his takeoff until after the plane landed.

"Are you saying the plane coming in is my dad?"

"Yep. Should be dropping in within five minutes. Said he'd only be here long enough to refuel, though, so it's a lucky thing you're here."

She stepped back. Her dad. Here? Today? Why didn't he let them know? "He's only stopping to refuel?"

"That's what he said when he called." Sam turned as once again a voice came over the speaker. "Cessna F6548 Juliet, midfield, right downwind for runway 18."

Livy stared at the radio as Sam cleared him to land. The voice held the barest hint of her dad. He had time to call Sam but not his family? He hadn't intended for them to know he was here. How many times had he done this in the past? Just breeze through and never call? She started for the door.

"Aren't you going to wait and see your dad?"

She hesitated. If she left now, Sam would duly report it all over town. "Just going after something in the car. But I guess it can wait." Besides, she looked forward to seeing the expression on her dad's face when he saw her.

"Let's watch from outside," Sam said. "He'll come from the northwest."

She stepped outside the terminal building with him.

"There he is," Sam said.

With a south wind whipping her body, she scanned the predawn skies. A tiny dot appeared in the distance and grew larger until it banked north and approached the runway into the wind.

"Nice plane," Sam said as he picked up a pair of chocks and walked out to the tarmac.

She supposed. All twin-engine planes looked the same to her. Alex's plane roared to life, and she waved to him as he taxied to the runway. With a shiver, she stepped back through the glass door to the terminal to wait for her dad to come to her.

The cabin door opened, and a man too young and too short to be her dad climbed out. He hurried inside, nodding as he passed her. A minute later Jeremy Reynolds emerged from the cockpit and hopped off the wing. Sam stuck out his hand, but her dad grabbed him in a bear hug, pounding him on the back.

Livy pressed her lips in a thin line. Didn't he know how much he was missed in Logan Point? Sam said something to her dad, and his face lit up. He turned toward the building, and when he saw her standing just inside the door, he jogged over and came inside.

"Olivia, what are you doing here? Never mind. I don't care why you're here, just that you are." He wrapped his arm around her shoulders and squeezed. "I would have let you know, but I didn't think you would be up. Sorry I can't stay any longer than to refuel."

Like a flashpoint, seeing him in the flesh triggered all the anger she'd stored up, and the words spilled out. "What's so important that you can't spend the day? It's been five years since I've seen you. You didn't call on my birthday, not even a card. You didn't come home for Thanksgiving or Christmas."

He dropped his arm and stepped back, his face a dark cloud. "That highway goes both ways, Little Bit. Why didn't you email me back when I let you know I was coming? And it's not like you can't afford airfare to Alaska."

Maybe she didn't email because she didn't expect him to follow through. "I've been busy with a case. Besides, I'm not the one who left."

"So it's okay for you to be busy, but not me? Why did you bother to come out here? To read me the riot act? Well, I don't need that. I already know I'm a miserable excuse for a father, but—" He broke the words off and spun around. "Just forget it."

"I didn't come out here to see you," she yelled at his back. Then she looked for Alex and realized he'd already taken off, and she hadn't even watched.

Her dad waved her off without looking back and stalked through the door, hurrying to where the plane was being refueled.

"Fine," she muttered. She whirled around right into the other pilot. "Oh, I'm sorry. I didn't mean to block the door."

"Quite all right. I couldn't help overhear, and—"

Her cheeks blazed. "I really am sorry about that."

"Well, you might want to cut him some slack. We really can't stay any longer than to refuel."

"What could be that important?"

"We're transporting a donor kidney from Alaska. It's for a kid with a rare blood type. I do think he planned to stop overnight when we returned."

A kidney? The words seared her conscience, and Livy winced. She wanted to slink away and find a hole to bury herself in, or just crawl under the faux Persian rug on the floor—she'd certainly have no trouble fitting under it. She glanced toward the plane where her dad stood next to Sam as he refueled. Why didn't he tell her he planned to stop on the way back? Maybe because she hadn't given him a chance?

Livy rubbed the side of her face. She hated that she was always so ornery around her dad, almost looking for something to find fault with. This time he had barely gotten into the building when she lowered the boom. She glanced out toward the plane. Well, this was one time she wasn't going to apologize.

By the time she had her seat belt fastened, her conscience needled her. She gripped the steering wheel. Why did she always have to be the one to apologize? Always? Well, not always, but still . . .

Go apologize. She blew out a breath. The hurt she'd seen in his eyes tightened her throat. She couldn't let him leave without apologizing. She scrambled out of the SUV. He was climbing into the cabin when she burst from the terminal. "Wait!"

He turned to his copilot. "Give me a second."

Livy rubbed her hands on her pants. "I, ah, I'm sorry. I shouldn't have jumped all over you."

She forced herself not to look away from his steady gaze, but she couldn't keep her face from flushing.

"No, you shouldn't have." A crooked grin slid across his lips, and he held out his arms. "Come here, baby."

She took a step, and he met her, enveloping her in his arms.

"I'm sorry too. I should've called last night. It just happened so fast, this kidney, and we've flown straight from Anchorage, stopping only long enough to refuel so we could get it to Jackson, Mississippi, in time to help the boy. If it hadn't been for the strong headwinds and then the thunderstorms in Oklahoma, I wouldn't be refueling here now."

Livy stepped back and wiped her eyes with the back of her hand. "It's a good thing, what you do."

"Yeah, well, I don't know. We'll talk about it when I stop by on my way to Alaska."

"Do you know—"

"Tomorrow or the next day. I'll call you."

Skepticism must have shown on her face.

"No. I promise. I'll call you." He glanced at the plane. "Look, we have to leave, but I want you to know I love you. I'm just not real good at showing it."

"I know," she said and hugged him again. "Be safe."

"You too."

He climbed into the cabin and closed the door. Livy backed away, then turned and walked to the terminal. She hoped he would call, but she wouldn't bet on it.

20

At six fifteen, the alarm on Robyn's phone went off. She rolled over and turned it off, then lay in bed, listening to the sounds of the house like she had every morning until she'd married Chase.

Water pipes knocked as someone ran water. Her mother, making breakfast for Abby, probably. Her daughter had stayed the night. That was why Robyn had set her alarm. She wanted to see for herself that Abby was okay after what had happened to her dad.

A picture of Chase in the pickup filled her mind. He'd been so pale and still. He hadn't looked much better a few hours later after the doctors had removed the bullet. At least no vital organs had been hit, but if she hadn't come back to Logan Point, he would not have been shot. For the hundredth time, she asked herself if she'd made a mistake coming home. Would it have been better for everyone to go on believing she'd just run off?

A board creaked on the stairs, and Robyn smiled. The more things changed, the more they stayed the same. Her mother was coming upstairs to wake Abby just like she had years ago when she had four girls to get up. Her footsteps stopped just on the other side of Robyn's room, and a soft knock followed before the door to Abby's room creaked open. Robyn listened to the muffled voice.

"Abby. Time to get up."

"I'm awake, Nana. Do you know how my daddy is?"

"He was sleeping when I called earlier. We'll call again before you leave for school. Do you have your clothes ready?"

"Yes ma'am."

It was decided last night that Abby would go to school as usual, and then one of the grandmothers would take her to the hospital. Chase should be sitting up by then, and hopefully looking much better than he had last night.

Robyn swung her feet over the side of the bed. If she wanted the bathroom, she'd better get in there before Abby did. She turned on the lamp, and the soft glow dispelled the darkness. A quiet knock at her door startled her, and she reached for her robe, but it was draped across the chair. Her pajamas would have to do. "Come in."

The door opened, and her mom stuck her head through the doorway. For a second, Kate stiffened and her eyes widened, then she smiled. "For a minute, I—" She shook her head. "Never mind. I didn't wake you, did I?"

"No, I have several things to do today, so I set my alarm." How in the world did her mother manage to look so put together this early in the morning? She'd French braided her hair and appeared to have a smidgen of makeup on. Not that she needed any with her olive skin and thick lashes that fringed her dark eyes. Why couldn't she have gotten her mother's coloring instead of her dad's Irish fairness?

"How are you this morning?" Real concern echoed in her voice.

"Sad about what happened to Chase." She eased off the bed. "I want to go see him this morning."

"If you need a car, you can borrow mine. I'll be working in the pottery room all day."

"Livy is going, and I'll ride with her." It was so hard, being in the same room and talking to her mom like she was a stranger. Robyn had finally convinced Ben that they needed to tell her mother the truth, but he'd wanted her to wait until this morning when he could be present. It was all she could do not to blurt it out.

She hadn't been able to talk him into letting anyone else in on her identity . . . unless something happened at the hospital, and it became necessary to tell Chase. She both dreaded and looked forward to seeing her husband. Last night before he was shot, they'd made a connection, and she'd seen admiration in his eyes when they talked about college. Would they find common ground again once he knew who she really was?

"Does Ben have any leads on the shooter?"

Robyn hesitated. Ben was coming to the house at eight, and he and Livy were going to lay out their plan. "He's working on it."

Her mom nodded. "I won't hinder you any longer. Breakfast is almost ready."

After the door closed, Robyn heard her mother knock on Abby's door again. She smiled as her daughter responded that she was getting up.

Robyn made it downstairs and had a cup of coffee before Abby bounded into the kitchen. The desire to hug her daughter clogged her throat.

"Oh, good, you're up. Can you tell me what happened last night? Nobody else will. Why did someone shoot my daddy?"

Robyn glanced at Kate.

"No one knows yet, honey." Kate set a bowl of steaming oatmeal on the table. "Eat your breakfast, and then we'll call the hospital. If your dad's awake, you can talk to him."

"I hope he is."

Robyn did too. But more than that, she hoped they caught the monster who shot him. She was so tired of living in this barren never-land. But at least Abby seemed to be handling her father's shooting pretty well. "Do you have a busy day?"

She crossed her eyes. "We have tests. It's not fair to have tests on Monday and especially during the week of Valentine's."

Valentine's Day was this week? "What day is it?"

"Friday."

"Are you having a party?"

"Mm-huh. And TJ Logan said he was going to give me a box of candy. But I'm not going to take it. Boys are icky."

Robyn coughed to keep from laughing, and for a second the ache from wanting to wrap her arms around her daughter eased.

"Are you still helping Mr. Alex with that case?"

She'd forgotten how fast Abby could change subjects, and nodded.

"Are you finished?" Kate said, looking at Abby's half-empty bowl.

"Yes ma'am." She took a sip of milk. "I want to be a detective like Aunt Livy and Mr. Alex when I grow up."

"You do?"

"I'm already working on a case. I saw this man hanging out near the playground two times last week. If I see him today, I'm going to report it to the principal."

Cotton filled Robyn's mouth. "What did he look like?"

"He was tall and skinny. And when he saw me and TJ watching him, he hurried away. TJ's helping me on the case."

"Maybe he was cold," Kate said. "Or . . . maybe it's your wild imagination."

Robyn hoped that was all it was. Tall and skinny. That description could fit a number of the men who ate at Johnny B's. "Did you notice anything else about him?"

Abby looked up toward the ceiling. "He had on those camo clothes."

Just in case it wasn't Abby's imagination, she'd call Ben just as soon as Abby left for the bus. But what if this man was real and what if he snatched her while she waited at the end of the drive? "Hey, how would you like it if I drove you to school? If your nana will let me borrow her car." She turned to her mother. "Would that be okay?"

Kate folded a dish towel and hung it on the rack. "I suppose, even though she usually rides the bus."

"Let's make today special."

"Yay! I like you, Miss Sharon."

Her chest swelled. If only Abby felt the same way after she discovered she wasn't Miss Sharon. Robyn shifted her gaze to Kate. "What time does Abby need to be there?"

"At least seven twenty. School starts at seven forty."

She checked her watch. Twenty minutes. "Finish your breakfast and scoot upstairs and brush your teeth."

Abby gave her a strange look, and so did Kate. "What?"

Her mother cleared her throat, but Abby answered first. "You sounded just like my mommy."

Her heart sank to her knees. "I'm sure all mommies say things like that."

"Are you a mommy?"

She'd stepped into her own trap again. "Ah . . . yeah, I have a little girl, and right now she's with her grandmother. I hope we can be together real soon."

Abby continued to stare at her. "Why are your eyes blue today? They were a different color yesterday."

Oh no! She'd forgotten her contacts. No wonder everything was slightly off-kilter. She always put them in first thing in the morning, but when her mom came into her room earlier, Robyn had forgotten all about them. She floundered for an answer. "Oh, I'm wearing my blue contacts today."

"You have contacts that will change the color of your eyes? Cool. Is that so you can help Mr. Alex?"

"Yes. Now run brush your teeth."

Kate continued to study her. Finally, she nodded. "I'll get my keys."

"Thanks." She was a lousy actress. While she was alone, Robyn dialed Ben's number, and when he answered, she told him what Abby had said about the man near the playground.

"I'll send a deputy to patrol the area," he said. "Is Livy up yet?"

Robyn glanced around as her cousin entered the kitchen from the back door. "She's up."

"Just let her and Alex know I'll be there in thirty minutes."

Robyn hung up and turned to Livy. "Where's Alex?"

"On his way to Nashville. When his car wouldn't start, I took him. I'm starving. What's for breakfast?"

Robyn pointed toward the stove. "I think there are scrambled eggs and biscuits in the warmer. That was Ben. He said he'd be here in half an hour. But I thought he was going with Alex."

"He decided not to go with him after the shooting."

"There's strawberry jam in the refrigerator," Kate said, then gave Robyn another long look before handing her the keys. "I'll be in the pottery room when you get back."

She swallowed. Maybe Ben would be here by then. "I'll bring them to you."

Livy's face wrinkled in a questioning frown.

"I'll explain when I get back from taking Abby to school."

"Why—" Livy stopped. "Never mind. I saw Daddy at the airport when I dropped Alex off, but he didn't have time to come home."

"What?" Robyn and Kate said the word simultaneously.

Robyn winced. Sharon would not have been so upset. Hopefully, Kate hadn't noticed. "I'll be back as soon as I can."

She puzzled over Livy's statement as she waited for Abby to come downstairs. If her uncle was at the airport, why didn't he come home with Livy? Then, Abby clattered down the stairs and Robyn didn't have time to think about it as she ushered her out the door to the car.

For a few minutes as she drove Abby to school, it was almost like she'd never been gone. They'd forgotten to call the hospital, so she let Abby call on her cell phone, but Chase was still asleep.

They talked about him getting well, then Abby chatted about her friends and more about Valentine's Day coming up.

"I think it's so neat, TJ's mom and dad getting married on Valentine's."

"It is neat. Are you making cards for everyone?"

She nodded. "And Nana says I have to give everyone a card, even the boys."

"You wouldn't want to hurt anyone's feelings, would you?"

"But boys don't care."

"You never know." She pulled into the drop-off lane, and Abby gathered her book satchel. When she climbed out of the car, Robyn said, "Did you remember your lunch money?"

Abby pressed her lips together and looked at her strangely. "You sure do say a lot of things my mom always said."

This time it had to be a Freudian slip caused by the ache in her heart. "It's what I always say to my daughter when I drop her off at school, but I'll try to do better."

"No, I like it. Bye, Miss Sharon."

As Abby ran inside the school, Robyn blinked back the tears scalding her eyes. It had to get better from here.

Because she didn't think it could get any worse.

■ ■ ■

"What do you mean, you saw your dad at the airport? What were you doing at the airport?" Kate stared at her.

"Alex's car battery is dead, so I took him to the airport. While I was there, Dad flew in to refuel on his way to Jackson with a kidney for a transplant."

"That would explain why he didn't have time to visit."

"Yeah. I sort of read him the riot act before I learned about the kidney."

Her aunt winced. "Oh, Livy. I wish you could cut your dad some slack."

"I know. It's just that he's never here."

"He had a bad time dealing with your mom's illness and then her death."

Livy folded her arms across her chest. "That was over fifteen years ago. Evidently we're not worth his time."

"Livy Reynolds, that's not true and you know it. His work is in Alaska now."

Her dad had a great job as a pilot for one of the top airlines until he walked away from it. "Don't worry. I apologized, and he said we would talk when he stops by on his return flight. If he stops."

Her phone dinged with a text, and she glanced at it. "Ben is on his way." Livy scooped up scrambled eggs and then grabbed a couple of slices of bacon. "Can I fix you a plate, Kate?"

"Goodness, child, I ate an hour ago. And if Ben is coming, I think I'll get out of your way, go work in my pottery shop."

"Stick around, Kate," Livy said. "And where's Charlie? We have something to talk to you about, and I think Ben would rather Charlie wasn't here."

"He stayed at the hospital with Chase last night." Kate cocked her head. "I don't much like the sound of this."

She would probably like it even less after she heard what they planned to do. Except the part about who Sharon really was. Livy was glad Ben decided to go ahead and tell Kate. If anyone could keep a secret, she could, and with Charlie gone, this would be a good time. The back door opened, and Robyn came into the kitchen. Close on her heels was Ben. He sniffed the air.

"Wow, is that bacon I smell?"

Kate nodded her head toward the cabinet. "You know where the plates are. And what's this you want to discuss with me?"

He held up his hand. "Food first—I haven't eaten."

Robyn sat across from her at the table, and they exchanged glances. On the way home last night, they had decided to tell Kate the same way Susan had told her and Alex last week. Had it only been a few days ago that she got involved in this case? Or exactly one week ago, she and Mac were pinned down by gunfire in that warehouse? That seemed like a month ago. Or a year, even. The past seven days had passed at warp speed.

As they ate, Ben filled them in on what they'd discovered in the shooting. "Jason, Timothy, and Bobby had all left the restaurant when the shooting occurred, and none of them have an alibi—they all said they were on their way home."

"How about Johnny B?" Robyn said.

"He'd left to check on the game room and arcade."

"Did you retrieve any of the bullets?"

"Three, including the one in Chase. Looked like .22 long rifle shells. If it'd been a deer rifle, he would've had more damage to his body."

"Do any of our suspects have .22 rifles?"

"None of them claim to. Jason has a couple of 30-06s, Timothy has a shotgun and a 30-06, Bobby has a 270 Winchester, and Johnny B has a Maxwell 270. And they didn't take kindly to me asking about their guns."

Livy drummed her fingers on the table. Dead ends. That's all they seemed to run into. She glanced at Robyn. As they'd discussed the investigation, color had drained from her face.

Ben poured another cup of coffee, and then he held the pot up. "Anybody?"

"I'll take some," Robyn said. He found a cup and filled it. Her hands shook when she took the cup from him. "Thanks."

Kate looked from Ben to Livy. "Which one of you is going to fill me in on what's going on?"

"We all are," Livy said. "And I'll start. Remember when Alex came here looking for Samantha Jo Woodson?"

"And I thought Robyn's case might be similar."

She nodded. "Then Alex and I flew to Bristol to talk to a Susan Carpenter, and that's where we met Sharon here." She glanced toward Robyn, who had her arms wrapped around her stomach. "But before we met her, Susan told us a story about finding a woman at a rest area on the highway outside of Bristol. She'd been battered and beaten and had a concussion, a broken nose, three broken ribs, and she'd been drugged with GHB, so she didn't remember what happened.

"Months passed before she was well enough to leave the rehab place she was put in after the hospital discharged her. She was afraid to go back home," Livy said. "So she went to stay with Susan, who runs a women's abuse shelter."

"Why was she afraid to go home?" Kate looked from Livy to Robyn, and slowly recognition bloomed in Kate's eyes.

Robyn stood and walked closer to Kate. "She was afraid no one would believe her." Robyn had dropped the western Virginia accent. "But she really wants to come home."

Livy's heart nearly broke as tears filled her cousin's eyes.

Kate stared up at Robyn. "This morning, it crossed my mind that you surely did know a lot of the phrases that my Robyn knew . . ." She pressed her lips together as tears rolled down her face.

Robyn wiped her eyes and knelt beside Kate. "Oh, Mama, I've missed you."

Kate's arms went around her daughter. "You could've come home, honey. I would've believed you."

"I know, Mama, but I was afraid to."

Ben cleared his throat, and Livy glanced toward him. His eyes were as wet as hers. Now, if they could just have a happy ending for everyone.

■ ■ ■

Livy leaned back in her chair. The past half hour had been spent filling Kate in on all that had happened to Robyn. Alex had texted that he'd arrived in Nashville and that as soon as he rented a car, he'd check out the lead on the purse. If the kidnapper—no, killer—did turn in the wallet as a red herring, maybe Alex could get a description of him.

"So we can't tell anyone else that Sharon is actually Robyn?" Kate asked.

Ben shook his head. "Whoever kidnapped her is still out there, plying his trade. I got a hit on the fingerprints just before I came. Our victim is the waitress from down in South Mississippi. She went missing December 29 after a fight with her husband."

"We have another plan." Livy took a deep breath. This was going to be the sticky part. "For a little while longer, Robyn will continue to go by Sharon, and I'm going to be Robyn. She and I are leaving in a little while to find a red wig and some clothes the old Robyn would wear."

"What?" Kate almost rose out of her seat. "No! It's too dangerous. Don't you think someone will recognize who you are?"

"I'll make a deal with you. I'll let you decide after I get in disguise. If you think someone will see through our scheme, I won't do it." She was certain she could pull the disguise off. "Besides, it's too dangerous not to. We believe this guy lives in the area. And he's fixated on Sharon now. Taylor thinks he shot Chase because he's jealous."

Kate gasped. "Is Chase in danger?"

"I have a deputy guarding his room now—just in case."

Kate's eyes grew round. "Abby. Do you think the man she saw at the school was him?"

"What man?" Livy demanded.

"Abby saw a stranger dressed in camo clothes hanging around the school."

She directed her gaze to Ben. "Has anyone reported seeing someone hanging around the school?"

"No," Ben said.

"It could be Abby's overactive imagination," Robyn said. "She thinks the undercover role I'm playing to help Alex is pretty exciting. She even told me she wants to be a private detective one day."

"I've considered that, but we're not taking any chances. I have a deputy stationed there as well, and all outside recess for the fifth grade has been canceled." He turned to Robyn. "Have you called in to quit yet?"

She shook her head. "Livy thought it might be better if I waited until she was ready to talk to him about a job."

"Kate, do you think you can explain to Charlie that Livy is going to play the part of Robyn?" Ben asked.

"I'll take care of Charlie, and Allison, but who's going to tell Chase? And Abby?"

"We are." Livy pointed to herself, then Robyn. "Chase, right after we get the wig and clothes."

"I think tonight will be better for Abby—after she sees her dad," Robyn said.

"Are you going to tell him who you are?" Kate raised her eyebrows at Robyn.

"It depends on how it goes. I'd rather not. He doesn't need to deal with my homecoming right now."

21

Chase clamped his jaw together as the nurse dressed his wound, the pain overriding the morphine. He focused on the white and black name badge. Kathy something or other—his eyes blurred before he could read the whole name.

"That's it for today." Kathy straightened and wiped the sweat from his face with a damp cloth.

He swallowed the nausea that threatened to make him lose his breakfast. "Thanks." Panting, he slumped against the bed, wincing again as his whole shoulder throbbed.

"I'll tell your mom she can come back in."

He nodded and closed his eyes, just wanting the pain to be over with. He'd like to know why someone shot him, as well. No one seemed to know, or if they did, they wouldn't tell him.

"Chase?"

That didn't sound like his mother. He opened his eyes. "Sharon?"

He'd had crazy dreams about her all night.

"Look, I'm really sorry about what happened."

Her blonde hair fell softly around her face. "Wasn't your fault. I understand you stopped the bleeding."

She lifted her shoulder in a shrug. "You didn't have a towel or anything in your truck so I used my jacket."

He shifted in bed and winced as pain shot through his shoulder. "I'll be happy to replace it."

Sharon's eyes widened. "No! It was my fault you were shot."

"How could it be your fault?" Every time he'd awakened in the night, he tried to puzzle out why someone shot at them, but not once had he thought she was to blame.

She sat in the chair beside the bed. "I've made such a mess of everything. Ben hasn't told you what happened?"

He didn't realize she knew Ben well enough to call him by his first name. "No one's told me anything. What do you know about it?"

She chewed on her bottom lip, and something about the way she did it was so familiar. Almost like Robyn when she didn't want to tell him something. "What are you afraid of?"

Her shoulders slumped, and she hugged her arms to her stomach. "I thought I could do this, but I can't. I'm just so sorry. I'll get Livy."

He stared at her retreating back. Maybe Livy would make more sense. A few minutes later, the door opened, and Sharon returned with Livy in tow. His mother followed on their heels. "I hope you can tell me what's going on," he said to Livy.

"First, how are you feeling?"

"Like someone shot me with a cannon. Spill the beans. Who shot me and why?"

Livy sighed. "We don't know who, but we're pretty sure we know why."

"Don't start talking in riddles. Start at the beginning—wherever that is—and don't leave anything out."

Livy glanced at Sharon as if to ask if she wanted to tell him. She gave a small shake of her head. "Okay," Livy said. "You know Alex is trying to find Samantha Jo Woodson, the waitress who worked at Johnny B's before she went to work at Molly's?"

"And Sharon was helping him," Chase said. "I never understood how, though."

Livy held her hand up. "I'll get to that. We know this guy's MO, and Alex and Ben believe the same man who stalked Sharon and beat her up is the one who kidnapped Samantha Jo."

He ran his hand over his face, the day-old stubble prickly to his fingers. "This doesn't make sense. Sharon lived in Bristol. Why—"

"I escaped from the man just outside of Bristol. He abducted me someplace else."

"We believe the man lives in Logan Point," Livy said. "Sharon doesn't remember what he looked like, but she hoped he would do something to trigger a memory. That's why she came back and went to work at Johnny B's."

"But won't he recognize you?" Allison said.

Chase glanced at his mother.

Sharon picked at her thumbnail. "No. I don't look the same."

It was what she'd said last night, but how different could she look? *Please don't die.* Something else she'd said before he lost consciousness. "Where did he abduct you from?"

Sharon shot a nervous look at Livy. "I told you we couldn't just tell him part of the story."

What were the two of them talking about? A memory nagged at his brain. Something else Sharon had said, words that eluded him. "How long ago were you kidnapped?"

"Two and a half years ago." The whispered words filled the room.

His mother gasped.

It's me, Robyn. The words exploded in his brain. A band constricted his chest as his gaze held hers. It couldn't be. "Robyn?"

Tears streamed down her face as she nodded. His mind rebelled. It couldn't be. This woman looked nothing like his wife.

"Robyn?" His mother crossed the room and cupped her daughter-in-law's face in her hand, turning it first one way then another. "I never would have guessed . . ." She wrapped her in an embrace. "Have you told your mother?"

"Yes." Robyn stepped away from his mother and walked closer to the bed, her gaze locked on him. "I didn't mean to tell you like this."

Anger clogged his throat. "When did you mean to tell me?"

She flinched at his harsh tone. "I don't blame you for being angry—"

"Abby. Have you told her?"

Robyn shook her head.

"Don't you dare tell her, not until I'm able to be there. And until I can, stay away from my daughter."

"She's my daughter too." Robyn turned to Livy. "I knew this was a mistake. I'll be in the waiting area when you're through."

Robyn bolted from the room without another glance his way. His mother threw him a pleading look, and he jutted his jaw. "She should have called, let us know something."

"You should at least give her a chance to explain, son." She followed Robyn out the door.

He sank lower into the bed and closed his eyes. He had every right to be angry.

"She was afraid you wouldn't believe her." Livy spoke softly.

His shoulder throbbed as conflicting thoughts chased through his mind, but the ache in his heart weighed heaviest on him. "Does everyone know Sharon is Robyn?"

"No. Only six people know who she is. We're not even telling Charlie."

"Why not?"

"Until this man is caught, it would be too dangerous. He almost killed her once. Besides, this guy is more than a kidnapper. We think he's responsible for the death of the woman who was pulled out of the lake yesterday. He has to be stopped."

"How do you think you're going to do that? You don't even know who it is."

"This afternoon, I'm going to pose as Robyn and ask for my

old job back at Johnny B's. I believe this guy lives in fear that she'll return to Logan Point and identify him, so I thought I'd make his worst nightmare come true. He'll come after me as Robyn, and we'll get him."

He lay back on the bed. "But you don't look anything like her."

"By the time I put on a curly red wig and clothes she would've worn before she lost so much weight, I'll look more like her than she does now. As for the nose, I'm going to tell people I had plastic surgery. And I'm going to say things only Robyn could know."

"How did she manage to get plastic surgery, anyway?" Evidently his wife had been having herself a good old time.

"Like I said earlier, he almost killed her—the jerk beat her so badly she had to have reconstructive surgery to breathe."

Chase closed his eyes. Maybe he was the bigger jerk.

■ ■ ■

Alex thanked the secretary and marked the last recording studio off the list the Woodson family had faxed him. Samantha Jo had not visited any of them. So far his trip had been a bust. The waitress the kidnapper took last October had moved and left no forwarding address. Not that he blamed her.

His cell phone beeped a text. Ben with the name and address of the person who turned in the purse. A Mrs. Alma Rogers.

Alex had tried to get the information, but the cop wouldn't divulge it. He put the address in his GPS on his phone. Five miles from where he was.

He checked his watch. One o'clock. His shift at Johnny B's started at four. It would be pushing it to drive the rental car to the address and talk with Mrs. Rogers. He looked at the text again. Oh, good, her phone number. He dialed and identified himself, and then spent the next five minutes convincing the woman he was a private detective, and then waited while she called the precinct where she turned in the purse to check him out. At least she didn't hang up.

"I'm so sorry, Mr. Jennings, but a body can't be too careful these days," she said when she returned to his call. "The policeman said he had been talking to you."

"Yes ma'am. You did right to call and check." And cost him ten minutes of time. "How did you get the wallet?"

"I was sitting at the bus stop, and this nice young man pointed it out, asked me if the billfold was mine. He could've just taken it, you know. No one would have ever known. When he found out it wasn't mine, he suggested that I take it to the police station." She paused, and he heard the unmistakable flick of a cigarette lighter. "Did the woman who lost the billfold claim it?"

"No, not yet. What did this young man look like?"

"Very nice looking. Wore those clothes hunters and the military wear sometimes."

"Camouflage?"

"Yes, I believe that's what my grandson calls them."

"Do you remember what color hair he had?"

"Young man, I may sound old, but I'm not senile. I would have remembered what his hair color was if I'd seen it, but he wore one of those black toboggans pulled down over his ears. And before you ask, I didn't see his eyes either. He wore sunglasses."

"Was he very tall?" Getting information from Mrs. Rogers was like pulling teeth.

"He was taller than I am."

"Ah—"

"And before you ask, I'm five six." Exasperation had crept into her voice.

"Thank you so much for your time, Mrs. Rogers. You've been a great help. The young man. He didn't give you his name, did he?"

"He did." She took a deep draw, and he pictured a seventyish, blue-haired granny smoking a pencil-slim cigarette. "Why are you so interested in him? If he was a criminal, why didn't he just take the billfold and run? There was money in it—I saw it when I looked for a name. I can assure you we both just want the billfold returned to its rightful owner."

"Yes ma'am, I'm sure you do. The name?"

"John Douglas—that's the name he said."

He thanked her and hung up. So now the guy was playing games with them. But at least now Alex knew the billfold was a plant and that their killer had Samantha Jo.

■ ■ ■

Two hours later, Alex had picked up his new rental car and was back at the bed and breakfast staring at a very unfamiliar Livy.

"How do I look?" She pushed the black-framed glasses up on her nose, and then she turned away from the mirror and rested her hand on her hip.

Alex tilted his head and looked her up and down. "Are you . . . padded?"

She nodded and smoothed the plain white shirt. "You like?"

Heat crept up his neck. "You certainly don't look like Livy."

He couldn't believe the way the long, curly auburn wig changed how she looked. Or how much the rectangular black-rimmed glasses and loose-fitting clothes over the padding had transformed her into a resemblance of the Robyn in the old photos.

She turned to Robyn. "Do you think I can convince Johnny B that I'm the old you, only skinnier?"

"He was so upset when I called in and quit, he won't care," Robyn said.

"We have one more person to get approval from, and she was in her pottery shop when I arrived," Alex said. "But let me call Ben first."

After he made the call, they went to find Kate, and Livy questioned him about his trip to Nashville. "So you think the wallet was a plant?"

"Yep. While I flew back, Ben had Wade and another deputy find and call all the John Douglases in Nashville. None of them knew anything about the billfold."

"John Douglas," Livy said. "That name sounds familiar."

Alex opened the door to the pottery shop. "He's a famous FBI profiler. Wrote a book on profiling."

Livy snapped her fingers. "That's where I remember it."

"So he's playing with us," Robyn said.

"Yes, and he'll get overconfident and make a mistake."

She shivered. "I hope so."

Kate looked up as they entered.

"Well," Alex said. "What do you think?"

She wiped the clay from her hands and studied Livy. "It might work with the explanation that she's lost weight and had a nose job. There is a family resemblance."

Livy turned to him. "Then we're good to go."

He wasn't sure he was ready to put the plan into action. "Ben said to tell you he'd have a deputy stationed at the plaza."

22

After Livy left for Johnny B's, Robyn wandered out to her mother's pottery shop where she was unloading the kiln. She needed something to keep her mind off Chase.

"Hey, Kiddo."

The nickname wrapped around Robyn like a warm, fuzzy robe. She didn't know why her mom had such a penchant for nicknaming everyone when they'd been kids. Kiddo for her, for Taylor, Pipsqueak, and Livy had been Little Bit.

She admired a still-warm porcelain vase. "This is beautiful."

"That did turn out well. In fact, everything did."

"Like Christmas?" All her life Robyn had heard her mother say when she opened the kiln after firing a load that she didn't know if it was going to be Christmas or Halloween.

Her mom laughed. "Yes. You want to work in the clay?"

Robyn had hours stretching before her until Livy and Alex returned. "Sure."

She surveyed the bags of clay. "Does Daddy still dig this for you in the field behind the house?"

Kate nodded. "Makes him feel useful. He's going to be upset we didn't tell him."

"I know. But Ben thinks we should wait." She hesitated. "Thanks for not pushing me to talk about what happened."

Her mom's smile didn't erase the sadness in her eyes. "You'll tell me when you're ready."

Robyn cut off four pounds of clay and took it to the wedging table, where she kneaded the clay into a cone. "I use clay when I work with victims of abuse."

"I'm glad you took something I taught you and put it to good use."

"I don't think I ever thanked you for teaching me."

"You did. In a hundred different ways." Kate glanced at the clock on the wall. "Oh my! It's almost four, and I promised Abby I would pick her up from volleyball practice and take her to the hospital." She took off her clay-stained apron and hung it on a peg. "Would you like to go with us?"

She wanted to, more than anything. "I don't think Chase would be happy about that. I'll stay here and work." She pounded the clay into a rounded ball and set it beside the wheel. "Will you bring Abby back here?"

"Yes." Then, with her eyes bright, her mom put her arms around Robyn. "I'm so glad you're back. And it will work out between you two. God didn't bring you through the fire to deny you your husband," she said softly.

Robyn leaned into her mother's embrace. "I know. Just don't know if Chase is on board."

Her mom squeezed her shoulders. "It's going to be all right."

After she was alone, Robyn took her seat behind the wheel and centered the ball, loving the feel of the cool, wet clay as she coaxed the sides up in a cylinder. When she'd pulled it as high as the clay would allow, she bellied the cylinder out into a vase, then cleaned the bottom up before lifting the bat off the wheel to admire. Her mom would be surprised. When she'd made two more vases, she cleaned up the wheel.

Robyn didn't use the wheel with the women she counseled. Instead, she taught them how to sculpture, and now she pinched a small ball of clay and set it on the table beside a bowl of water.

Her fingers moved quickly, shaping the ball into a lamb. By the time her mom returned with Abby, she had a flock of sheep.

Abby gently touched the small animals. "Wow! How'd you do that?"

Robyn brushed a stray curl from her daughter's face. "It's not hard. I can show you, if you'd like. How was your dad?"

"He said he was coming home tomorrow."

So soon? She'd thought he would be there at least a week—long enough for Ben and Alex to catch her abductor. "Your dad is a good guy."

"Yeah, I know. And so is my mommy."

Abby's words cut her breath off. How could the child feel that way after she'd been gone so long? Two and a half years was a lifetime to a kid. *Tell her.* What would it hurt? But then she would have to tell Abby she had to keep it secret, and that was too much to ask any child to do. Surely it wouldn't be much longer. "I'm sure she would be proud to know you feel that way."

"Sometimes I think someone is holding her prisoner. You know, like Samantha Jo at the diner. And she'll escape and come home to us."

"What do you know about Samantha Jo?"

She shrugged her thin shoulders. "Just what I hear grown-ups say when they think I'm not listening. TJ says his daddy's going to find her."

"I hope he does." Sooner rather than later too.

"My mommy used to make things with clay." Abby touched the clay sheep again. "How come you know how to do the same stuff my mommy and Nana do?"

"I had a good teacher, and I'll tell you about her sometime."

Abby turned and looked into her eyes. "I bet she's not as good as Nana."

"I don't know . . . Has your grandmother taught you how to make things from clay?"

"I've been helping Nana since I was little. Mommy would bring me over here sometimes when she helped her. I make crosses and soap dishes. Sometimes TJ comes over, and I show him what I've learned."

"I see. You've talked about TJ before. Who is he?"

"You wouldn't know him. He came to live here last summer with his mom, Dr. Leigh." Her eyes grew round. "He's Sheriff Logan's son. Only he didn't know about him. But now he does and TJ's mom and Sheriff Logan are getting married."

So that's who TJ was. She had a vague recollection of him at Ben's house that first day back. "Really? I tell you what, why don't I show you how to make sheep and you can make them a wedding present."

"I like that. But Nana said you were going to tell me something about Aunt Livy."

"I'll tell you while you work." As she showed Abby how to sculpt sheep, Robyn explained how Livy planned to play a role at the restaurant.

"Aunt Livy is going to pretend she's my mommy? But how? She's so skinny like you, and my mommy . . . well, she wasn't so skinny. And how would that help Mr. Alex find this lady?"

It touched Robyn that Abby didn't want to say she'd been fat. She would make a good diplomat someday. "Your last question first. I can't explain everything that's happening, and we wouldn't have even told you this, but we were afraid someone might tell you they heard your mother was back. We're hoping what Livy is doing will help Mr. Alex."

"Is my mommy ever coming home?"

"I believe she is, Abby. Soon too."

"Are you going to stick around?"

"I hope so, Abby. I hope so."

■ ■ ■

Livy adjusted her blouse. All day she'd immersed herself into the role she had to play. Remembering Robyn's mannerisms, like twisting a strand of her hair around her finger and chewing on her pencil. Small things. The way she never looked people in the eye. At least they sounded alike when Robyn wasn't using her Bristol accent. She had to make this work.

With Ben in the parking lot and Alex in the kitchen, she was as ready as she'd ever be, and she pushed open the door to the restaurant. Johnny B sat at the cash register. Livy approached him slowly, walking hesitantly like the old Robyn rather than her normal, confident gait. "Evening, Johnny B."

He looked up from his receipts. "Do I know you?"

"I think you do." She held out her hand. "Robyn Martin. I used to work here."

His mouth dropped open and his eyes bugged open. "You don't—"

"Look the same." She looked down at the floor and ran her hand through her hair, catching one of the strands and twisting it around her finger. "I know. But I lost weight while I was gone. Got my nose fixed. And now I'm back and need a job."

"I don't know . . ."

Livy looked around the restaurant. "You're busy and it looks like you don't have enough help. I'm experienced. What's the problem?"

"Got a little sass while you were gone too."

Oops. She'd have to watch that. The black glasses she'd picked up at the drugstore slipped down her nose, and she pushed them back. "I was a good worker for you."

"I can't believe you're back. Why did you leave in the first place?"

"You know how it is. Things get bad at home, you look for a way out. But it never turns out like you think."

He nodded. "Heard your husband got shot last night. He okay with you working here again? If I remember right, he had a little problem with it before."

"We ... . we haven't worked things out yet. I need the job." She lifted her gaze and tried not to react as he stared at her.

Johnny B smacked his hand on the counter. "I do believe I see a little of the old Robyn in your eyes, the shape of your face. Never knew you looked so much like your sister."

Bailey. *Stay in character.* Livy lifted up the corners of her mouth in the hesitant gaze she'd seen Robyn give all her life. "Yeah, she was the pretty Adams girl. Can I have the job?"

"Can you start now and work until eight?"

"Yes sir."

"It's the evening rush so fill out the paperwork later." He jerked his head toward Callie. "See her about an apron and whatever else you need. You know what to do after that. And welcome home."

"Thanks." Livy pasted Robyn's uncertain smile on. "Hey, Callie," she called. "Johnny B said you'd get me an apron."

The waitress turned, and her penciled brows almost met. "Do I know you?"

"You should. We worked together a year." She twirled a curl around her finger before tucking it behind her ear. "It's me, Robyn."

"Robyn?" Callie's mouth gaped, and she blinked and then stared at her as though she didn't believe what she saw. "You had a nose job!"

A few diners looked up from their meals as Livy nodded. "Yep."

"It looks good, girl. How much weight have you lost?"

She stood a little taller and squared her shoulders. "A little over fifty pounds."

Callie tapped her on the arm. "Get outta here! Girl, you're going to tell me how you did that."

"Sure." Just get your jaw wired together. That's how Robyn had lost the weight.

"Come on back here and we'll get you an apron and ticket book. And, start spilling the beans about how you did it." She patted her ample hips. "I have to lose a few pounds myself."

"Exercise and dieting, that's what I did." Livy tied the apron on and slipped the ticket book into one of the pockets. "You want me to work the front section or the center, like I used to?"

"Center section will be fine. We had a new girl working it, but she was involved in an accident last night and she up and quit." Callie beamed at her. "Sure glad you showed up."

"Thanks." Livy surveyed the back section. "I see the Three Musketeers are here."

Callie looked to see who she was talking about. "Oh, Jason, Timothy, and Bobby. I declare, I think they'd starve if we closed. They'll be glad to see you. All three of them ask about you every now and then."

She looked them over. It was hard to believe one of them could be a killer. She'd much rather think it was one of the truckers she didn't know as well. She turned to Callie. "How many of the same big rig drivers still eat here?"

"Let's see . . . Bobby's not actually a driver, but other than those three? I don't think any. Long-haul truckers come and go—they find a new place to stop for a while, then they come back. I think those three only eat here regularly because they live here. And I see Bobby raising his cup. Better take care of him."

Livy grabbed a full pot of coffee and took a minute to familiarize herself with the menu. Robyn had drawn a diagram of the restaurant and shown her which section each waitress worked. Livy counted her customers. Seven and three empty tables. Maybe she'd have time to work in a few questions with the Three Musketeers.

Two hours later, Livy found Alex alone in the break room.

"Tired?" he asked.

She nodded. "I can only take a minute. I don't know how Callie does it day after day."

"Working in the kitchen isn't too much fun either. How did our four suspects react to you?"

"I didn't seem to set off any alarms. Robyn had filled me in on each of their favorites and gave me little tidbits about them that I threw around. They all seemed to buy that I was actually Robyn. Surprise that I came back was the prevalent reaction, even for Johnny B. Timothy left right after I arrived. Jason was nervous, as usual, and Bobby was overfriendly."

"Do you think Timothy was afraid you'd recognize him?"

"He'd finished his meal, and there wasn't any reason for him to hang around. Jason left soon after—said he had a delivery to pick up and take to Nashville, but he did seem more nervous than usual."

Alex leaned forward. "It's just hard for me to believe it's Jason, even though he wears camos all the time. I think if he planted the billfold, he would've worn something else."

"Our guy is smart. Maybe he figured you'd think that way." She massaged the back of her neck. Unless he made another move, she didn't know how they were going to catch him. Her cell phone dinged an incoming text, and seconds later, Alex's phone chimed. Livy read her text. "Ben wants us to stop by the jail on our way home."

"Looks like he has the logs for our truck drivers."

"Good." She checked her watch and groaned. "Time for me to get back to work."

"Me too." He squeezed her hand. "You're doing a great job."

"Thanks. I do think everyone bought it."

He tilted his head toward her. "Friday is Valentine's Day. Do you think we could take an hour and do something special?"

Warmth spread through her chest. Sometimes she got so caught up in the case, she didn't think of anything else. She was glad he did. "As long as we're back in time for Ben and Leigh's wedding. What do you have in mind?"

"I almost forgot their wedding." A grin played around his lips. "I'll surprise you."

That could mean trouble. "I hope we've solved this case and

Samantha Jo is home with her parents so we get more than an hour," she said. "Otherwise, this guy is liable to kidnap someone else."

■ ■ ■

He stood in the shadows of the parking lot, torn between finding Sharon and waiting for Robyn to come out. *Robyn*. After all his looking, she plops in his lap out of nowhere. If it was really her. Certainly didn't look like Robyn. Well, maybe some. The hair was right, and the best he remembered, she was about that height, but she wasn't that size. He supposed she could have lost weight. He had a photo of Robyn from before he kidnapped her. Maybe he'd slim it up and see how it compared to the new waitress.

His thoughts drifted to Sharon. Why hadn't she shown up today? She hadn't been hurt last night. He'd followed her to the hospital and watched as she'd paced the surgery waiting room.

The door opened, and Robyn came outside. Here was his chance. He felt inside his coat pocket for the syringe. All he had to do was grab her and pop the needle in. Then he'd take her to the farm. Samantha Jo would probably like a roommate. He eased between the cars until she was only ten feet away.

The door opened again. "Wait up."

He clamped his jaw. The guy staying at the bed and breakfast with Sharon. Alex somebody. He'd seen him working in the kitchen the last few days. He slunk back in the shadows as they passed by him.

"I'll follow you to Ben Logan's office." That was Alex. His heart plummeted. Robyn was going to the sheriff—she must have made him. But if that was the case, why hadn't the sheriff arrested him?

"Check your cell phone."

Robyn stopped at her car. There was a subtle change in her stance. The man pulled his phone out and then looked around, like he was searching for something. *She'd seen him.*

He ducked down, and footsteps came his way. He dropped to the ground and rolled under a car, gravel digging into his back. It was too dark to see who had passed, but he wasn't waiting around for them to come back. He scooted his body to the next car, feeling every rock.

"Let me get a flashlight." The man again. He had to get out of here before they found him. The parking lot backed up to a wooded area. If he could get to the woods, he could get away.

Wait. Why was he running? If they knew who he was, he would have already been arrested . . . unless she'd just made him. But if that were the case, he'd be hearing sirens. He slipped out from under the car and darted between the shadows to the overhang of the building.

The door to the restaurant opened again, and a group exited. Perfect. When they passed him, he eased in behind them and walked to his car. Once inside, he waited until one of the other cars pulled from their parking space, and followed them out.

When he arrived home, he booted up his computer and pulled up the photos he had of Robyn. He didn't have many, but there was one that was pretty good, although in it, she looked nothing like the skinny waitress at the restaurant tonight. In the photo, Robyn's plump figure and Roman nose made him think of the beautiful women in a Rubens painting. The "new" Robyn was too skinny for his taste. He went over each of her features. The hair was the same and the eyebrows—they both had strong, arched brows . . . and the glasses were similar.

He opened his browser and typed in a weight-loss simulator website. After he uploaded Robyn's photo, he clicked on the weight loss selector and chose forty pounds and then hit enter and waited. The image revealed from the top down, and as it did, he blinked. Not an exact match, but if he imagined the photo with the nose smaller, it would be close. Maybe if he adjusted a little here . . . and here. He bit his lip, concentrating on the picture that emerged on the screen. Slowly, he nodded. So, Robyn *had* found her way home.

■ ■ ■

"Who do you suppose was in the parking lot?" Alex walked with Livy toward the sheriff's office. Was it possible they'd been that close to the man who had Samantha Jo?

"I don't know. I'm beginning to think it was my imagination." She slipped her cell phone into her pocket. "I called Robyn to let her know nothing out of the ordinary happened tonight."

"Good. I'm sure she was anxious to know how things went." The droop of Livy's shoulders and dark circles under her eyes advertised her fatigue. The strain of the case and pretending to be Robyn was getting to her. Or maybe it was something else. "Have you heard from your dad about when he'll arrive?"

"Oh, my goodness! With everything going on, I forgot to tell you. This morning, when you had to wait to take off, it was my dad in that twin prop."

"You're kidding. That makes me feel better about getting you out of bed so early."

"Go back to feeling bad about it. He only touched down to refuel. Hadn't planned on letting us know he was in the area." She rolled her shoulders. "I sort of came down hard on him until I learned he was transporting a kidney to a kid in Jackson."

"From Alaska? That's at least a ten or eleven hour flight. I didn't know a kidney would be viable that long."

"I think there's a forty-eight-hour window, but the sooner it's transplanted, the better."

"Is your dad coming back through here?"

She nodded. "Don't know when, though. How about your dad and granddad? Have you heard from them?"

Livy was an expert at rolling the conversation away from herself. "No, which is a good thing." He would just as soon not hear from them. The bar exam hanging over him was enough.

Alex held the door open for Livy and followed her in. Ben's

chief deputy was at the front. "Is Ben in his office, Wade?" Livy asked.

"He's in the conference room." Then he looked up and his jaw dropped. "Wow! Ben told me what you were doing, and while you don't look like the Robyn I remember, you do remind me of her sister, Bailey—except for the dark hair."

"That's what everyone says."

They walked down the hall, and once again Alex held the door open for Livy. He hadn't realized how much he liked the atmosphere of a small town, where knowledge of someone extended to the whole family. It seemed to Alex that everyone cared for and looked out for their neighbors. At least everyone except the man they were after. Ben looked up from the stacks of paper on the table when they entered. "Livy?" He gave his head a shake. "Well, you were right. No one will mistake you for yourself, but did they buy you were Robyn?"

"The customers seemed to, especially when I knew things about them, like their favorite dessert and the kind of coffee they liked. I just slid right into place."

"When we came out, Livy thought she saw someone lurking in the shadows." Alex pulled one of the chairs away from the table for Livy. "We never saw who it was, but it could've been our guy, stirred up because he thinks Robyn is home."

Ben tapped his pencil on the table. "Maybe he thought he could catch Robyn alone."

"That's what I think." Livy slid into the seat. "Tomorrow night, Alex can hang back, and I'll go out by myself. Just make sure you have a deputy or two there."

Alex picked up one of the papers on the table. "Are these the log sheets?"

Ben nodded. "I'm trying to get them organized."

"I can help—I'm good at organizing," he said.

Two hours later, they took a break, and Livy stretched. "I wish these were on the computer."

"That would be nice," Ben said. "As it is, it's going to take until sometime tomorrow to cross-reference them to see which trucker not only had routes to the cities where the girls were abducted but also cities where they were dropped off."

Alex sorted through the stacks he'd organized by drivers. "Have you seen any logs for Timothy? I've found Jason's. And did we get a schedule of Bobby Cook's salesman route?"

Livy glanced through her stack. "I don't have anything for Timothy. How about you, Ben?"

He shook his head. "He has his own truck and contracts out for different companies. Said he'd get them to fax his logs over." He picked up his cell phone on the table. "I think I'll give him a call and get a list of the companies he drives for. Maybe we can hurry them up." After a minute, he laid the phone back on the table. "He doesn't answer. I'll catch him tomorrow."

"It's after eleven," Livy said. "He may be asleep."

Alex tossed a folder on the middle of the table. "Here's Bobby's itinerary. Looks like his sales route carries him through Nashville to Kingston, Tennessee. There's no record of him being in the other areas. I think we can rule him out."

"Who has Jason's logs?" Ben asked.

"I do." Livy opened the folder and glanced through it. "He doesn't have regular runs, and he only works a couple of days a week. When he was at Johnny B's, he said he was making a trip tonight and wouldn't be home until tomorrow afternoon."

"Jason's an odd one," Ben said. "I doubt his taxidermy business brings in much money. I think he only drives the big rigs to support his hunting and fishing obsession."

Livy's lip curled in distaste. "I'm like Robyn. Stuffing dead animals gives me the willies."

"He does good work." Ben's phone rang, and he picked it up. "It's Timothy Nolan." He slid his finger across the screen and answered. "Thanks for getting back with me. Your companies haven't responded. Can you give me a list of them so I can call and see what the holdup is?"

Ben was silent for a minute. "I see. Okay, tomorrow will be fine." He disconnected. "It seems Mr. Nolan is in Cullman, Alabama, on his way to Birmingham to deliver a load."

"Explains why he left the diner so soon after I got there," Livy said. "That makes two of our local boys on the road tonight."

"Does it eliminate them from being in the parking lot?' Alex said.

"Cullman is two hours from here. It would be difficult for it to have been Timothy, unless he's lying about where he is now." Livy rubbed her temples. "How about the drivers who don't live here? Are any of them a possibility?"

"It'll take a few more hours of research to know that," Ben said. "I think I'll send a deputy by Timothy's place to see if he's there."

Alex's phone vibrated in his pocket, and he fished it out. A quick look at the ID made him groan. It must be a life-and-death matter for his dad to pick up the phone and call him. He excused himself and stepped out into the hallway. "Hello."

"I thought you'd want to know your grandfather is having by-pass surgery at seven in the morning." His father's hollow voice reflected the shock that reverberated through Alex.

"What happened?"

"He's been having pain that radiates down his left arm. It got bad enough to send him to the hospital this morning."

The pain must have been really bad—his grandfather hated hospitals. Alex chewed on the inside of his cheek. He'd fueled up when he returned from Nashville. Could he leave the case? He felt in his bones they were close to a breakthrough. But this was his grandfather. "I'll be there as soon as I can, probably around one."

"Good."

The line went silent, and Alex looked at the screen to see if his father had disconnected. Then he heard him take a deep breath.

"Be careful, son. I hear night flying is dangerous."

Alex was almost too stunned to answer. His father, concerned about him? That was a new one. "I will, and don't worry, I'm rated to fly at night."

His mind raced. What had the weather report said earlier tonight? He opened his weather app and checked the weather between Dallas and Memphis. A low-pressure area was moving from west to east with thunderstorms preceding it. It might get a little turbulent. Livy looked up as he reentered the room. "I have to leave. My grandfather is having heart surgery in the morning."

"Oh, Alex, I'm so sorry," Livy said. "Is he in the hospital now?"

"Yeah. I'll be back tomorrow as soon as he's out of the woods."

23

The smell of cleaning solution stung Alex's nose as he walked through the door into the darkened ICU waiting room. All hospitals smelled the same, even at one in the morning. In one corner, a faint light glowed—a few people were still awake. He glanced around for the doors to the patients' rooms. He'd already called the number his dad had given him and talked with his grandfather's nurse. She'd said he could see him if his grandfather was awake when he arrived. He approached the area that was lit, and a woman who looked as though she hadn't slept in a week glanced his way.

"Do you know where the call box is?" He kept his voice low.

"Follow that corridor." She pointed to a hallway to his left.

"Thank you." The black intercom was just outside double doors that he assumed led to the unit where his grandfather's room was. He pressed it and asked for his grandfather's nurse, and when she answered, he asked to be admitted.

"Sure. He's waiting for you. Won't go to sleep until he talks to you."

He viewed her words with mixed feelings as the stainless steel doors opened and he passed through them. The corridor led past rooms where curtains were drawn into a spacious nurse's station.

A nurse at the desk frowned when she saw him. "May I help you?"

"I'm looking for Josiah Jennings's room. His nurse—"

"Around the corner, second room on the right."

"Thank you." He approached the room, picturing his grandfather pale and weak. A nurse sat at a small desk situated between his grandfather's room and the next one, which appeared to be empty.

She looked up from the computer screen. "You must be Mr. Jennings's grandson. Go right in."

"Thank you." He stopped just outside the door and sucked in a fortifying breath, then rounded the corner.

"You came."

"You had to wonder? You should have known I would come. How do you feel?" His grandfather looked better than Alex expected, even though he was getting oxygen.

"Better than when it felt like an elephant was sitting on my chest."

"I hear they're going to fix that in the morning."

"Yeah."

Alex looked for a place to sit and dragged a chair to the bedside. "Where's Dad?"

"He went home to get some rest."

For a minute neither spoke, and then both spoke at the same time.

"I—"

"You go first," Alex said.

"I don't want to go into this surgery with anger between us."

"And I don't want you to. I want to apologize again for being rude Sunday."

Josiah nodded. "That's pretty much what I want to do too. I want you to know that I hope you find the Woodson girl. And I want you to consider something else."

The boom was about to be lowered.

"I have every confidence you'll find her. Been checking around and discovered you're a pretty good detective."

Alex managed to keep his jaw from dropping. Praise from his grandfather? Must be the meds. "Thank you, sir."

"I want you to promise me something."

Alex swallowed the anxiety that statement brought. "If I can."

His grandfather nodded. "The operation tomorrow is a little tricky—"

"People have bypass surgery every day. You're in great health other than blocked arteries. There won't be any problems."

"It's not just bypass surgery. They're replacing a valve. And I know what being under anesthesia for that long does to someone my age." Alex started to protest, but his grandfather cut him off with a wave of his hand. "Anyway, I'm ready for whatever. But I want you to promise me you'll finish the application process while you're here and take the bar exam in July."

Alex's shoulders sagged. They'd had a deal. He bit back the words on the end of his tongue. Just like Josiah knew he would. His grandfather took advantage of every situation. "Can we talk about this later?"

"There might not be a later. I want it settled before I go into surgery."

No, what he wanted was for Alex to agree. And the old man knew he would, because otherwise his grandfather's blood pressure would go up, along with his heart rate. "Why? Even if I take the bar and pass it, I still don't want to be a lawyer. I like what I'm doing, I'm good at it. I'll never be a good lawyer."

"I don't care whether you practice law or not. It's a matter of finishing what you start."

Alex didn't know whether to believe him. "If I take the bar, you won't pressure me into practicing law?"

"Just because you take the bar and pass it doesn't mean I expect you to work for the law firm. At least not as a lawyer. Like I said,

I've been checking up on you, and we can use a good private investigator. And who knows, someday you may want to join the firm."

Alex didn't know why he was arguing with him. Alex knew he'd agree, and his grandfather knew it too. "All right. I'll apply before the deadline. It might not be tomorrow, but I promise, I'll take the bar in July."

"Thank you. Now get out of here so I can get some sleep. They'll be back in a couple of hours, sticking me and drawing blood."

"I'll be in the waiting room if you need me."

"Why don't you go home?"

"By the time I got there, it'd be time to turn around and come back. I'll see you in the morning before you go in to surgery."

Alex found an unoccupied recliner in the waiting room and settled in with a blanket and pillow. Funny how life changed with one phone call. If it weren't so serious, he'd be tempted to accuse his grandfather of staging the whole thing just to get his way. He chuckled. Even Josiah Jennings wouldn't go that far. He shifted in the chair, trying to get more comfortable.

His cell phone vibrated in his shirt pocket, and he pulled it out. A text from Livy. He'd texted her when he landed and wanted to call after he saw his grandfather, but it'd been so late.

Thinking of you. Let me know how your grandfather is.

He responded, letting her know when the surgery was scheduled. His phone lit up again. *Will be praying.*

Yeah, so would he.

■ ■ ■

Alex leaned forward and braced his arms on his knees and stared down at the floor. His dad stood at the window, looking out. His grandfather had been in surgery for four hours with at least one more to go, but reports from the surgical team sounded good.

"Dad said you were going to take the bar."

Alex jerked his head up. His dad stood in front of him. "Yeah."

"Does that mean you're going to put this private investigation foolishness behind you?" His dad might be named after his grandfather, but evidently his grandfather's tact and diplomacy didn't come with it.

"It's not foolishness. Right now, a girl's life may depend on whether I'm good enough to find her before her kidnapping goes south."

"That's what cops are for."

"Hey, that's an idea. I'll become a cop."

His dad's face flushed, and an arrow pierced Alex's conscience. Now was not the time to fight with him. "I'm sorry. I didn't mean to sound sarcastic. I just don't understand why you can't respect what I do." So much for not baiting his father.

"Oh, come on, son. Anything but a private eye." Josiah—Joe—Jennings looked down his nose at Alex.

"What's wrong with being an investigator? Granddad approved."

"What are you talking about?"

"Last night he told me he thought I was a good investigator. I make a difference, Dad. Whether it's finding this girl or locating a long-lost relative or tracking a money trail for a bank. Or—" What was the use? His father wasn't listening to him. "And I wasn't being facetious when I said I might become a cop."

That got his attention.

"You're kidding."

"Don't think I am." The idea had been floating around in the back of his head for a while. It just didn't have a name on it until now.

The hospital phone rang, and they both turned to look at it. When it rang again, Alex hurried over and answered. "Jennings family."

"This is the OR nurse. Mr. Jennings is doing well. They're closing him up now. The surgeon will be out to talk with you shortly."

Yes! Alex's fist closed tight. "Thanks."

He hung up and repeated what the nurse had said.

"He's okay then?"

"Sounds like it."

His dad slapped him on the back. "I knew he was too ornery to die."

Their gazes caught, and awkwardness stretched between them. Alex swallowed. Blast it. Why couldn't they be like other families? Without overanalyzing it, he wrapped his arms around his dad. At first his dad's arms hung limply, and then Alex felt a tentative pressure on his back.

His dad stepped away. "I wasn't sure he'd make it."

Alex chuckled. "And I knew he would. If for no other reason than to make sure I take the bar."

■ ■ ■

The crowing of a rooster mixed with a screaming woman in his dreams. He turned over and pressed the pillow over his head, but the echoes of the screams stayed with him.

His eyes flew open. Robyn was back. That wasn't a dream. He pressed his hand to his head. He had to figure out how to silence her.

Wait, though. Why hadn't she identified him? Reasons ran through his mind, and he locked in on one. Maybe she didn't remember who he was. Maybe she hadn't even seen his face that night.

He tried to remember. It was dark in the cab of the truck. She was in the sleeping compartment, knocked out, he'd thought. Then the drug wore off much too early. He'd just been lucky he had the big rig parked at a truck stop and away from other trucks when she'd come screaming out of the sleeper into the cab. His stomach turned sour when he thought about how he'd lost it. The anger he hadn't been able to control.

But it wasn't his fault. She made him hit her with her yelling and fighting. What he had to do now pushed thoughts of that night away.

He had to get her and bring her to the farm. But how? She was always with someone.

He'd just have to follow her and wait in the shadows for her to come outside, hopefully alone. Keep the filled syringe handy.

■ ■ ■

"I'm going in to work this afternoon." Robyn picked up Livy's plate and rinsed it before placing it in the dishwasher. She'd go mad if she continued to sit around doing nothing.

"You don't have a job. You quit, remember?" Livy sipped her coffee. "And don't take my cup. I'm not finished with it."

Robyn made a face at her cousin. "I called and Johnny B said that virus had made another waitress sick, and I could come back. I go in at six and work until eleven."

"How do you propose to get there? I have to be there at five."

"I don't mind going in early. I keep hoping something will happen at Johnny B's to trigger a memory."

Livy sighed. "I understand how you feel. And if you want something to do, come with me to Ben's office and help compare the drivers' logs against the dates the waitresses went missing. With Alex gone and his deputies on patrol, it's just me and Ben—if he doesn't get called out."

"That would be great." It would beat sitting around the house all day. "How is Alex's grandfather?"

"He came out of surgery an hour ago. Alex said it was a success, and the doctors were pleased. He's flying back now." Livy stood. "I'll be ready to leave in twenty minutes."

Robyn spent the rest of the day with Livy and Ben, cross-referencing logs from the trucking companies with the dates she and the other waitresses had been abducted. She didn't realize so many truckers stopped at Johnny B's. So far, no hits.

"Ben," Livy said. "Did you get the information from Timothy Nolan?"

288

"Not yet. He said he'd be in tonight, so I'll give him a call later."

Robyn checked her watch. Four fifteen. She fingered the bracelet watch, a present from Chase on their seventh wedding anniversary. She'd had it on the night she'd been abducted, and it and her wedding band were the only personal items she'd had for the entire time she'd been gone. Until now, she'd been afraid to wear it, but now that Chase knew who she was, there was no need to hide it or the ring. *What about Abby?*

How could she have forgotten that her daughter might recognize it? She glanced at the watch again. It was simple, nothing fancy. Abby probably wouldn't even recognize it. Nevertheless, she'd take it off as soon as she returned home.

She nudged Livy. "We're going to be late if we have to be at work by five."

"We?" Ben shot her a questioning look.

"I'm going crazy with nothing to do." It gave her too much time to think about Chase. "At least if I'm at Johnny B's, I feel like I'm doing something constructive. Livy will be there and Alex will arrive later, and you do have a deputy patrolling, don't you?"

"A couple of them, including me and Wade."

"See? I'll be safe."

In the end, Ben agreed to her request, and she went home with Livy to dress. As she came down the stairs, she met her mom. "Did Chase get home?"

"Yes. I just came from there, and he asked me to give you a message."

Dread inched down her spine. He probably wanted her to go back to where she came from. "W-what did he say?"

"He'd like to see you."

Was it possible he wanted them to have another chance? "When?"

"Now, if you have time."

He probably only wanted to chew her out again, and that wouldn't take long. "I was going to work, but I don't have to be there until six. Livy could drop me off at his house if you can pick me up and then take me to the restaurant before six."

"I can do that."

Robyn went looking for her cousin and found Livy in her bedroom, brushing the wig. Livy looked up. "I can't get used to your hair not being this color."

"I kind of like the blonde. Not sure if I'll keep it straight—takes too much time. One thing I'll be glad to change back is my brows. Don't like them blonde." She glanced in the mirror and smoothed her eyebrow. "Can you drop me off at Chase's? He wants to talk to me."

A quick smile spread across Livy's face. "You bet."

The afternoon light faded into dusk as Livy dropped her at Chase's door. "I'm running late, so tell him I'll come see him tomorrow."

"I will." Robyn turned and faced the door she'd gone through so many times. She didn't know which emotion was strongest—anticipation, hope, or fear. What if he said he never wanted to see her again? She rubbed her sweaty palm on her pants, remembering too late that she was dressed to work at Johnny B's. If Chase noticed, she was sure it would irritate him. She'd forgotten to take off the watch too. If Abby was here, she'd just have to keep it out of sight.

Robyn raised a shaky finger to press the doorbell. Her whole insides were shaking. When her mother-in-law opened the door, relief washed over her as her warm smile encouraged Robyn. At least Allison was glad to see her, and he wouldn't be ugly in front of his mother.

"Come on in. Chase is in the den, and Abby and I were just leaving to pick up dinner at Molly's Diner."

"Oh. If I'd known, we could have gotten it." The jitters returned. She paused inside the doorway to look around. He hadn't changed anything. That was a hopeful sign.

"Abby," Allison called. "Let's go!" Then she gave Robyn a quick hug. "I'm praying for you two," she said softly.

Abby's eyes lit up when she saw her. "Hey, Miss Sharon. Don't leave 'til I get back. I drew a picture of that man at school, see?" She held up a sketch. "Granna Martin made a copy and I'm taking it for Aunt Livy."

Robyn slipped her left hand into her jacket, hiding the watch, and glanced at the paper, but tears blurred her eyes. What if Chase insisted that she not see Abby again? She would fight him on that. She drew a shaky breath. "I'll try to be here."

When the door closed behind them, deathly quiet settled in the house. Her feet dragged as she walked down the hall to the den. Why did she think this would go so badly? Because she knew her husband.

Chase sat in his recliner watching TV, and in the fireplace, logs burned, heating the room. When he saw her, he muted the sound but didn't turn the television off.

"How are you today?" Her voice was as shaky as her insides.

"I've been better. Sit down." He motioned to the chair opposite him.

She licked her lips, wishing for a glass of water to wet her dry mouth. How should she begin? There'd been a time when talking to Chase had been the easiest thing in the world. Not so much in the months before she'd been abducted. And definitely hard right now.

"I . . ." He sighed. "This isn't easy, but I want to apologize for yesterday. I don't think I was very nice. Can't be sure because of the pain meds."

"You weren't."

His face flushed, and at the same time his eyes widened. Good. He might as well know that she wasn't the same person she'd been before.

"Why didn't you come back?"

"I was in the hospital for a month with my jaw wired shut. Then there was the surgery on my nose."

"That wouldn't have mattered."

He wasn't going to be satisfied with surface answers, but how did she tell him she'd been so scared she hadn't left the shelter for six months even to go into the backyard? A log shifted in the fireplace, sending sparks shooting up the chimney. She stood and crossed the room. After she opened the screen, she used the poker to rearrange the wood, then turned around to face him. "I couldn't come back. I had no idea who kidnapped and beat me. I was afraid he would find me again, and this time someone else might get hurt. Like Abby. Staying away was the hardest thing I've ever done."

"I would have protected you."

"How? I didn't know who did it."

"If you were so afraid, why are you here now?"

She twisted the watch on her arm, wondering if he'd even notice she was wearing it. "I probably wouldn't be if Livy and Alex hadn't found me. When I found out other women had been kidnapped, it made me sick to think that if I'd come back and reported it, this man possibly could have been caught already."

Chase seemed unmoved by her words. It was like he'd built a wall between them. She walked back to the chair and sat down again. "There's another reason I came back—I want my life back."

"That isn't happening." His words, cold and harsh, filled the room. A shadow darkened his eyes. "Until yesterday, I thought you were off 'discovering' yourself. That hurt. It did damage. Not only to me, but to Abby."

"I—"

"Let me finish. Do you know what it was like around here after you left? Abby cried herself to sleep every night for six months. I walked around like a zombie. I'm sorry, but don't think you can waltz back into our lives like nothing happened."

She jumped up. "But it wasn't my fault." The words came out

sharper than she intended. "I wanted to come home. But things weren't the greatest around here. You want me to be honest? I didn't think you'd believe me, and if you did, you'd find a way to put the blame on me."

"Well, if you hadn't worked—"

"Fine. Blame me. I don't care. But I don't have to stand here and listen to you." She wheeled out of the room.

"Wait! I'm—"

Robyn slammed the front door and flew down the steps. Why had she thought he would understand? At the edge of the driveway, it hit her that she didn't have a way to leave, that she was supposed to call her mom to come get her. And when did it get so dark? She turned in a circle, searching the area. Seemed safe enough to walk home. Or she could call her mom and go back inside to wait for her.

She glanced at the door, remembering Chase's angry face. No. That wasn't an option. She remembered the pathway through the woods. It was less than a quarter of a mile to the bed and breakfast.

An outside light guided her to the edge of the yard, where she found the path. The wind moaned through the bare limbs overhead, sending a shiver down her back. She could still go back to the house and wait. A twig snapped to her left.

Get out of here! She turned and bolted for the house.

An arm snaked across her neck and jerked her back, pinning her to a rock-solid body. She screamed and the arm tightened. She couldn't breathe. A sharp sting hit her neck as she struggled to free herself.

"No!" She fought against the darkness that clouded her mind. Numbness started in her face and spread to the rest of her body until her knees buckled and unconsciousness covered her like a blanket.

■ ■ ■

He grunted as he hefted her over his shoulder. He had to hurry. The Versed he'd given her wouldn't last long. Adrenaline pushed him to move quickly to his truck parked on a dirt side road. By the time he made the half-mile hike, he was sweating. Now to get her to the farm without getting caught. He didn't know how long he'd have before anyone realized she was missing, but he wanted to be at Johnny B's when it happened. He couldn't wait to see the look on Livy Reynolds's face.

The detective had done a good job of making herself look like Robyn, but the photo in the weight-loss simulator looked enough like Sharon to prompt him to edit the photo in another software program, changing the hairstyle and color.

Robyn had come home all right, but she wasn't the waitress at Johnny B's last night. It hadn't been too hard to figure out who that waitress was, and once he had Robyn safely stashed, maybe he'd go to the restaurant and take care of the nosy detective.

A thought nagged him as he pulled out of the side road and sped toward the farm. *Samantha Jo.* What was he going to do with the two women? When Robyn didn't show up at work, the whole town would be out beating the bushes. These women were becoming a liability. Maybe it was time to cut his losses. Dismantle the cage. Take Mama and relocate.

Maybe it was time to take another boat ride.

This time with two black bags.

24

ivy checked her watch. Ten after six. Where was her cousin?

"Robyn, table six needs a menu and water," Callie said as she passed her.

She glanced toward the back of the room. "Timothy Nolan doesn't need a menu, but I'll get his water."

She grabbed a tray and filled the water glass, then saw Jason hold up his cup. "Coming," she muttered and grabbed the coffeepot as well. Didn't these guys ever cook at home? The only missing member of the Three Musketeers, as Robyn called them, was Bobby. And he'd probably show up any minute.

She set the glass on Timothy's table. "You want the usual?"

"Nah, I think I'll try something different. How about a rib eye?"

She erased the burger and fries she'd scribbled on the pad and then cocked her head. "Celebrating?"

"No, just hungrier than a sandwich."

"Sure. How do you want it cooked?"

"Medium rare."

She took the rest of his order and then took the coffeepot to Jason's table.

"Thank you, Ms. Robyn." The soft-spoken hunter folded a piece of gray paper and put it beside his plate.

"Invite to a party?" she teased. The card looked familiar.

He stuffed the paper in his pocket. "No."

A man of few words. After she entered Timothy's order into the computer, she checked her phone. Robyn and Chase must be working things out. Maybe Robyn would answer a text, though. Her fingers flew over the keypad. *Are you coming to work?* And hit send. Then she went searching for Alex. She found him in the kitchen, behind on orders.

"If you have time to come back here and jaw, you can help me," he said.

"No time. Just wanted to see if you'd heard from Robyn."

"She's not here yet? Have you checked with Kate?"

That was a good idea. One she should have already thought of. Before she could dial, her phone rang and Kate Adams showed on her ID. "I was just about to call you and see if you'd heard from Robyn," Livy said.

"She's not there?" Panic edged Kate's voice.

"No. Isn't she still at Chase's?"

"I just called him, and she's been gone from there at least an hour."

Livy fought the panic that unleashed in her throat. "She didn't call you?"

"No. Chase said she left angry. Do you think—"

"I don't know. I'll get back to you." Livy pulled her apron off. "Robyn's missing," she said to Alex.

He yanked his apron off. "Have you called Ben?"

"You can call him while I drive."

She bolted from the kitchen, almost running over Callie. "I have to leave. And I'm taking your cook with me."

"You can't. What will—"

"I'm sorry. Johnny B can cook."

"But he's not here."

Livy stopped. "What?" Johnny B was always here. Two of the

regulars were missing. Bobby Cook and Johnny B. That was where they needed to start their investigation if they didn't find Robyn in the next few minutes.

Alex insisted on driving her SUV to the Martin farm, and she gladly relinquished the keys. Kate was leaving with Abby when they arrived, and the look on their faces sent Livy straight to them.

"Aunt Livy, please find Miss Sharon!" Abby's bottom lip quivered, and Kate looked like she was about to fold.

Livy put her arms around Abby. "I'm going to try, honey." It would do no good to tell either of them not to worry. She lifted her gaze to her aunt. "We'll do everything we can to find her."

Kate swallowed. "Thanks."

Livy gave them both a hug. "Have you seen Ben?" she asked her aunt.

"He just went in the house to talk to Chase and Allison."

She nodded and turned to go to the house.

"Livy . . ."

The heartbreak in her aunt's voice echoed her own. She looked back at Kate.

"Bring her home."

"I will." As she trekked across the yard, lights scoured the ground near the wooded area where Ben's deputies searched for any sign of Robyn.

In the den, Chase slumped in the recliner. When Ben asked what time Robyn left, he shook his head. "I don't know." He glanced at his mother. "What time did you and Abby leave?"

"A little after five. Robyn and I talked, and Abby showed her a picture she'd drawn." Allison's hand flew to her lips, and she turned to Livy. "It was of the man she saw lurking at school. She was taking it to Kate's for you. I made a copy of it—I'll get it."

Livy knelt beside his chair. "What happened?"

"We talked, and everything seemed okay. Then . . . I don't

know . . ." He rubbed his forehead. "She didn't think I believed her, and that made me mad. And I said some things. If he hurts her, I—"

"We'll find her, Chase. And you can tell her how you feel."

"We don't know that he's kidnapped her," Ben said.

Allison hurried into the room with a sheet of paper. "Here's the picture she drew."

Ben and Alex crowded around Livy and the drawing that depicted a lanky man in camouflage. It was good for a ten-year-old. "Skinny shoulders, which lets out Bobby Cook if the guy lurking around the school is the kidnapper. I wonder if she saw him today?"

"I asked her that when we were going to Molly's Diner, and she said she hadn't."

"Ben!" Wade Hatcher burst into the room. "We found this." He held out a bracelet watch. "Do you know if it belongs to Robyn?"

A strangled cough came from Chase. "It's hers. I gave it to her for our anniversary."

Livy's stomach lurched. "She had it on today."

■ ■ ■

"Hey! Are you okay?"

Robyn groaned. *Don't shout. And please stop with the shaking.* "Go away," she muttered.

"Wake up." The voice was insistent.

She cracked her eyelids, suddenly aware she was lying on something cold and hard.

"Oh, thank goodness. I thought he'd killed you."

Why was her head so fuzzy? She rose to a sitting position, and everything whirled around her. Robyn closed her eyes and then slowly opened them. This time the room stayed still. Dim light covered the area from a naked lightbulb that dangled on the other side of wire bars. "Is this a cell?"

"More like a cage."

She shifted her gaze to the speaker. A woman, actually a girl with long, red hair, knelt beside her. "You must be Samantha Jo."

She sat back on her feet. "How did you know?"

"We've been looking for you. Do you know who kidnapped you?"

"No. He wears a ski mask and baggy camouflage clothes."

"Has he—" Robyn couldn't bring herself to finish the question.

Samantha Jo hugged her arms to her stomach. "No. He made me dye my hair this awful shade of red. Said if I didn't, he would. I couldn't stand the thought of him touching me. I haven't slept in days. I've been so afraid he'd come into the cage. I don't even know how long I've been here. Are people really looking for me? He said nobody cared."

Robyn squeezed her arm. "I thought that once, and it cost me two years of my life. A lot of people care about you. Your family hired a private detective to find you. They found me instead, and I've been helping them."

She didn't mention that a certain truck driver cared very much. For all Robyn knew, Jason could be their captor. "We've got to find a way out of here."

Samantha Jo's shoulders slumped. "There's not one. He takes the key to the door with him, and it's the only way out."

"Does he bring knives and forks with the food?"

"Yes, but he makes sure they're on the tray when he picks it up."

Robyn examined the cot for springs—or anything she could use as a weapon. No luck. The bottom was made out of the same wire as the walls. She stood and examined their enclosure. The cage was in the middle of a barn. The steel wire stretched flush against the ground, too tight to crawl under. Wooden posts sunk into the ground served as cornerstones.

A good ten feet away, a shovel and pitchfork hung out of reach on the wall. She paced the small enclosure, stopping to shake the side of the cage, her fingers barely fitting through the spaces between the wires. It was the kind of wire used to make dog cages. She lifted her gaze toward the ceiling, but she couldn't tell how far it went. "Does this thing have a top?"

"That's why I call it a cage. The sides go all the way to the rafters. I thought about climbing to the top once to see if I could get out, but my fingers won't fit through the wire." She held her hands up. Samantha Jo had large hands.

Robyn shaded her eyes against the lightbulb. She made out the rafters and estimated the height around sixteen feet. Maybe her rock climbing would be useful for more than exercise. "How tall are you?"

"Five eight."

She was five six. Even if they used the cot and Robyn stood on Samantha Jo's shoulders, she wouldn't quite reach the top. She would have to climb the rest of the way.

But she needed to practice before she climbed on Samantha Jo's shoulders. She shed her socks and shoes. All the exercise and training Susan had drilled into her better pay off. She stretched her arms as far as she could and hooked her fingers through the bars.

The steel wire dug into her fingers as she pulled herself up and tried to get a toehold. *No!* Her big toe wouldn't fit through the wire. She dropped back to the floor. If only she had a rope. But all Robyn had was Samantha Jo and herself. She would have to get to the very top using only her arms to pull herself up. And even then it might be for nothing if he had secured the top as well as the sides.

"Let's try it. Get on your hands and knees."

Samantha Jo climbed on the bed and did as she was instructed, and Robyn eased onto her back. She reached as far as she could and stuck her fingers through the wire. The muscles in her arms protested when she pulled her body up long enough for Samantha Jo to stand, and then she put her feet on the girl's shoulders. The

300

two of them wobbled, and Robyn grabbed the wire. "You're doing great, but focus on your breathing. It'll help you to stand still."

The faint sound of a motor spiked her heart rate.

"It's no use," Samantha Jo wailed. "He's coming back."

"We have to try." Once again she stretched her arms and hooked her fingers through the wire. The top was no more than a foot from her hands. Her muscles burned as she pulled herself up. Twisting her foot, she managed to get a couple of toes in the wire. She let go with one hand and reached higher, touching the top of the cage. *Wire!*

She pushed, and it raised enough for her to slide her hand between the top and sides. She could almost grasp the rafter. She caught another toehold and pushed again. The wire panels separated. He hadn't tied it down. Relief surged through her body. He probably never dreamed anyone could climb the wire. She slid one hand between the panels, then the other one, and grabbed the two-by-four rafter and pulled herself out of the cage.

Robyn swung herself on top of the rafter and breathed.

A car door slammed.

"He's coming. Hurry."

She climbed to her feet and walked the rafter to the hayloft and climbed down the ladder. If she could get the shovel, she could knock him out when he came through the door.

A key rattled in the lock and she raced for the shovel and grabbed it off the wall.

The door swung open, and she ducked behind a stack of baled hay as he came into sight wearing a black ski mask and camos.

"Okay, ladies. We're taking a little—where's Robyn?"

He turned as she swung the big shovel from overhead, aiming at his skull. It crashed down on his arm instead. He swore and grabbed his arm.

She lifted the shovel again and lunged. He grabbed the end of the shovel and twisted it out of her hands. She turned and ran for the door. He caught her arm, spinning her around. She kicked at him. He backhanded her, and she staggered. He tackled her, and she hit the ground, feeling his knee in her back. Then the sting and burning in her arm.

And then nothing.

■ ■ ■

Livy paced the conference room at the jail. "I don't see why we can't search their farms."

"Without a search warrant, we can't go barging onto peoples' property. You know that, Livy." Ben folded his arms across his chest. "And if we don't find something incriminating in these files, we can't get a search warrant."

This was one time she'd like to be a rogue cop.

Wade looked up from his computer. "Ben, I may have something. Didn't Jason say he didn't have a .22?"

"Yeah."

"Well, according to county records, he bought one five years ago. Of course, he may have sold it."

"We have no evidence he did. And that will be enough for Judge Morgan to sign a warrant."

Livy stood up to go with Ben, and he shook his head. "Wade and I will cover this."

"Ben—"

"Jason may not be our man. One of the companies that Timothy Nolan drives for faxed their records, and I need you and Alex to go through them, see if he was near any of the cities when the waitresses were abducted."

He made sense, but she'd much rather go with him. One look at Alex told her he felt the same way. After the two left, Livy picked up the stack of logs and handed Alex half. "If we find anything that even suggests he's our man, I'm going out there."

"Livy . . ."

"Don't Livy me."

He laughed. "This from someone who dots every i and crosses every t? I've been a terrible influence on you."

"The man has my cousin, and I'm afraid he might be getting desperate." She glanced at the first sheet. The start date was Saturday, a week and a half ago, ending date Sunday noon. Didn't pertain to the time they were looking for. She discarded it and picked up a second sheet. Suddenly she reached for the sheet again. "Remember that first day when we talked to the truckers at Johnny B's?" She took out her notepad and flipped through the pages.

"Yeah. You talked to Timothy and Jason and . . . Bobby."

"What date was that?"

"It was right after I arrived in Logan Point, around the fifth."

"Well, I remember Timothy saying he saw Samantha Jo Sunday morning, but let me make sure." Livy flipped back to the first of the month. "Here it is." She raised her head. "He definitely said he saw her Sunday morning. But he couldn't have if he was on the road."

Alex picked up the sketch Abby had drawn. "You know, Timothy Nolan has narrow shoulders, and he's skinny too."

She stood. "I think I want to ask Mr. Timothy Nolan where he was earlier this evening."

"I think that's a good idea, partner. Are you going to tell Ben?"

"I'll call him on the way."

Fifteen minutes later, Livy pulled into Timothy Nolan's farm.

"Doesn't look like anyone's home," Alex said.

The house was dark. And it surprised her that Timothy didn't have any security lights. At least the skies had cleared and a half moon gave a little light.

"Are we waiting for Ben?" Alex asked.

"Jason's farm is thirty minutes from here. It'll be another fifteen or twenty minutes before he can possibly get here. I say we knock on the door and see if Timothy's mother answers. He says Mrs. Nolan never goes out anymore." She took a flashlight from the console before she stepped out of the SUV. With the light shining in front of them, they approached the front door through a row of hedges that circled the house.

"Livy." Alex's voice was low, intense. "Someone's in the trees on your left."

Her heart pounded against her ribs as she pulled her SIG from the holster. She wished for her vest. "Do you have a gun on you?"

"Yeah, my Glock."

"Stay here and back me. I'm going to circle around behind him."

"Got it."

Using the hedge as a blind, she crouched and eased along the side of the house. Leaves rustled. Whoever it was had moved and seemed to be approaching the front of the house. She slipped through a break in the hedge and a shadowy figure stood just beyond her with what looked like a pistol in his hand. She swallowed. Or was it? Blood pounded in her ears. A band squeezed her chest, cutting off air. Justin Caine all over again.

No! She had a job to do. "Drop your gun."

He whirled around.

"Drop it, or I'll drop you."

He dropped the gun and stepped out of the shadows. "D-don't shoot."

"Jason Fremont? What are you doing here?"

"L-looking f-for S-samantha Jo."

Alex appeared from the shadows and picked up the gun. "Why are you looking for her here?"

"Samantha Jo showed me the card some nut sent her. And tonight Timothy dropped this." He reached toward his coat pocket.

"Stop. Keep your hands where I can see them." Livy kept her gun trained on him. "See what he's talking about, Alex."

Alex pulled a small card from Jason's pocket and held it up in the moonlight. "It's gray like the others and looks like the same card stock."

Livy took out her cell phone and called Ben again. "Jason is here at Timothy Nolan's house."

"Doing what?"

"Looking for Samantha Jo, he says. He has a note card similar to the others. Says he picked it up after Timothy dropped it."

"I'm ten minutes away."

Livy slid her phone into her pocket and turned to Jason. "You come with us while we see what Mrs. Nolan knows."

They climbed the steps to the front door, and Livy rang the doorbell. No one came to the door. She tried the doorknob. "It's unlocked."

"Going in?" Alex asked.

"Mrs. Nolan has to be here, and she's not in good health. We need to check on her—she could have fallen." She pushed the door open. "Mrs. Nolan. It's Livy Reynolds. Are you okay?"

Silence answered in the dark room. Livy felt for a light switch. "If you find a switch over there, flip it on."

"Got it," Alex answered.

She blinked as light flooded the room. "What—"

Sheets draped every piece of furniture.

"Think he's planning on leaving?" Alex folded back the cotton muslin covering a sofa and coughed. "No, it's been here a while."

Why would all the furniture be covered? "Maybe it's their parlor," Livy said. She turned toward a door she supposed would lead to a hall and opened it. "Mrs. Nolan. Are you here?"

The house smelled musty. Alex found a light switch as Livy opened a door off the hallway. A room with more sheets covering the furniture. Another door in the hall revealed a bedroom. This one without sheets. Livy stepped inside as light from the hall illuminated a figure in the bed with long, dark hair splayed across the pillow. She heard Alex fumble for the light. "Mrs. Nolan?"

No movement; she walked closer. Light flooded the room, and Livy gasped.

"Oh no." Alex echoed her feelings.

"I told you he was crazy," Jason said.

Livy swallowed the revulsion in her throat. The dark red hair framed a skull. And in the middle of the forehead was a hole the size of a bullet.

■ ■ ■

Timothy nudged Robyn with his foot. Out. Just as well. He grabbed her arm and pulled her limp body where he could slip his arm around her and hoist her over his shoulder. He'd let his guard down again. He should have known better than to put the two women together. At least he should have gone inside the barn with his gun ready. Who would have thought she could climb out of the cage? Not many women could have done it.

He dumped Robyn in the passenger seat of his pickup. She should be out long enough for him to get rope from the house, and then he would bind and gag her before putting her in the semi. Samantha Jo would be fine in the cage for now.

Maybe he'd take them to a wilderness area. Yeah. Maybe the hills of East Tennessee. People minded their own business up there. And he knew exactly how to control Robyn. When she came to, he'd show her the photo on his phone of her little girl. If Robyn refused to cooperate, he'd make sure she knew how easy it would be to grab her child.

Timothy glanced toward the house and froze. Why was his house lit up? He never left lights burning. He scanned the drive, and his heart almost stopped. A white SUV sat near the porch.

Livy Reynolds drove a white SUV. More lights came on.

They would find Mother.

Timothy pressed his hands to his head. He was trapped.

His boat. It was the only way out.

The women. What would he do with them? Samantha Jo could walk, but he couldn't carry Robyn all the way to the river. Maybe he could drive—no, the January rains had washed out the road. He'd leave her behind and take Samantha Jo.

He ran to the barn door to get his ticket to freedom if they caught up with him before he made it to the river. But he needed a diversion. Like setting the barn on fire. A two-gallon can of gas sat in the back of his pickup, and he grabbed it.

He dragged Robyn out of the truck and inside the barn and left her lying near the door where she could be discovered. If given a choice of saving her or coming after him, he figured Livy Reynolds would save her cousin. Then he doused the hay with gas and found his acetylene torch and set it near the hay.

"What are you doing?" Samantha Jo screamed.

Timothy turned to her. "You want to come with me or stay here and burn up with your friend?"

"You can't kill her like that."

"I can and I will. Which is it?"

"D-don't leave me here. I-I'll go."

"That's a good girl." He pulled the gun from his pocket and waved it at her. "Just in case you change your mind when you get outside."

He lit the torch and set it a foot from the hay, then unlocked the door and grabbed Samantha Jo by the arm. At the door, he grabbed his .22 rifle and the night goggles.

The hay whooshed into flames just as he stepped outside with Samantha Jo in front of him.

■ ■ ■

Robyn struggled to free herself from the darkness that held her captive. Her nose burned. What was that crackling? She tried to turn over . . . too hard. Heat wrapped around her. The acrid scent of something burning forced her eyes open. Flickering shadows.

The crackling grew louder. Almost a roar. She heaved herself to her knees.

"No!"

Flames licked the wall. Over her head, the loft burned. She stood, and dizziness overcame her.

Gotta get out . . .

25

A quick search revealed Robyn and Samantha Jo were not in the house.

"There's a barn out back," Jason said.

Outside, a puff of wind brought the scent of burning wood. Livy turned toward the barn. Flames lit the night sky. "He set the barn on fire."

She raced toward the barn, but Alex beat her. The whole building was engulfed.

"I see Robyn. On the floor." Alex dashed through the doorway just as a beam dropped from the loft, barely missing him.

She started in, and Jason grabbed her. "No, you stay here. I'm going in. Samantha Jo may be in there."

Livy followed him through the door. The heat hit her like a wave. Alex had lifted Robyn and stumbled toward the door. She swept her gaze around the barn. The only part not engulfed was where they stood. If Samantha Jo was in the barn, it was too late. Flaming boards dangled from the roof. She yanked Jason back.

"It's coming down. Get out, Jason! She's not in here."

Livy stumbled out into the barnyard and sucked in fresh air. She knelt beside Robyn. "Are you all right?"

Robyn nodded. "Where is Samantha Jo?"

Jason dropped beside her. "Was she with you?"

"Yes. He must have taken her."

Timothy's truck sat ten yards away, so he was on foot. "How far are we from the river?" Livy asked Jason.

"Not far. I think he has a jon boat."

Sirens sounded faintly in her ears. Ben was on the way, but she couldn't afford to wait. "Alex, stay with Robyn until Ben gets here. I'm taking Jason and going after him."

"Let Jason stay here."

"No, he knows the woods and how to get to the river."

"Let me go in your place, then."

What if she froze again? Livy knew that's what he was thinking, because she was thinking it too. "I'm the cop here. Call Ben and have him alert the Coast Guard that he may be on the river." She turned to Jason. "You okay with helping me?"

"You couldn't keep me from it. I've hunted this land. Shine your light so we can find the road that leads to the river."

She scanned the woods and saw an opening. "There it is."

What little light they'd had outside the barn disappeared under the canopy of pine trees. She plodded behind Jason, letting him take the lead. "How far do you think it is?"

"Not more than a half mile," he said.

What if Timothy doubled back and ambushed them? She pushed the thought from her mind. He had Samantha Jo with him. Maybe she would slow him down.

They came to a fork in the road. "Which way?"

"I don't know. Let me have the flashlight."

He took the lane to the left. In less than a minute he was back. "No signs that he went that way. Let's try the right lane."

She followed him.

"Look, here's a broken limb," he said. "And another one. Maybe Samantha Jo is leaving clues."

"How much farther to the river?"

Gunfire answered her question.

310

"Get down!"

Too late as Jason crumpled to the ground.

■ ■ ■

Timothy laughed under his breath when the detective dashed behind a tree. She could run but she couldn't hide from him and his night goggles. He fired again, and bark split away from the tree. That ought to hold her until he could get away. He would have already been in his boat if it weren't for Samantha Jo slowing him down. He crawled back to where he'd left her hog-tied and gagged.

When Timothy reached her, he pulled the slipknot that was behind her back, releasing her legs. "Give me any trouble at all, and you won't live. Got that?"

She nodded, her eyes wide.

A twig snapped, and he whirled around.

Livy Reynolds was walking toward him.

■ ■ ■

Gunfire rang from the woods.

"Go after her, Alex," Robyn urged. "I'll be all right."

He hesitated. He'd moved her well away from the burning barn, but what if Nolan came back? The faint wail of sirens reached his ears.

"Go!" she said. "I'll be okay until Ben gets here."

"Tell him I've gone to the river to help."

He took off running where he'd seen Livy and Jason enter the woods. Once under the trees, pitch dark surrounded him. A branch slapped him in the face, stinging his cheek. He needed a flashlight. *Cell phone.* He slipped his phone out and tapped the flashlight app. Light flooded his path.

Another gunshot rang out. With his Glock in one hand and the phone in the other, he raced in the direction of the gunfire. A fork in the road. Which way? A groan to the right settled it.

He rounded a curve in the lane and almost stumbled over a body. His heart plummeted, lifting only slightly when he realized it was Jason. He knelt beside him and put his fingers against his neck. Fast but strong. Jason's eyes fluttered open. "Where are you hit?"

"Shoulder. Help Livy."

Alex punched off the flashlight and tried to call Ben. No service. "Do you know which way she went?"

"To the river . . . just ahead."

"Ben should be here soon."

"Go back to the fork and take the other road. Should bring you out above where he keeps his boat. Maybe you can get him from the rear."

"Thanks." Alex patted his shoulder, and then tapped the light app again. He backtracked to the fork and took the other road. When he came to the river and the trees no longer blocked the moonlight, he turned the app off. No need to broadcast where he was. He jogged along the rocky bank, looking for where Nolan kept his boat. Voices around the next bend reached him, and he froze.

"Drop your gun, or I'll shoot her."

He recognized Timothy Nolan's voice. He crept around the bend.

Nolan held a gun on Samantha Jo.

■ ■ ■

Livy slowly walked into the clearing. Near the riverbank, Timothy held Samantha Jo in front of him as a shield. He wore some sort of glasses. *Night goggles.* So he hadn't been shooting blindly, but now that they were out of the trees, he'd lost that edge. She estimated the distance at forty feet and moved in closer. She would only get one shot, and she needed every advantage she could get. But what if she froze when the time came? She brushed the thought away. This wasn't a dark alley, and Timothy Nolan wasn't some seventeen-year-old kid with a toy gun. But he *was* a living, breath-ing soul. Could she pull the trigger? Even to save Samantha Jo?

"Stop where you are, or I'll shoot her."

"Give it up, Timothy. We found your mother. It's over."

"Leave my mother out of it."

"Why did you kill her?" she asked, edging a little closer. *Keep him talking, give Ben and Alex time to get here.* Where was Ben, anyway? It seemed like this situation had gone on for hours. But in reality, she realized it hadn't been more than ten minutes since they'd found Robyn in the burning barn.

Timothy took a step back, taking Samantha Jo with him. The girl yelped, and he drew his arm tighter. "Shut up." He turned to Livy. "Don't come any closer."

"Do what he says, Samantha Jo." The girl stood rigid, the whites of her eyes showing. Livy needed her to relax, to remember the self-defense course she taught for the women at church. With her gun trained on Timothy, she moved to the left where the girl partially blocked his view of Livy. "Samantha Jo, it's going to be okay." She locked eyes with her. "Remember what I told you at church—"

"You shut up too."

"Sure, Timothy." Samantha Jo kept her eyes on Livy. "You never told me why you shot your mother. She was a sweet lady."

A strangled cough came from his throat. "Sweet. About as sweet as a rattlesnake. Sharon Nolan was evil. Pure evil. Locked me in closets when I was a kid. Beat me. People knew what she did, and nobody cared. Nobody tried to save me. She never even remembered my birthday."

"When is your birthday, Timothy?"

"January thirty-first."

That explained the dates some of the women were kidnapped. The notes had said something about taking care of the children. He thought he was saving the kids. "Is that why you sent the notes?"

"They didn't listen to me. If they'd quit their jobs, I never would have taken them. All they had to do was stay home and take care of their kids."

"But I don't have a kid!" Samantha Jo struggled to get loose.

He jerked her back with his arm and tightened it around her neck. "Yes, you do!"

He'd choke her to death if she didn't do something.

"No, Timothy. She doesn't."

In the pale moonlight, his brows lowered and uncertainty crossed his face. He relaxed his arm, and Samantha Jo took a breath.

"Yes, she does." Timothy's voice went up an octave.

He didn't sound too sure. She didn't want to shoot him. If she could just talk him into giving up.

"You're wrong. You took someone who is a child herself." She kept her voice calm. "What you've done to her is as evil as what your mother did to you. Did you mean to do that?"

"No! I just want to save the children."

"Then start with her. Let her go."

"Never!"

A rock sailed from somewhere to her right, hitting Timothy on the shoulder. He turned and fired.

"Drop, Samantha Jo!" The girl fell like a hundred-pound bag of feed.

Timothy swung his arm around, and Livy squeezed the trigger.

■ ■ ■

"You did great." Livy wrapped her arms around Samantha Jo's shivering body. Three feet away from them lay Timothy's gun that he dropped when Livy's bullet hit him.

"Is it over? Really over?" Samantha Jo's lip quivered.

"Yes." She'd done her job. Stopped a murderer. But knowing that didn't ease the tension of having to shoot him to do it. She looked over the girl's shoulder for Alex. He'd climbed down the rocks to the river's edge, where Timothy's body had landed.

314

Alex finally appeared, a cell phone glued to his ear. "Yeah, Ben, we need an ambulance for Jason. Nolan too. I don't think you can get a helicopter in here." He nodded and hung up.

"Timothy is alive?"

"Unconscious but breathing."

Relief coursed through her body. If he lived to stand trial, justice would be better served.

Later they walked out of the woods together after Ben and his deputies arrived and Timothy and Jason had been transported to the hospital. An ambulance had come after Samantha Jo and Robyn as well so they could be checked out.

"You handled the situation like a pro," Alex said. "Well enough to end your leave of absence, don't you think?"

"You might be right." While she would always regret the life that had been lost in the alley, what happened that cold December night no longer controlled her or filled her with guilt. She could even see the good that had come from the terrible ordeal. If she hadn't taken a leave of absence, she wouldn't have been at Timothy Nolan's house tonight, and Robyn might be dead. God did indeed work in mysterious ways.

Livy nudged Alex with her shoulder. "By the way, thanks for distracting him. That was a lucky throw."

"Lucky?" He cocked his head, and his brown eyes glinted in the moonlight. "I'll have you know I was an all-star outfielder on my college team."

"Yeah, but I told you to stay with Robyn."

"I figured that was just a suggestion."

"You would."

26

Chase smoothed Abby's curls back, hooking one behind her ear. He'd kept her home from school to tell her about Robyn, and it had gone better than he'd expected. Later after she had time to process the information, he was pretty sure there would be harder questions. His mother would be here soon to take her to Kate's, where Robyn was recuperating from her kidnapping. He would like to take her himself, but he seriously doubted Robyn would welcome his presence.

"Why didn't you tell me last night that Miss Sharon was Mommy?"

Looked as though the hard questions wouldn't be later, after all. "Because I wanted you to get some sleep, and it was too late by the time the doctors got through checking her out."

The intensity in Abby's face as she sat on the oversized arm of the recliner was so like her mother. How had he looked at "Sharon" and not seen his own child? Because he didn't expect to was no excuse. He should have inherently known.

"But you promise that she's okay?"

"I promise. Now, do you want cereal or eggs and bacon for breakfast?"

"Cereal, and I'll fix it. You might hurt your shoulder getting the milk out of the refrigerator." She hopped down from the chair. "And I'll fix you some."

"I think I can manage." Although his chest did throb. Gingerly he rose from the recliner and followed Abby to the kitchen.

"You sit at the table," she ordered, "while I do this. Do you want a banana in your cereal?"

He eased into his chair at the table as sweat popped out on his face. He wasn't as strong as he thought. "Yes, please, and thank you."

A few minutes later, she handed him his bowl, then tilted her head and stared at him with those eyes so like her mother's.

"Why didn't Mommy tell us who she was?"

Because I never provided a safe environment for her to tell us. But Chase could hardly tell his daughter that was the reason. Neither did he want to tell Abby the whole story. That would be for later, when she was older—if she really wanted to know. "She was protecting you. There was a bad man after her, and until he was caught, she was afraid if he knew who she was, he might hurt you."

"Like he did you."

"That's right."

"I want to go to Nana Kate's and see her."

"Granna Martin will take you after your mom has time to get up."

"Aren't you coming?"

Chase was certain Robyn would not want to see him, not after the way he'd acted. "I think you and your mom need some time alone."

"She is coming home, isn't she?"

That was a question Chase couldn't answer. So much had happened in the last two and a half years. They were both in different places, and Robyn had changed so much. She might not want to come home.

"Dad, you do want her to, don't you?"

Oh yeah. Last night after she'd been abducted, he realized just how much he wanted her back in his life, but he may have killed any feelings she had for him with his sharp tongue. "Yes, honey, I do, but let's give Mommy some time."

■ ■ ■

Robyn's fingers shook as she dabbed concealer under her eyes. She'd been strung too tight to sleep last night and didn't want Abby to see her dark circles. Allison had called her cell phone a few minutes ago and said she and Abby would be coming shortly. Finally she could hug her daughter and not raise questions. Although she imagined Abby had a million of them.

With one last glance in the mirror, she decided the way she looked would have to do. At the foot of the stairs, the front door opened and Abby burst in.

"Mommy!"

Robyn wrapped her arms around Abby as her daughter flung herself at her. "Oh, Abby!" Tears ran down Robyn's face as she buried her face into her daughter's hair. "I've missed you so much."

"I've missed you too!"

"Here, let me look at you, I mean *really* look at you."

"I'm sorry I didn't know who you were." Abby touched her face, then her straight hair. "But you look so different."

"I know, baby, and I'm so sorry I had to fool you." She looked past Abby to Allison. So her husband hadn't come.

Allison hugged her. "I'm going out to the pottery shop to talk to Kate so you two can be alone."

"Chase didn't—"

"He wants to give you some time."

More likely he was the one who needed the time, judging from his anger last night. Abby tugged on her hand. "Let's go into Nana's den and we can talk."

Abby had questions, and Robyn sent a prayer up for guidance. She'd already given a lot of thought about how much she would tell her and decided on a condensed version. Very condensed. If only Chase were here, it would make it easier. Tears stung the back of her eyes as she followed her daughter to the den, where she touched on being abducted and how Susan rescued her and made sure she went to college as soon as she was well enough.

"So there really is a Susan?" Abby asked.

"Yes, and I want you to meet her sometime."

"Why didn't you come home after you got well?"

Abby had never asked easy questions before and that hadn't changed. Robyn hesitated, trying to formulate an answer.

"Daddy said you were afraid the bad guy would hurt me."

That was sweet of Chase. "That's true, but I was mostly afraid for myself."

"But Daddy would have protected you. Are you coming home with me?"

Robyn froze. She'd been dreading this question most of all. "I . . . I don't—"

"I hope you will consider it," Chase said from the doorway.

"Daddy! You came!" She ran to him and grabbed his hand.

"Yes, honey, I came. Would you give your mom and me a minute of privacy?"

"Okay. I'll go see Granna and Nana."

Robyn's heart pounded in her chest as his eyes never left her face. "Do you mean that?"

He nodded.

"Why do you want me to come home?" As much as she loved her daughter, if Abby was the only reason he wanted her home, she couldn't do it.

"Because you're the only woman I've ever loved."

She pressed her hand to her mouth. "Oh, Chase!"

He held his hand out. Robyn took it, and he pulled her into his arms. She gently laid her head on his chest, avoiding the bandage. "I don't want to hurt where you were shot."

"You're fine. More than fine, and I'm sorry for all the things I said . . . even before you were kidnapped. We'll go to counseling, and I'll move into the guest bedroom until we work things out."

She pressed her lips together, but that didn't keep the tears from flowing from her eyes. He lifted her chin and used his thumb to wipe the tears from her cheek. "I love you, Robyn Martin. Will you give us a second chance?"

She closed her eyes and leaned into him. "Yes," she whispered. "And I love you too."

With a sigh, he lowered his face until their lips touched.

27

Alex pulled the rental car beside Charlie's old truck. He'd run all over Logan Point looking for Livy's gift and afterward talked a florist into selling him a dozen red roses. He put the bouquet behind his back as he searched for Livy and found her sitting in the kitchen, drinking coffee. He was returning to Texas tomorrow, and he had decisions to make today. Decisions that involved this woman who made his heart beat erratically.

He took a few seconds to steady his nerves before making his presence known. "Happy Valentine's Day."

Livy glanced up, and a twinkle lit up her blue eyes. "That better not be candy you're hiding."

"Would I do that to you?" he asked as he pulled out the long-stemmed red roses.

She gasped. "For me?"

"For you."

A smile stretched across her face as she took them. "Thank you. They're beautiful. But I didn't get you anything."

"Don't worry about that. Now, for lunch, I found a restaurant about a hundred miles away near a landing strip. It has four stars and is supposed to be very quiet and romantic. I thought we might leave around ten thirty and fly over and have lunch. I would have made it dinner, but we have the wedding of a certain sheriff to attend." He held his breath as he waited for her answer.

"Fly, as in your airplane?"

"I told Abby I'd take you up on Valentine's Day."

"That you did." An email alert sounded on her cell phone, and she glanced at it. Her dad. *Arriving around noon. Can you meet me at the airport?* She showed Alex the message.

"We'll just have a late lunch. Do you want me to drive you out there?"

"No. He may need a ride. Or not, if he isn't hanging around."

Alex nodded. "Can I give you a little advice? Something I've learned since I've been here?"

She tilted her head slightly. "Sure."

"Accept your dad for who he is."

"I'll think about it."

He hoped her dad stayed for a few days, but if not, Alex hoped he'd make things right with Livy. He also hoped they didn't have to cancel their lunch date, but if they did, he'd work around it. "Any news on how Jason's doing?"

"He's going to be okay. The bullet missed anything vital. He should be out of the hospital tomorrow or the next day. I think Samantha Jo was released last night." She smiled. "Kate said Molly took her home with her."

"How about Timothy Nolan's condition?"

"I called Ben earlier. Timothy's condition has been upgraded to fair, and Ben has a guard posted at his hospital door. Oh, Ben also said Timothy has a hawk tattoo on his chest. Robyn must have seen it when she attacked him in the semi."

"Any clues on his motivation for doing what he did?"

"I talked with Taylor last night, and she said he probably killed his mother in a fit of rage—she said or did something that triggered all the anger and resentment he'd built up over the years, and he exploded. When he first began sending the notes, Taylor thinks he truly believed he was saving the children from the same thing he experienced."

"Why do you think he kept referring to Samantha as Sharon?"

"It was his mother's name. According to the preliminary report, she's been dead about five years, and because she had no friends, no one missed her. Taylor thinks that after her death, he started looking for a replacement, and six months later, he kidnapped his first victim in Mobile, Alabama. As far as Ben can tell, Robyn was his third. Timothy's logs put him in the right place at the right time for all the kidnappings." She cocked her head. "And did you know his birthday is January 31?"

At least Livy would not have to deal with killing Nolan. "Are you okay with what happened at the river? Shooting him?"

She nodded.

"How about the shooting that happened before Christmas?" He feared Nolan's shooting might have triggered more anxiety.

"I'll always deal with killing the Caine boy, but now I can see that it wasn't my fault. Caine died because of the choices he made. I hope I never encounter another situation like that, but because I chose to become a cop, it's a real possibility that I will."

"And you're okay with that?"

"I have to be."

■ ■ ■

Livy scanned the empty skies as she climbed out of her car. If her dad didn't come, it wouldn't be the first time he didn't show, but ten minutes later, his voice came over the radio.

"Logan Point Tower, Cessna F6548Juliet, five miles southeast, at 2,000 feet, landing Logan Point with weather information Bravo."

"That's him," Sam said. "Cessna F6548Juliet, enter right downwind for runway 3-6, report downwind."

"Cessna 48Juliet, midfield, right downwind for runway 3-6."

"48 Juliet, cleared to land runway 3-6." Sam turned to her, grinning from ear to ear. "Let's go meet him."

"You go ahead. I'll wait here." Livy remembered how the last time she'd almost taken her dad's head off when she discovered he was not staying. She didn't want a repeat of that performance, but already, she felt the tension building. Why couldn't she just accept her dad the way he was?

Maybe because, just once, she wanted him to show that she was worth spending time with.

The plane door opened, and her dad climbed down on the wing. He was alone. Maybe she was wrong and he was staying a few days. She nibbled at her thumbnail as he shook hands with Sam and then walked toward the terminal, his stride purposeful, and his broad shoulders straight.

"You came," he said as soon as he was through the doorway.

He thought she might not? "I figured if I wanted to see you, I'd have to. Where's your copilot?"

"Ned?" He hesitated a second before answering. "In Jackson."

"You're not staying, are you?"

"What makes you think that?"

She shrugged. "Just a feeling."

"Always said you were smart."

Flattery would get him nowhere. "Well?"

His shoulders drooped. "I'll be here long enough to visit with you and run to the house and see Kate, then I have to go back. We have a patient who needs a lift to the Mayo Clinic, and then we'll fly home. But she won't be ready to leave until four, so I decided to fly up here for a short visit."

"Why didn't you just use the courtesy van to come to the house?"

He dropped his gaze, then turned and glanced out the window. She followed his gaze toward his plane where Sam was refueling it. When he turned back to her, his eyes were bright.

"I wanted the extra time alone with you to ask for your forgiveness and to apologize for not being a better dad. Can you forgive me?"

His words pierced the wall around her heart. How long had she waited to hear those words? But were they too late?

Accept your dad for who he is.

She mustered a smile. "I'm glad you asked me to come after you."

He held out his arms, and she went to him.

"I've always loved you," he said softly against her hair, "and all these years, I've missed so much because I didn't know how to show it or get past your mom's death."

He stood back and lifted her chin, wiping away her tears. "I can't unscramble eggs, Little Bit, but maybe we can learn how to make an omelet together."

She blinked back more tears that threatened. "I'm a pretty good cook. Let's go visit Kate."

■ ■ ■

When Alex returned to the house two hours later, Livy fairly glowed as she pulled him into the kitchen. "Dad, I want you to meet Alex."

Alex stuck out his hand, and Jeremy Reynolds grasped it in a firm handshake.

"Do I need to ask—"

"Dad!" Livy's face matched her red cashmere sweater. "He's a pilot, like you. Has his own plane."

"Really." He gave Alex a more thorough look-over. "What do you fly?"

"Bonanza F33A."

Jeremy's eyes widened. "You're kidding. That was my first plane. Ever do any aerobatics?"

"A few times."

The look of admiration in his eyes gave Alex a boost, which quickly disappeared at the look of dismay in Livy's eyes.

"Is aerobatics where you do stunt flying?"

He held his hands up. "Just loops, nothing dangerous."

She eyed him skeptically, and her dad stepped in, saving him from deeper trouble. "Who's taking me back to the airport?"

"We both will, sir. I'm taking Livy for a late lunch."

Her dad slapped him on the back. "Good for you, Alex. Let me go tell Kate bye."

After her dad left the room, Livy eyed him. "You never told me you were into aerobatics."

He grinned. "I was afraid it would be the kiss of death if I did."

"You got that right. No loops today, okay?"

"Not even one little one?"

"Alex . . ."

"Okay. Not even one."

■ ■ ■

Back at the airport, Jeremy admired Alex's plane, and they talked a little about his trip to Minnesota later. "Are you affiliated with Angel Flight?"

"Yep," Jeremy replied. "You've heard of them?"

Alex nodded. "I've flown a couple of missions for them."

"You never told me that," Livy said.

"If you remember, we never talked about planes much." But maybe that would change now that she seemed to have forgiven her dad.

After they said their good-byes, her dad climbed into his plane and taxied to the runway.

"So, everything is good with you two?" Alex asked her.

"It's a beginning. He apologized for not being around, and I remembered what you said about accepting him for who he is. I think he means it, but time will tell. Either way, he was right about one thing. I don't have to wait for him to come to Logan Point. I can go to Alaska for a visit."

"And I can fly you."

"You'd be willing to do that?"

"Yes ma'am." That and a whole lot more. "Are you ready for lunch?"

"I'm starved."

The flight over to the restaurant was smooth, and although at times Livy was animated, often she seemed deep in thought. He didn't know if it was flying or if it had to do with her dad. Or something else altogether.

When they landed, a car waited to transport them to the restaurant that was everything it advertised. A crackling fire warmed the cozy area where they dined by candlelight on filet mignon and roasted veggies in their own private dining room.

"I can't believe you went to all this trouble," Livy said. "No one has ever done anything like this for me before."

He took her hand. "I'm glad. I wanted today to be special, not just because it's Valentine's but . . ." He ran his thumb over the top of her fingers. "I'm flying back to Texas tomorrow."

She took a deep breath and nodded. "Are you going to register to take the bar?"

"Probably." Alex stared into Livy's blue eyes. "So you will miss me?"

■ ■ ■

Miss him? Judging from the pain his words brought, Livy would definitely miss him. She should have listened to her head and not risked her heart with someone who wasn't sticking around. "You might say that."

"Then the way I see it, we have two options. You can move to Texas—"

"Or you can move to Memphis . . . or Logan Point." Her heart seemed to stop as she waited for his reaction.

"That may be a plausible solution in the future." His grin started slowly and then stretched across his face as he pulled a small box from his pocket.

She widened her eyes.

"It's not a ring," he said quickly. "Not yet anyway."

Livy unwrapped the embossed white paper and lifted the lid on the jeweler's box. Nestled against white satin was a platinum heart with an inscription on the back. *To Livy~As a token of my love~Alex.* "It's beautiful."

He took her hands. "I don't know what the future holds, but if you feel the same way, I want to explore the possibilities with you."

Her heart filled to almost bursting. "I would," she whispered.

He stood and pulled her into his arms. Briefly, they danced to their own music, and then he cupped her face in his hands and rubbed his thumb across her lips. "You are so beautiful," he said as his lips gently claimed hers.

Livy leaned into him, slipping her arms around his neck. This was one Valentine's Day she would never forget.

Acknowledgments

To my family, Barbara, Elisa and Carole, and Bryan, you have always believed in me. I thank you.

To my critique partners, Imagine That Writers—your input made the difference.

To Patricia, who listened to me moan and groan, then told me to get back to work.

To My Book Therapy Team and Susan May Warren and Rachel Hauck, you challenged me to be better.

To Dr. Amy Davis, my go-to for physician and hospital-related questions; Robert Hand, my blood technician; Sharon Buske, my nurse who keeps me honest; and Dr. Reba Hoffman, who answered my many questions dealing with psychology and police work, thank you all. Any mistakes in not getting the facts straight are mine.

To my wonderful agent, Mary Sue Seymour. One of the most inspiring women I've ever met.

To my amazing and gifted editors, Lonnie Hull DuPont and Kristin Kornoelje—a special thanks for your patience, kindness, and valuable input. And to the Revell art, editorial, marketing, and sales teams for your hard work—you are the best!

And most of all to my heavenly Father, who loves me.

Patricia Bradley is a published short story writer and is cofounder of Aiming for Healthy Families, Inc. Her manuscript for *Shadows of the Past* was a finalist for the 2012 Genesis Award, winner of a 2012 Daphne du Maurier Award (1st place, Inspirational), and winner of a 2012 Touched by Love Award (1st place, Contemporary). When she's not writing or speaking, she can be found making beautiful clay pots and jewelry. She is a member of American Christian Fiction Writers and Romance Writers of America and makes her home in Corinth, Mississippi.

Meet
Patricia BRADLEY

www.ptbradley.com

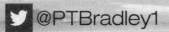 @PTBradley1

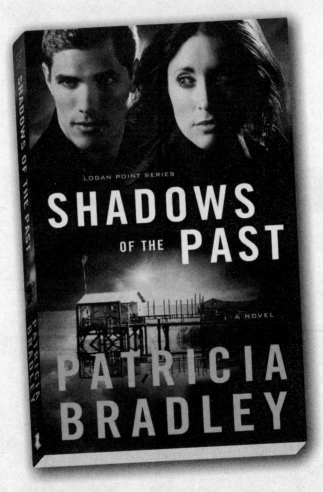

"A taut story of mistakes and betrayal, a mother's fierce love, revenge and danger—and the redeeming wonders of faith and love."

—LORENA MCCOURTNEY,
New York Times bestselling author of the Cate Kinkaid Files

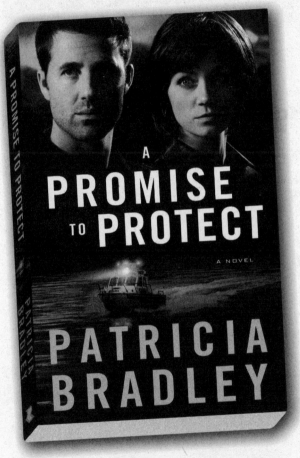

In a steamy small town of secrets, danger, and broken promises, Leigh Somerall reaches out to a former love to save her brother's life, while trying desperately to keep her own secrets that, if revealed, could change everything.

Revell
a division of Baker Publishing Group
www.RevellBooks.com

Available wherever books and ebooks are sold.